USA TODAY BESTSELLING AUTHOR
Dale Mayer

SIMON SAYS...
SCREAM

A KATE MORGAN NOVEL

SIMON SAYS... SCREAM (KATE MORGAN, BOOK 4)
Dale Mayer
Valley Publishing

Copyright © 2021

ISBN-13: 978-1-773365-66-4
Print Edition

Books in This Series

The Kate Morgan Series
https://smarturl.it/DMSimonSaysUniversal

Simon Says… Hide, Book 1
Simon Says… Jump, Book 2
Simon Says… Ride, Book 3
Simon Says… Scream, Book 4
Simon Says… Run, Book 5

About This Book

Introducing a new thriller series that keeps you guessing and on your toes through every twist and unexpected turn....

USA Today Best-Selling Author Dale Mayer does it again in this mind-blowing thriller series.

The unlikely team of Detective Kate Morgan and Simon St. Laurant, an unwilling psychic, marries all the unpredictable and passionate elements of Mayer's work that readers have come to love and crave.

It's taken some time, but Detective Kate Morgan's various relationships are gelling at work—and even at home. Until Simon starts screaming in the middle of the night. Worried and not sure she's up for this, Kate distances herself from him. When a tortured female body shows up, Simon's visions are of no help, until he describes one specific injury, ... the same injury on Kate's latest case.

A case getting weirder as more is uncovered. A similar tortured death happened more than a decade ago, where the killer was caught and served time. As a suspect he looks good for this current case because he's now out and back in society. Except he has a solid alibi ...

This isn't the only victim though, and, as the Vancouver PD Homicide Unit digs deeper, Kate's team finds several more cases—all with connections to the same suspect. But Kate's still not convinced.

Too much more is going on, and she's determined to get

to the bottom of this, before someone else dies a painful
death …

Sign up to be notified of all Dale's releases here!

https://geni.us/DaleNews

CHAPTER 1

First Sunday of September, Wee Morning Hours

A SCREAM FROM hell woke up Simon. He bolted from the bed and spun around in a panic. In the dark and nude, he tripped over his clothing on the floor, as he raced for the window. He didn't know where that scream had come from, but—

"Jesus Christ, what's the matter?"

He stopped, turned, and slowly reoriented himself.

Kate sat up in the bed and stared at him. "Simon? What's the matter?"

"An unholy scream." He held up his hands, so she could see them trembling.

"From where?" she asked, sliding out from under the covers. "The hallway? Your neighbor?"

She quickly pulled on her panties and jeans, then a top over her bare chest, as she walked to the front door. She stepped out into the hallway, coming back in again.

He stared at her. "I think"—he took a deep breath—"I think it was inside my head."

She groaned. "Not another one."

He gave her a lopsided smile. "Hey, Kate. This isn't my doing. Remember that."

"Hey, Simon. This isn't what we wanted either. Remember that."

"I know." He nodded. "And it's been a long time."

"It has, at least a couple weeks." And, with that, she gave him an eye roll.

"I know. Sorry."

"It's all right," she noted, "but it would be good if you could explain a little more."

"There's no explaining," he murmured. "This is just insanity."

"I get it," she agreed. "I really do."

"Good, because this is just too much."

"You don't know where or when or what or who?"

"No." His expression was grim. "Just the most horrific scream."

"A woman?" Kate asked, and he nodded. "In pain or fear?"

He looked at her, frowned. "Pain."

"I get it. Somebody being tortured." She sighed heavily.

He slowly nodded. "I think so." He paused. "I wish not, but I think so."

She nodded. "Oh, *great*. Here we go again."

CHAPTER 2

Sunday Early Morning

THE VANCOUVER SHOWERS just wouldn't quit as Kate stood over the remains in front of her. Puddles had formed on the sidewalk and down along the back of the alley. The rain poured down on the woman's body, tossed atop the full contents of a dumpster, left open. As for the victim's cause of death, Kate couldn't be sure just yet. She saw so many bruises, so many injuries, so much blood.

One thing was for sure though; her vocal cords and throat area had been slashed. The coroner would determine if the vocal cords themselves were actually cut. Kate didn't really want to get close enough to take a better look. But, in spite of herself, she knew she had to.

As she tilted the woman's head slightly to the side and up, Kate confirmed that her throat had, indeed, been cut. Swearing slightly to herself, she stepped back, muttering, "Torture is one thing. This is something else again."

At her side, Rodney looked at her. "What did you say?"

She shrugged. "Some torture is obvious"—she pointed at the dead body—"but this seems to be a step above."

"Is there a step above?" he asked cynically. "It looks just like murder to me."

"It does, but then why cut the vocal cords?"

He looked at the woman's bloody throat and shrugged.

"If it's her vocal cords, it was probably part of the throat slashing that killed her."

Kate frowned as she studied the body. "I don't know that we can put a cause of death to it yet."

He snorted. "I get that we have to wait for the report," he noted, "but her throat has definitely been slashed."

She nodded. "Yeah, and both wrists are broken. Both ankles are broken, and you can see bone on the back of that calf, where some of the muscle has been stripped back."

He looked, then turned back to her and frowned. "But again, none of those would be cause of death."

"No." She sighed. "I guess I'm just hoping that the ass-hole who did this had her so drugged that she didn't know."

Rodney swallowed. "You're thinking all that was done while she was alive?"

Kate nodded. "Yes, I do. But again, we'll have to wait to hear it from the coroner." Just then his vehicle drove up. She turned and nodded as Dr. Smidge got out. "He'll be happy with this."

"He's never happy with us," Rodney quipped with a half smirk. "But we're just doing our jobs."

"He's not even upset with us," she admitted. "We're just the messengers."

Smidge walked toward her, a glare in his eyes.

She nodded and gave him a bright smile. "Lovely day, isn't it, Doc?"

His eyebrows shot up, even as the rain poured over him. "I didn't bring a hat or an umbrella," he announced.

"Won't matter," she said. "You won't do much here anyway."

He continued to glare at her, stepped up, and looked down at the woman inside the bin.

"God damn it," he muttered. "We'll need to go through all that garbage too."

She nodded. "Absolutely. Forensics is on their way."

"Interesting." He shook his head. "As if she were the last thing tossed in."

"And no attempt to cover her up either," Kate murmured.

He nodded at that. "Was the lid open?"

She nodded. "It was open. Body was found by a homeless man." Kate turned to look around the corner, where the man should still be sitting. He was, thankfully, but he was tucking into a big bottle of some golden liquid at a pretty fast rate. Probably to haze out the scenes in his mind. It would be her job to pull those scenes back up front and center again, so he could tell her anything he might be hanging on to. "Shit. He's the one over there, drinking up," she murmured.

The coroner looked at him, nodded. "I would be too, if I were him."

She smiled. "Well, I'd like a coffee myself, and the dang coffee shops aren't even open yet."

"The street vendors aren't here either," he grumbled. He bent down, took a look at the body, without actually touching her, then pulled out gloves and started doing an exam. She opened her mouth, when he flat-out stated, "Don't even ask."

She snapped her mouth shut. "How do you always know?"

"Because you guys are all the same. It's the first thing out of your mouths every time. Cause of death, time of death, all of that." He snorted. "As if I've had a chance to even figure any of it out."

"Well, we were thinking cause of death was the slashed throat," Rodney suggested.

"He was," she clarified.

At that, Smidge turned and stared at her. "What's your vote?"

She shrugged. "I don't like very much about this one at all, ... so I won't hazard a guess."

His eyebrows popped up. "What? You won't go for the obvious?"

She shook her head. "No. The obvious in this case doesn't work for me."

"Explain," he barked.

"She has been too badly tortured," she detailed. "And I'm thinking those are severed vocal cords."

He looked at her in approval. "You're right. It cut her vocal cords. And this is a cut to her throat"—he pointed—"but I'm not sure it's what killed her. It's not very deep."

She nodded. "I was thinking he might have been almost killing her and bringing her back, almost killing her and bringing her back," she suggested. "And cutting her vocal cords meant nobody would hear her. He could torture her for as long as he wanted to."

At her side, Rodney muttered under his breath, "Jesus Christ. I didn't even think along that line. Who the hell would?" He turned and frowned at Kate, dumbfounded.

She shrugged. "It's a big city. It's dense, and who has a space private enough for a woman to scream—like she would have from the pain," she said quietly. "The severed vocal cords are a given."

"So what do you think killed her?" asked Smidge, as he continued to examine the body.

"Well, I'm really hoping," she added quietly, "a shitload

of drugs are in her system."

"There probably are. I just don't know what and how much yet." Smidge stood. "You'll get more when I get more."

She nodded quietly.

"Do you ever think of going into this field?"

"No." Her headshake was adamant. "I'm doing what I do now, and that's about as far as I can go."

"Hey"—he shrugged—"you're doing the part I don't do. We need all of it."

With one last glance at the body and the dumpster and the mess all around, she turned and nodded. "We need everybody on board for this one." Kate wrapped her arms around her chest. "It feels ugly."

"That's because it is ugly," Smidge agreed, giving her a look. He motioned at two guys, who lifted the body from the dumpster and placed it on the plastic laid out for that purpose. He added, "No clothing and no ID, nothing to identify her."

"Any tattoos?" she asked quietly.

He looked at the dead woman again. "No. Nothing I'm seeing at the moment anyway. But then the body's still a mess."

With the corpse in front of them, the gruesomeness of what had been done to her was even more apparent. One breast appeared to have been cut off, and chunks of flesh were missing from her thigh and her pubis.

Kate shook her head. "I really don't like the missing pieces."

"In what way?" Rodney asked, his tone snarky. "Just think about it though. It might give us something to go on."

She shook her head, frowning. "I mean, that's possible,

but why those pieces? Why there? Was he just experimenting? Was he curious? What the hell," she said in disgust. "Wouldn't it be nice if people would consider a human body as sacred and something to be honored instead of desecrated?"

"We're living in the wrong times for that," the coroner argued. He stood again, barking orders to his team. He walked toward her. "I don't need to tell you to catch this asshole, right?"

"No, you don't need to tell me," she repeated quietly. "It's at the top of my priority list."

"Damn good thing," he noted. "But it's not your only case, is it?"

She shook her head. "That would be way too simple to say that and to work each case in that way." She sighed. "We did just close a couple though. So, with any luck, we can get started on this one, while it's hot."

"You need to," he agreed. "I know we've had budget cuts. There are always budget cuts, but we need to make sure this doesn't happen again."

At that, Rodney turned and looked at Smidge. "What do you mean?"

He faced Rodney, his mouth firmed into a straight line. "Whoever did this had fun. How long will it be before he decides that he needs to get that same fix again?"

"It won't be long," Kate guessed, quietly shoving her hands into her pockets. "It won't be long at all."

And, with that, she spun and headed over to talk to the drunk. Unfortunately, as she got to him, his head bobbed against his knees, and he had passed out in a stupor. She groaned, reached down, shook him awake, but all she got was mumbles.

"Whoa, whoa. Whaa ... t do you ... you want?"

But he wasn't conscious enough to talk with her about this. She motioned to one of the police officers, standing off to the side. "Can you take him down to the drunk tank?" she asked. "He's the one who found the body, so we'll need to talk to him when he's sobered up."

Then she joined Rodney, still standing here, staring at the crime scene. "Forensics will be here for a while. Do you want to help go through the dumpster?"

"Hell no, I don't want to," he replied. "Chances are they won't find anything anyway."

"No, but we can't take that chance," she added quietly.

Just then the Forensics team arrived, and she was ushered to one side.

"There goes our chance anyway," she muttered. "You know how territorial they can be."

"Which is nice," Rodney noted, "because, honest to God, we don't want to be in their faces, and we don't want them in ours."

"Never quite works so nice and clean as that though, does it?" She gave him a half smile.

He shook his head. "If this is the only case, we do need to canvass everybody around here."

"I know. I was thinking of that," she noted. "This is mostly a business district, and it'll be dark in the evenings, but a group of homeless people should be up and down this area all the time." Kate frowned as she reoriented herself. "Maybe if we check out this alley, we might find somebody who saw something."

"Anybody who was here is long gone," Rodney stated. "You know that. It's the law of the land out here. Self-preservation means, *Get the hell out before the cops come.*"

"Unfortunately you're right about that," she agreed, "but it doesn't help when it comes to getting witness information. What about cameras?" she asked, turning to look.

"There'll be cameras on the main street," Rodney noted, "but not a whole lot when it comes to these alleyways though."

"Still, the main street will give us something." She walked to the corner and took a look. "An all-night coffee shop is up at the corner." She pointed. "Looks a little bit on the seedy side."

"Did you hear what you just said? An all-night coffee shop in this part of town?" He shook his head. "This is Hastings Street. I'm surprised anything is all-night here."

"Unless it's rented by the hour," she suggested.

"Only if they have somebody around to rent to," he muttered. "I'm not exactly sure anybody around here will be doing the tango in a coffee shop."

"Well, they probably are. They just won't admit to it."

He laughed. "True enough."

Crossing the street, they headed into the coffee shop. As it was, one woman, looking very tired and old, sat on a stool behind the counter. The coffee shop had only a couple tables, and it wasn't any bigger than a postage stamp. Kate pulled out her badge, identified herself, and asked if the woman had any cameras outside the shop.

The woman glanced at Kate and shook her head. "Nope. No cameras around here," she replied. "They did that for a while, monitoring the whole works. But, after so many break-ins, they couldn't get coverage anymore from insurance, and the equipment was so cheap that you couldn't tell who it was anyway. The owner figures it's cheaper to replace a couple tables and chairs, and they even bought these solid cabinets, instead of the glass ones, for when the break-ins happen. We post signs that we don't have cash after midnight, so nothing's in the till anyway." She shrugged. "It's a lot better that way."

"I guess," Kate offered. "We've got a body in the dumpster across the road."

The woman snorted. "Seriously? Again?"

At that, Kate's eyebrows shot up. "What do you mean by *again?*"

"Seems like every couple years one is found over there," she noted.

"Looks like a popular place, but with whom?"

"Everybody. Everybody who doesn't want to have anything to do with anybody," the woman replied.

"Explain what you mean by that," Kate said.

"The area's run-down. Anybody who's here doesn't really want to be here, but there are limitations as to how far anybody can go in this world, without some help."

"Why are you still here?" Kate asked.

"Because it's a job," she stated simply. "I get to eat for free while I'm here, and it pays the bills." She shrugged. "Nobody will hassle me. I'm well past being a looker, and, honest to God, most people are just grateful when they come in that they can get a cup of coffee."

"How is the coffee here?"

"It sucks, but, at two o'clock in the morning, when you're looking for coffee, you really don't care. It's a hot drink, and, on this rainy morning, people don't really give a shit. They just want access to something."

Kate studied the older woman, whose hair hung in thinning lengths down her head. It looked like she was balding early, whatever red hair she may have had was a more carroty orange, and her skull showed through. Her apron was dirty, but her hands appeared clean, and, although tired and worn-out, she looked like she could manage most verbally ugly clients. But there was nothing to her, if the customers became violent. The woman couldn't have had more than 110 pounds on her frame, and she looked more like an old junkie street worker, who couldn't find any more business because of her age.

"What was your clientele like last night?" Kate asked.

"The usual," the woman said, studying Rodney. "A few came in—a couple girls, a couple guys. A few people grabbed some ready-made sandwiches. Other than that, it was pots of coffee and not a whole lot else. Matter of fact, last night was on the quiet side. The boss won't be happy." She chewed on her bottom lip and then shrugged, with an almost philosophical attitude, as if to say nothing she could do about it.

"If the boss isn't happy, then what?"

"Hard to say," she replied. "He's been threatening to shut it down for a long time just because there's not enough business to justify keeping it open."

"I guess it's a numbers game, isn't it?" Rodney agreed sympathetically.

"It sure is," she muttered, "and my numbers say, I need to keep working to pay the rent. So, if this shuts down, it's not in my favor either. So I sure as hell didn't have anything to do with any trouble."

"Do you know anybody who would have? Any unsavory folks who came in last night who might have had something to do with the dead body in the dumpster?"

"No." She shook her head. "All kinds of unsavory players are around here, but nobody I know of is into murder."

"Right." Kate frowned. "No cameras and you can't ID

anybody who came in after midnight?"

"I didn't say that," she corrected, looking over at Kate. "I didn't say anything along that line."

"Excuse me. My mistake. Can you identify anybody who was here?"

She frowned. "I'm not sure I can, but I didn't say I couldn't."

"Okay, I'm confused."

"Well, you didn't ask," she explained, "so I didn't offer any information."

"Right." Kate tried to figure out this woman. "So, can you identify anybody who came in?"

"Sure. I mean, Louise was here. Sandy was here. Big Tom was here." Her face crumpled up. "And that psycho was here, Little Mitt."

"Little Mitt?"

"Yeah, he's that half-Asian something or other crazy martial arts guy around here. He's got some brain damage. He was pretty harmless for a long time, but lately he's getting a little more off his rocker."

"Where would I find this Little Mitt guy?"

"He hangs around the homeless shelters more than anything," she noted. "Other than that, you'll find him sleeping on a bench somewhere."

"He was in last night?"

She nodded. "Yeah, it surprised me too because he had ten bucks on him."

"Is that a lot for him?"

She nodded again. "It's a lot for most people around here. When they get a couple coins, they come in for coffee."

"What do you do at the end of the pot, when you can't sell it anymore?"

An odd look came in the woman's gaze, as she turned to face Kate again. "What do you mean?" she asked, her voice almost worried.

"I'm not here to tell on you," she responded quietly. "But surely, when a pot of coffee has been sitting there for too long, you don't serve it."

"No, I don't. We're supposed to dump it down the sink."

"And, in most cases, you would."

But she waited. As if she had a lifetime of waiting for others to speak first, never being the first to jump in with an answer. She just stared at Kate. "You got a point to make?" The woman finally caved in to the awkwardness, speaking with a note of challenge in her voice.

"I'm just wondering how many of these people know that a pot of coffee will get old after a while, so there might be free stale coffee available." The woman frowned and looked down at her hands, and Kate realized that she'd hit a vulnerable spot. "Again, I'm not here to tell your boss. I'm also not here to complain about you making good use of food that'll be wasted anyway," she added. "I'm just trying to get an idea of who was in the area last night, who might have seen something, and who we can talk to next."

The woman turned, looked out the window. "If he finds out, he'll fire me."

Rodney piped up. "For dumping old coffee into a cup instead of down the sink?"

She nodded. "He doesn't like these guys hanging around. Calls them freeloaders and says that they're a waste of space. He doesn't even want them in his place," she said. "He just doesn't get it."

"He doesn't get it because he's never been there," Kate

stated quietly. "You have, so you know what it's like to go without any hot coffee on a cold night, don't you?"

The woman looked at her and then nodded. "I do," she answered, "and I don't see the harm in not wasting something. Yet the boss would rather it be wasted than help someone who doesn't have the money to buy a cup anyway."

"Well, *some people*," Rodney noted, "are supposed to follow orders regardless."

"*Some people*, quite true," she snapped. The woman crossed her arms over her chest and looked at him. "And your point is?"

"His point is, it doesn't matter," Kate said, with a wave of her hand. "The bottom line is that a few people stopped by looking for coffee last night. Can I get the names of those people?"

"I guess." She paused. "They won't thank me for passing on their names."

"No, of course not." Kate nodded. "I get that. But the woman who died in that alley won't thank anybody either. Not unless we help her and at least give some meaning to her death, like by making sure nobody else goes the same way."

"You think he'll strike again?" the woman asked, scratching her arm.

Kate could see psoriasis patches, old ones, with dead flaky skin, and the woman just kept scratching. Kate reached out a hand and stilled the other woman's movements. In a calm voice, Kate spoke, while removing her hand from the woman's arm. "It's possible. We just want to do our job, so we can put a stop to it."

The woman frowned and pulled her sleeve over her scaly skin and leaned back a little farther. Obviously the contact was something she wasn't comfortable with.

Rodney walked toward the door, ready to leave. "All we need is a couple names."

The old woman looked at Kate first, then Rodney. She muttered a couple names in a soft and quiet voice that Kate couldn't make out.

"I didn't hear that," Kate said, pulling out her notepad. "Can you just write them down, so we can remember them?"

She frowned at that and then shrugged, as if to accept that, if she was in for a penny, she was in for a pound, so what the hell. She wrote down two names. "These two were in last night."

"You got the other names, right?" Rodney asked Kate, standing against the doorjamb, his arms across his chest. He looked down the street, then turned to the woman. "Looks like you might have some business coming."

"Maybe, or it's just my replacement."

"Who takes over after you?"

"Riley," she muttered. "He has been here since forever too. Honestly, if it weren't for the two of us, the boss couldn't keep this place open. Nobody else wants to work these hours."

"They're not the best, as hours go, are they?" Kate asked. She accepted her notebook back again, then asked, "How is the coffee now?"

"Shit," the old woman replied, "but it's all I have to serve."

"Got it." Kate hesitated. "Is it really bad, even if I'm desperate for coffee?"

"Yeah, it is," she stated. "You better go down around the corner and get something better."

Kate wasn't sure if the push-off was because the older woman didn't want them around any longer or if it really was ugly coffee, but Kate figured she'd take the hint anyway. "Good enough. Hopefully we won't have to bother you again. If you do hear any rumors, talk, or anything along that line, give us a shout."

"Why would I do that?"

"You're not in the business anymore," Kate noted, quietly taking a chance. "Yet you know a lot of women out there who are. We don't know for sure that the woman we just found was on the streets because she was in reasonably decent shape, but she sure could have been."

"She could have been new, or she could have been working high-end."

"She could have been either of those, and she also could have been somebody's mom. She was definitely somebody's daughter." Kate's gaze bored into the other woman's eyes. "Somebody has to care sometime."

At that, the woman looked down at her fingers and muttered, "Nobody ever cares."

"We care," Kate responded, "but we still need help in order to solve these crimes and to ensure we don't find another body in another alleyway."

"You'll find it anyway." She sighed. "Another body, another day, another alley."

"You're right," Kate agreed, "but let's do our part to make sure there isn't another one today."

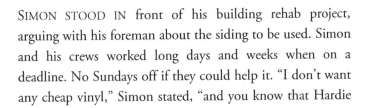

SIMON STOOD IN front of his building rehab project, arguing with his foreman about the siding to be used. Simon and his crews worked long days and weeks when on a deadline. No Sundays off if they could help it. "I don't want any cheap vinyl," Simon stated, "and you know that Hardie board lasts forever."

"Not really," he argued, "but it's got to look like it belongs in this historical area too."

"So what do you want to do?" Simon asked.

"Brick is expensive. Rock is expensive, and anything else looks like cheap plastic."

"If we want to make it look like the rest of the buildings on this strip," Simon noted, "I'll have to go with a mixed-media look." He groaned as he studied the tall building in front of him.

"Interesting that they made all these so tall and narrow," the foreman noted. "Reminds me of London."

"Only these are twice as tall."

"Right. Still, it's what we've got to deal with."

"Let me think about that. How's the plumbing?" Simon asked. Just as his foreman went to answer, Simon's phone rang. He pulled it out, frowned, then shut it off and put it away.

"Do you need to answer that?"

"I'll get it in a few minutes." Kate would wait. Normally he wouldn't *not* answer, but he knew he wouldn't like anything about the message she had for him, so he was just as happy to push it off. After that, Simon and his foreman got into a heavy discussion on plumbing and budgets, then adaptations and change orders. Simon was loath to do too many change orders on one building because that was a surefire way to ensure no profits at the end of the day.

He was in this work for a couple reasons. One was turning these old buildings back into something useful and new, while rehabilitating them for use by the public. Most often for low-income families, homeless shelters, and often women's shelters, although not everybody knew about them.

This town had a huge need for senior living facilities as well. Which is precisely what this one would be.

As Simon headed off, after this final meeting, and walked toward home, he pulled out his phone again. "You called," he said, when she answered.

"I did," Kate answered briskly. "Remember that nightmare?"

"Which one?" he asked in a hard voice. "There's been a few lately, and why the hell do I have to remember them anyway?"

"You don't," she acknowledged, "but you and I both know that whatever is going on in your psyche won't let you rest until whatever the hell is going on is solved."

"That's an awful lot of vagaries," he noted.

"Well, anytime you want to give me something definitive," she replied in a cheerful voice, "I'd be happy to have them." Her voice dropped as she added, "Especially right now."

"Ah hell." He stopped in his tracks; a person walking behind him bumped into him. With both of them apologizing and moving out of each other's way, he hissed into the phone. "What did you find?"

"A pretty ugly scenario," she replied quietly.

"I don't really want to deal with any more ugly scenarios."

"I get that," she noted, "but, in this case, I'm not sure any of us have a choice."

"Why not?" he snapped.

"Because her vocal cords were cut," she answered quietly. "To stop her from screaming."

A long, drawn-out hiss escaped as Simon realized which nightmare Kate was talking about.

"Ah, crap, the woman who was screaming but not screaming."

"Yep, that one. At least as far as I can figure, that's the one we're talking about."

"Meaning that I have more than one nightmare?"

"No," she stated, with a note of finality. "Just hoping that we don't have more than one murder victim."

"Isn't your desk piled rather high?"

"Too damn high," she groaned.

"So it's not like murder takes a holiday."

"No, it doesn't, unfortunately."

He groaned. "What do you need from me?"

"As always, anything you have to give."

"Wow, Detective," he said in a mocking voice. "I didn't know you cared."

"You know I care," she snapped right back in a pithy voice. "You just don't know if I care very much."

He shook his head at that because it was very true. He wasn't even sure where the hell their relationship was at these days. She was independent, and, as much as he wanted her to be less independent, she struggled with their relationship as it was right now. "Fine," he muttered. "What would you like from me?"

"A heads-up if you get any insights."

"You know I'm pushing them away."

"But I know that sometimes they won't let you push them away. And, Simon, I get that you don't want to do this," she said. "I really do. But I've got to tell you, I really don't want to stand over any more women who were in the condition of the one I saw today."

"That bad?"

"Worse," she replied. "I've got to go. Remember. Any

answers you get, I'll take them."

"You don't even believe in this bullshit," he argued.

"I don't know what I believe anymore," she snapped right back.

It was an argument they'd had many times, and he couldn't blame her because he was definitely on the same side in terms of not knowing what to believe. Obviously he was a believer, but sometimes it all just seemed too damn farfetched to be feasible. As he went to answer her, he realized she'd already hung up on him. He swore, staring down at his phone.

A man standing nearby, waiting for a bus, laughed at him. "Had to be a woman," he stated. "Those are the only calls that can screw us over so badly."

Simon looked at him, realized what the guy was saying, then chose to ignore him and walked away.

"You can run, but you can't hide," the guy called out with a laugh.

The trouble was, it was almost true. The guy was right in some ways, and it was all Simon could do to figure out how it would ever work with Kate. Simon was used to having his relationships be a little more amiable. He was wealthy, busy, decent-looking, and confident. Women tended to fawn all over him. Although his last relationship had ended with a less-than-stellar result, he'd firmly expected that, when he was ready, he would find somebody new, somebody better suited to him.

Kate was not even close to what he had imagined. She was contrary, cranky, independent, and she worked too damn hard. And he just couldn't get enough of her.

CHAPTER 3

DETECTIVE KATE MORGAN walked into the jail cell and asked for the prisoner she had sent to sober up. She was given the log-in book to take a look at. She identified the prisoner and asked to speak with him, then headed over to the interview room she had been assigned and sat down, waiting.

Soon the prisoner walked in on his own accord, looking a little sheepish and red-eyed. He sat down nervously on the chair across the table from her. "Good morning, ma'am," he started.

She looked at him in surprise and just waited.

He winced. "I've spent a lot of time in the streets, but I ain't never seen anything like that."

"Hopefully you'll never see it again either," she replied in a quiet voice.

He nodded. "I know. Look. It wasn't the right thing under the circumstances, but I just couldn't think of anything to do but drink enough to stop seeing that. Turns out it was burned into my brain." He wiped his mouth and cleared his throat a couple times. "Could I possibly get a drink of water?"

She nodded, then walked to the door and asked for water for the interviewee. When it was delivered in a bottle, he uncapped it and drank. She watched, as he gulped the bulk of it in one sitting, then wiped his mouth again.

"Thank you," he said. "Nothing like alcohol to make your throat dry."

She wanted to ask why he continued to drink, if that were the case, but she had come to accept it as one of those things. It didn't matter what answer he gave; the addiction was real. Or almost as uncontrollable as anything else in life. She pulled her notepad toward her and picked up the pen. "Now tell me. What did you see?"

"The devil," he replied instantly. "No doubt in my mind, the devil himself was there last night."

She put down the pen, crossed her arms, and looked at him.

He immediately held up his hand. "I get it. You don't believe me. But I'm telling you, it was the devil."

"And what was he doing?"

"Nothing good," he stated.

"Did you see him kill that woman?"

The witness immediately shook his head. "Nope, nope, nope, nope. I didn't see nothing like that."

"So then what did you see?"

"He came out of the alleyway, wearing a big cloak and a mask with horns," he told her.

"So this devil wore the devil's mask?"

"I don't know," he replied. "It looked really real."

She nodded and put down a couple simple notes. "Any idea how tall he was? How big he was? Did you hold anything in his hand? Did you see him bring in the woman?"

"Nope," he answered. "I was just sitting there, snoozing, then I heard a weird *thunk, thunk, thunk* sound and heard him saying something. When I looked around the corner—from where I was hiding farther down the alleyway—he stood in front of the dumpster, his hands on his hips like this." Her interviewee hopped up, put his hands on his hips, and glared, as if the table were the dumpster.

"So he was pissed?"

He nodded. "He looked like it. But he had on this weird mask, like I said. And the way he was standing there, I didn't really see his face. So I don't know if it was anger for sure, but that's what it seemed like," he explained apologetically.

"And, if you did see his face, what would you have seen?"

He shrugged. "Well, it would have been just the mask."

"Height?"

"I'm thinking around six foot," he guessed.

"And you figured that out how?"

"Well, he could rest his arms easily on the top of the dumpster."

That she wrote down. "Did he have anything in his hands or anything with him?"

He shook his head. "Not that I saw."

"Did he come past you?"

He shook his head. "Nope, nope, no way. I wasn't gonna let that happen. I would have been out of there beforehand, but, when I saw him heading down to the other end, I let him go, and then I called the police."

"But you didn't call the police right away, did you?"

He looked around nervously.

"Because first you wanted to see what he put in the dumpster, didn't you?"

The guy lifted his gaze, and she saw the haunted look in his eyes.

"Well, he cured me of that." His voice was harsh, almost guttural in tone. "Because what I saw is something I won't ever unsee."

As she remembered the poor woman with the visible torture evident on her body, she could only agree with him. "What else can you tell me?"

"Nothing." He laughed. "That was all."

"Did he stop on the way as he left? Did he throw anything on the way out of the alley? Did he turn and look back?"

"No, he just walked away."

She looked at him for a long moment and then nodded. "And there's nothing else you can tell me?"

He shook his head. "No, he wore this long thing that looked like a cloak and the mask, but that was it."

"Did he have the mask on when you first saw him?"

He frowned. "I don't know." He paused. "He also had this, you know, like a big hood on the long coat."

"So, was it a cape or a coat?"

He shrugged.

"But it had a hood? So how do you know he wore a devil's mask?"

"Because he pushed the hood off his head, when he looked up at the sky. Remember when I said he was standing, his hands on his hips, as if he was frustrated, angry, or something?"

"Got it," she muttered, wishing there was more. It didn't make a whole lot of sense, but when did any of this shit make sense? She wrote down the name of her witness. "Do you have an address? Somewhere you stay?"

"Not for a very long time," he answered.

"Do you stay at any of the shelters?"

"When I can get a bed. Other than that, I just go from park to park."

She sighed and sat back. "Was anybody else there around at the time?"

"Nope. Just me."

"You don't have any friends you hang out with?"

"I do, but I had a full bottle of booze," he explained. "Matter of fact, I was supposed to go share it, but I drank it all, after seeing that dumpster last night." He shook his head. "I knew I wouldn't be welcome if they found out I'd done that."

"Well, you also spent the day in the tank."

"And thank you for that," he said. "It was nice and dry."

She sighed. "You know that we could give you a hand to get you dried out."

"There have been lots of hands over the years." He sniffled, his eyes turning rheumy with emotions. "Ain't none of them ever took yet."

"Doesn't mean they can't," she argued.

"Maybe," he muttered. "But I'd have to give up the one thing that's been good to me."

"You mean, the bottle?" she asked gently.

He nodded. "Yeah, she's always there for me."

"But she's a bitch in the morning," Kate added, with a note of humor.

He looked at her, and a bright smile flashed on his face. "That she is," he noted affectionately, "but she's my bitch."

And that was about the truth of it. After he was gone, Kate returned to her department. As she walked to the bullpen, she picked up a coffee, wondering how, ever since the team had all come to terms, there was always coffee now.

As she neared her desk, her landline was ringing. She groaned, raced over, and grabbed it. "Detective Kate Morgan here."

Dr. Smidge was on the other end. "I've got your DB from this morning on the table."

"Already? It must be almost like a holiday down there."

"Not likely," he snapped. "A couple things you should probably go over."

"I'm on my way," she replied. "Give me half an hour."

"That's all right. I got lots of paperwork and plenty to deal with."

When he hung up the phone, she turned and looked over at Rodney. "That was Dr. Smidge. He's got this morning's victim on the table, and he wants me to go over there for some reason."

At that, Rodney looked up, startled.

"I know. Most of the time he's kicking us out of there."

"How did it get on his table so fast?"

"I asked him that and made a smart remark about it must be a holiday if he's already up to this patient, but he didn't seem to appreciate it."

"Well, that's nothing new either." Rodney hopped up to his feet. "I'll come with you."

"You got anything else to do at the same time?"

"Go back over the crime scene," he replied, with a shrug. "A couple statements that I wouldn't mind going over."

"Locals?"

"Some people saw something a couple blocks away."

"A couple blocks away?" She frowned as they walked out of the office. She looked longingly at the cup of coffee sitting and cooling on her desk.

He stopped her, pointing at the coffee. "Look. You can have a few minutes to drink it, if you want." She hesitated, and he said, "Stop. You know this isn't just about getting to the bottom of it. It's also about not killing ourselves in the process." She shot him a look, and he nodded. "Think about it. We won't be doing the victim any good if we get there out of sorts. It won't be any picnic to see that again. Best that we're calm, collected, and pulled together. And, for you, that means, grab your damn coffee."

She walked back to her desk, picked it up, and had several sips. Her computer wasn't even on yet. She looked around at the bullpen. "Where are the others?"

"Two were in with the sergeant," Rodney noted quietly.

"Problems?"

"No. One needs some personal time off. One's trying to arrange some holidays. Owen was in, and then he headed out to talk to a couple constables, doing some of the canvassing last night."

"On the same case?"

Rodney nodded. "He's the one who phoned in to say that somebody a couple blocks away had heard and seen something suspicious."

She shook her head. "Why a couple blocks away?"

He pulled out his phone, looked up the statement he wanted, and replied, "There was a pickup rumbling around the streets, going around the block several times, as if looking for something. He noted it because of a funky tarp in the back—something rolled up."

"So you're thinking it might have been the body in the back?"

"That's what Owen was wondering. Anyway, he went down to talk with our witness this morning before work and confirmed the model of the vehicle. It was an old Chevy with a rusted-out muffler, so it was making more noise than it needed to. A pickup bed with no liner, unless it was a sprayed-on black one, and then a bright green tarp in the back."

"We found no tarp at the scene," she murmured.

"And the Chevy was black, with a little bit of white trim around the rims."

"So, old rims?"

"It could have been. It's hard to say. They could have just been dirty. They could have been white rims and just really muddy."

She nodded. "And then what? He comes down to this area, starts running around, looking at things, looking for a place to dump a body maybe?"

"That's what Owen was wondering."

"Where is he now?"

"Remember the case we had last week? The one with a couple rocks thrown off one of the bridges and hitting a pedestrian down below?" he asked. "He got a line on that one."

"That pedestrian didn't die, did she?"

"No, but she was a friend of his."

"Ah, it's funny how friends completely change everything."

"Well, they're not supposed to," he noted, with a smile. "Yet there has to be a little bit of leeway in what we do. This isn't just a job for today. It's a long-term gig for us."

"Exactly." She tossed back the last of her coffee, put down her cup, and said, "Let's go."

As they headed toward the morgue, they found parking in the back of the hospital and walked down to the basement via the tunnel, where the morgue was situated. She knocked on the doors of the offices, and, when there was no answer, she turned the knob and stepped through, but the rooms were empty. She rolled her eyes and headed down to where the real action was.

"You were really thinking he'd be in the office?" Rodney asked, with a grin.

"He's never in his office, is he? But it's before the rest of it, so you always think you have to start there."

"I don't know. I think I would just completely ignore offices at this point and head down to his little corner," Rodney explained. And that's what they did anyway.

When she stepped through the double doors, Dr. Smidge looked up and frowned. "Gown up. Make sure you scrub down well."

She walked over, scrubbed her arms, put on a gown, grabbed gloves, and headed toward him. Smidge only ever requested this when he wanted her to see and to touch the body. She knew that Rodney would stay a little farther back because he couldn't stand this part. As she stepped up to the autopsy table, Smidge pulled the sheet off the victim. She sucked in her breath.

"What do you notice?" he asked her.

She shot him a look. "One of the first things is," she stated boldly, "now that she's been washed, what was done to her is so damn clear."

"Well, it's clear, but it's not clear," he argued. "You see the visible trauma without all the blood everywhere."

"The blood was bad enough," she murmured. "At the scene it looked horrific. Now it's like cold and clinical."

He nodded. "Which is a good thing because it allows us to see more. So what do you see?"

Kate studied the body, pointed out the wrists, with fractures, the ankles both broken. A shin fracture had a bone showing. The breast area she had to force herself to look at. "Completely cut off as a circle," she noted, peering forward.

"It's a weird hollow though."

"Yeah, that's what they look like after breast implants." Her gaze immediately went to the second one and then back to the first one, and he nodded. "She had both breasts done."

"Have you taken out the other one?"

"Not yet." He pointed. "Does it look like it's out?"

She could feel herself flushing because, of course, it wasn't. "You can ID her based on those, right?"

"Yep, when I get there," he stated. "What else do you notice?"

"Well, her throat." She paused. "But the wound looks odd. That didn't do more than cause her a lot of pain and possibly knock her out, but it's not the cause of death." She pointed to the higher-up slash.

"Vocal cords," he noted quietly.

"Right, so we were on target with that one."

"Yes," he agreed. "Therefore, she couldn't have screamed."

"Any idea when?"

"Probably midscream," he stated boldly, "realizing that he would have to minimize the noise."

"Or first off?"

Dr. Smidge shrugged. "Either way, it's effective."

"And doesn't she then feel like she's drowning in her own blood?" she asked.

"Absolutely, but she would have still been alive."

Kate winced. "Even with the heavy blood loss from all these injuries?" She shook her head. "The human body is amazingly resilient."

"If she'd been alive, we could have saved her, and all these injuries would have healed. Obviously the vocal cords would be an interesting conundrum to repair, depending on how much time had lapsed before we got her. But medicine has come a very long way."

"So, cause of death?"

He pointed at the missing right breast. "Besides the fact that it's got an odd shape, do you notice anything else?"

She bent over, and he pulled back the tissue against the bone, and there was a hole, right through to the chest underneath.

"Bullet?" Then she frowned. "No, what's that? It's almost like a—" She thought about it, shook her head. "It's almost like somebody took a knitting needle and poked it through her chest."

He looked at her in surprise and then nodded. "Bull's-eye."

She stared at him in shock. "Somebody rammed a knitting needle between her ribs and into her heart?"

"Yes, it punctured her heart and went right through into her back."

"Jesus," she muttered. "And I suppose ..." And she didn't even finish the sentence because, of course, the poor woman would have been awake—not awake necessarily, but she would have been alive when this was done to her. "That sounds terrible," she murmured.

"Yes. On top of that, we also have some burns." He raised one of the deceased's arms, so that Kate could see the back of the broken wrists. "These are cigarette burns. Found a couple on her cheek, a couple on her hand, a couple on her knees and—a couple on the pubis."

She looked down to see that, indeed, some pubic hair looked like it had been burned off. "He burned off her pubic hair?" she asked in astonishment.

"Probably wanted to see if it would burn," he noted

bluntly.

"*Great.*" She raised her hand to her chest.

"So we have a sadist, who wanted to bring maximum pain to this poor woman."

"That's what it would look like, yes. But—" She stopped, hesitating.

"But what?" he barked.

"Tox screen?"

"In progress," he replied. "And we can only hope that she was in some way drugged, but, because of her injuries, she wouldn't have done any fighting anyway."

Kate looked at the horribly broken wrists and nodded. "Even if she lifted her arms and tried to flail at him, she wouldn't have gotten anywhere."

"Exactly," he agreed. "It does look like her wrists were bound, so she was tied up—at least part of the time. The restraints would have been placed around where the fractures were."

"Any chance she'd have broken them, trying to get free?"

He looked at her with respect. "It's possible, except for the fact that these are open fractures."

"So, what happened?"

"In this case, I would suspect either a slice or a heavy object caused the fractures. The rest of her injuries were drier and less interesting. All it really reveals is that this guy held her for hours, possibly days, getting extreme pleasure in tormenting her."

When the coroner covered up the woman again, Kate finally stepped back, disposing of her gloves and gown. She stood at the doorway, her hands in her pockets, and looked at the rows and rows of bodies stored here. "Why did you choose this one?" He ignored her for the moment, and she realized something was important here. "Dr. Smidge," she called out, her voice slightly sharper.

At that, several other people in the same room lifted their heads and looked at her. Smidge looked up and glared.

She shook her head. "Here or your office."

His eyebrows shot up, and his glare heightened into almost fierce proportions.

Beside her, Rodney whispered, "Whoa, whoa, whoa. Cool it, kid."

But the doctor stepped back, took off his coat and his gloves, and followed her out to his office. When they got in there, Rodney stepped up close, not wanting to be left out. Dr. Smidge looked at him; his glare enough to force Rodney to immediately back up. Smidge let her into his office, as she shut the door on Rodney.

Smidge sat down at his desk, with a hard *thump*. "I wanted to," he snapped in answer to her earlier question.

"No, you *needed* to. Why?"

His fingers thrummed on the big pad atop his desk. "The knitting needle."

"Had you already seen that at the crime scene?"

He shook his head. "I didn't at first. But, when I was looking for a cause of death, the fact that one breast had been opened up caught my attention. I wasn't exactly sure what was going on, but I could see the hole."

"Have you ever seen that before?"

"Once." He paused. "Years ago."

At that, she stopped and stared. "What do you mean?"

"I had a case, a long time ago, where another young woman lost her life, with a knitting needle through her heart."

"I guess it's not a common murder weapon," she noted

carefully, "but it might have just been what was handy?"

"Maybe," he agreed. "It doesn't mean that it didn't happen since then. It's just nothing that I'm aware of."

She turned in her seat to look outside, but he was in a tunnel, so no windows were in his office, made even smaller with bookshelves upon bookshelves. "You think they're related?"

"That young woman's wrists and ankles were broken too," he stated.

"You're kidding. Vocal cords?"

He looked at her for a long moment and then slowly nodded.

She sank back in her chair. "Shit. Okay, ... we're gonna need to know what that case was. Was it ever solved?"

"Yeah," he admitted. "I'm pretty sure it was."

"Do you remember any of the details?"

He turned to his computer, clicked on the keyboard for a few minutes, and soon the printer spit out a piece of paper. He got up, walked around, picked it up, and handed it to her.

She looked at it. "Allison Lord."

"Yes." Smidge nodded. "Sounds familiar."

She read the details, which were almost exact. "So a copycat or a long sleep in-between."

"But, like I said, that doesn't mean there weren't others."

"Right, just no others that came across your desk."

He nodded. "And, if you think about it, a lot of other desks could have come across this."

"Back then, would everything have gone into the one database?"

"No." He shook his head. "Even now we're not the best at having a central depository."

"You would think that Canada would have something like that."

He snorted. "You know how much time and effort that would take?"

"And, if we started today," she noted, "in twenty years I wouldn't be looking back and cursing the fact that we didn't do it earlier."

He started to laugh at that. "Well, anytime you want to get on that, feel free."

She groaned. "Nobody will listen to me, and you know it."

"Nobody ever likes anything that'll involve a ton of money and that much work."

"I feel like it's more of a software thing." She frowned, as she thought about it. "I'll have to talk to the sergeant."

"You do that." Smidge's good humor seemed completely restored now. Having dumped everything on her, he stated he would be out for lunch.

She rolled her eyes at him, as she hopped up. As she walked over to the coroner, she asked him, "Anything else about the case bother you, Doc?" He didn't say anything for a moment, but she pressed on. "Well?"

"I never thought the guy they charged did it."

"Why not?"

"Her brother was blamed," he noted quietly, "but there was never a motive."

"That sounds pretty personal for a brother," she noted in astonishment.

He looked at her, tilted his head. "The kid was only sixteen."

"Whoa." She walked back over to the visitor chair and sat down. "Seriously?"

"He was sixteen when he supposedly committed the crime, and eighteen when he was put away, as I recall."

"Is he alive still? That is the next question. Because he was a juvenile at the time, so his sentence couldn't have been all that long. So, in theory, he could be out again."

"That's up to you to find out," Smidge replied.

"Yeah, I'll work on that." She shook her head. "I can't imagine doing that to a sister."

"Or anyone else for that matter. But, if I'd spent years in prison, thinking about it, it might be the first thing I'd do when I got back out again."

She winced, and, with that thought in mind, she added, "I'll leave you to your next patient."

"Other than getting some lunch, I'll be here all day and probably half the night," he grumbled.

"Sorry."

He shook his head. "We have a lot going on right now."

"It's not like there's ever a holiday," she reminded him.

"There never is."

With that, she walked out to see Rodney on his phone, texting away, as he leaned up against the wall. He looked up, and she could see the anger still evident in his expression.

"What was that all about?" he asked.

"Sorry about that. I'm not sure why he didn't want you in there."

"He doesn't like me," Rodney stated.

She stopped, looked at him. "Really no room for like or dislike when it comes to the job."

"You want to tell him that?"

"Nope, I do not," she stated. "You'll have to work things out with Smidge on your own."

"You're the only one he seems to get along with."

"I don't think so," she argued. "In this case, he had a reason to shift his schedule around."

"How do you know he shifted it?"

"Because that was this morning's body," she explained.

"And he got to it within what? Six hours?"

"Maybe." He rolled the back of his neck.

"Normally it would be days."

"Sure, but you seemed to be pretty determined that something was going on."

She shrugged. "Maybe just instincts."

He snorted at that. "That's BS."

"What? That I have any instincts?" she asked in a mocking tone.

"No, just that you confront him over it."

"I don't know." She shrugged. "Anyway, the reason he moved this one to the front of the line is because he remembered another case like this years ago." She handed him the printed report. "The brother was charged as a minor. He was eighteen when he was finally put away, sixteen when he committed the crime—supposedly. He proclaimed his innocence. The parents did too, and, of course, he and the sister were said to be close."

"And Smidge remembered all this why?"

"The cause of death. A knitting needle through the chest wall and on through the heart. Plus both ankles and both wrists broken, and the vocal cords cut."

"Shit," Rodney muttered. "God damn it. So a copycat or a repeat?"

"That's what we'll have to find out," she stated.

"Well, the first thing is to find out if he's still in jail."

"Given that he was a minor at the time, chances are he's free by now."

"But why would you do it all over again, especially if it was your sister—"

"Well, I guess the next thing is, does this woman look like his sister? Did he spend all those years waiting to kill her all over again?"

Wednesday, Early Morning Hours

IT HAD BEEN days since Simon had had the nightmare of the screaming woman that Kate then found dead hours later. Kate had been immersed in that case for the last three days, while Simon kept busy, terribly busy, working himself to the bone. That way, when he did finally collapse, the nightmares would either be too distant or his mind too exhausted to even dream them up. It worked for the first night or three, but last night it seemed to work in reverse.

This Wednesday, he woke up at two o'clock in the morning, screaming out loud, his body covered in sweat. Excruciating pain tortured every inch of his body. He dragged himself to the shower, where he quickly rinsed off the sweat, before coming back and pulling the sweat-soaked sheets off his bed, replacing them with clean ones.

But when he woke up at four in exactly the same state, he just laid here, letting the sweat cool on his body, his expression grim, as he gazed around his room. There was nothing, absolutely nothing that he could see or hear that would do anything to help this woman. And it was a woman; he knew that. It was another case for Kate; he knew that too.

For all he knew, it was old information, the torture of the same woman. Simon didn't know. Regardless, somebody was in extreme agony, screaming and screaming, but only in his head, although his vocal cords were doing the screaming.

He thought maybe she was screaming too, but he had no way to know that. His nightmare was just darkness, incessant darkness. He could almost hear her whimper in the back of his mind, as he lay here.

By the time six rolled around, he got up, had another long hot shower, and put on the strongest coffee he thought he could tolerate. Sitting at his dining room table and staring out at the beautiful horizon outside, he wondered how such a beautiful city could house so much horror. He hadn't seen Kate since she had caught this latest case. And that was life with Kate.

She showed up whenever and disappeared for days at a time. He could text her, and, if she had time, she'd answer him. However, if she didn't have time, he always stepped back into the background of her world. He had plenty to deal with on his own, so, in a way, it worked, Yet, in another way, it irked him completely because he wanted more. He needed more. And she wasn't having any of it.

He sat here, a notepad in front of him, as he worked out all the things he had to do today. Part of it was ordering supplies and going to the bank to move money. Some of it he couldn't do online, though he preferred to do all of it that way if he had the option. But, every once in a while, actually showing up with a physical presence at the bank was mandatory. It sucked, but that's what it was. He looked down at the notepad to see that he'd been drawing circles, some weird circles.

After a more careful survey, he realized that they were ropes knotted, with a wrist through it. Even as he watched, his hand continued to draw what looked like one single arm tied down flat. He immediately ripped off the page, crumpled it into a ball, and tossed it across the floor.

"No fucking way," he muttered. "It's bad enough to have all this crap penetrate my nightmares. It's another thing to have it get in the way of my working world."

He admitted a lot of the background emotion from his nightmares centered on fear, seeping into Simon too. He'd spent a long time not being a victim. A long time standing up straight and daring anybody to look down on him for whatever reason. He was well respected within his industry. He earned millions on a yearly basis, and, by now, it was actually every quarter. The money flowed quite nicely, as he worked to fix up the lower-end areas of the city.

He'd been asked by several people why he chose these buildings, and he couldn't say anything, except that they had heart and that the rest of the world had forgotten about them. It was foolish and even a bad business deal at times, since he was a philosopher, looking to reclaim lost souls and buildings. It was just BS, the whole lot of it. And yet, every time another one came up for sale, he found himself completely unable to do anything but buy it and then immediately turn around to fix it up again.

Speaking of which, he had an ongoing tag problem with a certain realtor. She had a property he wanted, and she knew it. But she was asking way too much money for it, so they were stuck at an impasse.

Periodically, once a week or so, she would reach out, asking if he'd thought more about that property. So far, he'd been ignoring her, but, yeah, he was considering it still. It was on his list to take another walk by it, just to see if he felt the same about the place. It was one of four that he had thought about getting. If he could get all four, he could just drop them and put up something nice. Something to help rejuvenate that part of town. But what she wanted for that one property was what he should pay for two, and agreeing to her price would set a dangerous precedent for the others on the block.

And, although money flowed through his fingers with regularity, he didn't get there by being a fool. So, when it came to actual money landing in his pockets, he knew that the more he had there, the more he could do. Only people, like this realtor, were intent on trying to take out every penny they could. He knew this was business, an industry on its own, but he now had less respect for these types who were greedier in this area than in most industries.

It was tough enough to deal with the various building trades. They promised they'd show up on a Monday, and, when they finally appeared on Wednesday, looking completely innocent, they would look you square in the face and say that you're the one who made the mistake. It was enough to make you want to rip out their hearts and toss them off the damn building. But Simon had been in this business for way too long and had a short list of contractors he would work with, and a secondary list of contractors he would consider trying again, providing they actually showed up as promised.

The problem was, he had so many buildings in progress right now—whether rehabs or tear-downs—that it was hard to find enough good workers. At that, he checked his phone and found a couple texts sitting there from his contractors, waiting to be read. He perused them, noting nothing was major. One was just an update, and the other one promised completion of a new section today. Simon wouldn't even say that he'd be there at the end of the day because, at this point in time, he wasn't sure he was going anywhere.

Then he looked down at the scratchpad. Once again,

he'd drawn a woman's wrist, tied to a table. He felt the fear jolt into his heart. "I don't need this," he said in a very low and threatening voice. He almost heard his grandmother's voice in the background, saying, *Tough shit. Deal with it.*

He got up, with a hard shake of his head, then ripped off the second piece of paper, scrunched it up, and threw it across the living room. That wasn't enough, so he grabbed both pieces of paper, stormed out to the recycling and garbage chute, and dumped them in. At least then they'd be gone, maybe not forever, but gone for the moment. He came in and sat back down, but, yet again, his hand immediately picked up the pencil and started sketching the same image. He looked at it and glared.

"What is it you're trying to tell me?"

And, at that moment, almost like he'd opened a damn door, a scream ripped through his mind.

CHAPTER 4

K ATE REACHED FOR the phone and called the parole officer and identified herself when he answered. "I'm looking into case file 127264D."

"Hang on," he muttered, as he brought it up on his computer. "Oh, right. Lord."

"Yeah, was the first name, Richard?"

"Yes, but he goes by Rick," he confirmed.

"Did he complete everything required?"

"He did actually. When he got out of prison, he came every week, and he never did anything wrong," he stated. "Why?"

"Just checking to make sure he's not a suspect in a current case."

"Well, I wouldn't have thought it of him," the parole officer replied. "He was a model inmate. He got his education and even earned a degree."

"In what?" she interrupted.

He checked through his notes. "English Literature."

She snorted at that.

"Hey, I think he intends to become a teacher, you know?"

"Is that even possible?"

"It is if he can get some job experience. They might hire him, if they don't do a record check."

"Doesn't he have to state that he has a criminal record?"

"He was charged as a juvenile, so that would have been expunged from his record."

"How is that even a thing?" she asked hotly.

"I wouldn't worry about it. He's no danger to society."

"I understand that he also maintained he had nothing to do with it."

"Even on his last visit, he turned to me, and he repeated, 'You know that I didn't do this. I'm as much of a victim as my sister.'"

"And you believed him?" It was hard to not question the parole officer because, when somebody was let out of jail, that parole officer was the one person who consistently saw the newly released prisoner over the following six months or one year.

"You know what? I do actually," he noted. "I think he got a bad rap. He was in trouble at the time, heading down a bad pathway. He made a good suspect, and they ran with it."

"There still should have been forensic evidence."

"The problem was, he and the sister lived together," he explained, "so hairs and fibers were all over the place."

"Of course. Did they ever find the location where she was held?"

"You tell me," he snapped, his tone turning hard. "As far as I'm concerned, the system railroaded this kid into confessing, and that ended his life."

"Or made it," she added quietly.

After a moment's hesitation, the parole officer grudgingly acceded. "Or made it. You're right. He was into drugs and gangs prior to this."

"Interesting. I wonder if it wasn't him. I wonder if it could have been somebody affiliated with the gang."

"Well, I'll tell you what. If you can solve it, then that kid has got some relief coming for all the years he sat in prison for a crime he didn't commit. Other than that, I've got nothing to offer."

When she hung up, she looked down at her notes, wrote them up on her file and sat back.

"What was that all about?" Rodney asked, as he walked toward her with two cups of coffee.

She looked at him in surprise. "What's this? I get served now?"

"Why not?" He shrugged. "You've bought me a couple."

"That's true." At that, she picked up the hot brew gently and replied, "I just talked to the parole officer. The kid was apparently a model prisoner. While he was inside, he got his degree in English Lit and is looking to become a teacher."

At that, Rodney's eyebrows shot up. "With a criminal record?"

"Well, he was a minor when he was charged and convicted."

"Right," he agreed, with an eye roll, "so everything gets expunged."

"Sealed, at least."

"Same diff," he muttered. "I wonder where the morality is on those, you know? When you apply for a job and when they ask all those questions, like if you can be bonded or if you have a criminal record? What do you actually say if it's been expunged?"

"I guess he could say no. How crazy is that?" she added, shaking her head.

"But then if he were to say yes, and then if they ask more about it, then go do a criminal record check, nothing will show up, so he just looks like a liar."

"Right," she noted. "I hadn't thought of it that way. The parole officer also said that he'd never done anything wrong. He followed all the rules and regulations, and, on his very last day, he walked out the door, saying he was innocent of all charges."

"Great, so we're nowhere."

"Not necessarily. I do have his last known residence."

"Where's that?"

"Well, that's the part I don't understand. It appears he has moved back in with his parents."

"Interesting."

"Well, the kid served ten years, has been out for five more, so has got to be in his early thirties by now—yet somehow he's still *the kid* to me, the kid who got caught killing his sister when he was only sixteen. And he's stayed clean, as far as we know," she muttered.

"Interesting."

"Only the two siblings in the family," she stated, "so, if the parents believe the son had nothing to do with her death, they must have welcomed him back with open arms."

"Of course. That's what would give them a sense of family again."

"I did ask the parole officer about this because no way her torture and subsequent murder could have happened to her without some place where she could have been held for a period of time, right?" Rodney nodded. She continued. "According to the file, the police believed the original crime was actually committed in the family home."

"I'm not sure how that works." Rodney frowned, looking through his copy of the file. "Looks like they sold that place and moved to a different one."

"Well, I sure as hell wouldn't stay in the same place

where I found my daughter murdered," she muttered. Kate brought up the address where they used to live. "Look at that. It's empty—currently slated for demolition."

Rodney nodded. "Looks like it's part of a rezoning area for a commercial development. That house is going down, and some mall or something is going up in its place."

"*Hmm.*" She looked at her computer screen a moment longer. "I'll call and see if we can get in there." With that, she quickly dialed the number for the current property owner and explained who she was.

The woman on the other end replied, "Well, the building is slated for demolition, but we probably won't get to it for about three weeks."

"I'm looking for permission to go in and to take a look at the old crime scene."

"You really think anything will still be there?" she asked in avid fascination.

"No, I don't think so, but I do want to go take a look, just so I can see it myself."

"Why would you want to do that?" the woman asked in disgust.

"You'd be surprised what we can think of when on the scene," Kate replied.

After a moment of hesitation, the other woman stated, "I have to clear it with my boss."

"Yeah, you do that. And who is your boss, by the way?"

"I'm not allowed to say," she answered, her voice turning cagey.

Kate rolled her eyes at that. "Fine. Get back to me, please. I'd like to get out there today."

"If not today, then tomorrow."

"It has to be at least tomorrow." With that, Kate hung

up, turned, then looked at Rodney. "It is slated for demolition. This woman is looking to get permission from her boss."

He snorted. "I just printed out the family history, work, employment, everything else we had on the daughter."

"Good." Kate nodded. "It's always interesting when we have a case that connects to the current one because, right now, we only have the victim to go by. We're still waiting for an ID on her." Just then her phone rang. She picked it up, checked her Caller ID, and smiled. "Hello, Dr. Smidge. Do you have any news?"

"Cherry Blackwell. At least according to the ID on the breast implant."

"Cherry Blackwell. Thank you."

"I'm sending through her file too," he added. "She was given knockout drugs. The pain would have kept kicking her awake, depending on the dose he gave her, it's cumulative, and it looks like she had quite a bit. But some of it's already out of her system. I would suspect repeated doses," he noted.

"Good enough. I'm just waiting on your report, and thanks." She hung up, turned, and looked at Rodney. "Cherry Blackwell. That's our victim. The report is coming through now."

His computer dinged at the same time hers did, as the reports landed in their in-boxes. She looked it up.

Rodney ran the information on her implant through the database. "We have the name of her doctor."

"With a doctor, we should get our victim's address. No address on Smidge's report." She picked up the phone and called the office of the doctor listed.

As soon as she explained who she was, the receptionist replied, "I'm sorry, but all the patient files are confidential."

"This patient is deceased," Kate noted. "So we're looking for an address."

The other woman gasped.

"We have the breast implant number, but we don't have anything else." Frowning at the silence on the other end of the phone, Kate tapped on her desk. "So, if you have any contact information, we need it."

"Oh my." The flustered woman rambled off an address and a phone number.

Making her repeat it, Kate wrote it down. "Good enough. When was she last in your office?"

"Two years ago," she stated, "so I don't know if the address and phone number are current."

"Her last visit was two years ago?"

"Yes."

"Good enough," she replied, before disconnecting the call.

Part of the information provided was also the insurance number for the medical plan she had used for some coverage of the original visits. With that, Kate tracked down some additional medical data. "She's twenty-eight years old, and the DMV still shows the same address," Kate told Rodney.

"Parents and two brothers, both back East. Address on Aspen?"

She quickly checked through what she had. "It doesn't look like it."

"You want to go to your address first or phone the family?"

"We should phone the family," she muttered, but she hated to. Those calls were always the worst.

"I can make that call, if you want," Rodney offered.

She looked over at him and nodded. "Do you mind?

That would be great. Find out if there's anything or anyone in her life."

"I know the drill," he added, with an eye roll.

She smiled. "I know you do. It's just habit." She got up and refilled her coffee cup, while he made the next-of-kin notification call. When she returned to the bullpen, he was still talking in a low voice, trying to calm down the family.

"I'm so sorry to bring you this news," he repeated, "and any help you can give us would be appreciated."

Once the call was done, and he'd scratched down all his notes, he turned to share what they had told him. "One of the two brothers is deceased, leaving just the one sibling behind. All the family lives in Toronto."

"Interesting," she noted, "so our latest victim had two brothers."

"The other brother had been deceased for ten years, from a motorcycle accident."

She winced. "Pretty hard to survive that kind of an accident."

"It happens," Rodney said. "But, more often than not, they don't."

She nodded. "Did they know anything about her current life?"

"She was working as a model sometimes. Other than that, she had a reception job at one of the offices downtown."

"Which office?"

He gave her the name, and she immediately typed it in.

"Look at that," she replied, with some glee. "The home address I have for her puts her just a couple blocks from this work address."

"A couple blocks?" Rodney asked.

"Right." Kate nodded. "So what are the chances that she was actually picked up at that location?"

"Pretty damn good, I would say. But she's wouldn't have been held at the same spot," Rodney noted. "All high-end businesses in that area."

She frowned, nodded, and added, "We need to talk to her boss."

"We do, indeed." Rodney hopped up, looked at her, and grinned. "You and your coffee."

"I know," Kate admitted, as she held her coffee cup. "Let's give it ten, and then we'll go."

He nodded approvingly, sat down again, while picking up his own coffee and taking a sip. "According to the parents, there was no sign of a current relationship."

"*Hmm*, she was pretty, a model. Surely a beautiful woman like that had dates," Kate added quietly.

Rodney tilted his head. "The parents did say she had a bad breakup about a year or so ago. They gave me the name—a Tyler Bjornsson—but, as far as they knew, the two had no contact ever since. So, a bad breakup, but not necessarily a bad aftermath."

"Possibly, yes." She typed in the name. "Did they give you any contact information?" she asked.

"Nope." Rodney shook his head.

She looked at her screen and frowned. "Looks like he's a day trader in Vancouver. ... And look at that. His office is in the same building where she worked."

"Not the same company though, right?"

She shook her head. "No, not the same company." Needing his contact information, she wrote down what floor he was on and added, "Maybe we can talk to him at the same time."

"Sounds good."

She tossed back the rest of her coffee and mulled over the emails that continued to pour into her inbox. "I don't know why people send emails all the time," she muttered. "Didn't they get the message?"

"What message was that?" he asked in surprise.

"I'm on a case," she snapped, her eyes glaring, as she turned to look at him. "I don't have time for the rest of this shit."

"What shit is that?"

"Plenty of review stuff coming up." She groaned. "And paperwork to fill out now that I am well past the three-month probationary period."

"You didn't do that yet?"

"Have I had time yet?" she countered.

He grinned. "Well, you might try telling them that but don't expect them to listen."

She groaned again, louder this time. "Okay, fine. I'll take it with me and work on it at home."

"How many times have you put it off?"

She grimaced at him, shaking her head.

He held up his hands. "Fine, fine, don't talk to me," he surrendered, "but you really need to deal with this review shit when it comes in. That way it's done, and you don't have to worry about it again."

"Yeah, until next year. Well, shit is exactly like that, isn't it? You get rid of it once, but you turn around the next day, and you have to handle it again."

He stared at her for a long moment, then he burst out laughing.

"It's not that funny," she muttered. But inside she was pleased. She rarely came up with witty jokes, and this one was not only witty but shitty as well. She even groaned at her own rhyme. But she hopped to her feet, grabbed her jacket, opened her desk drawer, and gathered her things. Picking up her keys, she said, "Let's go."

Still chuckling, Rodney finished his coffee. "You know what? You are starting to fit in around here."

"Why? Because I can add shitty jokes to the conversation?" she asked.

That set him off again, and she rolled her eyes and headed for the door. As they almost left the bullpen area, their sergeant walked in, looked at them in surprise, and asked, "Where are you two heading?"

"You know our victim found in the dumpster? We're headed to her place of work, as well as that of her ex-boyfriend, who works in the same building," Kate informed him, "to have a face-to-face talk."

"Good enough." Colby nodded. "I understand Dr. Smidge had something extra to add to this one." His gaze went from one detective to the other.

Kate turned and looked at Rodney. "Did you really say something to the sergeant?"

He shrugged. "Hey, all is fair in love and war, and we live in the war zone more often than not."

She turned back to the sergeant. "Dr. Smidge noted that he remembered a case—from about fifteen years ago—where the victim also died in a similar manner. The woman's brother was convicted as a juvenile, held in juvie from before and after trial, and he was released about five years ago now, after serving ten years." She shook her head as she tried to do the math. "He successfully completed all requirements of his probation and is currently on target with no problems. The parole officer believes his assertion that he was innocent."

"Interesting, but it's not like we haven't heard that one million times before."

"I know, and I do have the address for the family. I wanted to take a walk through the old house, which was the crime scene."

"He killed her in the family home?"

"Well, that's another part that doesn't quite fit. Anyway, the building is currently slated for demolition, and I've got a call into the development board, asking for permission to do a walk-through."

"That would be good," Colby agreed, "although I don't know what a crime scene from fifteen years ago would tell you."

"What it might tell me is whether it was even doable. Both these women were tortured, sir. Wrists broken, ankles broken, one breast removed, vocal cords slashed to keep them quiet, and finally a knitting needle through the ribs into the heart after the breast was removed."

He stared at her, shook his head, and frowned. "What a world full of sick people we live in."

"Well, there are sick people in this world," she agreed, "but I don't know that the world is full of them though."

"That's hardly making me feel any better." Colby waved them toward the elevator. "Go. Go get this one solved and out of my head. The last thing I want is to have a serial killer who's done two of these murders on the loose."

"Dr. Smidge did acknowledge that it's possible there could have been others in the meantime."

"In which case, the boy wouldn't have committed the crimes, right?" He turned and looked at her.

"Possibly a copycat killing in another area to keep it low-key, so the kid didn't get released."

"That would be lovely," he moaned. "What if the woman was killed to make it look like the kid did it?"

"That would be sick, sir."

"Well, I'm going right back around to what I said to begin with. It is a sick world." And, with that, he stormed down the hallway to his office.

Kate punched the button to the elevator, shoved her hands into her pockets, and rocked back on her heels.

"He's got a point," Rodney said.

"He might have a point," she muttered, "but we need more than points. We need forensic evidence. We also need a motive. That was the one thing Dr. Smidge said was missing before." She sighed. "That is a lot for a brother to do to a sister," Kate noted. "I don't care how much you think you hate her. When you think about it, you've spent a lot of time with her, shared meals, playtime, TV, holidays, vacations. You hear one getting berated by a parent. You hear the other getting smacked around. You hear about troubles at school. They're all connections. So, even though you may hate somebody, it takes a deeper level of absolute madness to turn that hate into something so dark that you're actually willing to torture somebody for hours and days before you finally kill them."

She continued. "And that's the problem with this case. I get that cutting the vocal cords provides a means to do this in any space. I mean, an apartment, a tiny room, or even a closet would probably be enough if you made it into a murder room. And that makes the location of the murder all that much more interesting."

"*Interesting?*" Rodney asked, his voice rising.

She shrugged. "The kid's bedroom? The kid sister's bedroom? Like the victim's room was maybe in the basement?

Maybe the parents were in Europe for six weeks. I don't know what to say, but that's why I want to go see the house."

"No, I hear you," Rodney agreed. "I don't have a basement."

"I've seen enough houses with basements," she added, "to know that, in some cases, they're really nasty-ass locations and would probably be good murder rooms."

"Especially if it was a cold-cellar-type basement," he mentioned. "The colder temps would keep her from bleeding too badly. And then ... wait. Was there a sexual connotation to this current victim?"

Kate frowned. "I don't know. I don't think Smidge answered that." She considered that, picked up her phone as they took the elevator down to the main floor, then sent him a message. **Was she sexually assaulted?**

Did you not read the report?

She winced at that. "Well, now you don't have to worry," she shared with Rodney. "I'm on his bad side too."

"Why is that?"

"I just asked if the victim was sexually assaulted."

He looked at her in surprise. "That's a fair question."

"Yeah, his response was fair too. He asked if I'd read the report."

"Ouch," he replied. "Yeah, nobody likes to have their time wasted."

Her phone buzzed again. She looked at the text and winced. "Jesus."

"What?" Rodney asked curiously.

"Well, she was assaulted with an object."

"Oh, great."

"Strong enough, hard enough, that it pierced the uterus." She groaned and immediately put away her phone and stormed out the front door of the station.

"Hey, hey, hey," Rodney called out after her.

She stopped and took a deep breath of fresh air, as if it would brush away all the nastiness clogging up her throat. "Why do people do that?" she asked, rounding on him. "No need to take it to that level."

He reached out, grabbed her by the shoulders, and stated, "There is a need. There has to be, and that's what we must figure out. What was the need inside him that drove him to this level?"

"It couldn't have been the brother in that earlier case," she argued, shaking her head. "I can't believe one family member would do that to another."

He stared at her and asked, "Really? After your years with the police force?"

She nodded slowly. "You're gonna tell me about way-worse cases, aren't you?"

"There *are* way-worse cases of horrible things family members do to each other," he stated, "so don't even begin to think that. You need look no farther than Simon."

She shook her head, grimacing at the reminder.

"In this case, we don't know because we don't know anything about the family. Right now you don't want to believe the brother could have done something like this. But something pinned him in that suspect chair. And there had to be something to convict him."

She nodded and tried to calm down and to get more oxygen into her lungs.

"Come on," Rodney said. "Let's go to our current victim's workplace and then meet the ex-boyfriend and see what we can dredge up."

"Right." She gave herself a mental shake. "And we also need to check the autopsy report from the old case and see if that sexual detail was duplicated as well."

"What's your guess on it?"

She shuddered. "Unfortunately I'll say it probably was."

"These details matter," he confirmed, "because, if this guy didn't do it to his sister, how does this guy who is doing it now know what happened?"

"You mean, if the brother didn't do it, the same killer is back in play. Yet, if the brother did do it, we have to know why. Plus, if the brother did one but not the other, it means he told somebody."

"Well, that would be a good way to analyze it." Rodney nodded. "Whichever way, we don't have enough to decide anything yet, so let's go get more data."

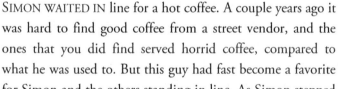

SIMON WAITED IN line for a hot coffee. A couple years ago it was hard to find good coffee from a street vendor, and the ones that you did find served horrid coffee, compared to what he was used to. But this guy had fast become a favorite for Simon and the others standing in line. As Simon stepped up, the guy with the weathered face looked up, saw who it was, and gave him a big grin.

"Coffeetime?"

"Yes, please." Simon put several coins on the window ledge.

"What size?"

"Make it a large," he replied. "It's a hot day out, but I've got a ton of work and could use the energy."

"You got to have more than just caffeine to live off of," the older man stated, with a shake of his head. "I have all kinds of food here too."

"It's just the wrong time to eat for me," he stated. "I had a late breakfast, so I'm not quite ready for more."

"Well, you know where to find me when you are," he muttered.

Simon realized he had yet to try any of this guy's food. He looked around to see several sweet items but also a chicken kabob that made his stomach growl. He frowned as he looked at the pictures. "So how close to the pictures are these kabobs?" he asked.

"I've got a dozen just coming off the oil," he said. "Hang on a moment." He disappeared around the side of his small outdoor street cart, where it had a cooking area in the back. He came back with a paper envelope, and he handed it over.

The kabob was hot enough that Simon's fingers were already complaining.

"This one is on me," the older guy stated.

Simon put the kabob on the counter, immediately shaking his head, as he dug into his pocket, pulled out a bunch more coins, and, without even looking at them, added them to his other coins. "Not needed," he said. It smelled delicious. "Cumin in this?"

The other man barked. "That's just one of a dozen spices in it."

"Good enough," Simon replied. "Let me give this a try with my coffee, and we'll see."

"Most people order a sweet."

"Not me," he noted. "I'm all about protein."

The older man gave Simon a wicked grin, scooped up the coins, then put them into a container on the other side. "Let me know how you like it."

And, with that, Simon grabbed the wrapped kebob,

some paper napkins, and his coffee, then headed off to a small bench nearby. He could keep walking, but he had something in each hand. He reached the bench, where he sat down. He took the lid off the coffee to let it cool ever-so-slightly and blew on the edge of the meat treat in front of him.

He thought about what the old guy had said and looked up to see several people walking away with some version of a cinnamon bun, coated in white icing. He looked down at his choice. Never having had much of a sweet tooth, he was always much more about protein. With that thought in mind, he took a tentative bite. The flavors immediately crashed through his mouth, making his senses sit up straight in shock. He smiled.

It was good. Not only was it good, it was really good. It always amazed him when he came across something so very different in taste. He had another bite and then another, thoroughly enjoying the completely different and almost foreign taste to the meat. It was crusty on the outside and moist and flavorful inside. Simon caught the vendor's eye and raised his treat with a smile and a nod. The coffee was cool enough now to at least have a couple sips, and, polishing off the treat in his hand, he stood, put the lid back on his coffee, and carried on to his next job.

When he arrived twenty minutes later, the foreman came out of the building and lifted a hand in greeting.

"Don't you ever get tired of walking?"

"Most of my projects are downtown at the moment," Simon explained. "If I lived anywhere else, then I probably would drive. However, down here, it's more of a pain to park anyway, so I might as well just keep walking."

"I get it, but you must put on a lot of miles."

"I'm used to it." Simon shrugged. "No different than a mailman who walks all day."

At that, the foreman nodded. "I hadn't considered that," he admitted. "It just seems to me that a man in your position could drive."

"A man in my position could drive," he agreed gently, "or even be driven, but this one chooses to walk."

With that out of the way, the foreman got down to business. "We've got a couple problems."

"Is there ever a time when we don't have a couple problems?" Simon asked, with a groan.

"Well, when it comes to these old buildings, you know that they tend to spring leaks and to open up all kinds of grizzly problems."

Simon frowned, turned, and looked at him. "What do you mean by *grizzly?*"

"Well, this one is not too bad," the foreman confirmed. "I've had a couple that were pretty rough but none of your jobs."

"Well, let's keep it that way." Simon shook his head. "How long have you worked for me now?"

"Two years, I think, or close to that anyway."

"Well, no shortage of work up ahead either," he added.

"Did you ever get that building? Are you still after that one you've had your eye on for quite a while?"

"No, the realtor still wants too much for it."

"You know the market has been going up steadily, right?"

"Sure, it has," Simon noted. "But it needs to rebalance itself when what they're asking for one is what I'd be willing to pay for two."

"The trouble is, they're all about location, location, location," he quoted.

"Yeah, but somebody will still have the money to turn that location into a moneymaker," he muttered. "And too often these are just crap."

The foreman laughed. "You've made money," he stated. "That's what the realtor thinks. How many have you bought from her now?"

"Probably too many," Simon admitted. "I might have to set up a new real estate deal with somebody else and make it look like there's competition sniffing around."

"Then she'll just come back at you and tell you there's even more interest."

"Maybe," he noted, "but that building is falling down, so we'd have to drop it and start fresh."

"You've only done that about twice that I can recall," the foreman noted, considering the clipboard in his hand. "But if you want to build a third one from the beginning, you need to pick that location pretty carefully."

"I know. That's why I was thinking about buying all four buildings, then at least, if we support and rebuild one of the middle ones, we might as well be fixing up the ones on the other side at the same time."

"That'd be a big job." The foreman pushed back his hard hat, as he studied Simon with interest.

"We're talking a couple years anyway."

"Even the best of jobs end up being a couple years."

"I'm not sure that it isn't bigger than I want to take on right now." Simon reached up and gently massaged his temple.

"Still not sleeping well?"

"It seems like I haven't slept well in six months," he said, with a laugh.

"You could go to a doctor and get something."

He immediately shook his head. "I'd rather do anything but that."

"Work out in the evenings instead of the morning?"

"I do that sometimes, maybe with a swim." He turned almost unconsciously toward his place. "One of these days I might buy a single-family home and have a pool, where I could go out in the evening and rest and relax in the privacy of my own place."

"You don't have a pool where you are?" the foreman asked.

"One's in the building. That's not the same as having one to yourself."

The foreman immediately nodded. "I agree with you there. My brother-in-law has this place with a gorgeous pool and a hot tub, but they never go in either. Half the time they're not even in the country."

"That's where most of those people are," Simon agreed, with a laugh. "That never really appealed to me. If I would leave the country, I would go do something fun and exciting, then come back and relax. It's still home for me here."

"I hear you there." The foreman tapped his clipboard. "But we do have a few hours of shit you need to go over. We should get started." And, on that note, he led the way back into the building they were rehabbing. "Let's start here." And he pointed out some of the structural problems they had discovered. "This is too far off square. We'll either need to refloor it, or we'll have to build up some of this support structure on the side," he noted. "The plumbing won't be sound enough to rest on here."

"We were worried about that in the beginning," Simon muttered to his foreman.

"Yes, and honestly the best answer at this point in time would be to start fresh and to get these supports in."

"We'll have to get the flooring and all of this reengineered. Better to do it now than later. You know how I feel about cutting corners."

"I know that," the foreman confirmed. "But I also know how you feel about projects taking way too long and losing money."

"Yeah, I get it," Simon agreed. "So, talk to the architect and see if we can get some of these flooring joists added in. Get that fixed, and we'll move on from there." He groaned as he looked around. "I wasn't really expecting this project to be done fast by any means, but it's had more headaches than any others on my plate right now."

"I'm only dealing with three of yours at the moment," he added. "And this is my priority right now, mostly because we haven't been able to get a clear shot at seeing real progress on it."

"No, and now the engineers need to come back in and take another look," Simon noted. "That'll just hold us up even more. But it's got to be done, and we don't want to end up with a bigger headache down the road."

With that settled, and a few other smaller issues dealt with, Simon headed off to his next project. He was still pissed off about the project he had just left, but only so much he could do. He knew it had been a gamble to take on that project, but it had been a building that Simon just couldn't walk away from.

So, as the rehab price went up, the headaches went up with it. Yet Simon was in, and it was one of those times where he basically had to spend his way back out again.

It would remain to be seen whether he made any profit

on that job or not. If it would be an obvious *hell no* result, then maybe he would just turn it over to something that warmed his heart instead. Canada didn't really have orphanages or children's homes, but there were certainly needs for women's centers, so maybe he could do something for single mothers, like put in some low-income housing to cater to that select market.

They wouldn't pay off the building by any means, at least not within fifty years at the rates that those single mothers could pay, but it would be one of projects he did on a regular basis just to give back to the world that had saved his life so long ago. He didn't want anybody else to end up in the same boat that he knew so many women did, so maybe that's what this one would have to be. He thought about all the apartments that could be created in a building that size, realizing it wasn't a bad idea at all. Which made it even more important that the building be structurally sound, so it would go the distance.

The last thing he'd want to do would be to endanger anybody, but to endanger children would be even worse. Simon wasn't the asshole kind who could turn around and take from the world. For him it was all about giving back and using his resources for good. But he also had to make money in order to keep those projects flowing, which meant it all had to be in balance. And keeping things in balance when it came to construction, well, that was a whole different story.

Heading to his next project, he already wished he'd picked up another coffee. It would be a hell of a long day at this point. His lack of sleep was definitely an issue as well, but it wasn't something that he would allow to slow him down. As he kept on walking, he heard almost like a knocking on the back of his soul. Maybe like the back door to his mind, although that thought made him feel like an idiot. No way he could have all this energy crap going on and keep it hidden, but he was doing his best to make it look that way.

Again he felt something in the back of his mind. He tried to ignore it but wasn't very successful. By the time he arrived at the next job, he had stomped on whatever it was pushing at his consciousness, which allowed him to focus on what he needed to do at the jobsite. He found a whole lot less headaches here, and things were actually functioning at a much better rate thankfully, so he headed on to his third one.

He was only a few steps away, heading around the corner to an alleyway, when he heard screams start in the back of his mind. He froze and took a quick glance around. It was early afternoon, probably about two o'clock, but he didn't have his phone in his hand. People rushed from place to place, and traffic was heavy, even in the alleyway. People were loading, unloading, and shouting up and down. He leaned up against one of the walls and took several slow deep breaths, trying to push back and get out of this psychic vision, so he could function normally.

With the sun beating down on his face, he turned ever-so-slightly, so that he was hidden in the shadows a bit more and took several deeper breaths. When somebody punched him in the shoulder, hard, he almost crumbled to his feet. He'd been stunned, caught by surprise, but he braced himself against the wall and turned to face his attacker. Two homeless guys looked a bit more ready for a fight than Simon would have expected.

"What are you doing in here?" one asked. "This is our place."

"Just took a moment to stop and rest," Simon replied in a mild tone. He was dressed in a three-piece suit, and it was obvious that he wasn't trying to take over the alleyway for himself. These two were just looking for trouble, more trouble than Simon would have been worth.

The one gave him a hard look. "You're just lying."

"About what?" Simon muttered in surprise. "I don't have anything to lie about."

"You all lie. You're part of the establishment, and every one of you are liars."

Simon rolled his eyes at that because there was really no arguing with crazy people. He looked over at the other guy. "Is that what you think?"

"Of course that's what I think," he agreed. "If my buddy says so, I believe him."

"Right, blind devotion," Simon muttered, "the blind leading the blind."

"I'm not blind," the first man snapped, getting even more belligerent.

"No, of course not." Simon looked at him and stated, "I was just leaving, and I really don't feel like getting into an argument with you."

"Too bad, you're in my space, so that means an argument's about to happen."

"Well, we could just avoid it," Simon replied quietly. "I really don't want to hurt you."

At that, the homeless guy's jaw dropped. "You think a little namby-pamby like you is gonna hurt me?" He snorted and nudged his buddy right beside him. "Did you hear that? He seems to think that he's a threat."

The other guy snickered. "Maybe he's got some money on him."

"Oh, so it's not just about the alleyway?" Simon muttered, straightening up. "It's all about stealing. So is this a mugging? Is that what you think this is all about?"

"Hey, we have to live too."

"Sure, you do. You could try a job. You could even try a homeless center and lay off the drugs and the booze and get your shit together."

At that, the first man glared at him. "Nothing's wrong with us," he sneered. "We're doing just fine."

"Right, as long as you can accost a few people, and you get to eat for the rest of the day, is that it?"

He shrugged. "We all do what we have to do," he stated, stepping closer. "Now just hand over whatever money you've got on you."

"Nope, ain't happening," Simon stated, "so don't even bother asking."

"You think I'm kidding?" And, just like that, he pulled out a switchblade.

"Ah, so it is a mugging and soon to be a stabbing. But you don't really care about any of that, do you?"

"I really don't," he said. "Assholes like you made my life hellish."

"Nope," Simon argued. "You were on your own journey down this pathway without me."

"You don't know what you're talking about," the man yelled.

"Maybe just get him to not talk so much," the other guy suggested nervously.

"Why? In case I say something that might make sense to you?" Simon asked, looking at him with interest. "I mean, you're with this loser, so obviously you're okay with his methodology."

"Well, we want the alleyway," he repeated. "We need it. With everybody here, it's all about turf."

"Maybe, but that knife is not about turf. That knife is about power, about hating the world around you. That knife is about, 'Hey, you got something that I want, and I don't want to go work for it, so I'll just take it off you instead,'" Simon explained, focusing on the less aggressive male.

At that, the guy glanced around nervously.

Simon went on. "Don't you realize, in this place, it's pretty easy for you to be seen in the act of committing a crime? Cameras are all over."

The second man stepped back nervously. "Maybe we should just leave him alone."

"That ain't happening," the first man snapped.

"But he's not like our normal guys."

"No, he isn't. That's why it's important that we teach him a lesson, so all the other guys like this realize they can't just talk to us any old way they want and expect us to back down and do their bidding."

"Yeah? Exactly what bidding did I ask you to do?" Simon asked, crossing his arms over his chest. He rested nonchalantly against the wall, waiting for them to make a move. The knife wasn't an issue, but the weird look in the knife-bearer's gaze definitely was. This guy was high on drugs of some kind; Simon wasn't so sure the second guy was though. He looked over at him. "Are you as drugged out as your buddy here?"

He shook his head slowly. "No, he's having a bad time today."

"Right, so, if this is a bad time," Simon noted, shaking his head, "I can't imagine what a good time is."

"Well, it's been a bad week, let me say that," he muttered.

"What are you doing hanging around with him? You know this guy will just get your ass thrown in jail."

He nervously moistened his lips. "Nah, he's my friend."

"Meaning, he gets you food and drugs, right?"

The guy looked at him, somewhat haunted.

"Stop talking," the other guy said in a hard voice to Simon. "You ain't got no truck trying to cause trouble between us."

"I'm not trying to cause trouble," Simon stated, looking at him. "Where'd you get that idea?"

"Yes, you are," argued the homeless guy with the knife. "You're making it sound like this is a bad deal."

"Well, it is a bad deal. I don't have to do anything to make it *sound* like that. Any idiot can see that it's a bad deal."

"I'm the one with the knife," he jeered. "So what will you do about it?" he asked, brandishing it in front of Simon's face.

Unwilling to waste any more time, Simon elbowed away the knife, clanging down to the alleyway, and flipped the guy around, until he was pinned against the building. "I'll do whatever the hell I want to do." Hearing protests from the second guy, Simon snatched him by the throat and slammed him up beside his buddy and squeezed. When the second guy started choking, the first man tried to move, but no way he could break Simon's grip.

"See? This is what happens when you attack somebody who is minding his own business and not causing you any trouble, and here you go pulling a knife and making all kinds of threats."

The second guy was still choking loudly.

"You'll kill him," the first guy cried out. "Leave him alone. Leave him alone!"

"Yeah, why is that? Is he your special buddy or something? You're the one who put him in this position. So this is all on you, man."

The guy looked at him and then back at his friend. "Please don't kill him."

"I don't plan on killing him, unless he has a heart attack or something right now. I mean, it's not my fault if he doesn't have any oxygen to breathe."

The first guy looked at Simon and then his shoulders sagged. "Please, just let him go."

With that, Simon slowly released his grip around the second guy's throat, who immediately bent over, gasping and choking for air. "That is your one and only warning," Simon said to the first guy. "If you ever come close to me again," he stated, "I'll take you down the minute I see you. Got it? I'm walking this area all the time, every day of the week out here. This is my turf. It's not your turf. So cross me one more time, and you'll pay for it."

And, with that, he shoved the man away from him.

The two men helped each other, and together they scrambled away. "Come on. Let's go." Shooting a glance of hatred toward Simon, they took off.

Simon looked down at the knife, knowing that, if he touched it, he would probably get completely engulfed in visions that he didn't want to see. But he also didn't want to leave it here. Pulling his handkerchief from his suit pocket, he picked up the knife and, with nobody else around to see anything at the moment, walked over to a dumpster close by and buried it in a corner. The last thing he wanted was to leave a weapon for someone else to pick up out here. The world was a dangerous-enough place to be without adding to it.

With one final look around, he turned and walked away.

CHAPTER 5

KATE STOOD OUTSIDE in the bustle of the downtown area, studying all the buildings, the traffic, and the parking around her. She was at a busy intersection, and people hustled up and down the streets. Vendors were on the corners, with storefront shops on some of the lower levels, and hundreds and hundreds of offices on the upper levels.

Rodney stood at her side and asked, "What are you looking at?"

"What would it take for somebody to actually notice a man kidnapping a woman out here?"

"It depends on what else is going on. It depends on what it would look like too. If she hopped into his vehicle, nobody would care. If he opened the vehicle door and held a gun against her so nobody could see, he'd get her inside without a fuss probably, and again nobody would know. If he came up and surprised her, and she didn't struggle very much, didn't cry out, didn't do anything, nobody would actually know."

Kate continued. "What *will* anybody notice? A woman having an argument with a man won't even cause a fuss out here. Just too much going on, too many people, and nobody wants to be bothered with getting involved. So, even if somebody were having a hard time down here, how much support do you think they would get from the crowd?"

Rodney replied, "If anybody noticed a problem and if

they weren't in a busy rush to get out of here or if they weren't on a bus or due in a meeting or something else that was keeping their attention focused somewhere else, the bulk of the time she probably would get some help in that scenario. But lots of things gotta line up for that to happen."

"Not really," Kate argued. "All you need is just somebody who cares."

"Maybe, but if you're the one who notices, you don't know that she didn't recognize the guy. You don't know that this wasn't the love of her life. Maybe everybody saw them together and smiled, thinking it was a picture of true love."

Kate nodded. "Right, that's part of the problem. We don't know anything about it." As she walked into the front of the building, she looked around and noted, "High-end."

"Most of these business offices look high-end," Rodney agreed. "They're paying thousands a month in lease rates, so people want it to look like they're worth a lot of money. That way, when clients come in, they won't balk at what they charge them."

"I guess it's all part of the mirage, isn't it?"

"Well, I don't know about *mirage*," he stated, with a laugh, "but it's definitely a part of the image."

She smiled. "Same thing. Maybe with different connotations though. *Mirage* makes you think that it's tenuous, that it may not really exist and could go *poof* right before your eyes. Whereas *image* is all about projecting an aura of success and making the people believe."

"You mean, like projecting, *Hey, we can make you a million bucks if you just give us your money?*"

"Same diff." She nodded.

He agreed, "On that you are correct."

"And it's just sad," she added. "So many people come in

here, hoping and believing that these people can help them, but so often it's just a crock."

"But not always," Rodney argued. "Some really good solid investment firms are here too."

"But how do you tell the sharks from the good guys?" she muttered.

"Well, presuming that you're asking because you have an awful lot of money that you think you need to invest somewhere," he replied, with a laugh, "I think personal recommendations are often the best bet."

"And then you and your friend share in the rook," she replied, with a shrug.

He burst out laughing at that. "I forgot how negative you are."

"I am negative about a lot of things in life," she admitted, "but I really don't want to be that way about everything."

"The trouble is, once you go down that pathway, it's hard to not let the taint of it carry over into everything else, isn't it?"

She nodded. "Yes. Especially when you do the job we're doing."

"Which is apparently the job that you always wanted to do."

"It is," she admitted.

"Is that because of your brother?"

She sighed. "My brother was a big part of it." Kate shrugged. "So was being in foster care. Being raised that way, and seeing the crime going on all the time, I found it really hard in school to see people cheating constantly, yet nobody seemed to care. Nobody would ever call them out. Nobody would ever get them in trouble. And, even when they were called out or caught, nobody really punished them. It was like, *Oh, well.* It was almost like, *Too bad you got caught. Cheat a little better next time.*"

"I think that's very prevalent in a lot of schools." Rodney nodded. "Unfortunately the way of our world these days isn't about doing it on your own. It's become more about stepping on somebody else to get what you want."

"There should be better things in life than just climbing vertically without giving a damn about who you take down in order to make it happen."

"I don't think everybody is like that," Rodney stated. "I'm sure enough are out there to challenge your interpretation."

She looked over at him. "Do you know anybody you'd invest one hundred thousand with?"

He snorted. "One, I don't know anybody who deals with that kind of money. Two, I have never even seen that kind of money. And, three, I wouldn't invest it with somebody else even if I did have that kind of money."

"What would you do with it?"

"Real estate," he stated instantly.

At that, she stared at him. "Have you checked out the prices of real estate in Vancouver lately?"

He nodded. "I have a small condo," he shared. "I was looking to get a house but with the current prices?" He whistled, shaking his head. "It's out of reach at this point."

"Yeah, the days of owning your own home went out about twenty years ago."

"I think it's been longer than that," he muttered.

"Right, so how is anybody supposed to get anywhere in life right now?"

"I think it takes family at this point," he suggested. "I

know my parents were talking about giving me a hand with the very hefty down payment required, but I'm not even sure that's a good idea."

"Sorry," she muttered. "It sucks, doesn't it?"

"It does," he agreed, "when you always wanted to have that perfect little house, picket fence and all that."

"What about moving up to the valley?"

"If I do," he replied, "I'd also have to transfer my job out there, so I'm not doing the crazy commute."

She winced at that. "I get that." Kate nodded in agreement. "Who the hell wants to spend their life commuting?"

"And there's just as much crime out there in the valley as is here downtown."

"Well, I hope not," she muttered, shaking her head. "Hopefully it depends on where you go. In Burnaby you've got an awful lot of gang fights," she muttered. "I guess the answer is, do what you have to do to suit yourself and your family, and then, if the job doesn't work out, you can always transfer to get another one."

"Well, that was a thought, but, so far, I haven't done anything about it."

"Good," she said. "I'm not all that comfortable with everybody else on the team yet. Seems like I've only been working with you."

"And that's mostly on you," Rodney noted, "not pulling any punches."

She glared at him, and he laughed.

"Seriously," he continued. "You still have a bit of a chip on your shoulder."

"Do not," she snapped.

"Do too," he snapped right back.

She laughed. "See? That's what I'm used to. Somebody

who'll talk back and put me in my place."

"And the rest of the team will do that too. You just might not like the way it goes down."

She agreed. "Well, there's a way to do it so it doesn't bite quite so badly or so you don't feel like they're taking a lot of joy in it."

He laughed. "Sometimes taking joy in what you're doing is very necessary."

"But not if it hurts other people," she replied immediately, pulling open the door to the building.

"Excuse me, can we help you?"

Kate turned to look at the nearby security guard at the main entrance. She pulled out her badge and explained where they were going.

He nodded. "That company is on the fourth floor."

"Good, and we'll have to go from that site to another," she noted, then gave the name of the ex-boyfriend.

"Right, he's on the day trader's floor." The security guard stopped, shrugged, and added, "The reception desk is right over there."

"Good enough." Kate bypassed reception and walked to the elevators; she glanced back to see the guard staring at her. "Did you get the feeling that he wanted us to sign in before going upstairs?"

"Well, we signed in verbally with security, so that should be enough."

"I don't think he thinks it's enough," she muttered. "He's still watching us."

Rodney nodded. "When the cops come, everybody wants to know what's up. Remember. No matter what job you're in, the minute you start bringing in the cops, everybody wants to know why."

She smiled. "Well, depending on how this works out, I'll be more than happy to shout it from the treetops."

He shook his head. "See? Now that—going over the top—is what will get you in trouble."

"Oh, come on," she muttered. "Sometimes these assholes need to be taken down a peg or two."

"Most of them do," Rodney agreed, "but also remember how that's not our job."

"Oh, I remember." She yawned. "It's too bad too, by the way."

He smiled. "I agree, but it doesn't stop any of it."

"No, maybe not."

When they got to the fourth floor, they presented themselves at the front desk. Kate asked to speak to Cherry's boss.

The woman looked up at her in surprise. "I'm sorry. He's got meetings all day."

"It's important." Kate flashed her badge again.

The receptionist hesitated.

"You can get him now, or we'll check every office for him ourselves," Kate demanded.

At that, the woman immediately shook her head. "No, no, no. ... I just—I don't want to interrupt him."

"Well, the news I have will interrupt everybody," Kate noted.

The receptionist frowned. "It's just that we're really short on staff."

"I understand, and I know at least part of why that is, so let's deal with this, shall we?"

The woman swallowed, then got up from her seat and walked over several office doors. She entered one, closing the door quietly behind her.

Kate turned toward Rodney. "Apparently it's difficult to

even talk to people now."

He gave her a wry smile. "Just the sight of us is enough to set alarm bells ringing. And, if they're short-staffed because Cherry didn't show up for work, people will realize that something's going on."

When the door opened again, the woman came out, followed immediately by a tall man with sparse hair and a stern countenance. He approached, held out his hand. "I'm Tom Bergeron. What can I help you with?"

"May we speak privately?" Kate asked immediately.

He hesitated and then nodded. "Sure, come into my office." Yet he led the way past his desk to a meeting area. When they stepped into the small room, he motioned the detectives toward the chairs. "Take a seat, please, and tell me what this is all about."

Kate immediately spoke up, identifying their victim as Cherry, and he stared at her in shock.

"She's dead?"

"Yes," Rodney confirmed. "The information is being released now, since we've contacted the next of kin. So it's likely to hit the news media very quickly. Therefore, we wanted to let you know what had happened."

"Good Lord." He looked shaky. "I can't believe it." He reached into his pocket, pulled out a handkerchief, and dabbed his forehead.

She stared at him. "You had a personal relationship with her?" It was a stab in the dark, but she'd spoken from her heart and her instincts. When he turned toward Kate, she saw the shock in his expression, and his gaze darted from one detective to the other, as if he didn't know what to say.

"Of course you did, and you're married." Kate tried hard to trim the disgust in her voice, but it was difficult.

His shoulders sagged, as all the *oomph* that had been there—when Tom had first opened the conference room door—had walked out. He slid into the seat nearest him. "Yes," he confirmed. "I was planning on leaving my wife."

"You mean, that's what you told Cherry."

Tom looked at her with a frown and then shook his head. "No, I actually was."

"*Was.* But, of course, *now* you're not in a position to worry about that, are you?" she asked quietly.

He stared at her, his face blanching. "I would never have done that to her."

"I wonder." Kate pulled a pen and a notebook from her pocket to take notes. "I wonder if you actually would leave your wife or whether this was just a very convenient time to break up an affair that obviously wasn't appropriate at the office."

He stared at her, his throat working.

"Maybe you should start by telling us where you've been for the last week," Rodney said.

"The last week?" he asked, his voice rising in a squeak.

Rodney nodded carefully. "Yes, we're working on a time of death, but it's not been locked down just yet."

He stared at Rodney first, his gaze going from one to the other. "I was supposed to be at a conference this weekend," he stated.

"But you didn't go, right?" Kate asked.

He slowly shook his head. "I didn't go, no. I stayed here with Cherry instead."

"Interesting," she murmured. "And where were you?"

"At her place."

"Until when?"

"We had a fight Saturday morning," he admitted. "I left,

and I didn't go back."

"Where did you go?"

He hesitated, and she just stared at him.

"I took a room in a hotel in another building," he replied. "I couldn't go home to my wife without an explanation. I couldn't go back to Cherry because, well, we were still fighting. So I went to a hotel."

"What hotel was that?" she asked him flatly. "When did you arrive, and when did you leave? What did you do while you were there?"

"I checked in at noon on Saturday at the Hotel Vancouver. I left Sunday at four, so I could go home, which would be the normal time to return after the conference."

"And what did you do while you were at the hotel?"

"I sat in my room and drank myself stupid," he replied in disgust. "I was upset over the entire thing."

"What was the fight about?"

He hesitated, then admitted, "Whether I would leave my wife or not."

"So, you're telling us that you decided you would leave your wife, yet clearly it wasn't resolved if you were fighting over that very thing. But you don't have to deal with that whole problem now."

"I didn't kill her," he stated. "You know that, right?"

"What did you do when she didn't show up for work on Monday?"

"I sent her several texts, asking her to come in. I was hoping she would, but she didn't answer my phone calls or my texts."

"Today is Wednesday," she noted. "Have you had any contact with her since the fight on Saturday morning?"

He immediately shook his head no.

"And what time was it Saturday?"

"We fought very early that morning," he recalled. "I left about seven in the morning."

"You said you didn't check into the Hotel Vancouver until noon. Where were you for those five hours?"

He stared at her, shaking his head. "Surely you don't think I killed her?"

"It's looking good right now," she noted in a suspiciously bland voice.

The sweat built on his forehead, and he immediately dabbed at it again. "I didn't have anything to do with it. I loved her. I swear."

"Which is why you had a fight because you obviously hadn't made the decision that you loved her enough to leave your wife by then."

"No." He sighed. "And I will regret that forever."

As he stared out the window, she could see the visible tremors in his fingers as he played with a pen in his hand. He was trying to regain some semblance of control. He was obviously overwrought, but she didn't know whether it was because he was afraid he was about to get caught or because he would actually miss the love of his life. "Can you confirm where you were?"

He looked at her in surprise. "Well, I was at her apartment. I left. I didn't see anybody that Saturday morning," he added. "I was pretty upset. I stormed out of there. I took the stairs down, went out the back way, got into my vehicle, and I just drove around for a while."

"For five hours?"

He winced. "No. I sat at the beach, just thinking about what I was supposed to do with my life. It's a pretty major deal to get a divorce for an office romance. It's so cliché and so damn common and frankly just messy on many levels. It's not what I ever expected. I fell in love, and I didn't know what else to do."

"You're married, but do you have children as well?" Rodney asked.

Tom looked over at Rodney and slowly nodded. "I do. I have two daughters and a son." His voice heavy, Tom sagged even farther into his chair. "I'm not proud of what I did," he admitted, "and I get that you're probably judging me."

"We see it all the time," she said, with a wave of her hand. "Marital vows apparently don't matter anymore."

Rodney looked at her sharply, but she ignored him. Her suspect, now skewered in place, twisted in his seat even more. "I get it," Tom acknowledged. "God." And he buried his face in his hands.

"Well, now you get to backtrack, don't you?" she said cheerfully. "I mean, once you explain to your wife the fact that your girlfriend has been murdered, I'm sure she'll take you back, with no problem."

He dropped his hands and stared at her. "Murdered?"

"Oh, yes, murdered after being tortured for days."

The color completely drained from his face. He shook his head. "No. God, no. Please, not her."

"What was she like?"

His voice trembling, he replied, "She was an angel. She was the most beautiful, heart-warming soul I've ever met."

"And yet somebody hated her. Any idea who?"

He shook his head. "She was very popular with all our clients, very popular at the office. I have no idea." His voice went hoarse, as he caught tears at the back of his throat. "I need—I need to go home." He stood.

"Yeah, interesting to see how you explain to your wife

why you're so emotional."

He stared at her and slowly sank back down on the chair. "Jesus, I can't tell her." He looked at them. "Please don't tell her."

Kate shrugged. "Should we need to speak to her, just what is it you expect us to say?"

He took several deep breaths, as if trying to hold back a heavy shock.

She watched him with interest, wondering if he'd have a heart attack over this. She was also being on the bitchy side, but she was damn tired of listening to all these men having a little piece on the side, supposedly loving these women, yet leaving both women in their lives stranded in a terrible in-between state. It's not how Kate would like to have a relationship. Rodney looked over at her with that look again, and she eased back slightly.

"Again, we need to know exactly where you were. So far, we don't have an explanation for the missing five hours, and, when you left her, did you leave her alone? Did you leave the apartment locked? Did you notice anybody else hanging around, either in the building on the way down or outside in the parking lot?"

He shook his head. "No, I was horribly upset. We'd had a terrible argument, and I raced out of there. I just ran down the stairs, got into my vehicle, and took off. I didn't see anybody." He looked at her. "Are you thinking she was killed there?"

"Good question," Kate noted. "And it's more than just that. Somebody kept her for a while, so, if we could find her phone, that would help."

"As far as I know," he replied heavily, "she had it with her when I left."

"Well, no sign of it when we found her body." Kate got up. "We still need an explanation of those five hours."

He stared at her blankly. "I don't have one. I literally just drove around, and then I sat at the beach for quite a while and got a coffee from one of the street vendors, just trying to get my head on straight."

"What was the decision?" she asked.

"I was honest when I told you originally," he repeated, "that I would leave my wife."

She nodded. "Any chance your wife knows about this already?"

He shook his head immediately. "Dear God, no."

She nodded. "Well, I hope not. Maybe you'll have a chance to make good on it after all."

"Make good on what?"

She looked at him and replied, "Your vows."

With that, she turned and walked out. She stopped at the front desk again. "You'll find out soon enough," Kate explained, "but your coworker Cherry Blackwell is dead. I need to know what she was like. How her working relationship was with people in the company and with customers."

Rodney hadn't come back out with her, so she presumed he was still talking to the boss. Maybe it was a man thing; she didn't know. She was just damn sick of cheaters.

The woman in front of her gasped in shock. "Oh my God, she was wonderful. She was so easy to work with. What happened to her?"

"She was murdered," Kate stated bluntly. "You'll hear about it in the news, I'm sure."

The woman just stared at her, still shocked, and her bottom lip trembled.

It seemed like, all of a sudden, the word was passed

around the office, and suddenly sobs were audible from several areas in the room.

She looked around, then asked the receptionist, "Was anybody here particularly close to her?"

She nodded and, still sniffling, grabbed several tissues from a box on the counter and led Kate to another young woman, sobbing into her hands.

Kate looked at her and identified herself. "I understand you were a good friend?"

The woman sobbed even harder.

Kate grabbed a chair and plunked down in front of her, then said, "I'm sorry, but I do need to ask you some questions."

Still blubbering, the woman tried to pull herself together and whispered, "I'm so sorry. I tried to call her. I texted her several times, but she didn't get back to me. I was getting really worried. I did phone her family, asking about her, but they said she was probably fine. And then well ..."

"What?" Kate asked.

She shrugged, then continued. "I figured she was mad at me."

"Why?"

"Because I had told her to break off the romance," she whispered, looking around in a panic to make sure she wasn't overheard.

"Ah. Okay, well, I do know about that," Kate admitted. "Was there anybody else in her life?"

The woman shook her head. "No, it was just Tom, and he was really jealous."

"Interesting," Kate replied. "What can you tell me about her?"

"She was beautiful, inside and out," she whispered, still

in tears. "She didn't deserve this."

"Did you see anybody here who was interested in her? A client who caused her problems? Anybody in the building?"

She shook her head, then frowned. "Her ex-boyfriend is here in the building. She was quite devastated for a time after they broke up."

"Did it end badly?"

She shrugged. "Is there ever a good breakup?" she asked, with a wry and teary smile. "It was a problem, but she got over it, and eventually they could at least be in the same elevator when they were going back and forth among the floors here," she noted. "She seemed to finally let it go."

"And yet this office relationship came on the heels of that one."

"Exactly. That's just what I told her. That's why she went into it too quickly and without thinking it through ... because she was on the rebound."

"Was she looking at breaking it off?"

She shrugged. "I wanted her to. But she wasn't really happy with the idea. She didn't want to be alone."

"Do you have any idea who might have wanted to hurt her or who hated her enough to kill her?"

She started tearing up again, wrapping her arms around her chest and rocking slightly. "No," she whispered, "she was a really nice person."

"She didn't complain about anybody following her? Nobody watching her? Or was she getting strange texts or emails from anybody?"

The woman immediately shook her head. "No, I never heard about anything like that." Then she asked, "How—how did she d-die?" Kate hesitated, then the woman teared up yet again. "It was bad, wasn't it?"

Slowly she nodded. "Yes, it was bad. That's why I'm wondering if anybody suspicious was in her life."

The other woman sighed. "No. She was really close to her family, but they'd seemed at odds this last bit after they found out about her relationship, you know, with her boss." She again took a quick look around the office.

"Does anybody here *not* know about the affair?"

She looked at Kate, horrified, and then she thought about it. "You know what? Probably not. But we all tried to keep it quiet because of his wife. She really is sweet," she added on a sad note.

"And Cherry's nice too?"

"Very nice. Oh, gosh, she would never willingly do something like this."

"I hope not," Kate replied, with a hard tone.

The woman looked at her and offered, "If there's anything I can do ..."

"We'll be contacting her family for questioning as well," Kate explained. "It is a problem though." She stood and handed over her card. "If you think of anything, please contact me."

The woman started to cry again, as she wiped her tears impatiently, then added, "It's so unfair. Cherry had a lot of life to live."

"We all do," Kate noted, "so please be careful. I don't know if there's any association with this company, with the people she worked with or anything. Just be super vigilant about your own safety."

The woman looked at her, clearly horrified, then snatched her card and replied, "I will." And started to cry again.

When Kate walked toward the front desk, Rodney was

talking with the receptionist. He looked over at Kate, smiled, and asked, "Ready to go?"

She nodded. "Yes, let's go upstairs."

And, with that, they headed out of the company's entrance door toward the elevators. As they got onto the empty elevator, she asked, "What did you stay and talk to the boss about?"

He sighed. "Pictures of his family were all around his office. I wanted to know if he really had made that decision to go with the girlfriend versus the wife, and, as it turns out, he hadn't."

"So he lied," she stated, as she turned and looked at him.

"I think he thought that you were sympathetic to the victim and that it would look better if he sided with her."

"It doesn't matter what I think," she snapped.

"Well, that's the problem. He couldn't make a decision regarding Cherry, which was the problem."

"But not making a decision *is* making a decision," she snapped.

"It is, but he wasn't brave enough to tell our poor victim that it wouldn't be her."

"Of course not, and, after the fight with her, that would have just cemented the fact that he wouldn't leave his wife. So, did he actually drive around and spend time at the Hotel Vancouver or did he go home to his wife?"

"He did spend time at the Hotel Vancouver apparently, and he did go home to his wife at the time that he said he did, supposedly anyway. We'll still have to confirm the story and see if it holds up."

"Right. Well, a quick phone call to the Hotel Vancouver should confirm that part at least."

"We'll probably need to stop there in person anyway

though, to get copies of records and to have a look at the camera footage and all, right?"

She groaned. "At least maybe we can cross another suspect off the list."

"Yeah," Rodney agreed, "though it would be nicer if we found one viable suspect because, right now, we don't have much. Though we still need to see our model parolee."

"I know," she noted, "but first the ex-boyfriend, since we're right here."

As they took the elevator up to the day-trading office, Kate looked over at Rodney. "You know what? It would be revenge served cold if this one came back and killed Cherry after all this time."

"Unless he only just found out she was having an affair with the boss."

"So, would it be the affair with the boss because it's the boss or just the fact that she found somebody else?"

"Probably just because she found anybody else," Rodney suggested. "Unless this Tyler guy was the super jealous type and would assume that she'd been seeing the boss all along or something."

When they identified themselves at this day-trading office and asked to speak to Tyler Bjornsson, the receptionist immediately picked up the phone and dialed his extension, saying that he was just about to leave.

"Well, hopefully he's still here."

She nodded. "He is."

When a tall, handsome, thirtysomething man, his hair slicked back, wearing an expensive three-piece suit, stepped forward and looked at Kate, she could have pinpointed his type right off the bat. She walked over, shook his hand, and identified herself. "We need to speak with you privately."

His eyebrows shot up, and he shrugged. "Sure."

Just something was a little too smooth, a little too slick about him for her peace of mind. But then he was never her kind of person. As they walked into his office, she took a seat and then asked him when he'd last seen Cherry Blackwell.

He looked at her in surprise. "I don't know. I haven't had a relationship with her in over a year."

"That's not what I asked you," she said smoothly.

His gaze went from her to Rodney and back to her again. "Probably in the elevator a couple months ago, I guess," he replied cautiously. "Why?"

She studied him for a long moment and then answered his question. "She was found dead Sunday morning."

He stared at Kate, and she watched him as almost shock and then maybe a hint of grief came into his eyes.

"I'm sorry to hear that," he said quietly. "She was a lovely person."

"And that will also explain why we're here," she added.

Immediately he shook his head. "I don't follow. We literally haven't had a relationship in over a year."

"Maybe so," she replied, "but you were her last boyfriend."

"No, that's not true. She was having a relationship with somebody in the office."

"Do you know who that was?"

"No," he stated. "I just saw her coming out of the offices late one day with this guy, and they were a little too cuddly. At least too cuddly to be just coworkers and too cuddly to be strangers."

"I see," Kate noted. "When was this?"

He frowned, grabbed his phone to check his appointment calendar, and said, "It was probably about three weeks ago. I was staying late," Tyler explained, as he flicked through the screen on his phone. "Yes, it was that Tuesday, three weeks ago. Normally I'm not even here in the afternoons. We work really early mornings. But I was having issues with some accounts, so I was here late." He shrugged. "When I went down, they came out themselves. She flushed, as if she were embarrassed, and even stepped back a little bit from him. So it was obviously one of those relationships that she either wasn't ready to make public or didn't want me in particular to see."

"Did you say anything to her?"

He shook his head. "No, I've had several relationships since I broke up with her," he admitted calmly. "Now, if you don't have any other questions ..."

She immediately asked for his whereabouts over the last week.

He stared at her in surprise. "Really?"

"Really," she said blithely. "The sooner we have all the information, the sooner we can work on this."

"Wow, I don't know what to say," he replied. "I was at my girlfriend's house on the island over the weekend. We took the five o'clock ferry out Friday, and we came back Sunday night. You can confirm that actually." He checked his phone again, clicked through some emails, and then added, "Here's our ferry tickets. I have receipts." And he held up his phone for Kate to see.

"Can you send me a copy of that?"

He nodded, tapped on the phone a few times, asked for her email, and then sent it to her.

"Good enough. And these last few days?" Kate asked.

He replied, "I'm here at four o'clock in the morning every day of the workweek, and, usually in the afternoons, I go home and do a workout. Then I spend some time with my girlfriend. She works nights," he added. "Yes, you can check with her," and he gave Kate the girlfriend's name and phone number as well."

"Thank you," she replied. With the information in hand, she said, "We appreciate your willingness to provide the answers we need."

"The sooner you get me out of the mix," he noted, "the better. I had a lovely relationship with Cherry, and I'm very sorry she is gone because she was a really nice person, but I didn't have anything to do with her death."

"Do you know of anybody who might have had an argument or some problem with her?"

"No—oh, wait, one of the other women in the office," he added. "She was jealous or something, but I'm not exactly sure when. But that would have been a long time ago. They had a problem, but I don't even think she's there anymore."

"Do you know her name?"

He shook his head. "Cherry just said somebody didn't like the fact that she was there. And the person left soon afterward. I guess you could ask down there and see if anybody knew about it. I don't think it was a big deal though," he noted. "You asked if there was anybody who didn't like her, and I supposed that would qualify, but did the woman hate Cherry? Enough to kill her? No. I can't imagine that."

And, with that, Kate nodded and took her leave.

As they headed back downstairs, Rodney looked over at her. "I'd say he's clear."

"He was pretty willing to offer information," she admitted, "so chances are that he had nothing to do with it. I don't know about the other girl that Cherry had a problem with though."

"Do you think this is the work of a female?"

"Well, I don't want to be sexist and say a woman *couldn't* do it because I'm sure that's not true," she explained, "but, no, I don't think that at all. But we can't go by what we think."

"No," Rodney agreed. "It would be easy enough to stop back by the office and talk to the one good friend."

"Or even the receptionist," Kate said, with a nod. She hit the elevator button suddenly to take them back to the fourth floor. As they got out and walked into the office again, the receptionist looked up and frowned.

"Hello again. I'm surprised to see you back again," she said.

"I understand that our victim had an issue with one of the women who worked here at one time," Kate stated.

The receptionist frowned. "I don't know about how much of an issue it actually was," she replied, "but that person left soon afterward."

"Can we get her name and number, please?"

She looked at Kate and said, "I have to ask the boss."

"You do that. We'll wait." Kate stood here with her arms crossed.

The woman disappeared and then came running back, with the information on the back of Tom's business card. "Here it is. She was only here for a week or two."

"Do you know what the problem was?"

"No." The receptionist shook her head. "I really don't, except that they just didn't hit it off. They were different personalities."

"Good enough." Kate took the information and walked back out again.

She wasn't sure that it would lead anywhere, but, in a case like this, every thread had to be followed, every *T* had to be crossed, and every *I* had to be dotted. Loose ends tended to create problems down the road. They had to chase down every detail, so the wrong person didn't go to jail for a crime he didn't commit. Kate was already afraid that may have happened once. She'd do a damn good job to make sure it didn't happen twice to the kid.

SIMON FOCUSED AS much as he could on his work, only to find his feet taking him toward Kate's office on Graveley Street. He found a street vendor within a block and grabbed a coffee and a hot dog and continued on. He shouldn't be here, but he knew that. The last thing he would have set out to do would be to pursue any relationship with a cop, and he sure as hell didn't want to end up with a group of cop friends.

Yet he also knew that he couldn't walk away from Kate.

Finding a bench, he sat down and put the coffee beside him, then proceeded to eat the hot dog, somehow managing to get it down without sending mustard all over his suit. He wasn't even in his Canadian suit today. He had a mental laugh at that because his favorite outfit was jeans and a blazer.

But today he was more dressed up, as he'd been meeting clients and investors. Not that he gave a shit what they thought, but it made him feel a little more powerful as he dealt with the other side of his business. Rehabbing buildings was one thing, but, once they were rehabbed, they had to be filled, either rented or leased, or in some cases purchased. He didn't want to be the largest property owner in Vancouver, but, with over twenty-two buildings completed, he was getting there.

As he polished off the last bite of his hot dog, he watched several people walk by. A couple looked at him casually, most of them rushing past, head down, anxious to get to wherever they needed to go. He understood, and he'd been spending an awful lot of his last few days with his head down himself, trying to stay focused and to forget the scream, whatever the hell that scream was, because it kept coming back, but it seemed fainter and fainter. He was also afraid it was connected to the case that Kate was currently working on, with the poor woman who had been tortured so badly before she died.

All he could think about was that this screamer could be another victim, yet that made no sense. He didn't know if there were any other victims, but the fact that there could be another one, a woman Simon was actually connecting with, sent his spine stiffening ramrod straight—if only to stop it from turning into quivering molded jelly.

To connect with someone in trouble, yet to be so helpless, that was a completely different thing.

Simon stared down at his hands, realizing just how different it was for him, as a big strong male in his prime, to have these particular feelings. They were not about insecurity because it went way past that to helplessness. This was about being a victim of somebody's agony, pain, and torture, yet Simon had no target to reach out and hit. No way to assuage that pain and that devastation inside these victims. He couldn't help the fact that he didn't know anything about this woman. In that moment, his grandmother's voice seemed to slip into his brain and whispered, *But you could.*

He stiffened, looked around, and, taking a chance, whispered back, "Is that you, Nan?"

He thought he heard the faintest sound of a laugh before it disappeared from his brain. Unnerved, he bolted to his feet, snagged his coffee, and stormed down the block. He would either cross the street and see if Kate was at the office or keep storming around the block, and the cops in her circle might very well end up saying something to her. Would she understand? He didn't know, but it didn't matter if she did or not. He was compelled, like they shared this umbilical cord between them.

If he didn't see her for several days, he got antsy and wanted to send her a dozen texts in a day, but that sounded more stalkerish and creepy than anything. It seemed like they slept together when it was convenient, and that drove him crazy too. He wanted more; he wanted to wake up to find her beside him. The times that she did sleep over, he found himself not even wanting to sleep.

Sighing, he just kept walking, pacing around the corner and back. All the time a voice so much like his nan's kept whispering in his ear.

You can run, but you can't hide.

Finally he stepped into an alleyway and hissed out loud, "What the hell do you want?"

You came the whisper, and then complete silence followed in his head. Shaken and not sure what the hell to think, yet only able to consider that maybe it *was* his nan, he slowly returned to the bench where he'd been sitting. As he sat down again, he looked at his hands and realized somewhere along the line he had completely misplaced his coffee. Struggling with that and really wanting the hit of caffeine to jolt his senses, not to mention the comfort of the hot brew, he got up and walked back to the block where the vendor was. As he bought a second cup, the vendor frowned. Simon shrugged. "I lost it somewhere."

The vendor just laughed, gave it to him, and told him to keep his money.

He looked at him in surprise. "You don't have to do that. It was my fault."

"It doesn't matter if it was or not," he replied. "You're a regular, so enjoy."

Appreciating the gesture, Simon added a tip to the jar, then turned and walked away. More nice people were in the city than not, as far as he was concerned. Although he certainly heard an awful lot from other people about how it was so hard to get to know anybody or how cold and uninviting the city was. It was truly a beautiful location, but that didn't always make for warm bedfellows.

In his case though, he'd been blessed on so many fronts for many years. Of course he made money, and money was always a strong reason for people to put a smile on their face. Either you could do something for them or they wanted you to do something for them. It was a strange thing about money, but he was acclimating himself to having it. It had been a few years since he had come into such strong success, and it was now second nature. He certainly wasn't born to it, and he was working his way up, dealing with as much as he could. But he kept most of his business quiet and under the radar, trying to stay out of trouble. Because, once trouble started, it never ended well.

That was always the lesson; it never ended well. You had to do what you had to do to stay clear of it. So Simon tried to stay on the straight and narrow and to not get involved with any of the very distracting and often very profitable side businesses that went on around town here—side businesses that were anything but legal.

He stayed legal because it was easier and because it helped him sleep at night. The last thing he wanted was to lose everything he'd worked so hard for. He knew others who took a lot of fun from that whole aspect of cheating the system, and Simon could admit there were times when cheating the system might not be a bad thing. The system sucked, and sometimes it was as corrupt as anything else in this world, but long ago he'd made a promise to his nan to not get into any of that trouble. She'd saved him at one point in time and had dragged him out of the foster care system, when he'd been in desperate need.

After her death, when Simon was only ten years old, he'd gone back into the system again, where he'd become a handful, as a sad and frightened preteen who acted out, guaranteeing he would never be adopted. And unfortunately Nan could do nothing to stop the foster care system from having responsibility for Simon that time.

CHAPTER 6

WALKING INTO THE office at the end of the day, Kate plunked down in her chair and stared at her monitors blankly.

"Before you get involved in anything, you may want to go outside and talk to your boyfriend," Owen said from the other corner of the room.

Boyfriend? What on earth? She turned and looked at Owen—the happily married family man in the team, truly an exception in their profession—wondering if she would ever really be accepted here. "What are you talking about?"

"Simon. He's been pacing outside for a while."

She frowned, got up, and walked over to the window Owen pointed at. She stared down at the street, and, sure enough, she found Simon, but he sat on a nearby bench, drinking coffee.

"He's just sitting there," she muttered. Of course, for him to be on her block, chances are he wanted to talk to her, but he hadn't texted her or come to her office. Then again he didn't really want anything to do with the cops, and she couldn't blame him. If she wasn't one, she probably wouldn't either.

Every time her presence wrought fear in others, she cringed. That part of her job she absolutely detested. Just the sight of her showing up on somebody's doorstep made them anxious. But Simon was made of sterner stuff than that. Of course it had to do with his history that, so far, they hadn't fully discussed—and probably wouldn't, given her profession. It was likely to rear its ugly head at some point in time and was part of the reason she held back from getting even more involved with Simon. Besides, he was just a distraction she could often ill afford.

She shrugged, then turned and walked away.

Owen watched her and asked, "You'll leave him hanging out there? Not the best way to handle a relationship." When she frowned at him, he shrugged. "Just saying."

"He hasn't texted me. He hasn't done anything to suggest he wants to talk to me," she replied. "For all I know, he's buying a building in this area."

"Is that what he does? Buys and sells real estate?"

"I think he buys, rehabs, and then sells," she explained.

"You think?"

"Yep, I think," she stated. "Or maybe he keeps some. I don't really know."

Andy chimed in now. "How the hell is it you don't know more about this guy?"

"Because I don't know anything more," she stated, with a shrug. "It's not like you know anything about any of your one-night stands."

"You've been dating him for a while though," he replied quizzically.

She shrugged again and headed back to her desk. The last thing she wanted to do was discuss her relationship with reluctant psychic Simon among her coworkers. They had bugged her about it a lot when they first found out, some asking questions that, even now, Kate didn't have answers for. Things like, whether he could read her mind or if it bothered her to think that no real privacy could be had between them.

It never bothered her when she was with him, and she hadn't ever asked him those questions. The fact that she hadn't made her wonder *why* she hadn't thought about it. Was it because she didn't believe it was even possible or because it wasn't a possibility she could contemplate? Which was it?

The fact was, none of it made any difference to her. If he said yes, that he could, what would she do differently? And, if he said no, it would just be the same as always. Besides, would she even believe him? That made her wince more than anything because, if she didn't believe or trust the guy even that much, she shouldn't be sleeping with him. She slowly rotated her neck, wishing that this, along with everything else, would go away for at least a few minutes.

Rodney joined them in the bullpen. "I think I'll call the ex-employee the victim had trouble with."

"Good," she noted. "We have a few things to follow up on but not too much else."

"Almost nothing at all," Rodney stated. "We do need to confirm with the hotel where the boss was."

She nodded. "I'll do that." And she reached for the phone. Only twenty minutes later they had managed to confirm the stories related to the office, including the ex-boyfriend's account of watching Cherry being friendly with Tom at work. "Great," Kate muttered, "so absolutely no joy here, and I've got copies of documents and even the security camera footage for that time frame, just so we can confirm that Cherry's boss was at the hotel and at work when he claimed he was."

"Nothing here," Rodney added. "Nothing from the other employee. Her name is Julie, and she told me that the two of them were antagonistic toward each other right from the beginning. She was mostly apologetic about it, saying that they were basically just too much alike."

"Did you believe her?" Kate asked Rodney, turning to look at him.

He nodded. "You know what? I did. And I don't see much in the way of motive there either."

She nodded. "Fine then, that means we have literally nothing to go on."

"Except the kid, the parolee."

"Right." She nodded. "The kid." She grinned at that. "We need to set him up with an interview."

"That'll be a little hard, since we don't have any forwarding address."

"The parents will know where he is," she stated.

"Yeah, but if the parents think we had put him away for murder, and it wasn't him, we won't get any address out of them."

"Wasn't he living at their place?" she asked, frowning.

"At first he was, but he's not required to check in anymore, so we have no confirmation yet."

"I know," she agreed. "Still, that's a place to start." She picked up the phone. When a woman's voice answered, Kate identified herself and asked to speak to the woman's son.

"He doesn't live here," the other woman replied tartly, "and I wouldn't give you the number anyway." Then she promptly hung up.

Kate stared down at the phone. "Well, somebody feels pretty strongly about it."

"That's what I meant," Rodney stated. "People get pretty irate over what they consider a wrongful conviction."

"And yet he also confessed."

"But he was a kid, so, from their perspective, it would have been coerced because that allowed them to believe their son. And he recanted the confession too."

"So then why confess in the first place?" she murmured in surprise.

"Well, that's what we'll have to find out, along with everything else."

"Great," she muttered. "We need to track him down." She typed in search parameters. "He's got to be working somewhere." It took a bit, but she finally found his last known employment. "He worked at a mechanic's shop. One of those *drive in and change your oil* places. Maybe he still works there."

Rodney looked over at her. "Good."

She nodded. "Well, it's the end of the day, and I think it's about time I got my oil changed." She gave him a smile and walked out.

"You be careful."

"I will," she replied.

But Owen added, "Could you at least put lover boy out of his misery before you go? Next time you have an argument, maybe tell him not to hang out at your place of employment."

She snorted at that because not only had they *not* had an argument but Simon wouldn't listen to her in the first place. She did walk out through the front door instead of the back, where her car was parked, and went toward Simon. He appeared to be on his phone, texting somebody, so, when she sat down beside him, he didn't even look at her.

Finally she said, "Is there a reason why you're here?"

He looked over at her and nodded. "Yeah, it's dinner-time," he stated, one eyebrow raised.

"I have to get an oil change."

He stared at her flatly.

She shrugged. "I'm hoping to find somebody who may have been wrongfully convicted for murder," she explained. "Either that or he's just committed a second one."

Instantly Simon stood. "Fine, I'll go with you." She frowned and remained seated, but he shook his head. "I walked. You at least owe me a ride home."

She shook her head. "I don't owe you jack shit," she stated calmly.

He burst out laughing, tugged her to her feet, slipped her hand through the crook of his elbow, and had her walking to the crosswalk, where they went around to the parking lot. "Look. I shouldn't be here. I know that," he muttered. "I don't even know why I'm here, except that you're one of those faces I can't stop coming to see."

"No, you shouldn't be here," she snapped. "I caught complete hell from the guys over your presence today."

"They saw me?" Simon frowned.

"Of course they did."

"I could be doing business in the area."

"You could be," she agreed, "and I did tell them that but—"

He nodded. "It wasn't enough for them, huh?"

"Everybody wants something to bug me about," she replied, "so you're it."

"Of course I am," he noted. "Besides, I'm also the psychic and, therefore, the resident target."

"Absolutely, and the fact that I'm sleeping with you," she added, after a moment's hesitation—as if trying to find the right word—"just adds to it."

"Is that what we're doing? Sleeping together?"

"Well, we're not doing all that much sleeping," she noted, with a smirk.

"Right." He nodded. "Good point."

Something odd was in his tone. "You don't like that phrase?"

"No, I can't say that I do," he replied. "I'd like to think that something more is between us."

She frowned, shoved her fist into her pocket, then finding her keys, pulled them out, and walked to her car. She didn't know what to say, so she didn't say anything. And the fact that she didn't say anything seemed to send him into a deeper, darker mood. Finally, when they were inside her car, she turned and looked at him. "Of course it's something more."

"But what?" he asked.

"I don't know," she said in exasperation, "and, if you need me to tell you that, then something's wrong."

He took a long deep breath and then nodded. "You're right. It means something is wrong."

She didn't like him when he was like this. It was unusual for him to sound insecure. "What happened?" she asked, suddenly realizing more was behind this than what she'd originally assumed. It was stupid of her to not pick up on those clues. She'd been irritated because the guys at work had been bugging her.

He shrugged. "Nothing." And, of course, that meant the opposite was true.

"Stop lying," she snapped.

He glared at her and pointed. "Just drive."

"And if I don't want to?"

"Then you don't have to," he replied. "I'll walk home."

He went to open the car door, but she reached out and grabbed his wrist. "Stop."

He glared at her. "I'm not someone to be ordered around."

Ya think? The two of them stared at each other, both of them strong-willed and probably not the easiest people to get along with. And neither one of them was very good at backing down.

"I'm sorry," she said. "It didn't help to get bugged by my team because you were outside, waiting for me."

"I got it," he noted. "And believe me. If I'd had any other place to go, I would have."

She closed her eyes, sank back against the seat, then turned off the engine. "Tell me what's going on."

When he didn't speak, she opened her eyes, rolled her head toward him, and added, "Please."

He frowned and hesitated again. "It's stupid. I mean, it's really stupid," he repeated, "but very few people are in my world that I can actually talk to about this."

"I'm hardly the one to talk to," she stated. "I can barely even believe half of what I hear coming from your mouth."

"Very true," he agreed, with a quirk of his lips. "Sometimes I don't either."

"I think that's why I keep hanging around," she suggested, "because sometimes you appear to be completely thrown off by it all, and I worry about you."

"There's no *sometimes* about it," he snapped. "I don't get what's going on at the best of times, but I have to deal with it because it's my life. I can't just close my eyes and walk away. This is just what happens."

She nodded. "And I get that. So tell me what happened this time."

Slowly, grudgingly, and a little bit at a time, he managed to tell her about the voice in his head, the woman still screaming, and the feeling that she was dying. And because Simon couldn't help her, he shared the complete frustration of being frozen, lost, and helpless.

"This isn't how I'm used to feeling," he burst out, waving his hand. "You know it's not like somebody comes and picks on me at a bar or on the street. It's not like anybody out there is attacking me. At least not now, not at this stage of my life, not when I'm fully grown and can fight back," he added in frustration, glaring at her. "This insight into these women's worlds isn't something I'm comfortable with, not at all. To know that they are in pain and are as helpless and as victimized as they are is … it's devastating."

When Simon's words finally stopped rolling, she realized that the person facing her was the real reason she was with him. This man was all heart. It was too big and soft, so he kept it encased in iron, so nobody could beat it up. But these victims were attacking it from the inside, and he had no defenses against them. He had no way to protect himself; he had no way to deal with the onslaught of these visions.

Whether his visions were right, whether they were wrong, whether they were true, whether they were lies or somehow made up in his mind, they were the real deal, and having seen just enough of the examples he'd given her and the help that he had offered her, she knew that some of this psychic business of his had to be real, that some of this had to be true. And the fact that it was scared her to death.

But it also scared him, and she knew that. She didn't know whether it was just the fact that it was possible or it was more about these particular cases or maybe because he'd lost his own grandmother, but the pain rang true, and it tore him apart. She realized that instead of gripping his wrist like she had been, she was now holding his huge calloused hand in hers. She gently stroked his palm and his long fingers, soothing him, somehow trying to find that place between them where they could meet and talk, without getting angry, without boiling over into something that was so much more.

When he finally fell silent and just turned to stare at her, she could see the guilt, the horror, and the terrible conflict inside him. She could also see that he was waiting for her to berate him for something.

"Are you expecting me to tell you to do more?" she asked quietly. "Are you thinking that I'm your grandmother or your mother or some unknown sister, who will either tell you it's all stupid and you should ignore it or that you have to do something about it? I can't be any of those people. I can only be me."

He closed his fingers around hers, let his head fall against the headrest, and nodded. "And maybe that's the attraction," he guessed. "That you're just you. You don't put on airs. You don't try to be something you're not. You're here. You're doing a job, and everything else around you is either black or white because that's what your life has been up to this point. You're no longer *not* open to the possibility of something else because you can see that there is something else. Yet you can't believe in it because it's not yours *yet*."

When he emphasized the *yet*, she winced. "There have just been so many things that you've told me that have been true," she murmured, "that I have to consider the possibility that there is something else."

"And because you're willing to consider the possibility," he admitted, "I feel compelled to always be nearby, knowing that at least you're willing to hear me talk."

"And where does that leave us now?" she asked. "I don't know how to find this woman in your head. I'm doing everything I can on the ground, and, if she's related to my cases, it means my case is even worse than I thought because we had hoped that this was a one-off from many years ago. The fact that it's happening again and that we don't know whether it's an imitation, like a copycat, or the same person causing trouble again, is frustrating all of us on my team," she murmured. "What I can tell you is that I just don't have any answers."

"And again, that's what I like about you," he said. "You don't try to push me off with a nice little PR statement that you're doing your best. You tell me that you don't have answers. It's black, and it's white, so far for you. And when color is there, you'll tell me."

She nodded slowly. "That's exactly what I'll do," she confirmed. "In the meantime, I'm doing everything I can to find out what's going on. And, if this woman connecting to you is a current victim, if this woman, indeed, needs help, I need you to reinforce that connection as much as you can, so you can tell me what you can about her. So maybe we have a chance of saving her. If not today then at least tomorrow."

His lips twitched. "Good enough," he said. "Let's go get your engine oil changed."

She smiled. "Is that because you want to see who this guy is?"

"Yes, I want to get a feel for him."

"Oh." She turned the key to start the engine. "Have you ever done that before?"

"I've gotten the feel of lots of people," he said, with a wicked grin.

She rolled her eyes at the innuendo. "I meant on a psychic level, as you well know."

"Oh, so now you're asking me about my psychic skills?"

"Well, according to you, you don't have any," she retorted, "so I haven't wasted the energy asking, up until now."

He snorted. "And you probably shouldn't even now," he noted, "because I'm damned if I do and damned if I don't. I can't ever get enough information to help, and, what there is, I find to be sketchy at best."

"And yet it helps to confirm. In many ways it gives us a direction, and maybe it's just enough information to make us go after something so that we do find these people," she noted. "There's nothing I can stand you up in court over. There's nothing I can give to my boss and say, *Hey, look. Simon said this or that.* You know?"

"No." Simon shook his head. "And I don't want that anyway."

"Neither do I," she agreed. "I can't imagine anything worse than bringing that circus into town, into the office, or into the courtrooms."

"Neither can I," he replied, with horror.

"The fact of the matter is, there isn't a whole lot we can do about a lot of things. So, the best we can do is deal with what faces us and take it one day at a time. When I took the oath to become a police officer, I didn't realize the emotional commitment," she shared, "and the sense of finality, when I have to walk away from a case, because there's nothing else to go on or because I can't find anything else to do or any more leads to follow or even another thread to tug on. Knowing the family is still there, waiting, asking if there is any news, and all I have to tell them is, *I'm sorry. We have nothing else. We know nothing else.* It's devastating on so many levels."

"Yes, I can see that," he noted. "I don't think I've given that aspect even a little bit of thought. I'm sorry."

"Why would you?" she asked, with a half smile. "Like everybody else, that isn't part of your reality. Your reality is you get up, you go buy property, you fix them up, you sell them, and, every once in a while, some person screams in your head and tells you that they're in trouble. And I'm not part of that reality until you bring it to me and tell me that somebody out there is suffering."

He stared at her. "Doesn't it make you wonder about how the two of us are so different?"

"Often," she stated shortly. "And then honestly I brush it aside, realizing that maybe it's the differences that make it work."

"And is it working?" he asked curiously.

Her stomach clenched. "Are you saying it's not working?"

"I'm not saying anything," he clarified. "I'm sitting here, studying you for the oddity that you are, the uniqueness of who you are, realizing how very blessed I am that you're in my life."

Startled, she could only stare at him. When she heard a honk, she quickly turned her gaze back to the traffic. "You want to just not say shit like that when I'm driving?" she muttered.

"Nope, I think I probably still will," he stated, "because something about you releases whatever is in my mind."

"Well, I don't know if that's a good thing or not," she muttered to herself.

He laughed. "You know what? With anybody else I'm confident, suave, debonair even, if that's the role that they want me to play," he explained. "However, with you, I'm not anything but me, and that's what's so unique about us. We can both be who we need to be and not put on airs or make it look better than it is. And we'll still forgive each other because we accept the reality of where we're at."

And, with that revelation, he sat back and fell quiet.

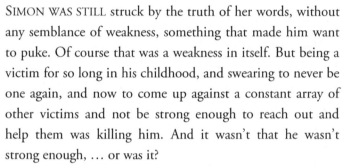

SIMON WAS STILL struck by the truth of her words, without any semblance of weakness, something that made him want to puke. Of course that was a weakness in itself. But being a victim for so long in his childhood, and swearing to never be one again, and now to come up against a constant array of other victims and not be strong enough to reach out and help them was killing him. And it wasn't that he wasn't strong enough, ... or was it?

He scrubbed his face and noted that Kate was pulling into one of those speedy oil change places. "I've never used one of these," he murmured. She looked at him in surprise, and he shrugged. "I like to take my car in to the dealer."

"Of course you do," she said, with an eye roll. "There's quite a price difference between the two." She pulled up into the bay, following the employee's instructions, and rolled down her window. She proceeded to go through the check-in process, sharing the current odometer reading and confirming her account.

"Have you been here before?" Simon asked her.

She nodded. "I come here every once in a while."

"Good for you," he muttered. It wasn't his style at all, but, hey, whatever worked. It was a different life that he'd built for himself, and seeing that, at this level, made him appreciate it all the more.

As they proceeded, she looked over at the employee assigned to her car, and, seeing the name on the pocket of his uniform, she asked, "Are you Rick?"

He nodded.

"Rick Lord?"

He nodded again and looked up at her in surprise. "Yes, do I know you?"

She shook her head. "Nope, you don't." She hesitated and then pulled out her ID.

He froze, stared at it; then his gaze narrowed as he looked at it again. "I haven't done anything fucking wrong."

"Good," she replied. "I'm glad to hear that."

He kept working away on his computer keyboard, but it was obvious that he was distracted.

"I tried to call your parents to find out where you were," she explained, "but they wouldn't give me any information on where you live."

He winced. "No, they wouldn't."

"I do need to ask you some questions. So either we can do it here or I can meet you somewhere. Or you can come down to the office."

"I'm working every day this week," he replied, with a note of desperation.

"What time are you off work?"

He looked up at the clock. "Twenty minutes."

"Good," she stated. "That'll finish my car." He glared at her and disappeared under her hood. She sank back and looked over at Simon.

"How did you know he was in this bay?" Simon asked.

She shrugged. "I phoned."

He nodded. "Do you expect him to still be here at the end of his shift?"

"Well, I hope so," she replied, "but do I expect him to

pull a runner? Maybe. In which case then I'll have to go to his boss and find out where he lives and let him know what's going on. And that'll make it even harder for the kid."

"Exactly," Simon muttered.

And it seemed like they were getting somewhere on her case, until she realized that this oil change was taking way too long. She looked over at Simon. "Stay here." She opened the car door and hopped out. And, sure enough, nobody was under the hood of her car. She swore, looked back at Simon, and said, "He did pull a runner." At that, she walked over to the office door and pounded on it. When a guy popped out, she pointed to her car in the bay. "Your guy just took off running."

He looked at her, shocked, then at her car, as they walked over to it. "I don't understand." She quickly explained, and he raised both hands. "Goddammit, he's a hell of a worker. What the hell did he do wrong now?"

"What do you mean by *now?*"

"Wouldn't hire him because of his record, but I figured, what the hell? He came with great references, so I did."

"And I just need to talk to him, but he has taken off on me now."

"Well, first let's get you back on the road," he began.

"And then you can get me his address and phone number and any other contact information you may have."

He swallowed and then nodded. "Yep, I can do that. But I sure as hell hope that whatever this is about just ends up being nothing because I really don't want to lose him."

"I hope you don't too." She stood here, hands on her hips, fuming. Yet she realized just what a sly thing this kid had done. Her vehicle was up on blocks, and it's not like she could just take off in pursuit of him. She stuck her head into her car, and Simon shook his head, then grinned at her.

"You have to at least appreciate his resourcefulness."

She rolled her eyes. "We'll get this done. Don't worry. I'll track him down, but this time I won't be half as nice."

"And that's something he'll have to face," Simon said quietly.

She nodded.

At that, the kid's boss turned from under the hood. "Is he really in trouble?"

"I don't know. Can you tell me when he worked the last few days?"

He nodded. "He has been here for the last four days."

"Every day?"

"Yes, every day, and doing a good eight-hour shift, if not longer," he admitted. "He's been a really good worker."

"Well, that helps. Do you know where he's living?"

"At his parents' place," he replied. "I have the address and phone number."

She nodded. "In that case, you can give me the address and the phone number. I'll pay for this, and then I'll go track him down."

"Will he show up for work anymore?" his boss asked.

"I don't know." She shook her head. "Depends on what he's done wrong."

He frowned and looked over at her. "I don't even know what he did wrong in the first place. But he did tell me that he had a criminal record, but that he was falsely accused."

"It's in his juvie record, so the fact that he even brought it up is a surprise."

"That's what I thought. I didn't ask for too many details. He said not to worry, that it wasn't theft or anything major."

She snorted. "Nothing major? How about murder?"

The boss's eyes grew wide. "Jesus."

"Yeah, but we're not sure that he did the crime. I'm trying to investigate that right now, but he's not cooperating."

"Why would you go after him?"

"Because a second woman has turned up dead with the same MO."

At that, the boss started to shake. "Maybe I don't want the kid back."

"Depends on if you're *sure*," she noted with emphasis, as she studied him carefully, "that he was here for the last four days."

He nodded. "Yeah, he was. Today is the end of his week. But I don't know what he does in his own time."

"And that's a very valid point," she noted.

"He never seemed like the person who would do anything wrong. He's really quiet, shy even."

"And you don't know what any of these guys do when they're off work?" she asked.

He nodded and quickly wrote down the address and phone number for Rick Lord, then handed it to her. "What do I do if I see him?"

"You call me," she stated. "I'll let you know if I find him and talk to him, and then I can get some answers."

"I really hope he comes back because I need him as a worker."

"I get that, and he might still return. What I don't know is where this is going yet."

He nodded slowly. "I am torn about him. Can't say I feel all that great about it now."

"Understood." She turned her attention to Simon, who had been listening in. "We're just about done here," she told him.

He nodded and looked over at the boss, who was still finishing off the paperwork for the service of Kate's car and taking payment. "You might want to tell the kid that, if he did anything wrong, he should just talk to her. She's not here to nail his ass to the wall, unless he did something bad."

"I don't think he has any trust anymore," the boss noted.

"And the problem with that is that he confessed last time," she shared.

The boss's jaw dropped open. "Oh, shit," he replied in a squeaky voice.

She got into her car and motioned at Simon. "Come on. Let's go."

He hopped in, and they tore off out of the building. "That's a great way to keep things calm and quiet."

"What am I supposed to say? He did confess, and confessions have consequences."

"Yes," he muttered. "I know."

"And I get that not everybody likes the law, but, at the same time, it's not exactly easy for us to handle murders either. This guy confessed to murdering his sister, and he did time, and now we've got a second body, but he's free. What am I supposed to think?"

"You can't think anything but what is right there, staring you in the face. ... And yet I hear you trying to justify your actions," Simon replied.

"That's because I don't think the kid did it," she stated bluntly.

He looked at her in surprise. "You don't?"

She shook her head. "No, I don't. You have to really hate your sister to do what was done to that woman."

He sank back and nodded. "You know what? That's a level of hate I don't understand myself, but that doesn't mean it's not out there."

"Nope, not at all," she agreed. "It's one of the things that has to be dealt with."

"No, I get it." He looked at the piece of paper that she handed him. "This address is not very far from here."

"No, it isn't, like five minutes around the corner." She took several turns, turned around, then pulled up in front of a small house, with curtains closed in the front windows. The driveway led to a very old beat-up garage. She looked at this place and shook her head. "Not what I expected."

He hopped out beside her. "No, not what I expected either."

"But," she added, "in the last however many years, it's probably cost them a lot."

"In many ways," he added.

"People who commit crimes never think about the consequences to their actions that can affect their family," she noted. "The stepfather lost his job and couldn't get anything at the same level. He has been working at a security job for the last five years."

"What was he before that?"

"He was a business CEO and got fired because of his involvement with his stepson's case."

"Well, they had to have a reason for that too."

"I guess he lost it, after his stepdaughter's death, and then lost it again when his stepson was convicted," she explained quietly, as she walked up the front steps.

"And you can't really blame him for that."

"No, and the mother was working as a cleaning lady for one of the hotels, and her health has become a big issue recently."

"Damn good thing there's free health care here."

"It may be free," she said, with a wave of her hand, "but there are wait times involved, and some stuff is still out of touch with what you can get, if you only had the money."

"I know," he muttered. "But, believe me, one of the main focuses when I managed to get out of my situation was that having money meant that I wouldn't be left behind anymore. I would have the power to do what I wanted because money really does give you a lot of freedom, a lot more choices."

"It may give you freedom"—she knocked on the front door—"but it doesn't keep you safe. And particularly not when a shitty life comes knocking," she murmured. "Sometimes there's just nothing you can do but try to handle the shit as it flies around you."

CHAPTER 7

W HEN NOBODY ANSWERED the door, Kate knocked again. Finally a cranky voice inside called out, "I'm coming. I'm coming."

The door was flung open, and a middle-aged—maybe early fifties—woman stood there, glaring.

Kate pulled out her badge and held it up. "We're looking for your son. May we speak with him, please?"

"He's not here," she snapped.

"We have intel that says otherwise. We also have intel that says that he lives here full-time." She paused. "May we come in and speak with you?"

"No, you sure as hell can't," she snapped. "I won't listen to you guys anymore."

"And why is that?" Kate asked, knowing that the situation would end up with this couple down at the station to be interviewed.

"Because of what you did last time," she snapped.

"I had nothing to do with that," Kate replied. "And your son confessed."

"He didn't do it."

"Potentially," she agreed. "Can you please confirm whether your son lives here or not?" Kate asked, hardening her voice. "And, if you don't want to talk here, that's fine." She nodded. "I can issue an order to have you come down to the station and talk with me there."

"Why are you badgering us?" the woman asked, some of her bravado starting to break down.

In the background Kate heard a man calling out.

"Who is it? Who is it?"

"Barney, it's nothing," the mother said, then immediately stepped outside, pulling the door shut behind her. "We don't need him to get involved."

"I need to ask some questions," Kate stated firmly.

The woman looked over at Simon, then back at Kate. "What do you want to know?"

"I need to know where Rick was these last five days."

The woman shook her head. "Why?" she cried out, so much pain in her voice. "Hasn't he been through enough?"

"Yes, I believe he has. This isn't the same house you lived in where your daughter was killed. Is that correct?"

Tearing up, the woman shook her head. "No, and that house is being destroyed, I understand."

Kate nodded. "Yes, I'll take a walk through the place myself."

The woman studied her in surprise. "Why?" she asked.

"Because I need to know what happened back then."

"I don't get it," she stated. "My son already did time for the crime."

"I know," she replied. "And you keep telling me that he didn't do it. So, I don't know whether he did or didn't." Then she took a deep breath and added, "Unfortunately we have another body."

The woman stared, and her jaw dropped. "Oh no, no, no, no." She shook her head rapidly. "I can't go through that again."

"It depends on if he had nothing to do with it," she stated firmly. "In that case, then he's free and clear, and everything he can tell us will help us find out how this all happened."

"What do you mean, another body? You mean like—" And she stopped, then she shook her head. "You don't understand. It was so terrible."

"And this one is terrible too," Kate told her, "with way-too-many similarities. So, either it's the same killer"—and she stopped for a moment, as she studied the other woman—"or it's somebody who knows all the details."

The woman looked so terribly frail that Simon reached out before Kate could and helped the older woman sit down in a rocking chair on the porch. Kate crouched in front of her.

"If your son didn't do this, then we can help clear him from the previous murder, if he didn't do that one. I need to know if he's told anybody in great detail what happened to his sister or if he had any other close relationships, maybe when he was in jail," she explained. "But first we have to clear him of this latest murder."

The woman looked at her in so much shock that Kate was afraid this would end up being a medical emergency. She looked over at Simon.

He patted the woman's hand gently and asked, "Can I get you a glass of water?"

The woman looked at him gratefully and then nodded.

Simon asked, "Is it okay if I go into your house straight to the kitchen to get it?"

She nodded again slowly and then leaned back against the chair, her eyes closed. "Dear God," she murmured, "the pain, you have no idea what it was like."

"No," Kate said quietly, "but I do have a pretty good

inkling."

The woman opened her eyes, looked at her, and asked, "Has anybody in your family been murdered?"

"No," she stated firmly.

"Then you don't understand," the woman snapped.

"Maybe not," she agreed, "but I had a younger brother kidnapped, and he still hasn't come home."

At that, the woman gasped, her hand going to her mouth, and she stared wide-eyed at Kate.

"So I do understand," Kate repeated. "No, it's not the same obviously. I wish that you never had to experience what you did, but, by the same token, I know what it's like to lose someone close. I know what it's like to have no answers—or answers that you can't agree with. And it still doesn't get any easier. It's been a lot of years for my brother. And, no, it does not get any easier."

The woman slowly dropped her hand. "Yes," she replied, "you're right. It doesn't get any easier. When Rick was in jail, I didn't tell anyone. I couldn't. I just ... I didn't even know what to say. We moved because we had to. I couldn't live in the same house. My husband lost his job. I had to quit working," she added. "And this"—raising a hand to the front porch—"is what we have now. I can't bear the thought of losing even this much."

"And there's no reason to think that right now," Kate stated. "We need to talk to your son."

"He's at work," she whispered.

"No, he isn't. He ran when he saw me."

The woman looked at her, and her bottom lip trembled. "You know he's terrified of the police," she replied, with hope in her voice that Kate would be understanding.

"And I get that." Kate nodded. "I really do, but running

away won't be the answer. I must talk to him, and, if he'll continuously avoid me, then I'll have no choice but to have him picked up and taken down to the station, and we'll have to interview him there. And you know it won't be nice, even compared to the other time."

"No," she whispered, "it'll be way worse."

"He already has a black mark against him. And, as much as I can be understanding," Kate added, "I can't let it go. We have another body in the morgue that resembles what happened last time, and it's way too close to ignore that comparison. If your son is not involved, then he potentially knows somebody who is."

"How could he know? He told me once that he had no idea what happened, and he doesn't know anything about it."

"And that's important too," Kate said, sitting back on her heels.

Just then, Simon stepped out of the house with a glass of water. He walked over and gave it to her.

The older woman took it gratefully and took several sips. And then she inhaled a deep breath. "What happened to my daughter was the most horrifying thing," she told Kate. "I could never have imagined that my son would have done that to her. There was no way."

"What was their relationship like?"

"Feisty," she admitted. "He wasn't the easiest person to live with. He was always in some trouble, but, at the same time, they didn't hate each other. And what was done to her? That was just ..." She shook her head and took another sip.

"I get it. I do. You know what was done to her. You also need to understand that I now have another woman, another daughter of another mother, who's facing the exact same thing right now."

The woman nodded slowly. "Dear God, I'm so sorry for her."

"Exactly, and I need to see what's happening, so we don't end up with a third."

"Oh dear God," she whispered, her hand shaking.

Once again Simon reached over and gripped the woman's fingers.

"We need to find Rick. We need to talk to him. We'll have more questions for you and for your husband, as well," Kate relayed quietly. "I don't want to rake up all the coals, but I'm coming at it from a very different angle now. And we can't have another body show up."

The woman started to shake. "I don't know where Rick's gone. He should be home. He's off work now, and normally he would come straight home."

"Yes, but once he identified me at his job," Kate noted, "he took off running."

His mother nodded. "But I don't know where he went."

"Can you find him?"

She looked at her in surprise. "Well, I can. But he might get angry at me."

"Would he ever hurt you?"

"Oh, no," she stated. "You don't understand. He's very gentle."

"I'm glad to hear that," Kate replied. "I need you to phone him then and to tell him that he needs to talk to me."

The woman nodded. "Okay." She pulled her phone from her pocket and picked a number and called it. Almost immediately it was answered. "What are you doing?" she asked. "You need to come talk to the police."

Shocked silence continued on the other end, until he

said, "I can't. I just can't. You know that I can't."

"You have to. We have to talk to them and to sort it out."

Kate held out her hand.

The woman looked at her phone and at Kate's hand and then slowly handed it over.

"Rick, I need to talk to you. So either come home where we can talk here, or we'll send somebody to pick you up and take you down to the station."

"No, no, no," he replied, "you don't understand."

"No, I don't, and it's up to you to tell me."

"That's not fair," he cried out. "I didn't do anything."

"So why did you run?"

"Because it's *cops*," he stated. "You think I care to have anything to do with cops anymore?"

"That's not the point," she replied. "When cops come calling, you need to answer questions."

"No, I sure as hell don't. Answering questions last time got my ass sent to prison."

"And yet you confessed."

"Of course I confessed. I needed it to stop."

"And, if that's the case, then I need to talk to you," she stated. "There's a good chance you know who did it."

"No, no, no, no, you don't understand."

In the background on his phone, she heard sounds of somebody delivering an order, as if he were in a drive-through. "You're not coming home for your dinner with your mom, huh?" Kate looked at the mom.

"No, I'm not."

"Fine," she snapped. "I would really like to pick you up and talk to you without any fanfare. But, if you'll resist, I don't have any choice, and we'll put out a BOLO and track you down."

"No," he cried out, "no, no, no."

"Then stop," she snapped again. "Get your ass home where you belong, and let's talk this out. I just need to ask you a few questions." At his silence on the other end, Kate returned the mother's phone to her. "If he doesn't come home, I'll have to haul him in." Then Kate walked over to the other end of the porch.

Simon joined her. "What do you do in a case like this?"

"Pull out an all-points bulletin on him and the vehicle, and someone will pick him up within a day or so." She shrugged. "And then he looks guilty as hell. We'll do everything we can to get answers out of him, but he'll get thrown in jail, and I can hold him for forty-eight hours."

"Even if he didn't do anything?" Simon asked.

"Even if he didn't do anything," she stated quietly. "Believe me. It doesn't make me feel any better."

"Of course not," he agreed, "and it's not your fault." He walked back to the woman, who sat there, holding the phone against her chest. "And?"

"I asked him to come home," she replied in a teary voice. "Please, please don't hurt him."

"If he comes home quietly and is cooperative," Kate said, joining them at that end of the porch, "there is no reason for him to get hurt at all. If it gets to the point where he resists arrest, you and I both know that things can go downhill very quickly."

The older woman started to sob gently, as the front door was flung open, and an older man stepped out. He took one look at Kate, and his back went up, and he looked angry, like in a flash of red.

"Hi," she greeted him calmly. "Just talking to your

wife."

"You made her cry," he yelled belligerently.

Almost immediately, the older woman got to her feet and headed to her husband. She wrapped her arms around him and patted him gently. "It's okay, Barney. Honestly it's okay."

He looked at her with concern, and yet something was a little bit off about his mannerisms.

The woman whispered to Kate, "I'll just take him inside." And she turned and led her husband back into the house.

Then Kate realized what was wrong. She looked over at Simon. "Did that look like his mental acuity was reduced?"

"Something is definitely wrong. Obviously there are some health issues. Neurological maybe, I'm not sure," he replied. "What a sad life."

"It is, indeed," she agreed. "Very sad when you consider what this poor woman has been through. To think that her husband is now failing as well just adds to it."

A vehicle pulled up almost ten minutes later, and a younger man hopped out with a bag of takeout food and walked up to the front door. With the overgrown vines taking over the trellises on the front porch, he didn't see Kate standing at the far end until he was already at the front door. Simon came in from one side, and Kate came in from the other. He looked at her in terror.

She held up both hands. "I told you that I just want to talk."

"Yeah, well, cops tell me all kinds of crap." He walked inside the house, and she raced in behind him, grateful when he didn't try to bolt out the back door. He stopped in front of his mom and stepdad.

"What's the matter with Dad?" he asked in concern.

"He got upset," his mom replied softly. "I was crying with the detective here, and he thought the detective hurt me."

"Well, she did," he snapped. "Anybody who has these kinds of conversations will hurt you. And yet it doesn't stop anything."

"Can we sit and talk?" Kate asked quietly. "Or maybe we should go back out on the porch, so we don't disturb Barney here."

The older woman looked at her gratefully. "Maybe you and Rick could go outside, could you?"

She nodded and asked Rick, "You ready to go talk?"

Rick frowned and headed out in an almost childish action of defiance. He then threw himself into the same chair his mother had just vacated. "What do you want to talk about?"

"Well, to start with, why did you run from your job?"

"My shift was over," he replied in a snide tone.

"Sure it was, except for the last ten to fifteen minutes. Your boss gave you a good reference, but, of course, he's bothered by your behavior."

He looked at her in alarm. "Did you get me fired?"

"No, *I* didn't." She stared at the young man. "Did you do anything to get yourself fired?"

He stared at her in shock and started shaking his head. "No, you don't know how hard it was to get a job when I got out."

"So, tell me about these last few days. Where were you?"

"At work, I was at work," he said. "What about it?" An honest bewilderment was in his voice.

She stared at him for a long time. "What time do you

leave the house to go to work?"

"I work seven to five usually," he replied, "but I've been putting in extra hours because we're short on people."

"I know your boss appreciates it," she noted quietly. "What time do you get up?"

"About fifteen minutes before I have to be at work," he answered, rubbing his eyes. "I stay up late gaming sometimes. I know I shouldn't because then I sleep in late, and I have to book it to get to work."

"And what do you do when you come home?"

"Usually I help Mom with a few chores and dinner and play a few games with my dad. He's really slipped. I don't know what it is. The doctor said he's regressing."

"Well, when you can't handle the stress of what's going on in the world, that makes sense."

"It's not like who he was at all," the son fretted. "Haven't they been through enough without you showing up now?"

"You mean, without you running away and making it all that much worse?" Simon said from the side.

Rick looked up at him, frowned, and then back at Kate. "What is this? Good cop, bad cop?"

"Nope," she argued cheerfully. "So did you go anywhere else on the weekend?"

He shook his head. "The usual. I took Mom grocery shopping. Other than that, I've been playing an online game all weekend."

"Well, as much as I could, I worked over my weekend," Kate noted.

"But it's not like I have any friends."

"Any criminal friends?"

He shrugged. "Most of them are still in jail."

"So it's lucky for you that you're out."

"Yeah."

"Did you ever give anybody details about your case?"

"Tons of us talked about our cases," he noted, with a sneer. "Sometimes it was all about whoever could tell the biggest story. And other times nobody gave a shit and just basically told you to shut up."

"I get it," she stated quietly. "Now you said that you didn't murder your sister ..."

"No, I did not," he snapped.

"Did you give any of the details of her death to anybody in jail?"

"No, not really." Rick paused. "I mean, I don't remember all the details. I didn't want to know."

"I'm sure you know a lot of them," she countered.

"Sure, some of them, but it's not like I'm the one who did it."

"Good." Kate nodded. "So, if you didn't kill your sister, do you have any idea who did?"

He looked at her in surprise. "Seriously?"

She just stared at him.

"Am I hearing things?" he asked.

"What do you mean?"

"I don't know anybody who would have killed her," he replied, "and honestly I don't think anybody ever asked me that question. Back then, I mean."

"Well, the question remains as pertinent today as it was back then," she noted. "Do you have any idea who else might have killed your sister?"

He stared quietly for a long moment. And then he slowly shook his head. "Honest to God, I don't."

SIMON WASN'T SURE if he believed Rick or not, but such a solid ring of truth was in the kid's voice that it was hard not to. He looked over at Kate to see how she was taking his words and was gratified to see her looking like she was seriously considering it.

"You've had lots of time," she said to Rick, "to think about what happened, to think about who might have done this. So, if you are innocent, I find it hard to believe that you don't have at least some idea."

He stared at her, and his lips curled downward. "Of course you don't, and, because I can't actually tell you who did it, I'm the guilty one."

"Not at all," she argued. "Somebody had access to your house. Somebody had access to your sister. Somebody knew that everybody was away. So how is that possible?"

He looked at her, shrugged, and sighed. "I don't know. I wasn't even there at the time. I was away with friends."

And he said it in such an emphatic voice that she asked, "And who were these friends?"

He sneered. "Friends who ran as soon as I got into a whiff of trouble."

"But they were friends who were part of your trouble, were they not?"

He nodded. "If you're trying to say in a roundabout way that they were just as quick to avoid law enforcement as I was, then yes. I spent a hell of a long time in jail thinking about all the things that I did wrong," he explained, "but not one of those things deserved what I went through."

"None of them," she added, "is anything your sister deserved either."

At that, he winced, then stared off into the distance. "No, we were as different as chalk and cheese."

"Tell me more," she said.

He shrugged. "What can I tell you? She was a good person, and I was a shithole. If somebody should have suffered, it should have been me. She didn't deserve to die like that."

"What was your relationship like?"

"We were siblings. We fought a lot. She kept telling me that I should turn a corner and change my path and all that crap. She was right, but I ignored her because, of course, I knew better." He shook his head. "And there is no remorse quite like the remorse of knowing that you were in the wrong and that maybe you could have done something to save her."

"Do you think you could have?"

He looked at her in surprise. "I've always thought that, maybe, if I'd been home," he explained, "this wouldn't have happened."

She nodded. "And maybe it wouldn't have. No way for us to know until we know exactly how and why she was targeted. There have never been any other cases like this before, and there weren't any—until now," she stated, with emphasis.

He stared at her. "*Now?*"

She nodded. "Until now. And the fact is, you're back out of prison again. So, if you didn't do the last one, did you do the latest one?"

His jaw dropped, and Simon could see the shock and the horror on his face, as if suddenly realizing what shit he was in.

"Jesus Christ," Rick said in a hoarse voice. "Somebody killed another girl?"

She nodded slowly. "And, in this case, a very similar methodology to what happened to your sister."

He swallowed hard, and his fingers clenched and tightened on his lap. "I didn't do it," he cried out.

"I'm glad to hear that," she noted calmly, not giving an inch either way. "If you didn't do it, then somebody needs to give me a little bit more detail."

"What do you mean?"

"Well, if you didn't kill your sister, and if you didn't kill our recent victim," she began, "who do you think did?"

"I don't know," he wailed. "Jesus, I can't believe this. I won't go to jail for something somebody else did, not again," he cried out.

"And I'm not planning on letting you," she replied in a firm voice, "but hysterics won't help."

He glared at her. "*Hysterics?* You ain't seen nothing yet," he said. "Anytime anybody threatens to put me back into that hellhole, I have a right to hysterics. I have a right to throw a temper fit. I have a right to be upset. I was railroaded into serving time for a terrible crime that I did not commit."

"And that brings up a really good point," she noted. "Why did you confess?"

He slowly closed his mouth. And his shoulders hunched. "I've never regretted anything quite so much in my life."

"Except for not being home to help protect your sister."

He stared at her, haunted. "And that's why I confessed. I was supposed to be home," he replied. "I was sure that it was all my fault because I was supposed to be home with her."

"And yet you weren't. So where were you?"

He winced. "I was scoring drugs. Like I said, I was a little shit back then. But she deserved a whole lot better than a shitty brother."

"Got it," Kate noted quietly. "So why confess? You felt

like it was your fault?"

He nodded. "Yes. I did feel like it was my fault, and I felt like this is what I needed to do to atone for it."

"And now?"

"Jesus, no," he replied. "I was a shit. I did not deserve to have her as my sister, but I didn't do that to her, and I've paid more than any person should have to pay for the lie of saying I did."

"Once you say something like that," she explained, "it's a lie that's almost impossible to come back from."

"Do you think I don't know that?" he asked bitterly. "I tried to recant my story. I tried to get them to believe me, but all they could hear was the confession that I'd made. It's as if they were just so locked on to that, there was nothing else to even consider."

"Well, think about it," she stated. "Why would there be? You were there. Your DNA was all over the murder scene, and the forensic evidence led to you. You confessed. As far as any law enforcement knew at the time, it was an open-and-shut case."

"I didn't do it though," he repeated. "I didn't have any motivation, and nobody would talk to me about that."

"That's because it's easy to consider the motivation was being siblings," she explained. "Whether I personally can see that much hate between siblings or not doesn't mean that it doesn't exist."

"I didn't hate her," he argued, tears welling up in his eyes. "Dear God, I didn't hate her at all. She was my sister, so why is it nobody can believe that?"

"Nobody can believe that because you confessed," she repeated. "So we get on this endless loop that just doesn't stop."

He shook his head, and his shoulders started to shake.

Simon glanced at Kate.

She understood what that look meant. She could see Rick was reaching his breaking point, and Simon could see it too. Maybe he wanted her to put a stop to this, and he probably saw this as difficult to watch in many ways. But this was her job. She tried to be compassionate yet a hard-ass as needed.

Simon cleared his throat to catch her attention again. When she looked over at him, he raised his eyebrows.

She just studied him for a long moment, then turned back to Rick. "I want you to come down to the station," she stated, "and give us a formal statement about where you were the last few days. I need an alibi to make sure that everybody doesn't immediately think you're the suspect."

"Too late," he snapped. "Isn't that why you're here?"

"I came to simply talk to you. Then you ran, which didn't help your case. And now you're sitting here, giving me guff again," she noted quietly. "So you tell me how you want to play this. Last time you got belligerent and difficult, which made things tough for everybody. And nobody could get to the bottom of the truth. Then, once you confessed, you sidelined all the search for the real culprit," she explained. "You do that again, and all those man-hours to find the murderer will cease on this case too, and it becomes something that you don't really want to deal with again."

Rick shook his head. "I tried to recant."

"And like I said," she added gently, "it's a one-way street. Sure, you can recant, and you know what? With any luck, we might do something about it, but chances are good that it won't make a damn bit of difference because, once you say those words, and everything else points to you ..."

She shrugged and left it there.

"What do you want me to do?" he asked. "You've got to understand that no way in hell I can go back to jail."

"I hear you. It all depends on if you've kept your nose clean and out of trouble all these years since you got out," she explained. "And then we really need to tear apart your life."

He stared at her in shock. "Why? What did I do?"

"Somebody waited all this time, until you got out of jail, before they turned around and committed another murder— just like one you were put away for. Making you the perfect patsy for this again. All to avoid prison themselves."

He shook his head. "But why? I didn't do anything to anybody."

"If you had a bit of a shady history at some point in time, what are the chances you pissed somebody off, and they're just out for revenge?"

He stared at her. "I didn't think anybody hated me like this."

"Maybe they don't. Maybe they're just playing with you. Maybe you took a girlfriend from them. Maybe you screwed them over with somebody else. Like a drug deal or something, and they've been waiting a long time for this. Maybe it has nothing to do with your sister, but it was a way to get back at you."

At that, his face whitened. "That would be unconscionable," he whispered.

She looked at him and said, "When it comes to murder, the motives are interesting. There always is one, but sometimes you have to dig a little deeper to find it."

He shook his head. "But what you're saying is that I could actually be to blame for my sister's death."

Her eyebrows shot up. "I'm not saying anything about that," she argued. "If somebody killed her to get back at you, that still doesn't mean that you're at fault. Whoever did this is at fault. So don't go getting hung up on the blame game," she warned, "because that can go wrong very quickly."

He shook his head. "If they did it to get back at me, then I am to blame."

"And again, that could be something you can look at, but it's an indirect blame," she explained. "You don't get to turn around and confess again to say that it's your fault in order to appease your own conscience after all this time, when it's quite likely that somebody else did this, and it has nothing to do with you."

He shook his head. "What do you mean?"

"What if they got away with it last time, laughing their fool head off because you were convicted. And now the urge has been something that they can't hold back, knowing that you're out of jail, and here it happened all over again."

"But I've been out for five years."

"Yes, but how long were you actually given as a sentence?"

He stared at her for a long moment and then slumped into his chair. "I was just thinking about that last week," he admitted. "If I hadn't gotten out early for good behavior, I wouldn't have been out until this week." When the reality of that statement sunk in, he blanched, and all the color drained from his face. "Dear God," he murmured. "Somebody timed it so that I would look guilty again."

She nodded. "Exactly, which also means that you are our best bet for finding this person because whoever it is knows what's going on in your world. But apparently they aren't too close to you, since they don't know that you got out early. But they had to have known how to get ahold of your sister."

He shrugged. "She was a good person. She was out doing good deeds all the time. She wanted to marry a minister and do God's work," he whispered. "I used to laugh at her all the time, thinking it was such a foolish thing to want to do, but she just gave me that gentle smile and told me that everybody had a pathway in this world, and that was hers. But she never even got a chance to have that." He shook his head. And again his bottom lip started to tremble.

"Well," she noted, "now it's time for you to do your part and to get the answers that we all need for your sister."

He stared at her, with tears in his eyes. "Okay, so what do I need to do again?"

"Good, I'm glad to see you get it," she added. "You'll come down to the station, where you'll give us a full statement. Then you'll help us figure out who could have had access to your place back then. And who would know what happened back then—enough to know that you were out of prison now."

"Where was this woman? The one who you just found?"

"Downtown." Kate pulled out a photo and held it up. "This is the victim. Do you know her?"

He stared at the image in shock, and then he started to bawl.

She slowly lowered the picture, looked over at Simon, then back at the kid. "And I guess that's a yes, isn't it? I'd like you to come down to the station with us now."

He continued bawling, shaking his head, as he slowly stood.

Simon and Kate watched the young man carefully. They both shared a look and really hoped Rick wouldn't do anything stupid. When the mother stepped out the front door, she was bawling too. The son rushed forward, and the mother engulfed him in a big hug.

Kate stood, looked over at the mother, and explained quietly, "I'm taking him in, so he can give us a formal statement. We are not charging him or anything like that. But I do need him to help us figure out who else could be involved in this."

The woman looked at her, a hint of suspicion in her gaze, but nodded. "And you're not keeping him, right?"

"No," Kate replied. "I'll take him down now, and I'll bring him back later this evening."

The woman stiffened, patted her son, and said, "You go do what's right this time."

He looked at her and, in a teary voice, said, "That's what I thought I was doing last time."

CHAPTER 8

KATE WAS GRATEFUL that she was getting Rick down to the station to give her a statement and to answer more questions. Even as she drove, her mind was full of all the questions she needed to ask. As they headed down the street, she glanced in the rearview mirror, frowning when she saw a muscle car pulling behind a little too close. Getting suspicious, she called back to Rick, "Know anybody who drives a muscle car?"

"Not now," he replied. "I told you that I don't really have any friends."

"Any come into your shop?"

"Sure, all the time," he noted, "but none I really know."

"Anybody who was overly friendly or overly curious the last couple times?"

"Lots of times they're friendly, but why are you asking?"

"Because I think we're being followed," she replied quietly.

He gasped and spun around and then immediately ducked. "Good God, why would somebody follow us?"

"Well, considering that we just picked you up, maybe it has to do with you." She reached for her phone on the dash and called Rodney.

When he picked up, he asked, "Where the hell are you?"

"I'm just coming into the office. Why?"

"The sergeant has been looking for you."

She sighed. "I'm trying to do a job. Remember?"

"I get it, but he does like regular check-ins."

"Yeah, I know. I'm bringing Rick Lord in for questioning."

"Have you found him?"

"Yes." She studied her rearview mirror, as she changed lanes. "I also think I'm bringing in a bogey." There was a pause at the other end.

"Say what?"

"I think I'm being followed," she spelled out. "Can you head down to the parking lot and get yourself in a vantage point where you can take a look as I pull in?"

"You really think somebody is coming in behind you?"

"Well, he is, but I don't know how far he'll travel. And I don't know whether they're interested in me or my cargo."

"You didn't arrest him, did you?"

"No, I didn't. But somebody is very interested in my passenger."

"Or in you," he offered. "You have a tendency to make a lot of enemies."

She laughed. "Good point. Anyway, can you do what I asked?"

"I'm already there," he stated. "How far away are you?"

"About four minutes." She kept driving, steadily changing lanes, and the other driver kept up with her. She studied Rick in the darkness. He looked seriously scared. She glanced at Simon, who was looking at his side mirror at the guy following them. "Do you recognize the car at all?"

Simon shook his head. "No, I don't. I'm trying to get a bead on the driver."

"Yeah, let me know if that works. All I see is a baseball

cap and sunglasses."

"Which is pretty cheesy," he muttered.

"But effective," she countered, "and that's why people do it."

"Got it," he noted, "but you'd think they'd be a little more original."

She laughed. "Nope, not in this world. They're all about making it work." After several quick turns, she then pulled into a side street and drove slowly. And, sure enough, not very long afterward, the muscle car came in behind her. "I can see the first two letters of the plate," she noted. "Can you get the rest?"

"Yep," Simon replied. "Wish I could take a picture."

"You might in the rearview mirror," she murmured.

He nodded. "I'm already on it." And just then, he said, "Got it."

As they came into the police station, at the back entrance to the parking lot, a shot was fired, and hit the side mirror of her car. She immediately turned, with the kid screaming in the background, and pulled into a parking spot, where they were surrounded by other vehicles. She told Rick to get his head down and to stay there, as she got out of the car. She raced to the entrance, but the muscle car had already taken off down the road.

As she got to the corner, Rodney stood there, staring at her in shock.

She nodded. "Yeah, that was him."

"Well, shit. Did he just shoot at you?"

She nodded. "Sure did."

A black-and-white came up at the same time. She immediately pointed and said, "That old Oldsmobile that just turned left up there? He just shot at my car."

They nodded and took off in pursuit. She wanted to go after them herself but not when she had the kid with her. She returned to her car to find Simon outside, studying the parking lot. "You don't take orders well, do you?"

"The order was for the kid," Simon noted, "not for me."

"Are you sure about that?"

He nodded. "Absolutely sure."

She smiled, opened up the back door, and motioned at the kid to get out. "Come on. Let's get you inside."

"You don't think they were after me, do you?"

"I'm not sure," she noted. "Could be you, me, or Simon here."

He looked over at Simon. "You got people who hate you too?"

"When you live," Simon replied, "you get people who hate you. It doesn't matter whether you think you deserve it or not."

"I didn't do anything—honest," he said.

"Good." Simon nodded. "In that case it should be pretty easy to clear this up."

"I don't know," Rick replied. "This is making me more than a little scared."

"Did you ever get death threats when you were in jail?" Kate asked him.

"Yeah, I got as many death threats as marriage proposals." Rick raised both hands in shock. "Who the hell does that?"

"Lonely women," Simon answered. "Women who have their own issues and who think they can save you. Being young and cute and sometimes misguided, these women think that you would be theirs and that they could fix you."

"But there's nothing wrong with me," he said in disgust.

"Yeah, just don't tell them that." Simon laughed.

The kid just shook his head. "It makes no sense."

"A lot of times these things don't make any sense," Kate said. "It doesn't make sense until we get to the truth, and then it makes way too much sense, and you wonder how you couldn't have seen it in the first place."

Rick stopped, looked at her, and then nodded. "It was like that about confessing," he admitted. "I mean, it seemed like the right thing to do at the time. I was so guilt ridden, and then all of a sudden it was not the right thing to do at all, but it was way too late to change it."

"Life is like that," she noted. "When you do things impulsively, you really need to step back and to try to think about what you're doing."

"But I just react," he admitted quietly. "I don't think. I just react."

"I get it." She nodded. "Yet you also have to consider that, by confessing, and you being a really good suspect, the police stopped looking for anybody else."

"I assumed they weren't looking to begin with," he replied.

"But, if you didn't actually kill her, don't you think they should have been sure?" And they were originally keeping their options open, but then they stopped looking because, of course, Rick confessed, making it a slam-dunk deal. She didn't say anything more but led them to her area and into an interview room. She pointed Rick to a chair. "Take a seat. Simon, are you hanging around or leaving?"

He said, "I'm leaving."

She nodded. "You want to wait here for a minute?" He nodded in understanding, taking a step outside the room, and she looked at the kid. "Do you want a coffee?"

"If there is Coke, I'll take that," he replied. "I didn't even get dinner."

"Hopefully we can get you home real fast," she told him.

With that, she disappeared and got him a can of Coke from the vending machine and poured herself a coffee. She should have brought one for Simon. As she walked back to the interrogation room, she held it out to him, and he looked at her in disgust. "Right, plain old coffee is not exactly your style, is it?"

He shrugged. "Let's just say I'm not desperate enough."

"Same diff." She smirked, as she returned to the interview room, shutting the door behind her. She gave the kid his Coke, put down her coffee cup, then dug into her pocket for her pad of paper and a pen and dropped both on the table. She set her phone on Record and got his permission to tape this exchange. "Okay, let's go, from the top."

Rick looked at her in surprise. "Top of what?"

"The top of this nightmare," she stated, "way back to the day that your sister was killed. Where were you a couple days in advance of that?"

He looked at her in shock. "I can't remember way back then."

"Your sister was held in your house for more than twenty-four hours."

He slumped in his chair. "Seriously?"

She looked at him. "You didn't know she was tortured?"

"Sure, I know she was tortured. My parents were away. They took a week's holiday and went over to the island to visit with friends. It was their one chance to get away, and I don't remember how many anniversaries it was, but they almost never went away."

"And you two were supposed to look after each other, I

suppose."

He nodded. "Yes, exactly."

"And you took off with your friends into your world of drug deals?"

He took a long slow deep breath. "Yes," he admitted, "and the trouble is, I was under the influence for so much of that time that I don't have answers for you."

She nodded. "Which is why the cops couldn't get anywhere because the one person who was supposed to be there with answers wasn't there mentally."

"No," he agreed, "and that's also, as you know, why I confessed."

"So, when you got home that day, it was the first time you'd been home in how long?"

"Several days, but, no, I don't know how many."

"Two, maybe three?" she asked, making circles on her pad of paper. "You didn't hear anything when you first got home?"

"Remember that whole 'under the influence of drugs' thing?"

"I get it," she noted. "I'm trying to figure out if the killer was actually in the house at the time."

"I don't know," Rick replied, "and, to be honest, I've thought about it a lot. I just don't have any answers."

She nodded. "Okay, so from the top, let's just go. You tell me what happened, and I'll take a fresh statement."

"And what, compare it to the last one to see if I lied?"

"Sometimes, after the passage of time, that distance jogs memories, or sometimes it clouds it," she noted. "Remember. I'm not here looking to pin this current murder on you. I'm trying to figure out why and how somebody would choose to set you up for it."

"And I don't fucking know either," he cried out, reaching up to scrub his face as he took a deep breath. Taking a few deep breaths, he continued. "Okay, let's go. Our parents left for a week on a Friday night. They were supposed to be coming back Friday or Saturday of the following week. My sister and I had a big fight that first Friday night, and I took off. She didn't want to be home alone." His voice hitched for a moment. Then he took a deep breath and kept going.

"I came home Saturday afternoon, she was doing laundry, cleaning the house, and we weren't exactly friendly because I called her a bunch of names because she was being this Goody Two-Shoes."

"Carry on," Kate said.

"I stayed there Saturday night, but I left about four o'clock in the morning on Sunday because one of my buddies called me to say they had scored a deal, and, if I could come down and give him a hand, I'd get paid in drugs." He shook his head.

"It seemed so simple and like such a great deal at the time, but who knew it would cost me so much? Anyway I went downtown and met them. They had broken into a store and stolen a bunch of stuff, so they needed to sort it by pawn shops, get the deliveries out, and they needed somebody with an unmarked car. So I did the rounds with them and helped them dispose of the items." He sighed, as he rubbed his face again.

"Then I got high on the proceeds. And I stayed high for the rest of Sunday and all of Monday and Tuesday," he explained. "I think it was Wednesday when I finally went home again. I was wasted when I got there. It was late, I think. I don't know. I was looking for food, so I went into the kitchen and didn't find anything. That pissed me off, but

I just went upstairs to my room and fell asleep.

"When I got up on what was probably Thursday morning, I felt a bit better, but it was already about noon. By now I was in the kitchen, making peanut butter and jam sandwiches, and there was just this weird haunted silence around me. I didn't know what the hell was going on, and I didn't know where my sister was. I started calling out for her, but she didn't answer."

He stopped and took a deep breath.

"I had checked her room that previous night, and it was empty," he noted. "And then I got really worried because her room was a mess. As if she had just walked away from the laundry that she had been doing when I was there on Saturday—which was very unlike her. She also didn't have any friends who she would take off and do anything with. I don't think it really set in at the time," he added. "I was still flying on my own. You know? Like I'm a big man or something, and I wasn't really thinking about where she was, although I was getting concerned because she wasn't answering my phone messages. I sent her several more texts, and, at one point in time, I was close to her room when I sent one, and I heard her phone *ding*. I went into her room and saw her phone there. That's when I really got worried. I checked it, and there hadn't been any activity on it, beyond the messages I had just sent, since that Saturday when she had been there doing laundry."

Kate sat back and looked at him. "That's a long time."

He looked up with tears in his eyes, and he nodded. "I know," he whispered, "way too long."

"Go on," she said gently.

He nodded. "I did a full search of the house, at least I thought I did. I didn't see her. I knew my parents were coming home the next day, and they would be frantic. I didn't have any explanation. I didn't know where she was. I didn't know what had happened. I went downstairs to the basement, and there's a cold room in the back. It was just on an off chance that I went inside and checked." He stopped, swallowed, tears welling in his eyes. "And I found her," he whispered. He shook his head. "God, that's a sight I wish I could unsee."

"No," she stated, "when something like that happens, there is no unseeing it."

"I know," he replied, "but I wish it were possible. Nobody should ever have to see somebody they love like that."

She nodded. "While you were at home that one day, did you see anybody else? Did anybody come to the door? Did you see anybody in the backyard or anything?"

He shook his head. "No, I think the cop told me that she'd already been dead for a day though."

"Maybe," she noted. "I'll have to check the autopsy, which just means that this guy either saw that you came home and finished her off or that was the natural climax of whatever he had planned."

"The fact that it was in our home with her there is what I think my parents could never quite forgive."

"Why is that? Because in their mind you were there to look after her?"

"Well, I was supposed to be," he said bitterly. "And, as you know, I'm well-known for screwing up big-time."

Such bitterness was in his voice, and she understood entirely. "What did you do at that point?"

"I called the cops," he said. "All of a sudden all my transgressions and reasons for never wanting to deal with the cops seemed so petty because here I was, staring at my dead sister. But, even still, I'm trying to formulate a lie, something, some reasonable excuse for what happened, before my parents came home, because that would be the end of it for me—once they realized what had happened and that I had been gone."

"What did you tell them?"

"I told them that I'd been out on a job, trying to make some money, hoping they'd be proud of me, and instead it backfired, and I wasn't home to protect her."

"Instead of, you *were* on a job but definitely not one that would make them happy."

"No," he admitted, "they would never be happy with that, and I think they knew it. They just wanted to believe me." He shrugged. "You do anything you can to try and keep the faith alive, even though you know it's unjustified."

"When you're a parent," she noted, "I imagine that seems like the only answer available to you."

He nodded. "Once the police came, it was just chaos."

"So, at no time did you see anybody in the house that entire week, understanding that you've noted that most of the time you weren't there. Did your sister say she was meeting anybody? Was she the type to have a friend online or on the internet? Was she somebody who got involved in online groups or chats?"

He shook his head. "Not that I know of. She was fifteen, really sweet, like I said, and she just wanted to marry a pastor and do good works."

"Did she belong to any religious groups?"

He looked at her and nodded. "Yes, of course she did."

"I'll need to know which ones," she stated.

He shrugged. "My mom can probably tell you better than me."

"Okay." Kate wrote down a note. "Keep going."

"There's nothing else," he stated. "We never found out who did it, outside of them saying I did it because I went and said I did." He shook his head. "I didn't think at the time that, by confessing, by saying it was my fault, which is what my guilt was telling me to do, that they would stop looking for the real killer."

"But, in their heads, they had already found the real killer," she stated, looking at him.

"And I didn't think that far ahead," he explained. "And, all this time, this asshole has been free and living large, and I'm the one who's been locked up."

"Not only that," she added, "now he's come back around to bite you in the ass again."

SIMON NEVER DID go back into the interview room. That was definitely her domain, but, at the same time, it was fascinating to watch Kate work. She was both compassionate and a hard-ass, and the combination was fascinating. It was also difficult to watch in many ways. Simon headed outside, then stopped and took a deep breath. Something was just so very sad and dirty about the kid's tale.

Simon hadn't heard it all; he hadn't sat in the interrogation room or even in the viewing room to the side. It's not like it was his job or his area, and he didn't want Kate to get in trouble for having him there. His curiosity was pretty strong, but he'd seen tales like Rick's time and time again. Kids looking for excitement, something different, the call of drugs, and then a young woman left alone for the predators of the world.

Didn't have to be just women. It just had to be somebody vulnerable, as Simon well knew. He shook his head, knowing how something like that would have torn apart the Lord family and how little there was to recover from it. Changes like that were permanent—the pain, the torment, the guilt, the what-ifs—all permanent. And, although you did the best you could to try to move forward and to recover, it was largely impossible to do so. He hoped Mr. and Mrs. Lord and Rick could get past this, but, with another crime to dredge it all up again, and this kid being the obvious suspect, Simon didn't know how they would survive.

Across the street, a taxi sailed past. He hailed it, and, when it stopped, he raced forward, hopped in, and ordered a ride back to his house. There was something about that muscle car. Simon knew that there would be a big search going on for it. But where did it come from, and why was it after them? Was it just because of the kid? That made the most sense, but, at the same time, it was a stupid move.

Nobody knew anything about this guy driving the muscle car, so what difference would it make? Unless he was trying to kill the kid before he talked, in which case the kid actually knew something. But what the hell did Rick actually know that was that important? Because that was half the problem. The kid didn't seem to know anything about this latest murder. Hell, he didn't seem to know much about his sister's murder, just probably what others had told him.

But the other half of the problem was, when someone still thought you knew something, still were afraid that somebody, like Rick, would turn around and cheat or snitch or lie or do something that would get the driver of the muscle car into trouble, but Rick didn't even seem to know anything about the muscle car or its driver.

Simon had seen that a couple times too. Not everybody

was following everybody else's business. You just thought they were, and it was guilt that pushed you in that direction. And still, where were the answers to this? Where was the answer to any of it? There really wasn't any, in Simon's opinion. It was just another sad case of bad decisions, bad judgment.

If that kid had been home to help out his sister, would he have ended up dead too? That's one of the things that Simon wondered if anybody had ever considered. Maybe it was just dumb luck that Rick wasn't there because there could have been two dead bodies. But, of course, being stronger, Rick might have had a chance, and maybe just his presence would have chased away the killer, and his sister would have survived.

This was one of those endless *what if* scenarios that would never go away. You would be constantly plagued by the worry that you could have done something to change the outcome. Whether there actually was something the kid could have done to stop his sister's murder or not wasn't the issue. Simon sympathized in so many ways and wondered how Kate could do this day in and day out. That she could continue to do it with compassion and strength and humor just blew him away.

But the fact was, it was a hard life as a detective, and it would wear on her, particularly when she had no cushion, no release, no way to diminish some of this pain. He thought about all the things in her world that she had suffered through personally and had just pushed past, instead of finding a way to deal with it in some sense of normality.

She needed holidays; she needed to find some way to seek something else in life that wouldn't kill her like this. And yet he knew it would be almost impossible to talk to her about it because she was so adamant about doing things her way.

In that moment, he realized that he himself was just as bad.

How many times had people told him that he needed to get help before he cracked under the pressure and stress of what he was doing? Sometimes it was good, and sometimes it was just crap. In her case, what she really needed was somebody who cared—and so did he. With that, his ride pulled up in front of his place. Simon paid the cabbie and hopped out.

As he walked into the lobby, Harry, the doorman, looked up and smiled.

"Did you forget to bring dinner again?"

Simon stopped, looked at him, and asked, "What time is it?"

Harry shook his head. "Man, you need a keeper."

"Hell no," Simon snapped. "And, for the first time ever, I'm wondering about taking on that role myself."

Harry looked at him in shock. "Seriously?"

Simon shrugged. "I know somebody who spends so much of her time trying to fix things and to help others that she doesn't look after herself properly," he noted.

"Yeah, sounds like you," Harry pointed out, shaking his head. "Better not take on any more. Looking after yourself appears to be hard enough right now."

Simon just glared at the man, who was grinning at him. "Good thing I like you. Otherwise I might have to punch you out for that one."

"Nah," he argued, "you know I only mean good for you."

"I do. But what the hell do we do when there's a woman

driving herself into the ground with these cases?"

"Ah," Harry noted, "the lovely detective."

Simon nodded. "That she is. But she's also constantly in danger and running on the edge of her sanity all the time."

"And she's probably doing it because that is what she loves," Harry reminded him. "Remember. She probably wouldn't take it kindly if you were to try to take that away from her either."

"No, she wouldn't," he agreed. "Matter of fact, she'd get downright pissed."

Harry laughed. "I'm pretty sure she would."

"So, what do I do?"

"You make her life as easy as you can, so that she can get out and do that job every day," Harry suggested. "Then you make it so you can cover what she can't do herself." At that, the front desk phone rang, and Harry stepped back to answer it.

Simon took Harry's advice with him up to his penthouse, wondering how Harry got to be so wise. Because it was a hell of a good idea. Simon didn't know that she would like it, but, if she didn't know what was happening, she couldn't argue with him. Feeling much better, he headed into his place, and, starting with a shower, he rinsed off the stink of the day, before it took over the rest of his life. He could at least shower off his stink. He wasn't so sure in Kate's case. He thought getting out and facing that stench of humanity day in and day out was probably something that was a struggle for her to wash off every night.

Not his worry right now. But, if he were to take Harry's advice, Simon would have to figure out how he might help Kate with that.

CHAPTER 9

WHEN KATE FINALLY collapsed into her bed late that night, her mind was spinning so much that she was afraid she wouldn't sleep. So much was going on. They hadn't been able to find the muscle car, but they had run the license plate and had a name, though it wouldn't do them much good because it had been stolen early that morning out of a garage. She closed her eyes, willing everything to disappear.

Thursday

BEFORE SHE KNEW it, she was sound asleep and waking up to the sound of birds outside her window. She lay in bed for a long moment, wishing the aches and pains in her body would go away before she moved and had them all jumping up and screaming at her. She needed a couple days of downtime, though she didn't even know what she would do with them. But the thought of staying in bed and doing nothing appealed at the moment.

The cases were always hot and heavy. Though some would go on for months, some would show progress in two days and be solved in three. However, far too many of them were just a terrible twisted mess, like this one. She knew that time was running out for that window of closure, and, once a case lasted for months and months, it became one of those that you worked on the side because new cases were always coming in and taking priority.

She just never caught a break and could put them aside. Always another case and another one came after that, getting in the way. She shook her head and pushed herself into a sitting position, groaning as her body screamed at her. She needed to go for a workout, but several files at her office were calling her; plus she needed to check on her emails to figure out if anybody had found that car.

She groaned and pulled herself upright and, with a final push, stumbled toward the shower. Once in the hot water, she slowly felt her body loosen and her brain start to wake up. Coffee, that was next. Wrapped in a towel, she headed to the kitchen and put on a pot of joe, hoping to get a couple cups down before her phone erupted. She got dressed, then came back out, snagged her first cup of coffee.

She headed for the couch to enjoy the hot brew. She laid the cup down gently and then basically curled up in the corner and closed her eyes. She didn't want to check her phone. She didn't want to check the news; she just wanted a moment to recuperate. When her phone buzzed with a text, she just knew it was Simon. She snagged her phone and looked to see a heart, followed by a couple more messages.

Hi.

Good morning.

She smiled and replied. **Good morning. Any more nightmares?**

When there was no response right away, she felt bad, yet, at the same time, not bad enough. Then a message came in.

Yeah. A bad one last night.

She hit Talk, and, when he answered the phone, she asked, "The same one?"

"Yeah," he noted. "Except the scream is silent now."

"Wasn't it before?"

"Yes, but it's different."

She frowned at that, wondering how could it be different. "If you say so," she muttered. And then yawned.

"Are you just up?"

"I'm tired, worn out, and need a rest."

"And I'm sure you'll get it," he noted.

"Not until I finish this damn case," she muttered.

"And how close is it? Was interviewing the kid of any value?"

"Well, I hope so, but we still have things to sort out."

"Good enough," he replied. "I'm heading out in a few minutes."

"Off to buy the world?"

He laughed. "Nope, only a couple more buildings." Then he disconnected their call.

She smiled as she sipped away at her coffee. She needed to check the traffic cams to see if that muscle car showed up anywhere and to figure out why it had located her and was following them. She was hoping that maybe they could pin it on the garage where Rick worked, if somebody had followed him home or something. There was a slight chance that whoever was in that muscle car wasn't after Rick but was after her or even Simon. She had to admit something about Simon probably pissed people off fairly often, but then money and power had a way of doing that. Simon was very understated, but the wealth and the in-charge attitude were definitely there.

The fact that she saw a more vulnerable side of him

made him more human to her, but she knew he hated it. Of course he did. From his perspective, it made him seem weaker. To her, the opposite was true, and it just made him seem stronger. Because anybody who could survive all the shit that he went through on a regular basis was nothing short of a superhero.

Finally she grabbed her holster, shoved the gun into it, grabbed her jacket, and headed out.

She hadn't had quite enough coffee for her day but would grab some as soon as she got in to the station. She'd driven the kid home last night. His mom had opened the door with tears in her eyes, so happy to see him. Kate had promised to get him home, and he had been a help. It's just that it wasn't enough for her to do anything with yet.

They still needed to ask a ton more questions, and the problem with asking questions was not everybody wanted to give you the right answers. As a matter of fact, if they could get away with giving you something that would appease you and get you out of their hair, it was good enough for them. As she walked into her office, the sergeant called out to her. She detoured and headed his way.

He took one look and said, "Sounds like you need coffee first."

"Sounds like or looks like?" she muttered.

He grinned. "Maybe both."

She nodded. "Yeah, probably both."

"Go get coffee and then come on back in."

She nodded, walked into the station area, grabbed a coffee, and headed back toward Colby's office. She plunked onto a chair and asked, "What's up?"

"Does something have to be up?"

She shrugged. "Well, I haven't done anything wrong

that I know of, so I'm not sure why I'm here."

"I just wanted an update," he replied, "and to make sure we don't have anybody doing any maverick moves."

"No time for maverick moves," she muttered. "Too busy chasing bad guys."

He smiled. "I've noticed and appreciate it."

She rotated her neck slowly. "Thanks, but just so many of them are out there."

He gave her a sharp look. "Is it getting you down?"

"Nah, it's just frustrating. We put two away, and four more come out of the woodwork."

He nodded. "I get it. Believe me. I do. It's just a matter of plugging away, while making sure that you find balance in your life."

"Balance? What's that?" she quipped.

He looked up at her. "You've also hit some pretty hard and ugly cases recently. Do you need to talk to somebody about it?"

She looked at him in horror. "Hell no."

He laughed. "I'm not kidding."

"I know. That's why I'm so shocked," she explained. "Because really it's a hell no. I don't need to talk to any-body."

He frowned and looked as if he would argue the point but then shrugged. "Just make sure I don't see any signs of it getting to you."

"If it doesn't get to me," she replied gently, "I'm in the wrong business." And, with that, she got up and started out the door.

"That's a good one-liner," he noted, "but I mean it. You need to have a life outside of this work."

She looked at him. "I have a life."

"So maybe you need to make that more important in your world," he suggested. "I can't have you wearing down."

"I won't wear down," she argued. "I do need to take more breaks, and I need to get out a bit more. I was thinking about that last night. But it's also the nature of the job—the hours we keep, the work we do, and the cases we deal with. The victims, their families, the people who have been incarcerated, and the ones who were incarcerated who didn't need to be."

"You're talking about Rick Lord?"

She nodded. "I don't think he did the murder that he did the time for."

"It wouldn't be the first time an innocent man was convicted," Colby added, "but I sure hope you're wrong."

"I do too. The problem is, if he didn't do it, who did? Because I don't even have a lead on that yet."

"If you believe it," he noted, "then this one should be enough to help you break the other case apart."

"Should be, yes, and being shot at yesterday definitely adds to its intrigue."

"I heard about that," he stated. "I'm glad nobody was hurt. What the hell was Simon doing in the car with you?"

"He'd been out with me," she replied, waving a dismissive hand. "We were getting the oil in my car changed. And I recognized the kid at the service station. He was the one handling the oil."

"And you just happened to be there, right?"

She gave him a flat look. "Of course. I'd never involve a civilian in a case like that."

He groaned. "I'm not a fool, you know?"

"I know you're not, sir," she said in a bright tone. And, with that, she walked out of his office. She could feel his eyes boring into her back as she left. He was a good man and cared about his people, and that mattered. There was always a need for somebody to be at the helm, somebody to steer the ship in the right direction and to bring some order to the chaos because, God knows, it had to be like herding cats. They were all off, immersed in their own projects, their own methodologies, their own ways of solving all these problems. And it didn't help that each of them was a bit of a maverick, but it came with the territory. It should be part of the job description really.

She headed back to her desk, and she saw Rodney there already.

He looked up, grinned, and said, "You look like shit."

She rolled her eyes. "One of these days you'll say I look like a million bucks."

"Oh, I don't know about that," he teased, chuckling. "There'll have to be a hell of an improvement before that happens."

She snagged a pen on the desk and threw it at him.

He laughed. "So, with all that excitement yesterday, did you end up with anything that makes you think we've got some answers here?"

"Nope," she replied. "Just one million more questions that we have to find the answers for. To start with, who the hell knew that the parents would be away and that the kid would be off on the streets with his little thug friends?"

Rodney thought for a moment. "Well, anybody who watched the house, I guess. Or somebody who worked with the dad, who might have known they were taking off for the holiday. Any of the neighbors might have known. The parents probably warned them about it and asked them to keep an eye on the place or something."

"You know what? That's a good thought." She sat here, thinking about it. "It takes a pretty shitty person to go after your neighbor's daughter though."

"Honestly it just takes somebody who doesn't give a shit," Rodney replied. "Not necessarily a shitty person. They just do what they want to do, and they don't care. This was probably an opportunity they couldn't let slide."

She nodded. "So I still want to do a walkthrough of that crime scene in the original house though. We didn't get that done yet." She frowned and reached for her phone, but it rang beneath her fingers. When she answered, it was the woman from the building development corporation.

The receptionist said, "I spoke to the boss, and he's given permission for you to go into the house."

She flashed a smile over at Rodney. "Good, we'll be there in the next twenty minutes."

"How long do you think you need?" the woman asked hesitantly.

"I don't know," Kate replied. "I'll let you know after I've been there." She hung up, bolted to her feet with more energy than she'd had all morning, and told Rodney, "We got the go-ahead to get into the house."

He looked at her in surprise, slowly getting to his feet. "Seriously?"

She nodded. "Yeah, maybe this will be the break we're looking for."

As they walked out, he looked over at her. "Are you and Simon doing okay?"

She nodded, with a shrug. "Sure, why not?"

He frowned. "That's hardly a good answer."

"It's the only one you're getting."

"It's just hard on relationships—this business, I mean."

"Is everybody out to warn me to get some balance in my life today?" she snapped.

He looked at her in surprise.

She shook her head. "The sergeant was just on my case about it."

"Which also means that he's seen it too."

"Seen what?" she asked, glaring at him.

"That."

She slowly sighed. "Look. I'm fine. Simon and I are fine. But this case? It's getting to me."

"There'll always be a case," he reminded her.

"I know," she acknowledged.

"But if you have plans to spend a good amount of time in this profession, then you have to pace yourself."

"I know. I know." She slowly rotated her head, as they headed out to the parking lot. "I'm just tired today. Listening to Rick talk last night, it—" Her voice broke off.

"Yeah, it's tough, but don't be so sympathetic that he fools you."

"No," she noted. "I don't think that's the case here, but we do need to figure out what happened. What pisses me off is that, by confessing, he completely derailed the original investigation. Nobody looked anywhere else because they already had the right guy. Now we look around, and we see that maybe we don't have the right guy, and we have literally nothing to go on because so many years have passed."

"But it's not all lost," Rodney stated. "We're still waiting on forensic evidence on this latest case."

"Great," she muttered. "They didn't find anything last time, so let's hope they find something this time. But you know what? I wouldn't put it past them to actually have evidence there that puts this kid in the right place."

He looked over at her. "But what would his motivation be now, some fifteen years later?"

"I did talk to him about that," Kate noted. "He wasn't supposed to be released until this last week. So, in theory, if somebody was just doing the math, they would assume that he was just now out. But anybody who watches the news or TV would know that a lot of these guys get out early. But again, maybe our murderer didn't know about Rick's early release. Maybe the killer didn't look. Maybe he doesn't care. Maybe that was the timeline that he gave himself permission for, and, when the time was up, he went out and took another life because he wanted to."

"Imagine"—Rodney shook his head—"just doing something like that because you felt like it."

"There has to be a motivation for it, and that's what I don't get."

"Well, it seems to be tied up with the kid somehow," Rodney suggested.

"We'll find out soon enough. But, if the evidence comes in, pointing to him, it won't be a slam dunk in my mind that he's the culprit."

"Yet you'll find a lot of other people thinking that it *is* a slam dunk."

She nodded. "Oh, I know. It'll just add to the pressure."

"Of course," he agreed, "but that's what we do, isn't it?"

She smiled and asked, "You driving?"

"Hell yes, I'm driving," he replied. "Last time you drove, you got shot at."

SIMON WALKED THROUGH the building, studying the repairs that had been done. No flooring was down yet, but drywall had started in multiple rooms. At least they had some sheets up, though nobody had started taping yet, but it would get done before long. He'd had several truckloads of drywall delivered; the forklifts were moving materials up and down the various floors, and the crane was out there putting stuff on the different balconies to move into each of the rooms. Everything scheduled to make it fast and efficient.

But, at the same time, the building had almost a lonely feeling to it. He stepped out on one of the balconies and looked down. It was a beautiful area that had a view of the harbor, and that was worth a lot. In this city it was worth so much more than you would expect, since everybody was after that golden slice of view. He could make a ton of money off this place. Well, at least he could, if things would ever stop going wrong.

At the moment every change order was killing him with upcharges, and there had been too many to count. He headed down to the next floor and walked around, checking on the work being done. His foreman would be here any moment, but, in the meantime, Simon wanted to see for himself. It seemed like the minute he gave over control to somebody else, shit went wrong. He had learned that the hard way and had no intention of ever doing it again.

He stepped into one room and looked around, and the scream caught him in the back of the neck, almost sending him flying forward. It was such a strong sharp noise in his head that it was almost visceral, sending him tumbling into the wall. He couldn't even cry out in that moment, his body bent over, warding off a blow coming at him from an unexpected source.

And yet, as he rolled and twisted, his martial arts training kicked in, trying to save him from this hidden threat, even though he saw nothing here. But his brain was slow to compute it and didn't want to acknowledge there was no physical threat because it absolutely knew something was wrong. He lay on the ground, the bare plywood under his back, as he stared up at the ceiling, where wiring was hanging at all angles, waiting for the electricians, who were still working their way around through the building.

He took one slow deep breath.

"I don't know where the hell you are," he said out loud, "but you sure as hell need to be found before this kills me."

The words hit him wrong immediately because it wasn't *his* life hanging in the balance; it was hers. He closed his eyes and whispered quietly, "I'm so sorry. Please forgive me."

He listened for any sound that would tell him something, but there was always just this scream and nothing else. He thought he heard a noise in the background, something that would jolt him. And then he swore.

He heard a hammer. He sat up slowly, intent on the noise that he could hear, yet the hammer sound seemed to be distant too. He frowned at that, wondering where it could be coming from. It could be at any construction site, and then there were voices.

The woman appeared to be in some zombie zone, probably knocked out from the pain. Another voice in the background spoke, but Simon couldn't hear. It was as if she was just, well, ... like she was not just unconscious but unconscious from the pain. "Tell me something," he whispered, "anything. I just want to help."

He heard a shout from down below. Groaning, he pulled himself up to his feet and brushed himself off, just as his foreman stepped around the corner, looking at him quizzically.

"I didn't know you were here."

"Just came to check out some of the work," he noted. "Then I got struck with a really ugly headache."

"Man, you and those headaches lately."

"I know, right? They're such a bitch." He shook his head gently and tried to refocus.

His foreman turned and noted, "Listen. I'm supposed to be meeting a couple guys and dealing with a few things. If it's all right, can we meet up in what ten minutes or so, maybe fifteen?"

"Make it fifteen," Simon replied. "I'll do a walk around."

When the foreman disappeared, Simon took another deep, slow breath. "Come on. Talk to me," he whispered. "I'm almost out of time here. I'll be surrounded by people, and then I can't talk at all."

Even as he said it, he winced, since it wasn't like she had control of this time frame so he could work with it better. She had whatever moments of living she could actually survive. But he could do absolutely nothing to push that timetable. He took another deep breath and nudged her. "Come on. Talk to me."

But, when she opened her mouth, it was a scream, a wrenching scream, and, through her eyes, he saw flashes of whatever reality was going on around her, as something snapped at her ankle. And then she blacked out.

He opened his eyes, then quickly sent Kate a message.

He is torturing her again. Her ankle was just broken for fun.

CHAPTER 10

B EFORE THEY GOT out to the parking lot, Kate's phone beeped. She stared at Simon's text and frowned, turning back around. "Damn it. The original crime scene will have to wait." She called the woman back to postpone her visit and to make sure Kate was notified before any demolition began.

This latest vision of Simon's was just a little too close to the case she was working on. Both victims—the death of Cherry and the kid's sister from the old case—had their ankles broken, seemingly just for fun. What were the chances of a third victim, one that Simon had connected with? It was all too much coincidence for comfort, and it made her blood run cold.

How was she supposed to find the killer if he was already off torturing another poor woman? And what would happen if they managed to pick up the guy but couldn't find her? She would die without care. She likely would die before they got to her anyway. Kate groaned out loud, reaching up to grab the hair at her temples and giving it a hard pull, yet already returning to her desk.

Rodney instinctively followed her. "Hey, hey, hey," Rodney said. "What the hell is that for?"

She showed him the text on her phone, not slowing down her stride.

He stared at it, then looked at her. "Jesus. Is that Simon again?"

She nodded. "Yes."

"He's connected with a victim?"

"I don't fucking know," she replied, raising both hands. They had reached the bullpen again. "That's what it sounds like though, doesn't it?"

He glanced back down at that text. "Oh my God." Rodney rubbed at the back of his neck.

"Yeah," she agreed. "Now you're getting the issue."

"Do we have a third victim?"

"If we do, I don't know about it," she snapped. "What could possibly connect these two except our bloody suspect? The kid is now at home with his parents. And where the hell would they choose to pick up another victim—and why? Especially if Rick Lord *won't* be a suspect?"

"But he will be," Rodney noted. "And the killer is probably thinking that we'll just run around like idiots, and he'll get away with it again."

"I don't think he even cares anymore," she stated, staring at Rodney, now seated at her desk again. "I think this is a good run, and he's having way too much fun to stop. I don't think he can stop now."

"But we don't have his victim."

"Missing persons' reports," she said, galvanized into action. "What do we have for missing people from the last … what?" She thought about it and then suggested, "Four days?"

"Let's go seven," he said, pulling up stats on his monitor. "Just to make sure."

"Narrow that down to females." And, with that typed in, she rolled her chair closer to him to tell him, "And let's choose an age range to narrow it down."

He looked over at her, his eyebrows up. "The two women he had were both young and very beautiful." He frowned. "What? Maybe fifteen to thirty-six?"

She nodded slowly. "Go as high as forty, just to be sure."

He typed that in and said, "You know that we're probably looking at fifteen to twenty-eight."

"Yeah, but let's take a look at who is missing."

He pushed the Search button, and, within a few seconds, the results flashed on the screen with twelve names.

She whistled. "Jesus, twelve women in the last seven days."

He nodded. "But remember? Just because they've been reported doesn't mean that they're actually missing. As adults, they have every right to wander on their own."

"I know," she stated, "but Christ." She looked at the list and was struck almost immediately by the looks of the third photo on the left. "Look at that one."

"Why her?"

"Because she resembles the other two victims."

He looked at the photo sharply and quickly brought up another screen, where he opened up the pictures of the two victims they already had, and he nodded. "That's her," he agreed. "Obviously our killer has a type. Now that he's three for three."

"Yes, I agree."

And, with that, Rodney printed off the photos, and she arranged them on the whiteboard, so they were beside each other, then shook her head. "We need to find out who this person is, when and how she went missing, and what the hell is going on."

Rodney added, "Based on Simon's message, it looks like

we've got an urgent scenario happening here."

Just then, the sergeant walked in. "What's all this?" he asked, motioning at the photos. She hesitated, and then he raised an eyebrow. "Detective Morgan, you're not trying to keep something from me, are you?"

"No, sir," she replied. "I'm not. I'm just not certain that I want to share it with you yet."

He just glared at her, setting his hands on his hips.

"Look. Just ten minutes ago I got this text message, and that brought us to this point," she explained, as she held up her phone, tapping it, so that Simon's text would come up.

"What's this?" he asked, looking at her.

"A text from Simon. He's been connecting with a female who has been screaming in his head. He hasn't been able to find any place or location or distinctive landmarks to locate her. Nothing that would tell us where she is or who she is, so it wasn't anything I could work with," she stated. "And, besides, it's not like I have time on my hands and am just sitting here twiddling my thumbs."

"No, of course not," Colby agreed. "Then Simon sent you this message. What is so important about it?"

"It's the ankle reference. Both of our prior victims had their ankles broken."

He looked at the board. "You have three women up there. Are you saying you already know who this third woman is?"

"We did a quick search of missing persons in the last seven days." She motioned over at Rodney. "We chose females between fifteen and forty, and almost immediately, out of the twelve women, I saw this one."

"But you can't rule out the others."

"No, but look at the three victims. See if she is the right

one," she noted.

Colby frowned at Kate, then studied the photos and nodded slowly. "He's got a type."

"Yes. At least if this is his third victim, he does. Of course we can't exclude the other possibilities, and we'll do our due diligence to make sure, but, if we had to guess, she's the one who fits."

"Do we have any information on her?"

Rodney hopped to his feet, a sheet in his hand that he'd just pulled off the printer. "She never showed up for work, but she'd had a fight with her boyfriend the previous night. She went to her girlfriend's, where she slept overnight. They were both headed to work for the day, but the friend said that our missing girl had been really upset and was talking about just taking off for a while. So we don't know if she took off on her own or if she got picked up by somebody else," Rodney explained.

The sergeant shook his head. "But the bottom line is, how does any of this connect to the other cases? How does this guy know who this woman is or that she'd be perfect for his cause? And did he know ahead of time that she was distraught?"

"Well, the only way we'll find that out," Kate noted, "is to find him. Or her."

Colby turned to Kate and asked her, "So what the hell are you doing sitting on your backside?" She just glared at him. Laughing, he said, "Get to it. But this is good. This is movement."

"We could be barking up the wrong tree completely," she added, as if warning him.

"That's true, so it's your job to make sure you're not." And, with that, he turned and walked out.

She groaned and turned to face Rodney, but he was grinning at her. "It's not funny," she muttered. "We could be wasting a ton of time on this, all because of Simon's text."

"This is what opened up as a lead," he reminded her. "We move on it because that's what's there in front of us."

"In front of us, yes, but, if we kept looking in other directions, more shit could show up there too."

"Well, we'll make phone calls and handle every one of these other people on this list."

At that, Owen hopped up to join them. "Give me a bunch of them. I'll run them down. At least I can get the stories as clear as I can, but I'm with you. I really do think this guy has a type."

"Two isn't a type," she warned.

"No, but this one is the same age category, same demographic, also young and vulnerable. Easy to pick up, easy to grab."

"And that's the sad part," Kate noted. "If that's all it takes to entice this guy, that means most of Vancouver is his type. Something is majorly screwed up if that's the case."

Rodney nodded, then he looked over at the girls' photos and said, "I got a feeling about this."

She stared at the board, her heart sinking, and added quietly, "Yeah, so do I."

"We need to talk to the girlfriend, her parents, her bosses, coworkers, anything we have," Rodney stated. "But most of all, we need to talk to the boyfriend."

"It won't be him, you know," Kate stated.

"Maybe not," Rodney acknowledged, "but this serial killer likes to leave possible suspects in nice neat little packages, so I wouldn't be at all surprised if that's how this will look, once it starts playing out, while setting up the parolee."

"But you don't think it's him, do you?" Owen asked Kate.

"Not necessarily, but I won't make that judgment now," she said. "Yet I won't be at all surprised if things start lining up against Rick." She grabbed her wallet and keys and looked over at Rodney. "You staying here to run this down, or are you coming with me?"

"Oh, I'm coming with you," he replied. "Life has been much more exciting around here since you showed up on the job."

She rolled her eyes and snapped, "Feel free to take over the excitement part anytime."

"Nope," he said, "this is good."

"You're driving, right?"

"Why is that?" he asked.

"No car."

"Ah, not a problem."

And they carried on their customary banter down to the parking lot and out to his vehicle. As they hopped in, he asked, "You got an address for me?"

"Yeah, the girlfriend first."

"Is she home?"

"We'll find out." Kate was already busy dialing. When a woman's voice answered, Kate explained who she was.

"Oh my God," the young woman replied. "Did you find Chelice?"

"Not yet," Kate answered, "but that's why we need to talk to you."

"I have no idea where she is," she wailed. "She was so upset, and she and her boyfriend were having a hell of a time. And I know she just wanted to take off, but I just don't think she would have."

"Would anybody know where she would have gone, if she had been of a mind to take off?"

"No, see that was the thing. She didn't really know anybody. She wasn't from around here, and she didn't have any family nearby."

"What about heading back East?"

"I don't think so."

Kate wrote down a note to check the airports and the bus stations, looking for any connection with Chelice, just in case. "And you've had no contact with her since?"

"No, and that's the other reason."

"What do you mean?"

"She wouldn't have taken off like that. She would at least have called me. She would have let me know."

"Unless she thought that maybe you would tell the boyfriend."

"But she knows I wouldn't," she said desperately. "I know him. He's an asshole. But no way I'll let her get hurt again."

"Did he beat her up?"

"Yes, but she wouldn't go to the hospital. She was sore, but, when we both left, she told me that she was heading to work. I was hoping somebody there would convince her to get medical attention. She wasn't in that great of shape."

"How bad?" Kate asked, with a snap to her voice. "Are we talking a black eye or a puffy face that would easily be recognizable?"

"No, he didn't hit her in a way that would readily be seen. Her wrist was quite swollen and red. I wouldn't be at all surprised if there wasn't a broken bone or two in her ribs, from the way she was moving. He had kicked her. He used cigarettes and burned her, but she was wearing a long-sleeve shirt, so it covered most of it. That asshole needs to be picked up."

"We're on our way to talk to him, but I needed to talk to you first. Do you have any of her belongings there?"

"Yes, she left all of it," she replied. "That's another thing."

"When you say everything, what do you mean?"

"Well, when she showed up here, she didn't have much with her," she explained. "She had her cell phone and her wallet, but that was all."

"And do you have those?"

"I have her cell phone, not her wallet."

"Meaning that she headed out to work and left her phone behind?"

"That's what I thought happened," she stated. "I mean, she was certainly not all that clear-headed about anything. She'd hardly had any sleep. I begged her to call in sick and to take the day off from work, but she seemed to think that she'd be better off if she went to work and kept her mind busy."

"And the boyfriend knows where she works, I suppose?"

"Of course. He used to drop her off too. She didn't even have a car."

"Right," Kate noted. "And are you working?"

"Yes, but from home. When she went missing, I got approval to work from home, just in case she turns up here, you know?" With that, she burst into tears. "Please find her," she said. "She's had such a rough time of it."

"How long was she with this guy?"

"Only about six months." She paused. "I didn't like him right off the bat. He has that arrogance so common in abusive power-hungry guys, so you know that women are meant to service him, and that's all they're good for."

"Sounds like a lovely man," Kate replied in a dry tone.

"*Not*, and it's so sad because Chelice is beautiful, inside and out."

"And is her blond hair natural?"

"Yes, and so are the curls."

"Interesting," she muttered. "Okay, and she was working at this office," and she read off the name on the form.

"Yes, that's where she was working and where she was supposed to be going that morning."

"And she just didn't show up?"

"No, as far as I know, she didn't show up, and she didn't call anybody," she explained. "And calling her phone doesn't make any damn bit of difference because it's sitting right here. I've never felt so helpless in my life."

"I know," Kate noted. "We're doing what we can."

"The cops already called me about it."

"Right," she replied, "but I've just become aware of the case because I work in a different area. But it is possible there may be a link to something that's going on in my world."

"I hope so," she said, "unless you're a homicide detective, and then I hope sure as hell there isn't a connection."

"Well, I am," Kate admitted, "but we don't have a body."

"Oh my God," she whispered. "Oh my God, oh my God. You think she's dead?"

"No, actually I don't at the moment," she answered, with sincerity in her voice. Because, of all the things that she might not believe about Simon and his abilities, if he said this victim was alive, Kate would go with that. "But, if she is being held somewhere, I want to make sure that we find her, before she ends up that way."

"Jesus, I can't even imagine. If there's anything I can do, just tell me."

"Well, I need her phone for one. We'll come right now and pick it up, so that we can run down her contacts. Do you know anybody who would hurt her?"

"Yes," she snapped, "that fucking asshole, her ex."

"What about anybody else? Was anybody jealous when she hooked up with him? Was anybody out there pissed off that she was with him, or was there another relationship before him?"

"I don't know," she replied. "Chelice was single for a long time. And I never did figure out what the attraction was to this guy. But, when they first got together, Chelice was over the moon and thought he was some Prince Charming type."

"Yeah, they put on that act very well at the beginning," Kate noted. "And it wears off pretty quickly."

"Not fast enough," she muttered. "She got suckered in really badly."

"Well, we'll keep that in mind as we keep working this case," she replied. "It looks like we should be at your front door in about ten minutes."

"Fine. I'll wait outside."

"If you have any other personal belongings of hers, can you bundle that together and have it ready as well, please?"

"Sure, I'll take a look, but like I said, she didn't come with much. I actually gave her one of my shirts because her blouse was ripped and bloody."

"Good enough." Kate hung up, and, as they approached the apartment a few minutes later, they saw a woman pacing outside, walking back and forth, looking nervously around.

They pulled up to the sidewalk, and Kate hopped out and introduced herself. "I'm Detective Kate Morgan."

The woman rushed over, grabbed her hand, and said, "Thank God, I'm even freaked just being out here."

"You got her phone?"

She handed it over. "Here. Now I'm going back inside, just in case that asshole knows what I did."

"And just what is it that you think you did?"

She stared at her in surprise. "I told you about him."

Kate nodded quietly. "Very true. Now go on and take care of yourself. Keep the doors locked, just in case this asshole does come around to start doing damage control over his temper fit."

"Oh my gosh." As she raced to the front door, she called back, "Please let me know what happens."

Kate nodded. She didn't dare tell her that she wouldn't share unless she had something to say—and, of course, *something to say* was likely to mean bad news. She could only hope that Chelice's body still had life in it when she found it. Kate turned, walked back to the car, then hopped into the front passenger seat, and started fussing with Chelice's phone.

"Now where?" Rodney asked.

"I'd planned to go by her work next, but now I want to meet Prince Charming first."

"Do we know where he works?" Rodney asked.

"According to the police report that the girlfriend put in, he's a mechanic." She stopped, thought about that, and whispered, "And there's another car connection."

He looked at her. "But a mechanic is a long way from somebody who works in those drive-through oil change places."

"But it's still a connection. With the muscle car thrown in, car clubs, maybe? I don't know," she admitted. "My mind is drawing a blank. But car dealership, car salesman, car hobbyist. I mean, who knows at this point?"

"Well, it's something," Rodney admitted. "Let's get to the garage and see if he's there."

It took another fifteen minutes to cross town and to pull up to the address.

"Well, he's making good money if he's working here," she noted, as she studied the Volkswagen dealership.

"Sure, but that doesn't preclude him from being an asshole."

"No," she agreed, "it doesn't seem like anything does that." As she walked around and found the service department, the service manager smiled, then frowned when she explained who she was and who she was looking for.

"That's interesting. He didn't show up for work today."

She stared at him. "Has he done that before?"

He shrugged. "Not that I remember. I mean, I guess it can happen to anybody. So I haven't seen him today, but he did call in sick, I understand."

"Do you have an address for him?"

He nodded and pulled it up from his file. "Is he in any trouble?"

"It depends, although we were told that he beat up his girlfriend pretty good."

He winced at that. "He does have a temper," he muttered. "I've warned him about it a couple times."

"Has he ever had an altercation here at work?"

The manager shook his head. "No, we won't tolerate something like that here, but he does have a tendency to lash out at people anytime he's thwarted, to be honest."

"Well, apparently he got thwarted, and he beat her up. Unfortunately she's missing right now, so we're trying to find her."

The manager looked at Kate in surprise. "Chelice?"

"Obviously you've met her."

"Yes, and I, for one, was under the impression they were deliriously happy."

"Well, they were, until they weren't, I guess," she said in a dry tone.

He nodded. "And that is what Henry is like. He's a really nice guy, and then, all of a sudden, he's not."

"As in scary?"

The manager thought a moment, then nodded slowly. "Yes, I guess so, though I hadn't thought about him in that way. I'm a guy though and quite prepared to push back if he's an asshole here, but—for a younger, more vulnerable female—I suspect he could be very scary."

"Did he have any criminal history or anything that gave you reservations when you hired him?"

"He has been working here for a long time, maybe ten years. We've never had any trouble with him, except for his temper."

"Any rumors about previous relationships?"

He nodded slowly. "He has been through a few over the years. It seems like they get to a certain stage, and then something happens, and he gets upset and ugly about it, and they break up soon afterward."

"Well, apparently something of that nature was happening. He beat up Chelice, and she took off, but now we can't find her."

"Are you thinking he did something?"

"I have no idea, but we need to speak to him." On a

hunch, she asked, "Do you happen to know a Rick Lord?"

He frowned, his fingers strumming on the countertop. "I don't think so," he replied. "Why?"

"Just wondering, and what about—" She pulled up the photos of the other two women. "Do you happen to know either of these women?"

He looked at them, shrugged, and shook his head. "Honestly, no, they don't look familiar at all."

She nodded her thanks, then turned and headed back out. She walked toward Rodney's car, armed with the address and phone number of her next target. Rodney joined her momentarily. She looked over at him, with an eyebrow raised. "Where did you disappear to?"

"I went to talk to his coworkers."

"And?" she asked, as she got in.

"Basically he's an arrogant asshole. Not well liked, but he shows up and does the job, so nobody is willing to get rid of him."

"Just an attitude problem?"

"Especially where women are concerned. If a woman comes in, he makes all kinds of sexist comments the whole time they are there, but just under his breath, so they can't quite hear. As soon as they leave, he's got nothing but lewd and crude remarks to say about them."

"*Nice*," Kate noted, shaking her head. "If that were me, I certainly would not be happy to know that people were talking about me after I left."

"Exactly," Rodney agreed. "It's a sad case all the way around."

"I've got his address, so let's go talk to him."

"Presuming he's home."

"Well, he's supposed to be sick," Kate stated, "but who

knows where he is. If he is our killer, then he could possibly be with his victim."

"Which is our girl Chelice."

"Yes," she agreed, "but it seems like that would be a little too obvious."

"And that's what we were wondering at the beginning though, right? In order to make this stick on Rick Lord, it has to look like it's somebody else. But it can't look too much like it's somebody else because it needs to look like the other cases too. This guy is continuing to use ammo that he used on previous cases. The fact that it is recognizable means that it needs to be the same killer. Otherwise it's none of these. He's just doing what he can to throw us off course. And doing a good job of it, at the moment."

"Not really," she said in a dry tone. "He's just an asshole, who's wasting my time and pissing me off."

He laughed. "I get that. But the bottom line is, we still can't get our job done because this guy is throwing smoke and mirrors."

"That's a good phrase for it," she muttered.

"And the question is, how long has he been doing this? Did you ever do a run for other victims like this?"

"I did," she replied, "but I didn't get specific enough. I knew it at the time, but I got distracted and didn't get a chance to run it yet."

"Call Owen and have him do it."

She picked up the phone and quickly told Owen what they needed.

Owen replied, "I'm on it. And Lilliana is here as well. She'll give me a hand to see if we can track down the status of the other missing persons cases."

Kate explained what they'd found out so far.

"You think it's him, this asshole Henry?" Owen asked.

"No, not unless we can pin the other two on him as well," she explained. "It makes no sense that we'd have three killers doing exactly the same thing."

"Unless they're doing that on purpose too."

She thought about that long after she hung up. "You know what? There is that long shot that somehow there are three killers, three people who know each other, and they're following the exact same MO in order to confuse the issue on these murders because, if it casts a shadow of a doubt, you know perfectly well we won't get a conviction."

"That's very true." Rodney turned another corner and pulled the vehicle up in front of an apartment building.

They got out and walked up to the front door. It was locked, but somebody was coming out, so they quickly slipped inside as the woman left.

"I always worry about that kind of security," Kate noted. "I mean, just look how easy it was to get into this place."

"Well, it's not supposed to be *that* easy," Rodney argued, looking at her.

"And yet it is. I mean, just look at that. We got in without even trying."

He nodded and didn't say anything else. When they reached the right apartment, they knocked on the door and heard a mumble on the other side. She raised an eyebrow and knocked again.

Finally the door jerked open, and a guy roared in her face, "What the fuck do you want?"

She pulled out her shield and shoved it right in front of his eyeballs. He backed up and shook his head, like a bull seeing red. "Whoa, buddy, slow down," Kate stated firmly.

"What the fuck do you want?" he repeated.

He's drunk. "Well, I can see why you're home *sick* from work. I guess that breakup with the girlfriend was hard on you, *huh?*"

He glared at her. "She's a fucking bitch," he snapped. "I don't need any of this shit."

"What shit is that?" she asked, with interest.

"Her parents keep calling me, asking me where she is. I don't know where the hell she is. She took off."

"Well, we know she took off. We also know why," Kate stated, with a meaningful look at him.

He continued to glare at her. "You don't know anything," he muttered. He stumbled backward, hitting the couch at the back of his knees and falling down.

She watched him in surprise, but then he reached for a bottle and took a long sip. "Is this how you handle the trouble in your life?"

"What do you care?" he snapped.

"I don't really care, but you know what? Just like the parents, we're looking for your girlfriend. Well, ex-girlfriend, I assume."

"Yeah, damn right, she's an ex-girlfriend piece of shit."

"Is that how you treat all your women?"

"No. If I had my druthers, I'd beat them to a pulp," he snapped, "and make sure they weren't around to piss me off anymore."

"Is that what you did to this one?" Kate asked curiously. "Because, when you think about it, we've got a missing woman here, and you are making death threats."

Somehow along the line, a note of caution seemed to enter his gaze. "I didn't kill her," he said, "and saying I would like to isn't the same thing."

"No, it isn't, but it sure does give us something to think

about."

"You're just cops," he replied. "You're not paid to think."

She stared at him in surprise. "And yet all you're doing is insulting us. *Smart.*"

He just glared and took another swig from his bottle.

"You should have left it in the paper bag," she noted, "then it looks more authentic."

He looked at her in confusion, then at his bottle and back at her.

She walked over to the window, looked out, and asked, "When did you last see Chelice?"

"You probably already fucking know, if she went to you whining and crying about me beating her up."

"Is that what she told you that she would do?"

He just shrugged and didn't say anything.

"I still need to know when you saw her last," she repeated.

"I don't know. I just went to bed," he said. "I was pissed off and fed up, so I went to bed."

"What, so when you woke up, she was gone?"

He nodded. "So don't ask me what time that was because I didn't go to work that day. It was Sunday morning," he added, "and I was sleeping off a drunk."

"Ah, so that's it. You got mad drunk, beat up your girlfriend, and she takes off while you're sleeping. Then you wake up to find your world has changed, and you're not happy about it. I'm so sorry," she said, with mock sympathy.

He glared at her, shaking his head. "It wasn't like that."

"Glad to hear it," she murmured. "So what was it like?"

He shook his head again. "You wouldn't understand."

"Try me." She walked over, gingerly picking a pathway

through the mess on the floor. "Do you live like this all the time, or only when there is trouble in paradise?" She motioned at the mess around her. "There's like two-day-old food here."

"Yeah, Chelice never cleans up," he snapped.

"But she hasn't been here," she corrected him.

He replied, with a mocking tone, "Yeah, back to that again."

Kate nudged him. "When did you last see her?"

"Saturday night," he snapped. "That's when we were fighting."

"Oh, and that's when you beat her up."

He glared at her but didn't say a word.

She nodded. "And did you try to call her?"

He just shrugged.

"You need to tell me," she stated.

"I don't need to tell you jack shit."

"We can take you downtown to the drunk tank and let you sober up there for a while, until you're ready to talk to us," she stated. "I'm good with that too, and the city is always happy to have guests in the jail."

His frown deepened. "I didn't do nothing wrong, so you got no reason to take me anywhere."

"Well, you beat up your girlfriend pretty badly," she reminded him, "so that's one thing we would love to have a serious talk with you about. But, more than that, she's missing, and we want to know where the hell you have her."

He stared, and it's almost as if she could see the moment when it registered that he was actually in deep shit. He started to sputter. "Whoa, whoa, whoa, whoa. I didn't do anything. I might have just tossed her around a little bit. But, I mean, nothing more than she deserved."

"*Deserved?*" Kate snapped.

He looked at her and nodded. "Yeah, she deserved it. I didn't do anything." And damn if he didn't start to sob.

She stared at him in horror, as she looked over at Rodney, who was leaning against the front door. "You don't need to cry now. It's well past time for that."

"I loved her," he mumbled.

"Was that before or after you beat the crap out of her?"

"I didn't mean to," he whispered. "I never mean to."

"Did you ever hear about anger management?" she asked, with a note of sarcasm.

He glared at her, coming out of his tears almost too quickly for comfort, making her wonder if they were fake. And yet they had seemed pretty real at the time. She'd seen many a drunk with mercurial mood swings, and this was definitely another example.

"I really loved her."

"What I don't like," Kate noted, "is that you're using past tense."

He stared at her. "Are you telling me that she's not dead?"

"I have no idea. Are you telling me that she is?"

He started to shake his head. "I didn't kill her."

"Maybe not, but you're not making me feel any more confident about that statement than I was when I first walked in here."

He stared bleary-eyed at the door. "Did I let you in?"

"Yes, you did," she replied, aiming for patience and failing.

He sighed, then curled up into the couch again. "Well then, you can just go and leave again. Because I'll just sit here and finish my bottle."

"Bury yourself in self-pity while a woman out there is suffering?"

"She shouldn't have left me then," he replied callously.

Kate wanted to beat him up herself. What an ass. But she also knew that wouldn't give her the answers she needed. "Do you know where she would be?"

"At her friend's," he said, "at least I would assume so."

"And which friend is that?"

"The one you already talked to," he spat, with a sneer.

"How do you know I talked to her?"

"Because she only had the one friend, so that's the only one friend who you would have gone and talked to," he explained. "Jesus, you guys are so stupid."

"Wow," she replied. "Once again, we're back to that lack of respect."

"Nobody else in this fucking world understands anything. Everybody is stupid," he muttered, as he took another swig.

She considered her next question, when her phone went off. She walked several steps over to the front door and answered Owen's call. "Hey."

"Two other cases."

She started to swear. "Damn it, around here?"

"No, in the province of Alberta no less. One in the city of Calgary," Owen added, "and they found one in Edmonton, the capital, about two years ago."

"Jesus," she said. "You want to keep going cross-country and let me know what you find?"

"Yeah, will do."

"So, we have at least four dead, and this missing girl is a possible fifth."

"But we don't know for sure, do we?" Owen asked.

"No," she agreed. "And why would he be back here in Vancouver again?"

"Depends on if he's doing a couple in each location and then moving on," he guessed.

"And the problem is, we don't have enough cases to know yet."

"I'm on it," Owen replied. "When you come back, hopefully we'll have more figures for you."

"Okay." She hung up and turned toward the suspect, only to find him snoring on the couch. She shook her head and whispered, "So much for Prince Charming." She walked over to join Rodney, who had done a full search on the apartment. When he stepped out of Henry's bedroom, he shook his head. She nodded. "Let's go. We know where to find him."

As they walked to his car, she told him what Owen had said.

"Two in Alberta?"

She nodded. "Now they're contacting other major centers across the provinces."

"Good God," Rodney said. "We really need to get these databases linked together."

"More than that," she added, "this is getting pretty rough. If these are all related in MO, we have a serial killer who likely started back at the same time as our original victim."

"But was Lord the ground zero case?"

"We don't know."

"That would help a lot too," he muttered, "if we can at least catch a break on something."

"Finding new victims *is* catching a break," she reminded him. "Of course we don't want there to be more victims. Yet, if these cases line up, now we'll see a pattern, and every crime scene will tell us something more."

"Depending on how old the murders are," he stated.

"We'll find out just as soon as we get back to the office."

And, with that, he suggested, "I'd say, let's head that way now."

They got into the vehicle, and he took off for the station.

———◦◦◦———

THE PAIN WAS almost incapacitating. Simon started out fine and managed to get through part of the day. However, by the time lunch came around, his ankle was killing him, and his wrists were killing him, and his shoulders were killing him. After about twenty minutes experiencing the extreme pain, he finally noted it wasn't his pain. It was hers. Her pain was enough to almost cripple him.

How ridiculous to know this was happening to somebody else and yet to be feeling exactly the same torture. It was also heartbreaking to realize what this poor woman was going through. And Simon could do nothing about it. It broke his heart and pissed him off, and yet, once again, he was stuck without the ability to help her.

"Not true," he muttered aloud. "We might help her. There's got to be something we can do, … some way to find her."

He just didn't know how, and he knew that, as far as law enforcement officers were concerned, Simon could give them nothing at this point that they could use. The fact that this asshole was torturing her just made it that much worse.

"Is there anything you can tell me?" he muttered. He had a Bluetooth in his ear, hoping he wouldn't appear quite as crazy if someone saw him talking by himself, but how much worse would it be if they knew that he was talking to an energy source? That sounded strange even to him.

An energy source? How the hell did that work? He used to ask his grandma about it, and she would say that we were all energy. Everybody was energy, and, therefore, you could talk to their energy. When Simon tried to call it spirit, she corrected him, noting that it depends on what you're talking to. If you're talking to *spirit*, you're talking to the soul of that person, to the creation inside of who they are.

Simon had been confused at the time, but he had gained more clarity as he grew up. And it still didn't make all that much sense, but he kept hoping that he would eventually figure it out—especially now that he was stuck with this nightmare. But, to date, he hadn't gotten very far on that clarity issue. He did understand there was a difference between trying to talk to her directly and trying to talk to her indirectly. Something about spirit walks and talking to the soul versus trying to talk to her consciousness. He was working on it, but it just wasn't going very quickly.

By the time he understood just where this agony was coming from, he sensed that it was easing up, and that made it all that much easier to understand. Simon shook his arms and legs as he headed from the last building and walked several blocks over. Time for food and he was tired and cranky and sore because, even though the direct pain was leaving, an ache remained, something so deep that it hurt.

He headed for Mama's, intent on getting a hot Italian meal and maybe some more to go home with. He was tired, and he doubted that he would see Kate tonight, and that added to his bad mood. He wanted more of a relationship than she was willing to have, yet it still shocked him that he was the one to say it. But here he was, the one waiting on every call, waiting on every moment that she might give him. And when he finally rounded the corner and came up to Mama's, he pushed open the front door and stepped inside, realizing the weather outside was turning ugly. Inside it was warm and cozy, and Mama, with one look at him, raced over to fling her arms around him in a big hug. He allowed himself to relax and to give her a hug back because this woman truly came from heart. She would feed the world and never charge a penny if she could, but they had bills to pay, like everyone else.

"Oh my," she said, "it's so good to see you."

He smiled. "It's been a few days."

"You think we haven't noticed?" she asked, giving him an eyeful.

He smiled. "Sometimes work gets in the way."

She nodded. "I get it, but you forget who you're talking to. You've got to realize that you still have to eat, even when you're out working all the time."

"I know. I know," Simon admitted, "and I'm here now because I'm really hungry."

"Of course you are," she agreed, "if you haven't had a decent meal in days."

He thought about it and then nodded. "You know what? I think you're probably right."

"*Tsk-tsk.*" Mama made her way to a back booth, as she seated him, and then took off into the kitchen. She returned with a glass of wine, one of his favorites, and placed it, along with fresh bread, in front of him. "Get started on this," she ordered. "How do you expect your body to keep up with your workload if you don't look after it?"

Bemused, he just let her carry on, as she completely arranged his dinner tonight. He didn't mind in the least, finding it comforting in a way, almost like having a mother, something he didn't remember at all. It broke his heart to see how appealing it was to have that mother figure in his life, even if only for a moment. He hadn't thought that he would ever be so weak, then had to remind himself that it had nothing to do with weakness and everything to do with family—a relationship he didn't have much experience with. So, if he missed it or felt like he was missing it, then maybe that was just enough of an explanation, and he didn't need to feel guilty on top of it.

When she finally returned, she asked, "The special?"

"I wasn't even sure you would ask me what I wanted," he joked.

"Well, I wouldn't normally," she replied, "but we have a really nice special tonight."

She proceeded to launch into a description of some *partigiano thingamajig*. Finally he laughed and said, "It sounds marvelous. Besides, I've never had anything of yours that I didn't love."

She gave him a beaming smile, snatched the menu, and took off again. It was true that he hadn't had anything in mind when he arrived, and he'd eaten here enough times that his words were completely honest. She'd fed him so often that there probably wasn't a meal he wouldn't like in her place.

He sat here, relaxing with a glass of wine, and started to unwind, feeling the aches and pains leaving his body. A bit of a chill remained, which he suspected was more of a psychic chill than anything. Leftover from a vision. He figured this was what his grandmother had referred to as the willies. *Frissons.* He hadn't understood then, but now he understood it all too well. It wasn't long before Mama returned with a huge plate of food. She put it down in front of him, and he wanted to laugh. It was just so ridiculously large. No way he could possibly eat that much.

He stared at it in shock and asked, "Are you joining me?"

She went off in a fit of laughter. "Nope, nope, nope. But, if you have too much, we'll send it home with you. And what about your girlfriend?" she asked suddenly, her hands on her hips. "Or did you scare this one off too?"

He looked at her in surprise. "I haven't scared her off," he replied cautiously, not sure where that was coming from.

"Well, good," Mama replied. "I like her."

He snorted. "I'm glad to hear that. But it's not like I've been *intentionally* chasing anybody off."

She stared at him. "When you work so hard, you do it in order to avoid having a relationship," she explained, wagging a finger at him. "You fill your life with busy work, so you don't have to deal with the emptiness. You think I don't know that? You need to stop. You need to settle down. You shouldn't be lonely all the time." And, with that, she was gone again.

He was left here, stunned, as she'd never said anything quite so personal to him before. But, of course, that was also the danger of becoming friends with somebody like that. Mama would never be the person who could hold back her thoughts, especially when she thought she knew better. And he couldn't really blame her because he kind of was the same way. Yet, at the same time, it felt odd to have that frank talk directed at him.

Though maybe it was for the best. He really wasn't ignoring or trying to bump Kate out of his life. It was the opposite, in fact, since he was always trying to figure out how to get more time with her. But she was seriously busy. As he dug into the massive pile of stuffed shells in a beautiful tomato sauce with some basil leaves and white chunks of cheese, he thought about Mama's words.

Is that what Kate was doing? Working to fill a void? But then again, Kate was driven and had started with that drive for a whole different purpose, and it would take a harder person than him to get her to stop. And why would she? She needed to find her brother, but, with all these other cases, when would that ever happen? It would be more a case of tripping over it, should that opportunity ever present itself. That had to be tough too.

It wouldn't be easy at any point in time to deal with something like that. He should know since he'd endured enough bullshit in his own life. And yet, at the same time, enough good things had made up for Simon's rough beginning. He was in the position now where he could do so much more for himself and for others. Kate wasn't there yet; she was doing a ton for everybody else because of her job, but she couldn't do anything for herself yet because she was still so caught up in guilt. He shook his head at that. Then remembering Harry's earlier advice, Simon looked down at his phone and sent her a text. **Did you eat today?**

He thought about it, then took a picture of his plate and sent it to her. It was probably mean, but, at the same time, maybe it would shake her out of that overworked awareness and make her stop and eat. He was fully prepared to take food home tonight and coax her to join him. Not that he could eat again, but, if she would eat, it would make him feel a lot better. When a response came in, his heart lightened.

No, so save me some.

He quickly messaged back. **Not an issue. Tons are**

here.

And, with that, he attacked his plate with a little more enthusiasm. Even if he did manage to get through it all, he'd be more than happy to pick up more to go home with. Just the thought that she was planning to come by and to eat was enough to settle him down and to soothe his depression.

So what if ghosts bugged him? So what if he was trying to help people out there with this weird gift of his? So far, he wasn't helping as much as he wanted to. At least he was on a path, trying to give help. With time he would get better, and maybe they could do more with these victims than he was capable of doing now. And just as he went to put the next bite into his mouth, another vision slammed into him.

A door opened right into his consciousness, and he could see outside a big huge window. It was French, with curved tops, and stared out onto a street, with maybe a church on the other side. Then the door shut as somebody entered, blocking the view, and Simon was once again in darkness. He snatched his pen and grabbed a napkin off the table and started to draw. When Mama came around to refill his wine and ask him how his dinner was, he was busy sketching away.

She looked at it and asked, "Are you building a church now?"

"No." He pointed at his drawing. "I wonder if one is around here like this."

She nodded. "There is, indeed. It's just around the corner."

He looked at her in surprise.

"There's probably more than one though in this city," she added. "You'll have to check."

He nodded. "I will."

With that, he took a photo of his sketch, as poor as it was, and sent it to Kate.

Just as he was about to take another bite, Kate called him and asked, "What is that?"

In a low tone he explained.

"You think she's in that room?"

"I don't know what else to think," he admitted. "Somebody is in that room, and somebody opened a door, so she could actually see that little bit."

"And that's what let you see it?"

"Right."

"Got it," she noted. "How many damn churches are there in this city? A couple hundred for sure."

"Might be more than that," he suggested, "but that window is very important. And I just spoke to Mama here, and she told me that one like that is around the corner here."

"It's not an uncommon window style," Kate agreed. "We can't just assume it's in that vicinity."

"No, but why not? It's local. It's close and convenient."

"It is," she replied. "But we still can't just jump in and see if he's on the other side of that building."

"Well, as far as I remember, considering that church, on this block, has nothing on the other side of that building," he noted, with a sudden realization. "I think it was actually demolished for an apartment complex."

"Of course it was," she groaned. "I'm at the office, going over the evidence now. I'll talk to you later."

With that, she hung up.

CHAPTER 11

KATE STARED AT her phone. Then she sent the picture to her email and, from there, printed off the picture that Simon had sent her. She returned to her desk to find several detectives standing around the whiteboard. "Simon just sent me this." They looked at the photo, frowned, and shrugged. "My reaction too. However, he says that"—and she held up her fingers in quote marks—"somehow he could see what the woman saw through an open door and caught a glimpse of that window."

"That's like a church," Rodney replied.

She nodded. "That was his take on it too. So she would have to be inside an apartment or a house somewhere across from one of those big windows."

"And how many of those are in this city?" Rodney asked.

"Probably hundreds. But how many buildings will have that window shape of a size large enough and have housing across from it?"

"Quite a few," Rodney noted, "but let me get the IT techs to help on this. They could access data and search this out pretty fast. Faster than us anyway." And, with that, he took off.

She sat down at her desk and sighed.

Lilliana looked over at her. "You doing okay?"

Kate looked at her, smiled, and answered, "As well as I

can be, considering we are operating on the theory that a woman is being tortured somewhere, while an asshole drinks himself to sleep on a couch, and we're stuck not knowing who and what."

"No, but we've got actual breaks on the case now," Lilliana reminded her. "And, if this is the same killer as these other two cases …" She let her voice trail away.

"True enough, I guess we do have the reports now." Kate hopped up and walked over.

Lilliana got up. "I actually made up a packet for you." She handed it to Kate. "I know how much you prefer print."

"I do," she agreed. "It's too much to be on the computer all the time." She leaned against her desk, as she flipped through the file. "Same MO."

"Yeah, and that's what we thought, with very little for evidence."

"Nothing on motive and no suspects, *great*," muttered Kate. "That's not helpful. Now it's also interesting that these were a couple years apart."

"A couple years?" Lilliana asked.

"No." Kate shook her head. "A couple days, sorry. Which would fit with what we've got right now. We're about a week apart with these two current cases. So, if just two there and now two more here, that's a pattern. But, after killing the kid's sister fifteen years ago here, why is the guy back again? Same town, same place?"

"I don't know," Lilliana admitted. "Maybe he figured it was unfinished business, or maybe it was because the original guy convicted is now out of jail, providing another fall guy."

"And nobody was targeted as a suspect in those others?" Kate asked.

"No, not that we're seeing," Lilliana replied. "I've got a

phone call into the detective who handled the two Alberta Province cases. I'll see if he's got any more insights."

"We need to talk to him," Kate agreed, with a nod. "Even if it's not in the report, he'll have some idea."

"Maybe not. Do you?" Owen asked, turning to look at her.

She winced. "Touché. I guess I don't. I wish I did, but I don't have squat."

He smiled and said, "And that's what some of these cases do. They blow up in our face, and then, before you know it, we don't have anything to go on. They run cold, and we're stuck looking like idiots, and the cases end up being something that we can't work anymore because there's no direction to work in."

"I'm tired of those," Kate stated, rotating her neck. "And this is too recent. We've got a killer and actually have a missing person on the hook right now. So, whoever has this woman, you know ..." She let her voice trail off. She reached up, rubbed her face. "I need to grab some shuteye."

"Good. I'm really glad to hear that," Owen cried out. "I thought you would never quit."

"I'm not quitting," she argued, "but I definitely need some sleep and some food." She thought about their current scenario again. "I just hate to leave when a woman is suffering out there."

"If we get any breaks, we'll call you," Lilliana offered. "I'll be here for a little while longer."

Kate looked at Lilliana in surprise. "Okay, good, if you guys don't mind."

They shook their heads. "Go," Owen said. "You've been burning the candle at both ends for too many days. Let your team carry some of this."

"I'd be happy to," she added, with a yawn. She stumbled to her feet and asked, "Can you tell Rodney?"

"Will do."

She stopped, looked back at them, and asked, "How does any of this fit with the guy who shot at us?"

They both looked at her blankly, then at crime scenes photos up on the whiteboards. Owen shook his head. "I have no idea."

"Unless it was the killer," Lilliana suggested. "Maybe we're closer than we think."

"And, if that's the case," Kate added, "we need to take another look at everything. It doesn't make a whole lot of sense though." She shook her head. "Not now. But it will. Let's go over this from the old case to the new one, while IT is working on those church window photos." She turned toward her desk again.

"You go crash," Owen ordered. "Get some food, and, if you want to come back tonight, fine, but make sure you don't return until you've had at least a few hours of sleep."

They got no argument from her on that. She grabbed her wallet and stepped out of the bullpen. Heading toward the front door, she stood outside, taking several slow calming breaths of the fresh air. She wasn't even sure where she was going, but she needed food and wondered if Simon was even at home yet. She wanted him to be. She opened her phone, called him, and asked, "Hey, where are you?"

"Just heading home. What about you?"

"I'm off for a few hours," she replied, yawning again. "I need food, and I need sleep."

"Do you want me to bring the food to your place?"

She thought about it and then answered, "Maybe I'll come to yours, if you're okay with that."

"I'm more than okay with that," he said quietly.

She turned in the direction of Simon's place. She didn't have wheels, and it was way too far to walk, as tired as she was. She caught the first cab she saw, and, as she arrived, Simon walked up the front steps.

He looked at her in surprise. "Hello, that was quick." He took one look and whistled. "You look like shit." She glared at him, and he shrugged. "You don't want me to hold back the truth, do you?"

"No, but you don't need to be quite so honest," she muttered. "But, yeah, I definitely look like shit. I'm tired. I'm not sleeping. I need food, and I've got an asshole of a killer who's tormenting women. Where the hell is the good news in that?"

"None of it's good news," he replied. "But the bottom line is that you'll get there. And you can't beat yourself up in the meantime."

"Which is why I'm here with you," she noted, "and I sure as hell hope you brought food."

He laughed and held up the bag in his hand. "It's right here, as promised."

"Pasta?"

"Yep, I was over at Mama's."

"That's awesome," Kate replied. "That woman has a heart of gold."

"She does, and then she believes that her food is the answer to everything."

"Food and family," she corrected.

He looked at her in surprise. "You're right. She did tear a strip off me tonight, thinking I had chased away my girlfriend again."

She looked at him and started to snigger. "Did you tell

her that you didn't?"

"I tried, but she didn't believe me."

"Well, she could be right, I suppose," she noted. "Yet it's not that easy to scare me off."

"Good," he said.

As they wandered into the front lobby and over to the elevator, she raised her hand at the doorman, adding a smile. "Good evening, Harry."

Harry nodded. "You two have a good night now."

She shook her head. "I've got to go back to work. I just need a little shut-eye and some food first." He frowned at her, and she held up her hands with a shrug. "When the cases come, the cases come," she explained. "We work on them because we need to."

He nodded slowly. "But you've still got to look after yourself."

"I'm working on that part." She gave him a half laugh. "And honestly it shouldn't be all that bad. I'll see how it is."

And, with that, she and Simon headed up to the penthouse. As she stepped inside, she walked over to the big picture window and stared out at the beautiful view. "You know what? From up here you can almost forget all about the underbelly."

"I can't," he argued, "because I work in it."

She looked back at him. "You do pick up some of the worst buildings in the city, don't you?"

He nodded. "I do. Sometimes I just can't help myself. Those buildings, they're all part of the soul of the city. It's up to some of us to help fix them up and to heal that soul."

She smiled. "I like the sound of that."

With that, she walked over into his open arms, which quickly closed securely around her.

SIMON HELD KATE close, the fatigue evident on her lean features. "Food for the body or the soul first?"

Tilting her head back slightly, she looked up at him in confusion.

He smiled gently and dropped a kiss on her forehead. "Food for the body first. Otherwise you will crash and won't eat." With a nudge toward the table, he quickly portioned out two plates, watching in concern as she started eating with an appetite, only to slowly sag in place.

"Keep eating," he urged, "then bed."

Maybe it was his voice, or his words, but she managed to polish off her plate to stare at him, with huge bags under her eyes.

"Now bed." He stood and removed the few dishes, quickly putting them in the sink, then turning to her, as she moved slowly toward the bedroom. His heart sank. He hated to see her work herself to the bone; yet he also knew nothing he could say would change it. Turning off the lights, he followed her to the bedroom, only to find the room empty. Surprised, he followed the trail of clothing to the bathroom and the shower. She was leaning under the water, her head resting against the tiles, letting the water rush over her.

With a tender smile he quickly shucked off his clothing and stepped in behind her. He picked up the bar of soap and gently rubbed it over her lean shoulders. She gave a start at his touch, turning her head to give him a half smile. He soaped her from head to toe. Afterward, in the same caring motion, he shampooed her hair, then added conditioner. It was easier to treat her as a defenseless child. And she stood quietly, letting him.

When he finally turned her around to face him, he

smiled down at her, a trusting look in her gaze. "Bed, before you fall asleep where you stand."

A light flared in her eyes. "Soon," she whispered, looping her arms around his neck. "But maybe a little of this first." And, with the water sluicing down their silky bodies, she stood thigh to chest against him, sliding sinuously from side to side.

He sucked in his breath, his body already on a knife's edge. She slid her hands down his chest between them to wrap one hand around his erection. He shuddered, staring, mesmerized at the knowing glint in her gaze. "Tease."

"*Nah*, this isn't teasing. It's a start of something memorable." With that, she tugged his head downward, as she surged upward, her lips reaching for him, consuming him.

Passion ripped through him. He lifted her, spun, and slammed her up against the tiles.

She gasped.

He froze.

She laughed and wrapped her legs around his hips.

He groaned and surged deep inside her. She nipped at his chin, as he grabbed her hips and pounded into her, feeling a lust he'd only ever experienced with Kate. He let it drive him forward, riding her to completion. For both of them.

Exhausted and out of breath, he leaned against her, the water still raining down on them. When he heard her lilting laugh, he smiled and looked down at her, one eyebrow raised. "Now it's bedtime."

CHAPTER 12

Friday

K ATE WOKE EARLY the next morning to find Simon was already out of bed. She checked the clock on her cell phone and realized it was only six. She sagged back into bed, as her mind started to wake up and to fire in all different directions. When she smelled coffee, she hopped out of bed, walked into the shower, and scrubbed down. By the time she was done and redressed in the same damn clothes, she shook her head.

She should bring over a change of clothes when she came next time. Now she would have to stop by her apartment to change before going into work. She walked out into the kitchen, where she poured herself a cup of coffee. Simon sat at his laptop, scrolling through data. She glanced at his screen. It looked like numbers to her, numbers that she wanted nothing to do with.

She took her cup of coffee and walked over to the big huge window and stared out at the city.

"You're up early," he murmured behind her.

"And I'll have to leave early," she noted, just as quietly. "I'll head home for a change of clothes and get to work."

"Because of the case?"

"Partly," she noted. "Partly because I can't help but feel that I'm missing something."

"You always say that."

"Because it's true. I try hard, but it's impossible to keep all these bits and pieces in your head all the time," she murmured. "Something is going on that I haven't gotten to the bottom of."

"It's not your fault."

"Of course not," she agreed, "but it is mine to figure out."

She knew he'd understand, and there was no point in trying to argue the point further. She finished off her coffee, then walked over, gave him a hug, and dropped a kiss on his forehead. "I'll see you later." She turned and walked out. She wasn't one for long goodbyes.

They both had a job to get on with, and, even though it was barely light out, since it was late summertime, the early morning was a beautiful time of day. She quickly headed home to her place, got changed, and put on some toast, while she finished dressing. After eating the toast in just a few bites, she headed out the door yet again.

When she walked into the bullpen not much later, she wasn't the first one in. She looked at Owen, her eyebrows raised.

He shrugged. "Couldn't sleep."

"I get that," she noted. "Unfortunately I get that far too well."

He nodded. "Seems like the longer you're on these cases," he suggested, "either you learn to deal with it or sleep becomes a luxury item."

She snorted. "I know, but the trouble with that is," she murmured, "sleep *isn't* a luxury item. We all need it badly and don't get nearly enough of it."

"Is it because of the nightmares or because you can't stop

your mind from racing around in circles?" he asked.

"It's both for me," she admitted, "but currently it's the racing-around-in-circles thing." Rubbing at her eyes, she asked, "So any new leads that you know of?"

He looked over at her. "Well, we've gone through the data on the other cases," he noted. "As far as we can tell, the old case here was ground zero."

"But if we could get DNA ..." she murmured.

He nodded. "We're cross-checking that right now."

"So let's get our lovely kid checked against it."

"That's in progress too," Owen added. "If we could at least wipe him off the suspect list, it would completely change the scope of the case."

She nodded. "So after all these years since the kid's sister was murdered," she asked, with a frown, "why come back here to kill again?"

"I was wondering about that myself. What I keep coming back to is the fact that the first case is where he got somebody else to take the fall for him," Owen shared. "But I don't know if that was the essence of it or if he has some connection to this kid."

"Another good possibility," she agreed. "As soon as we know on the DNA—which hopefully we can get a rush job on—then we could *potentially* completely reanalyze what's going on here." She thought about it and then said, "It's almost like we need to start right at the beginning again."

"That's where we have been," he stated in protest.

"Yes, but the fact that the two Alberta cases have some DNA changes everything."

"And do you think that's because the killer got sloppy?"

"Or were we sloppy?" she asked, looking at him.

"Or maybe any DNA from the first case just wasn't tested because we had the kid's confession."

At that, they both dove for the case records. "Most of it wasn't tested," she murmured.

"A ton of the kid's DNA was there, but he lived in the house, so most of it wasn't considered useful."

She raised both her hands in frustration. "And that's partly what clinched the deal. His DNA *was* everywhere."

Owen nodded. "Yeah, everybody and their proverbial dog had DNA there, but why wouldn't they? It was their home."

"Right, so everybody in the family had a reason to have their DNA there," she noted, "and no other DNA was found. So now what we need to do is compare all that DNA against the DNA in Alberta."

"Wouldn't it be in the database?" Owen asked.

"Not necessarily," she noted, looking at him suddenly. "Not if you think about it. The kid's DNA was everything, and yet it was nothing." He stared at her in surprise, but she shrugged. "He confessed, and that made it a slam dunk. Game over. So, what we need to do is make sure that the kid's DNA was even entered," she noted, "and, while we're at it, all the comparable DNA as well."

He shrugged. "I can check up on that. I know the whole DNA database concept was pretty early back then."

"Early, plus DNA wasn't trusted."

"Agreed," he said. "Leave that with me."

"Okay, good enough." She scrubbed her face. "I'll go through all the files—of the kid's sister, of Cherry, compared to those two Alberta cases—and see if I can come up with anything either different or so unique as to be the same killer here locally."

"It's all so unique that it has to be the same person,"

Owen stated.

"Maybe so, and I get that, but I need to see it all with my own eyes."

With that, she grabbed the folders that had been printed off, poured herself a coffee, and walked into one of the empty interview rooms. There she sat down at an empty table and spread out the cases. As she went through the details from the autopsy reports, she realized that they were almost identical. *Almost.*

A little bit more ingenuity with each successive kill, a few more burns on the skin in several places, as if he were experimenting to fine-tune maximum pain with each woman. Yet the rest remained consistent. Both ankles broken, both wrists broken, and once again, a knitting needle through the hearts. All these victims looked similar. The same as the current missing woman, Chelice. A missing woman who they were still trying to track down. And every clue that Kate could possibly find was desperately needed right now. As she wandered through the various facts and figures, she took notes.

By the time she closed the folders, she realized that she wasn't any closer to finding the killer, yet knew, without a doubt, that the same one who had killed the kid's sis had also killed Cherry and the two women in Alberta, as he was planning to kill Chelice. He'd cemented a pattern, with a little bit of experimentation on the side. She wasn't sure it was a sane mind that had done this because who could? Yet sociopaths were well known in the criminal world. They just didn't give a shit. With that, she got up, collected her folders, and walked back to the bullpen. Then she sat down and called someone she knew in Missing Persons. "Any updates on your missing girl, Chelice?"

"No, not yet," her friend said. "What's this I hear that she might be related to something going on in your world?"

"Rumors travel fast," Kate noted lightly, not knowing how to explain Simon's visions.

"Just because we have a missing woman who looks similar to other cases," her contact noted, "doesn't make it so."

"No, it doesn't. As a matter of fact, it's almost a red herring that takes us away from our cases."

"And yet you were tracking and talking to the witnesses and relationships in Chelice's world."

"Yes," Kate admitted. "We had to be sure that it wasn't related."

"Did you get that assurance?"

"No," she replied, "we didn't. Not at all."

The other woman groaned. "In that case, do you want to just stay out of it? If you find something, pass it on. Otherwise we're doing our job."

"Glad to hear it. Same thing for you. If you hear anything, let me know, will ya?"

"Yes."

At that, Kate contacted IT and asked, "Any update on those church windows?"

"I was just about to call you," Bowman replied, "and also sent a message to the Missing Persons Bureau. I know you didn't go through them originally, but that has a way of pissing people off."

"Yeah, apparently I already did that," she muttered.

"It's hard to stay on everybody's good side. In this case though, I think we'll need the whole team."

"Why is that?"

"We have nineteen church windows."

"Jesus, nineteen, huh?" She stood up. "All possible?"

"Yes, all with buildings across from them, either uninhabited office buildings or some occupied residential."

With that, she phoned her Missing Persons' contact again. "Hey, sorry I didn't tell you about the church window thing."

"I just heard," she snapped.

"Not trying to step on your toes. We're on the same side after all," she noted.

"Then keep me in the loop. There's a reason we're called Missing Persons."

"I get it. I'm sorry."

With that out of the way and the information from the IT people running through her mind, Kate added, "Listen. We do have nineteen locations to check out."

"We don't have manpower for nineteen. We need to narrow it down somehow."

Kate thought about it and winced. "Well, we can check power and see if any of them have been turned off because there's obviously still power at this one."

"I can do that. Most of them will probably still have power on, even if it's empty," she warned.

"I know, but we might take a couple off. We need to find out who owns and/or lives in them too. I'm hoping we'll find some connection or rule some out that way too."

"Yeah, I can do that too," she replied, "I'll get back to you in a bit."

With that, Kate hung up and looked over at Rodney, who had just come in, and quickly brought him up to date.

"Yeah," Rodney agreed, "we need to keep communication open between departments. When people start screaming at the sergeant, it has a way of coming down on us."

"And with good reason," the sergeant declared, having walked in, just in time to hear what Rodney said. "We don't have time to spend on turf wars and stepping on toes."

"Sorry, I didn't realize I was out of our lane and upsetting people. In our defense though, Missing Persons hadn't even been out to see the people we spoke to yet. They're probably pissed because we made them look bad."

"It's never wrong to help find somebody who's missing," Colby stated, "but you have to communicate and keep the right departments informed and moving through the process."

She nodded. "I get it. So, we've isolated possible locations for this missing woman and have it down to nineteen sites."

"Damn, that's a hell of a lot," Colby noted.

"Which is why we're trying to find a way to narrow it down before we start physically checking them out."

"And did you get Missing Persons in on it?"

"Yes, I did," she confirmed. "They're running down ownership or tenants to see if we can find any connection to our cases, plus also checking utilities to see if any of these buildings may be turned off. I would think our killer would be using power."

"If he needs a cold room, that is another angle," Rodney added. "Remember that blood flows at a slower rate when people are cold."

"Damn," Kate replied, "I was hoping that was a way to knock down the numbers."

"It might be, but I don't think we can discount it totally," Colby stated.

She nodded. "I went through the case files on the two Alberta cases, compared them to our two," she told him.

"The one thing I can say is that it's the same guy. DNA was found on the one set of clothing for one Alberta woman. Not on the other, yet some was on her body."

"Right, so we don't have DNA here, outside of the kid. But, if he was locked up when these Alberta cases happened, it's looking like we put the wrong person behind bars."

She thought about that, nodded slowly, and added, "Something is still so twisted about this."

"Nothing more than usual," Colby stated. "Twisted is pretty much the norm in these cases."

She thought about it and agreed. "I'm still looking for what the next plan of action would be."

"Well, if you have nothing else to do," the sergeant suggested, "there are always those nineteen locations."

She winced. "I guess there's no reason not to." She stood. "Until the utility/ownership data comes in, I don't have any other way but to do this on foot. I'm waiting on DNA too. So, it might be a waste of man-hours, but at least we could eliminate some of them. That would be something."

"That's a tangible accomplishment," the sergeant agreed, "and it would do you some good to get outside for a bit."

With that, she gave Missing Persons an update and walked out to her vehicle and looked up the addresses on her list. "Bloody BS," she murmured, as she looked at them. "Still, with this guy, maybe he's running a generator for power or stealing electricity off a nearby address." She didn't think so, but she picked the five closest to her and headed out.

As she walked up to the first building, she checked the location against the presence of that church window, then frowned and nodded, mumbling to herself, "You know what? It is possible, I guess. It wasn't a very good sketch, so we still have a lot of possible rejects here. But it's what we have."

As she wandered up to the apartment building directly across from the church, once inside, she hoped to see her target window from certain landings, then choosing the floors which were the closest match to Simon's vision. It still left an awful lot of options and a lot of interpretation between a couple floors—depending on the angle and how exact the drawing was.

As she stood at the end of her first chosen hallway, staring at the church through a small window here, she phoned Simon. "That sketch you gave me," she began, "were you looking directly at the window, angle-wise?"

"Pretty close, yeah," he replied. "Why?"

"Because I'm in an apartment building across from a church with a similar window, but I'm in a hallway landing, so I'm slightly off to the side of the church window."

"My vision was directly on."

"So, height-wise as well?"

"Yes," he replied, completely understanding the point of her questions, "definitely the same height."

"So seeing the lower part of the church window frame?"

He frowned for a moment. "Yes. The lower part of that large church window."

"Okay," she noted, "in some cases I might have to check apartments on the floors above and below."

"Yeah, I could see that," he agreed, "but I drew it as close as I could."

"Good enough." She disconnected from Simon, then turned and knocked on the first doorway. When a young woman answered, a baby in her arms, Kate introduced herself, with a smile. "Have you heard any disturbances in this area in the last week or so?"

The woman looked at her in surprise and shook her head. "No, it's a very quiet area. It only gets busy on Sunday for church, when we get a ton of traffic outside. Other than that, it's fairly calm and quiet."

"So, nothing disturbing, nothing unpleasant?"

The woman immediately shook her head. "No, not at all. It's one of the reasons we chose to live here. It's all about families."

"Okay, good." Kate handed her a card and added, "If you think of anything odd or unusual that's happened, give me a shout."

"I can," she said. "What's this about?"

"We're searching for a missing woman," Kate replied. "And we have a few markers that identify this area as one possible place, but we're definitely not saying this is the location. We're just checking it out to see if it's a better option than the other places."

The other woman immediately replied, "Other options should be better. This place never has anything wrong like that."

And, with that, there wasn't a whole lot more Kate could ask, but she did see through the young mother's doorway to the window where the church was. And, indeed, it was a pretty straight-on view. But, from Kate's point of view at the apartment's doorway, nothing shouted that anything was wrong in the apartment itself. Smiling, Kate nodded her thanks and walked down to the next one.

There could have been an ever-so-slight change in the angle of perception which was not shown in the drawing. What if Simon—through the poor tortured woman's sight—

hadn't seen the window head-on but maybe by a peripheral glance or something? And, God, Kate hated even thinking what she was thinking because it just sounded so bizarre that she didn't want to justify it.

When she knocked on the second door, a young man came out, a headset on his ears. He frowned when he saw her. "Hey, what's up?"

"Just wondering if you've heard any disturbance in the area recently," she asked.

He looked at her, shrugged, and said, "Nothing ever happens here."

"You're sure about that?" she asked, with a lopsided smile. "It seems like everybody who says that always ends up wishing they hadn't."

He laughed. "Maybe," he agreed, "but, in truth, it's not a great place for singles. It's a great place if you want to raise a family and to live a dull and boring life. Other than that, there's never any noise, no parties. It's stupidly calm and quiet."

She wondered about that but smiled and added, "There are good things about that too."

He shrugged. "Maybe. I wouldn't mind a little bit more life though."

"Yeah, you'd probably like a little more of a party scene."

"I'm young," he explained. "I don't want to go to my grave thinking that this is all there was to life."

"Interesting," she noted.

He shrugged, looked at her, and asked, "Why?"

"Just your perception."

"Yeah, my parents say that all the time," he agreed. "I like my music, but it'd be better if I had somebody to share it with."

"Nobody else around in the building?"

"No, not that I've seen," he noted. "Well, I'm not much of a dater, so maybe that's the problem."

"It can be hard to meet people," she agreed, with a nod.

"This town is dead," he told her. "Seriously it's almost impossible to meet anybody here."

She'd heard that complaint more than a few times, so knew what he meant. She got his contact information and handed him a card, telling him the same thing she'd said to the other resident.

With that done, Kate headed upstairs to the next floor and did the same thing. In one case nobody was there but in the other was an older woman, single and living alone, who was just way too chatty. But Kate had found that people like that were usually great sources of information. Only this one didn't really have anything to report. Just not a whole lot of information to be had.

"Everybody is lovely," the woman had gushed.

And, with that, Kate took her cue and marked this building off her list. She did the same with the next three buildings, and, by the time she came to the fifth one on her list, she was tired and feeling like she was truly wasting her man-hours on this excursion. Frustration was building because surely there had to be some other way of making this list shrink. Although with five buildings almost done now, it wouldn't take that long to get through all nineteen. She again updated Missing Persons. This alone should get her out of the doghouse with them.

As she walked up the stairs and got to the floor that she presumed would be pretty close to eye level with her target window—in this case, the third floor—she knocked on the first apartment. When there was no answer, she tried knocking several more times.

The apartment beside her opened up, and a woman stuck her head out and frowned.

"Sorry," Kate said, "I didn't mean to disturb you. I'm trying to find the owner of this apartment."

"Good luck with that," she replied. "He took off last night, and good riddance if you ask me."

"Why is that?"

"The noise that comes out of that place, it's been terrible. And then all of a sudden it stopped, and that was worse in a way."

"What do you mean by noise?"

"Sounded like a hell of a fight."

"Does he have a girlfriend?"

"Not that I know of. He's creepy, as in creepy-creepy. I don't know why anybody would want to spend any time with him."

"Well, just because we don't understand relationships doesn't mean that they didn't have a reason for hooking up."

"Of course they do."

Kate questioned her further. "Do you know who he is, like what his name is?"

"You're the cops. You can find out."

"I can," she agreed. "I just wondered if you knew who he was."

"Sure, but he's a bit weird."

"Weird in what way?"

The woman leaned forward. "He brings men home."

At that, Kate realized why the woman was having such a hard time with it.

Going through the same motions with each person at the rest of her targeted apartments, Kate slowly walked away from this fifth building of nineteen, looking at the surrounding area. It wouldn't be the right area for a torturing murderer, as far as she was concerned. How would you get a body in and out? How would you handle the screaming? And then of course she thought about the vocal cords and winced. That's the way that you would handle it. Inside these four walls, nobody would know the difference. Depressed, she headed back to her car and sat in her vehicle for a long moment. Then on a whim she contacted Rodney.

"Any updates?"

"No, nothing yet. How did you do?"

"Hit five so far," she shared. "None look really possible."

"But, with the vocal cords cut," he reminded her, "there won't be any screams to be heard."

"I know. The first building was just super sweet, as in absolutely nothing could possibly go wrong there."

He snorted at that. "Yeah, that sounds like a perfect place to look closer."

"And yet nothing really to look at. Short of a warrant I won't get into any of the apartments. And we have nothing other than a picture of a church window."

"And we don't even have a picture," he reminded her, "nothing you could put in front of a judge."

"I know, and that just adds to it, doesn't it?"

He nodded. "And we can't ever forget that. We must have something that's usable in a court of law. It can't be something that we're pretending to make good use of."

"No," she agreed, "I get it. At the same time, I've got five more not too far away, so I'll do a quick check on them before I call it a day."

"Good enough," Rodney replied, then disconnected the call.

With that, she turned and headed in the direction of the next building. Five down, fourteen more to go. If she had help, she could get them all done. And, if she was fast, she could get well over half done today. She'd take it. With that, she pulled out into the traffic and carried on.

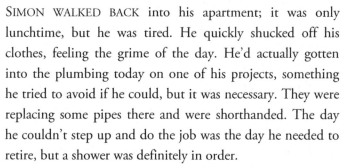

SIMON WALKED BACK into his apartment; it was only lunchtime, but he was tired. He quickly shucked off his clothes, feeling the grime of the day. He'd actually gotten into the plumbing today on one of his projects, something he tried to avoid if he could, but it was necessary. They were replacing some pipes there and were shorthanded. The day he couldn't step up and do the job was the day he needed to retire, but a shower was definitely in order.

Clean and dressed once more, he headed out to the living room, looking forward to the sandwich he'd picked up at his favorite deli. He sat down at the kitchen table and bit into it, and his gaze landed on the leftovers he had yet to clean up from last night. Frowning, he pulled the phone toward him and texted Kate. **How are you?**

He didn't expect an immediate reply. She would get back with him when she had time.

Yet he didn't get an answer even hours later.

CHAPTER 13

B Y THE TIME Kate made it back home again, she was worn out, having knocked off seven more places. Twelve down. Another seven to go. She had really pushed it at the end, hitting a drive-through and picking up burgers as she drove on. Her destination was home for a shower and a good night's sleep. She walked up into her apartment, unlocked it, and sat down, eating her burger. Just a few bites in, she stopped, burger in her hand, then shook her head and asked, "What the hell are you doing?"

She looked around at her sparse furnishings and noticed that dust had accumulated at least one-quarter-inch thick on the nearby bookshelf. She couldn't pull a book from it because she hadn't taken her books out of the boxes yet. She could be over at Simon's right now, sitting in front of that incredible view, having a cappuccino or a fancy coffee of her choice, looking forward to a good night's sleep.

Instead she came back here, alone. Why? She knew part of the answer had to do with the fact that Simon somehow centered her focus and made all the other things in life a greater priority. She found that dangerous when she was on a case, though everything about him was dangerous when she was on a case. He'd been a help in some ways, but she'd spent the whole damn day chasing down that stupid window. Although she'd seen plenty of them, there hadn't been enough details in Simon's paper napkin drawing to decide which window they truly sought.

That had become obvious because, very quickly, she'd recognized that, while all the windows were similar, they were definitely not exactly like the window in his picture. She needed something a little more definitive to add to his sketch. Yet what right did she have to call and to hound him for more information? And then she thought of the poor woman currently being tortured, plus the one she presently had in the morgue, with broken ankles, broken wrists, her vocal cords cut, not to mention the two cases she'd read about today in Alberta.

She picked up the phone and called Simon. When he answered, she stated briskly, "I need more details on the window."

"Good evening, Kate," he replied in a gentle voice. "Rough day?"

"Yes. I've been looking at churches," she explained. "Twelve of them today. I have seven more to go. All of them had big windows and similar looks, but none were exact."

"Well, of course not," he agreed. "They had all been built in different areas at different times, so they would have been designed by different architects."

"Which means I need more details in order to pinpoint a location."

Simon was silent on the other end for a moment. "So the drawing wasn't enough?"

"I just said that, didn't I?" She knew her voice was overly testy. She didn't mean it to be, but that calm, quiet voice of his was so very disruptive.

"You know I can't just turn it on."

"I know," she replied. "I get that. And when it's on, you

can't turn it off."

"I'm working on that part," he noted, and she heard fatigue in his voice.

"You know I wouldn't ask—"

"You would ask for the moon if you thought it would save your victims."

"Yes," she admitted, "I guess I would. I just keep thinking about Chelice, our missing woman, and Cherry, the woman in the morgue, and the two cases I read more about from Alberta today. All like the one from many years ago, when Rick Lord's sister was murdered."

"Were they exactly the same?"

"Close enough that it had to be the same killer."

"Or a copycat?"

"Or a copycat but it would have to be somebody who Rick shared very specific details with, and why would he tell anyone?"

"I'm not sure," Simon noted. "Maybe to save his own soul."

"Maybe. I don't know. I'm not a shrink."

"Do you have one at the station?"

"We've gone through a few," she explained. "After I managed to uncover the one who had been there for a long time but who had two pedophiles for brothers, they haven't yet hired a permanent replacement."

"Right, I forgot about her."

"Yeah, she's got her own trials right now."

"But you won't have anything to do with that, will you?"

"Well, I will if I get called to give testimony," she replied, popping the last of the burger into her mouth.

As she chewed, he asked, "Eating?"

"Yeah, I picked up a burger and fries."

"Good God."

"It was either that or come home and try to find something in my fridge."

"I already know your fridge is empty."

"There might be a few things moldy and growing inside it, but I haven't had much time to take a closer look."

"When you get into a case, you get into a case 150 percent, don't you?"

"Yes," she murmured, "and I have to. Otherwise we don't end up saving anybody."

"That's not on you," he reminded her. "You can only do so much."

"No," she snapped. "I need to do more. A woman is suffering right now."

Simon hesitated for a beat on the other end. "What if I'm wrong?" he asked in a diffident tone.

She stopped and stared at her phone. "Are you?" She hadn't even considered that. "You know that it says a lot about how far I've come," she noted, "because I didn't even question it."

"I know," he agreed, "but don't worry. I do enough questioning for both of us."

"The unwilling psychic," she teased, with a bitter laugh. "You know what? So far, your information has been accurate, although I'm not sure about this church window. However, I suspect, whenever we find the crime scene or this victim, this window of yours will have some pertinence."

"It might," he agreed, "yet I could be wrong."

"Because everything comes couched in *might be* and *could be*."

"I really wish I could change that."

"But you can't. Look. I'm not in any shape to talk to

right now, if you don't have any messages or information." She added, "I'm really tired, so I'll go have a shower and hit the sack."

Without waiting for an answer, she turned off her phone and got up. It wasn't fair to Simon, and it sure as hell wasn't fair to her, but, every time she talked to him, he made her want more. More than she could have. More information on this victim. More answers to the questions in her head. More of him. More time together. More of a life outside of work. Even though her work drove her, she didn't want to end up losing her sanity over this job.

Every night she woke up seeing these victims. Every night she went to bed, desperate to let them slide into the recesses of her mind, so she didn't go crazy. Then every morning she woke up vowing to get out of bed, determined to help them. And today, all day, what a waste.

She got up and headed to the shower. When she came back out, she threw on an old T-shirt, crawled into bed, and collapsed.

Saturday Morning

WHEN HER PHONE rang, she reached through the darkness for it and mumbled, "Hello." She heard Rodney's voice at the other end.

"Are you okay?" he asked.

"What time is it?" she asked, yawning.

"It's six."

She shifted upright. "Is it?" She pulled her hair off her face and stared around at the dimness of the room. "Why are you waking me up?"

"I found two more cases."

"Jesus," she said. "When?"

"In the last ten years."

"And where are they?"

"Saskatchewan."

"Why the hell would this killer be doing this in one province at a time?"

"I don't know," Rodney replied, "but I did find one correlation."

"What's that?"

He took a deep breath and said, "You won't like it."

"Maybe not," she agreed, "but, if it gives me a break in this case, I'll deal with it."

"The thing is, this kid that you think may be innocent, … he spent time in multiple prisons."

"Yeah, that's pretty common."

"Well, he spent time in Alberta," and, his voice deepening, he added, "and he spent time in Saskatchewan."

She pinched the bridge of her nose. "Please, God, tell me that he was actually in prison during these killings."

"He was, from a cursory check. I'll go deeper."

"I'll be in the office in twenty." She quickly slammed down her phone. It took her eighteen minutes to get to the office. And she was the first one there. She looked around, wondering where the hell Rodney was. But she saw no sign of him, so she put on coffee and headed to her desk. He wasn't in the bullpen and hadn't been here yet, from the looks of things. Groaning, she grabbed her phone and called him. "Where the hell are you?"

"I'm at home," he stated, "and, if you wouldn't have hung up on me, I could have told you that."

"Well, you could have texted me at least."

"Or you could have asked," he noted in exasperation.

"Well, I'm at the office at my desk," she explained. "Nobody's here, so maybe my brain can actually connect with something with no interruptions. Send me what you have."

"Already did," he stated. "I'll be in in a bit. I didn't get much sleep last night, so I'm not moving the fastest."

"Who the hell sleeps anymore?" she muttered.

"You sounded pretty well asleep when I called," he noted.

"And I was. Thanks for reminding me that you woke me up, and now you're not even here."

He laughed. "Didn't say I was coming in either," he teased. "You're the one who assumed that."

"Yeah, whatever," she snapped. "At least I have a whole pot of coffee to myself."

"Yeah, how about food though?"

"Don't even know what the hell that is anymore," she replied. "My stomach thinks my throat has been cut." At that, she remembered what happened to these women and winced. "Oh, crap, poor choice of words. Never mind the food. I'll just grab something in a bit."

"Okay, I'll see you in an hour or so."

With any luck, she might be up to speed in an hour; she hated being behind the curve on information. If Rodney—or Reese and her two assistants or the IT techs or whomever—had found something that could potentially help with this puzzle, she needed to know every detail. She printed off all the info Rodney had forwarded to her, then grabbed her first cup of coffee.

As she headed toward her desk, she picked up her print job and dropped that on her desk, then sat down, her feet up on her desk, and started reading. Not a whole lot here, but enough that she had to start several searches. By the time she was done, she could confirm Rick's location per murder site.

At the time of the two murders in Alberta, the kid had been in juvie. In Alberta. For the two murders in Saskatchewan, he was doing time in an adult prison. In Saskatchewan. She frowned as she thought about that.

He hadn't had an easy time in prison either. Did he have people who moved with him? Did he have people he knew from the system? Where the hell was this going? She frowned and realized it was pretty damn early to be making phone calls, but if Rick Lord was going to work today, she needed to see this kid before work.

She phoned him, and, when she got a cranky voice on the other end, she identified herself and said, "We need to have a talk."

"I've done all the talking I'm going to," he snapped. "My mother has gotten a lawyer for me. You want to talk, you talk to the lawyer." Rick promptly hung up.

She stared down at the phone. "Little prick." At the same time, that wasn't very helpful because he hadn't given her the name of his new attorney. She called him back. "In order to contact your lawyer, I need to know who it is."

He asked, "Really?"

"Yeah, idiot. How do you expect me to contact anybody if I don't know who it is?"

"So you'll actually talk to my lawyer?"

"If that's what you want, yes. It makes you look suspicious as hell but whatever."

"Hey, hey, hey," he replied, "what do you expect? You said I wasn't a suspect."

"I said that we were doing everything we could to clear you," she muttered, "so don't go putting words in my mouth."

He frowned. "That doesn't sound quite like the same thing."

"That's because it isn't, but, if you didn't have anything to do with it, you don't have anything to worry about."

"Oh, no, you don't," he replied. "I listened to that shit last time, and look where I ended up."

"You also confessed," she reminded him, "a fact that you keep trying to ignore."

"That's because I don't want to remember it," he snapped.

"So have you got a few minutes now?"

"Maybe. What do you want?" he asked in a grumbling voice.

"When you were in juvie," she began, "you spent time in Alberta, didn't you?"

"BC and Alberta, and I spent a couple weeks doing some special research bullshit in Manitoba and Saskatchewan."

"Did you go alone?"

"Sometimes my mom came," he replied. "Sometimes my dad."

"Anybody else?"

"Yeah, lawyers, probation officers, and scientists. Whoever it was who was trying to study my brain to figure out why I supposedly did this. You know they really could have saved themselves a ton of money and just listened to me."

"Don't forget that whole 'you confessed' thing. That in itself is something they probably want to study, to understand why you would confess. Especially if you didn't do it."

"What do you mean *especially*?" he snapped. "I told you that I didn't."

"And that's fine," she snapped back. "It would be nice if that was the truth because now we need to know exactly what did happen."

"And remember the part about I don't have a fucking clue?"

"Yep, I do," she stated. "But we've also found two similar cases in Alberta and two similar cases in Saskatchewan."

There was a moment of shocked silence from the other end. "What the fuck?"

"You heard me," she said calmly.

"Well, it wasn't me, and I'm sure somebody somewhere along the line should be able to prove that. And it also means," he added, his voice rising, "that you now have the proof that I need to have my charges cleared."

"Not so fast," she replied. "Aren't you the one who just told me that you spent months in Alberta, Manitoba, and Saskatchewan?" And she wrote down a note to check Manitoba for similar cases.

"Sure, but I was always supervised," he noted. "It's not like, once you're deemed a criminal, and you're in the system, you get to walk around free and clear."

"Did you get any day passes?"

"No." Then he stopped. "Yeah, I mean. Fuck!" he said. "I don't know. I had a couple day passes. I had a little bit of time out. Sometimes, you know, I was allowed to go visit my parents. When my mother had an accident, we weren't sure she would live."

"When was that?"

"It was in Alberta. You'll have to ask her when. I don't remember, honest to God. All that time in prison just runs into one nightmare after another."

"What happened to her?"

"She got badly injured and was in the hospital. They gave me special permission to go see her, no thanks to you guys," he snapped. "I fought like crazy and damn near had a complete breakdown when I wasn't allowed to see her at first. It was some special dispensation that they gave me at the time, and I was pretty damn upset when I had to go back, believe me. I kept kicking and screaming, telling them I didn't kill my sister."

"And we're back to that whole problem caused when you lied in the first place."

"I get it. I get it. Do you think I haven't regretted that all those years?"

"I'm sure you have," she said gently. "So, when you were in juvie, was there anybody you were close to?"

"Yeah, a bunch of people," he noted. "You asked me that before."

"Sure, but at the same time you also told me that you didn't have any friends."

"Not now," he stated. "Not when you're free because everybody hates your guts if you can't do anything for them. They all say they'll stay in touch, but really all they want to do is hate you because you're getting out, and they aren't."

"Did any of your friends go free?"

"A few of them, but I didn't stay in touch. Again, it's not a period of my life that any of us really want to deal with."

"Do you know others who did stay in touch?"

"Not with me but with other people. They all seem to make friends pretty easily," he murmured, with a jealous note in his tone. "I never had that ability."

"In what way?"

"My friends all seem to be shit," he replied. "I don't know what it is. Everybody around me seems to have good friends, people they can talk to and can do things with, you know? I got into the drug crowd, and it seemed like all they wanted from me was what I could do for them, you know? Like drive a vehicle or go check out a store. They made it look like nobody would ever know who I was, so I was asking questions about what goods they were looking to buy. Shit like that."

"Trying to further their crime area?"

"Exactly," he said. "I never did make good friends in juvie. Most of the kids there were pretty upset, pretty pissy in their own right." He shook his head. "I mean, obviously I made some friends, but it wasn't easy, and I was just trying to survive."

"I think that's what everybody in juvie is trying to do," she noted gently.

"Yeah, I'm sure they are, but it was not easy to do. Everybody's got an agenda, even in juvie, and it could be just to survive the day."

"Was that so hard?"

"Sometimes it was. A lot of the time it was just boring as all get out, following all the rules and instructions. Everything was structured so we couldn't make many choices for ourselves. We had worktime. We had exercise time. We had computer time. We had some classroom time, like life instructions. We had everything that we needed, I guess, but what we didn't have was our family, any real friends, or any personal freedom."

"What about group coaching to make friends?" she asked curiously.

"Didn't I just tell you that?"

She thought about the other murders. "Who would know that you were in these different prisons?"

"I don't know. Anybody who could search the system or

the database, I guess. Can people get a hold of that stuff?"

"Sometimes." Her mind was thinking rapidly.

"Well, maybe you should talk to them. If you found other cases, I'll talk to my lawyer about having my case cleared. And then you can bet this goddamn city owes me some fucking money for the years they incarcerated me."

"And again, not so fast," she said. "It could be the shoe is on the other foot."

"What are you talking about?" he roared.

"Hate to keep saying this, but you confessed, which wasted a lot of time and money, not to mention that other people were killed afterward."

"Jesus," he said, "it would be just my luck to have it turn out that way."

"And again, I don't know how any of that works," she admitted. "Let's deal with one thing at a time. We need to catch a killer."

"And what good will that do me?" he snapped.

"Well, for one, it'll clear you. Two, you won't be hounded by the police anymore, and you'll have a halfway normal life maybe for the first time ever. A life where at least you can hold up your head and say you didn't do this."

"You think anybody will believe me?"

She thought about what she'd heard in his voice, when he had told her about his sister's case. "You know what? I don't think it would take very long. Once people realize the truth, the tide will turn in your favor."

"Jesus, I hope so," he said. "My parents have been through enough shit."

"What about you?"

"I'm young, and I can handle it," he stated. "At this point in time, I'm getting more and more bitter and worried about them. It was just my sister and me, and, with her gone and me in jail, there was nothing for them."

"No, that's a tough deal all the way around. How did your dad handle it?"

"He didn't. How does any dad handle seeing his son go to jail for something like that?"

"Yeah, a tough deal. I'm sorry." She didn't really know what else to say. "I'll look into your case and get the records for your transfers and when, and just see what we can come up with. But, if you think of anybody you spoke to about your sister's murder, anybody who might have been a little too interested in the methodology used, I need to know their names," she stated. "Somebody out there knows the details."

"Yeah, but that could be any cop too," he suggested. "Anybody who's seen the case files would know the details."

She hated to admit it, but he was right. "That's one aspect, yes," she agreed, "but there's also the fact that it could have been somebody close to you, somebody you told, either in one of your therapy sessions or in some of your treatments, or when you guys were just joking around and trying to tell the world you were a tougher nut than the next guy."

"Yeah, that happened a ton too," he agreed, groaning.

"Of course it did. You were still kids with egos, trying to survive in a place where a hierarchy was even more important."

"Well, if you didn't survive that," he noted, "you were pretty well stuck for later on in life."

"Of course," she agreed. "And, as much as we don't like that aspect of society, it's pretty common."

"I think in any group," he added, "even at work, I mean, there's a hierarchy."

"There is, indeed," she agreed, "and that includes my

work too."

"And you're at the bottom, I presume," he said, with a laugh. "Otherwise, you wouldn't be calling me."

"I don't know about the bottom," she replied. "No, I'm definitely not at the bottom anymore, but I'm not at the top either."

"Do you want to be?" he asked.

Hearing a sense of real curiosity in his voice, she replied, "No, I'm doing what I want to do, and that involves being on the streets and handling these cases. I don't do well with politics and all that bending and bowing that's needed to make shit happen."

"No, I don't imagine you are." He laughed. "Listen. I've got to go to work. So do me a favor. Maybe, this time, you guys could work to set me free instead of putting me away."

"Do me a favor," she replied. "This time, don't confess to something you didn't do." And, on that note, she ended the call. She sat here, staring at her phone for a long minute. When she looked up, Rodney stood in front of her. She gave a start. "Jesus! I didn't even hear you come in."

"I came in around the back," he replied, lifting the cup of coffee in his hand. "You didn't even finish the pot."

"Nope," she murmured, "just got off the phone with the kid."

"Are we calling him in?"

"I'll do some research first to see if I can get a timeline on when he had visits outside."

He looked at her and nodded. "Are we thinking he did these other murders?"

"No," she replied, "but somebody knew his schedule, and somebody knew when and where was a really good time that Rick could be pinned for murder again."

"And yet nobody looked at it at the time," Rodney noted.

"No, and I'm thinking that's probably because all these cases weren't linked closely enough. But, at any point in time, like right now, when somebody finally got around to connecting all this shit, Rick does look like a really nice viable option."

"Yet he was a kid and in juvie at first, right?"

"Yeah, but, like we know, he moved around to other prisons," she noted. "Plus he did some therapy sessions in a special program in Alberta for eight weeks—over the same time period of those two Alberta cases."

"So he was there at the time?"

She nodded slowly.

"Well, Jesus, let's bring him in."

"He was in jail though. Remember that," she noted.

He nodded slowly. "So he didn't have access then."

"That's where the problem comes in," she added. "His mother was in a bad accident, when his parents came to Alberta for a visit, but the kid didn't give me the details of what happened to her. Anyway she was in the hospital, and he eventually was given dispensation to go see her. But I can't imagine that he was given enough free rein to go kidnap, torture, and kill somebody, much less *two* victims."

"No, of course not," Rodney agreed. "So either it's somebody close to him or somebody who knew him."

"We'll have to run down everybody who handled his case and who brought him to Alberta for the counseling program and all that special dispensation for hospital visits."

"Jesus." Rodney shook his head. "Okay, I'll start with the probation officer and see what he can tell me."

"You think that'll give you anything we don't already

know?"

"I don't know," he admitted, "but we'll have to go deep into his probation file to get something. So the probation officer might know more about it than we do."

"Maybe, let's see what we can dig out of these murder files. I wish they didn't have just the basics," she moaned.

"But it's the basics that we normally need. When you start talking this kind of stuff, however, we need to go that much deeper."

"At least it's there, and it's just a matter of digging for it," she muttered to herself.

"Yep, it is—or it should be." With that, he settled at his desk.

She picked up her phone and made a call to Dr. Smidge.

When he answered, his voice was as testy as usual. "You know that I just walked in the door."

She grimaced, then checked the time on her cell phone. "Sorry, Doc. My colleague just came in, so I figured maybe you were at work too."

"We're not all night owls, you know?" he growled.

"No, but we pull enough all-nighters in our world," she noted, "that sometimes it's hard to determine night from day."

"What's happened now?" he asked.

"Two similar cases in Alberta and two in Saskatchewan."

"How old?"

"All over the last fifteen years."

"Then your convicted suspect couldn't have done those, if he was in jail."

"And yet," she explained, "he was in those same provinces at the same time those crimes were committed."

At that, the coroner whistled. "Well, that's interesting."

"That's what I thought," she stated, "hence the call."

"What can I do for you?"

"From the files, clearly the injuries look very similar to our cases, but could you take a closer look at these related four and see if there's anything here that would be different enough to suggest it was a separate killer or a copycat or something like that? I know I'm grasping at straws, but I don't care because straws are what we need."

"If nothing else," the coroner noted, "we need to knock that potential off the list."

"Exactly," she agreed.

"Have you got the files?"

"I do," she replied. "I'm attaching them right now."

"You could just give me the case numbers," he reminded her. "I've got access."

"Oh, duh, sorry. I should know that." She gave him the related case numbers.

"Fine then. I'll get back to you." And he hung up.

As she got off the phone, she looked over to find Rodney staring at her.

"Was that Dr. Smidge?"

She nodded. "I figured he should take a look at the other cases."

"Good idea," Rodney stated. "I wish some billionaire would provide enough money to make a full-on real-time database across Canada."

She looked at him, shooting one eyebrow skyward. "Like you? Wouldn't that be nice," she joked. "I know it's something that they're talking about, and a certain amount is functional, but it's not complete."

"It'll never be complete at this rate, and why the hell can't we take DNA when kids are born? And I think that job would take deeper pockets than I have."

"Uh, something to do with, ... you know, their rights," she said in a sarcastic tone.

"Their rights, until they kill someone," he noted. "And then we're all screwed."

"Isn't that the truth?" she muttered. But there was no point in arguing about their lack of tools.

"At least we have the kid's DNA," Rodney muttered. "It's the first positive thing we've gotten, and yet there's none in this case from last week on Cherry."

"I know," she admitted. "It also doesn't make sense that the kid has been back here five years though."

"Right. I agree."

"More questions, no answers," she grumbled. "It's always this way."

"Then one day it breaks, and we get to the bottom of it, and the pieces fall together, and it all makes sense," Rodney noted.

"It's the getting to the bottom of it that's driving me nuts," she replied.

He laughed. "What? You? You're the persistent ferret that gets in here and digs into all this information until you find out what's going on," he noted. "We're all learning from that, you know?"

She stared at him in shock. "Seriously?"

"Hell yeah," he replied. "You're the one who found those kids lost in a pedophile ring. You're the one who hooked the suicides as assisted murders or whatever the final criminal charge will be. We didn't see this."

"Not at first, but you did soon enough."

"*Soon enough* isn't the same as being the one who saw it. You look at things differently," Rodney stated. "Don't ever change that. I get that you're frustrated, and it's hard at this stage, and it sometimes seems completely fruitless, but you have a knack for seeing things that we don't. We need that on the team." Then he fell silent and returned to his computer.

"You'll make some phone calls?" she asked him.

He rolled his eyes. "And you're very focused."

"Have to be. A woman's life is in danger."

He looked over at her. "Do you think Simon is telling the truth?"

"I believe Simon is telling the truth as much as he understands the truth to be."

At that, he started to laugh. "Isn't that like hedging your bets?"

She gave him a half smile. "Definitely. But I also think it's the truth. If he's not telling the truth, then he doesn't know what the truth is. This is the closest thing to the truth that he does know, which still doesn't help."

"No," Rodney agreed, "it doesn't."

"But it's all we have."

"A lot of man-hours."

"Don't even go there," she snapped. "I'm the one who spent all day yesterday running around, looking at bullshit windows."

"I know," he stated. "I thought that was actually a good thing for you to understand."

"What? That all of this is bullshit?" she asked, with half a laugh.

"No, but, when you're pushing for things—like Simon's story to be believed—you also need to understand what the cost of the man-hours is in terms of wild goose chases."

"Yeah," she agreed, "if that was part of the lesson, I got

it, but it still sucks."

"I know." Rodney nodded. "We got it too. And you're right. It sucks. But, at the same time, maybe something will come out of it."

"While I still have however many more to go ..." she muttered. "Seven, I think."

Rodney nodded. "You could ask the sergeant for some assistance."

She winced.

"See? You don't even want to talk to Colby because it came from Simon."

"I know, dammit, and yet it's information, and something we need to follow up on."

"What information?" came the question from the doorway.

She looked up to see the sergeant there. She frowned at him, and he frowned right back. "Just about the church windows."

"So did you take a look?"

"I hit twelve yesterday, and there's seven more."

He nodded. "And? What do you want now?"

"We have two more cases found in Saskatchewan."

He looked at her and asked, "Really? Why across Canada?"

"I don't know, but there's more," she stated. After taking a deep breath, she explained about the kid's travels while incarcerated.

He stared at her. "So the killings happened in the same towns where the kid was?"

She nodded.

"You'll bring him in for questioning?"

"I've already spoken to him this morning. He's gone to

work."

"And what'll stop him from taking a run out of the country?"

"*A*, he doesn't have the money. *B*, I don't think he will because he's hoping to get his case cleared now because, don't forget, all the time, no matter where he was, he was in jail. It's not like he could just sign himself in and out and run around without supervision."

At that, the sergeant frowned and leaned against the doorjamb and crossed his arms. "Am I hearing a *but?*"

"Yeah, and it's a big one. He also had day passes, and he had some free time."

"So you're thinking he just walked out of jail, did his thing, and walked back in? If these cases match up, it was a brutal crime and would have taken some time to torture his victims, not to mention planning."

"I know, and he was doing some special training therapy research BS in Alberta in order for them to understand why his juvenile mind would have killed someone like his sister."

"Oh, great. So what did they decide?"

"That he needed some, you know, special time with his family or something, so they went for a visit. Well, that was part of it anyway. At the same time, his mom was in a bad accident or was injured somehow. I need to confirm with her just what happened. Anyway Rick was allowed to go to the hospital to see her."

"So special dispensation for good behavior or something?"

"He described it more like he pitched a fit, and they eventually gave in," she explained, "but, at the very least, we have to see at what point in time those visits happened as compared to the murders."

"But keeping in mind that these women were all tortured beforehand."

She nodded. "And what I don't know is how long of a torture this would be."

The sergeant looked skeptical. "Could he have done something like this? Found a woman, kidnapped her, tortured her, then left her for days, only to not come back, and that's when she was found? I mean, is that part of this?"

"I don't know. I asked Smidge to take a look at the files."

"Good, maybe he'll have some insight into this mess."

And, with that, Colby turned and walked out.

She looked over at Rodney. "That didn't go too badly."

He stared at her. "You're still alive, so that's good."

She nodded. "I know. He's not too happy with this scenario."

"None of us are," Rodney noted. "Just, well, it's rougher on some of us than others."

"He didn't work any of these cases, did he?" She had looked for the officers involved in the original case that sent the kid to juvie, then prison, but thankfully it wasn't the sergeant. She didn't recognize any of the other names either.

Before Rodney could answer her, Kate's phone rang, and, when she pulled it out, she saw the call was from Simon. Wondering if she should answer the call, she got up, then walked a little farther away, ignoring the smirk on Rodney's face. "What's up?"

"Can you give me the addresses that you didn't hit yesterday?" he asked in a tight voice.

"Listen. I can't have you going in and causing any trouble."

He snorted. "Let's just say I had another vision," he replied. "I think I might recognize the location if I could see it."

"I'll give you the addresses, but you can't go in," she stated. "Promise me." There was a hesitation, so she pressed him. "I won't give them to you then."

"If you want me to find this woman, I have to get in there," he replied.

"Fine, but again you have to promise that, as soon as you see the building that you think is the right one, you have to call me."

"Fine," he snapped.

"I'll text them to you." She raced back to her desk and sat down, then pulled out her list and copied the ones that were yet to be done. She quickly sent Simon those. When she sat back after hitting Send, she frowned, thinking about the wisdom of it. She should probably have gone with him. She looked at her watch, looked down at her phone.

Rodney asked, "What's the matter?"

"It's Simon. He's had another vision, and he wants to see the possible addresses that I didn't get to yesterday."

"Interesting that he thinks he'll recognize it. So, what's bothering you?"

"Well, for one thing, I can't have him going in and causing chaos, if he thinks he's found it. I'm just wondering if I should go with him."

"You have to trust your instincts," Rodney noted. "If you think you should go, then get going."

WHEN SIMON ANSWERED his phone, he was already in his car, heading to the first one on the list.

"Come pick me up," she ordered.

He snorted. "Don't you mean, *Hi, Simon. How you doing? How about we go together?*"

"No, it's more like, I need to see these churches and the nearby buildings too. How about picking me up?"

"Well, that's a little bit better. Less of an order, more of a request," he explained, having already turned the corner, heading toward the station. "Did you eat breakfast?" he asked. He heard silence at the other end. "Then we're picking up food on the way."

"I don't have a problem with that," she admitted, "but I need to hunt down these places too."

"You don't have to explain anything to me," he noted. "I'm on the way."

"How far away are you?"

"Oh, ten minutes maybe."

"Good," she said. "I'll get a coffee." And, with that, she hung up.

He would tell her to get two, but she was who she was, and either she would or she wouldn't. And he knew it wouldn't be a reflection on how much she thought of him. It would most likely be a reflection of the fact that she was already focused and wouldn't think past that. But he wouldn't worry about it. When he pulled up, she was holding two cups.

He smiled as she put the cups on the roof of his car and opened the door before handing him one.

"I was sitting here, thinking that, if you were in a better mood, I could have asked you to get me one too, and I was thinking it was fifty-fifty as to whether you would think of it or not."

She looked at him in surprise. "I was already there, so it was a simple thing."

"It is a simple thing," he agreed, "but you don't usually think of it."

She frowned, as she slammed the door closed. "Are you saying that I don't think of others?"

"You do sometimes," he admitted, "but generally our relationship hasn't been all that open to thinking of things like that."

She shook her head. "I'm still not exactly sure what you're trying to say."

"Not certain I am either," he stated, "but how about I just say *thank you* and let's move on."

She nodded. "That works."

But her voice was a little distant. He wondered if he had insulted her. It wasn't something that he ever really worried about with her. "I didn't mean to insult you."

"Whatever," she replied. "What church are you heading to first?"

He pointed to the map he had printed off, on the dash, with seven numbered circles noted thereon.

She grabbed it and nodded. "That should work."

"Glad you think so," he teased, shaking his head.

She glared at him. "Look. I'm just focused on one thing."

"I know," he stated. "I get it."

She groaned. "But I don't have to be a bitch about it. I get that too. Thank you for picking me up and for letting me come with you. It's something I need to keep an eye on."

"What's that?"

"You're not a cop, so you can't go barging around doing cop things."

"Well, I can," he noted, "and I do on a regular basis, in case you didn't know that."

She stopped, looked at him, and asked, "What do you mean by that?"

He shrugged. "It's hardly like I do any superhero type stuff. But, in my work, I see an awful lot of shit, and, if I can fix it, I fix it. If I can't, I can't. And, in this case, whatever you want to call this ability of mine, it is screwing up my life, so, if I can't fight it, then maybe I need to join it and to just accept it."

"That might be easier for you," she stated cautiously.

He heard the tone of her voice and smiled. "Go ahead. You can insult me."

"It's not about insulting you," she argued. "It's about making sure that your perspective is squared away."

He laughed aloud at that. "How can one have a squared-away perspective regarding psychics?"

"I don't know," she replied, with half a smile. "It just sounded right."

"Says you." He pointed up ahead. "Here's the first one."

As he drove around the block, she stared up at the top. "Well, I can see where the window is," she noted, "but that looks like a pretty deserted building across from it."

"Is that a problem?"

"No, actually it looks promising." At that, she got out, studying the church. "It's a similar window, but it's not exactly like the other ones I saw."

"Well, that's the thing about church windows. I know vanity is supposed to be something that you don't really want to encourage when you're religious, but it seems like the churches were always these huge monuments to the god of their choice at the time."

She nodded. "That's not exactly the way most people would like to hear it described though."

"Maybe not," he agreed, "but it doesn't change the fact that it's pretty well what it is."

She smiled. "At least in this case, we will do a quicker check because the building is empty." She looked at it and asked, "Why don't you just buy it?"

"Why? Do you think I have nothing better to do than buy more buildings?"

"Well"—she shrugged—"yeah." And, with that, she laughed and headed toward the building across from the church window.

He smiled and followed. At least, she was in a good mood. Kate in a good mood was a dynamite force to be reckoned with. Kate in a bad mood was hell on wheels. Get out of her way, or she'd steamroll over you. But, man, she got the job done, and you had to respect that. You might not like it, but she got it done and got it done well.

All he could do was follow in her wake.

CHAPTER 14

NOT EVEN AN hour later, Kate studied this old ramshackle building, the second one on their list of possible locations where the latest missing woman may be held for torturing. "Has this been slated for demolition, I wonder?" She noted the Hazard and Danger signs and the big fence around it.

"Not necessarily. They do this to keep people off the property," Simon explained, "but there's always a way in."

"You want to find me one then?" she asked on a laugh.

He pointed to where the fence was separated off to the side. "There's an easy one."

She nodded, and, following him carefully, they walked through the fence.

"So now we're trespassing," he stated, turning to look at her.

She nodded. "I get that, but it's not like anybody's here to be disturbed."

"There is, and then there isn't," he replied. "There'll probably be a certain element of homeless men."

"Maybe," she agreed.

As they entered the building and climbed up to the other floors to be in alignment with the nearby church window, she looked around. "The walls aren't completely here."

"Nope, and that's something to consider too. The noise

factor."

She looked at him. "Yeah, well, the noise may or may not be an issue."

He stared at her with a raised eyebrow.

"He slices their vocal cords."

He winced at that. "Just another reason to capture this asshole."

"We don't need any reasons," she argued. "We've got so many victims right now that we're all just itching to get this guy off the street."

"And yet nobody else noticed?"

"Different territories, even different provinces, over a multitude of years."

He shook his head. "And what was the draw for our killer to come back here? Why Vancouver, BC, again, if he killed in multiple provinces?"

"I don't know," she admitted. "I really don't know."

"Do you have anything to go on?"

She nodded. "I do." She hesitated and then explained a little bit about it.

"Jesus, so the killings are happening at the same time frame that this kid is out and about in the same province and technically could have been available."

"And yet technically, not really," she added, "because he should have been supervised."

He laughed. "Anybody with any decent stealth ability will slip through that noose pretty quickly."

She looked at him. "But then it should be recorded in this file."

"The only people who will record it in a file are people who won't get in trouble. And what happens when they lose a prisoner for a day or for a few hours?"

"Well, they would get fired probably," she noted, "depending on what the prisoner did while he was out."

"Right," Simon agreed. "What do you think this guy is doing while he's out?"

She winced. "We don't know. That's the problem."

"And how long would he need to do the damage that was done?"

"Not long," she murmured. "The problem is, I've sent the evidence on these other seemingly related cases we found to our coroner to see what he's got to say about these cases, and we're still waiting on DNA results from one of the crime scenes."

"That's important," Simon stated, "and it takes time. And you're impatient."

"We have a woman who could be dying," she reminded Simon.

"I know," he acknowledged. "That's something that weighs on my mind constantly."

"But she's still alive?"

He shrugged. "I'm still getting visions, so I'm hoping so."

"Any chance your visions are old?"

"Yes," he admitted.

She looked at him, startled.

He frowned. "I haven't told you anything other than the truth. And I really don't know what to say about this case."

"I get it," she replied. "At the same time, it's frustrating."

"You and me both," he agreed. "Look where we're at."

She wandered around deserted floors. "It would only be these couple floors that would have the same view that you're talking about."

"And, of course, one big thing is missing," he muttered.

"What's that?" she asked turning to look at him.

"Doors."

She frowned, not following what was on his mind.

He explained, "Remember how this woman opened her eyes, and a door opened?"

"Ah." Kate understood, as she looked around at the deserted building. "Really not much left here for structure, is there?"

"Nope," he noted, "and no doors that would lead to that one room."

"So let's get on to the next one," she stated. "Maybe we can get through all of them today."

"And what if we go through all of them and find out it's none of them?"

"Then it's none of them." She shrugged. "And I'm back to the drawing board."

"Meanwhile I'll be feeling even worse because I put you on this pathway."

"Sure," she noted, "and I'll probably take a lot of ribbing because of the man-hours spent following this down."

"Which is also why you did most of this alone yesterday."

"Yet," she added, "there's a responsibility to follow the information too."

He nodded and didn't say anything.

"Let's go," she muttered. "The sooner, the better."

With that, they turned and headed to the next building on the list.

By the time they'd gone to four more, she was feeling beyond desperate. And defeated.

"We need food," he stated.

She nodded and didn't argue.

"I'm surprised," he said, "that you haven't mentioned it before."

"No appetite," she replied, staring out the car window. "And it's hard to have an appetite when you know somebody is suffering."

"And yet again I could be wrong."

"You could be, but it doesn't feel like it."

He looked at her in surprise.

She shrugged. "Yeah, I know. I'm not supposed to have *feelings* like this," she admitted.

"I don't think anybody is supposed to have or to not have anything like this," he argued. "The fact of the matter is, you have whatever you have."

She snorted. "How philosophical is that?" Something vicious was in her tone that she was desperately trying to crank back down because she wasn't mad at him; she was mad at the circumstances. She looked up when he pulled into a restaurant. "The Italian place?"

"I come here at least once a week, and, if I don't, Mama gets worried."

She smiled, and, as they walked inside, Mama raced over. When she saw Kate with Simon, Mama's face broke into an even brighter smile.

"I told him not to lose you," she shared. "You're too good for him."

Kate just looked sideways at Simon.

He smiled at both women. "And I brought her, didn't I? She hasn't eaten all day."

Mama immediately gasped in horror, ushered them to a table, and said, "You must sit. You must sit. I'll bring food." And she raced away, as if afraid that Kate would faint on the spot.

"You know I really don't need this coddling, right?" Kate murmured to Simon.

"Well, you're the one who didn't eat today," he noted. "So you'll have to take the punishment as it comes."

She groaned. "That sounds like blackmail."

"Maybe," he admitted. "On the other hand she comes from heart."

"I know, and I appreciate that. I know you do too."

He smiled. "I do. And it worries me when you get so involved in a case."

"What? Do I get bitchy and miserable?"

"Well, the misery I understand—and even the bitchiness to a certain extent. When you don't eat, it's hard to maintain a decent mood," he explained. "But you give so much of yourself, that it's worrisome."

"Not really," she argued. "Sometimes it feels like I don't give enough."

"And I'm sure you don't—in some totally human ways—but you're doing the best you can."

"And it's not enough," she cried out sadly.

He nodded. "To you, of course not," he agreed, "and that's half the problem. You just give everything you've got, and, when it isn't enough, you don't know what else to do."

"There's nothing worse than that sense of defeat."

"And," he replied, "you're doing everything you can. So you need to cut yourself some slack."

She lifted her head, looked at him, and retorted, "You first."

He stared at her in surprise.

"Isn't that why you're out here?" she asked. "Isn't it because you feel for this missing woman who's out there, and you're frustrated that we still can't find her? Isn't that why

you're out here because you won't cut yourself some slack?"
A slow smile crossed his face. He nodded. "Touché."

She shrugged. "It's not even a competition between us.
We both want the same thing," she noted quietly. "And it's
hard to do anything else but push toward that end, even
knowing that it may not be the one that we want to see."

"No, but it will give us answers, and it will stop the
search," he replied. "I don't want to see this woman on a
slab, and yet I'm not sure what else I'm expected to do."

"You can't do anything other than be who you are," she
noted. "Isn't that what you just told me?"

He laughed. "I did. You're very good at turning the tables on me."

"No." She shook her head. "It was good advice, so I'm
just reminding you to take it yourself."

At that, Mama returned with two large platters, not even
asking them about menus.

Kate stared down at the plate in front of her and gasped.
"Enough food is here to feed four people." When Mama was
long gone, Kate whispered to Simon, "How am I supposed
to eat all this?"

"I think she deliberately overloads us, so we have leftovers to take home to eat again later. I think, in her mind, the
worst thing that could ever happen to anybody is to starve."

Kate nodded. "It'll never happen around here."

He chuckled. "No, it won't, and that's a good thing."

She reached for a fork, filled it with what looked like
homemade ravioli, and took a bite. Almost instantly her
stomach screamed for more. "Oh my God," she whispered,
"this is fantastic."

"Like I've told you before," he muttered, taking in a
mouthful, "I come here often."

"I know you said that," she replied, "but I really didn't understand what *often* meant. But, in this case, I guess I do. Just not often enough for her, huh?"

"I don't think that's possible," he noted, with a smile.

When Mama came back a few minutes later, she brought French bread and a big tub of garlic butter and never spoke a word. She refilled their water and checked to see that they were actually reducing the volume of their servings, and then, with a satisfied smile, she took off again.

Kate just watched her in amazement. "She has so much energy."

"And she's always here, but she also has a ton of passion for what she does," he muttered. "And that's what keeps me going sometimes when I get a little depressed and fed up. I have to remember that we all have our purpose in life, even if it seems not so noble as other purposes in this world. People like Mama—who do what they do best for the rest of us so that we can function—allow us to do what we do best."

She nodded slowly. "And I've thought about that a couple times," she admitted. "It's just hard when it seems like I'm making no progress."

"And you know that it can come in a flash, and, before you know it, you'll have so much progress that you'll be slamming against criminals, catching the bad guy and locking him up. And you'll be sitting there, with a calm, quiet sense of pride, because that asshole's been taken off the street."

"It just can't happen soon enough," she muttered, "particularly in this case."

"I hear you there," he noted. "This guy needs to be stopped, and we'll do our best to make that happen. But, in the meantime"—he motioned at her plate—"let's eat."

With a laugh, she picked up her fork yet again and dove in.

SIMON DROVE TO the last possible building per the church windows chosen.

"It would be ironic if it were the last address on the list," Kate murmured, with a nod.

"Yeah, and just makes you realize you should have started at the other end," he teased quietly, as he looked up at the apartment building. "Do you really think it would be something like this?"

"No, but it's the only one left on my list," she stated, staring up at him.

"Who did the list?"

"Rodney and Owen, I think," she muttered. "Well, technically, our IT crew, maybe with the help of our analyst and her people."

"You can always check with them and see if they have any other addresses."

She sent off a quick text, which reminded her to update Missing Persons as well. "We still have to check this one out."

He nodded, and, as he opened the driver's side door and stepped out onto the sidewalk, he turned, then looked around and frowned. "I wonder if this church has windows on the other side."

"Well, we usually drive around the whole building first," she noted. "You want to do that?"

He nodded, "Yeah, I do." She wasn't even out yet, so he got back in and started the engine, then headed around the side.

"What made you bring that up, anyway?"

"Well, because we did drive around the other churches first. I don't know why I parked so fast. I just saw the address and stopped. We should have taken a quick gander around to see."

She didn't say anything.

He looked at her. "Why?"

"Nothing, just your instincts."

He shrugged. "I don't know about instincts. But this looks like something major."

As they headed around the church, she pointed at another apartment building. "That one looks like it's slated for demolition."

He nodded. "I think you're right. Usually it'll be demolished at some point in time when it's behind a construction fence like that," he explained. "This looks a little more possible than the other side. Let's check this side first." He hopped out and walked closer. As soon as he headed into the building, her nose lifted. What?" he asked.

"Something I don't like." She picked up the pace, as she raced forward.

"We need to figure out what's here," he added, following her. "Don't you want to take your time?"

"No," she snapped. "I already have a damn good idea." She had her phone in her hand.

By the time he squared up behind her, he gasped in shock. "Jesus." He immediately turned away from the gruesome sight.

Kate was already on the phone, making calls. She watched Simon as he pivoted and forced himself to take in the body. What it must look like to a civilian to see this much devastation done to a fellow human being. It was hard for her, even now, after all her years as a cop and now as a detective. She hated to think that this poor woman, this mutilated body, had once been human. The damage done to it was incredible. And he must feel worse, since he had that psychic connection with her before she died.

He took several steps back, looking around the area. By the time Kate got off the phone, she looked at him. "I have to stay here," she stated. "You don't." He looked at her in shock, and she walked over and said, "This isn't your fault."

"No," he agreed, "but the thing is, I don't think that's my victim."

"What do you mean?" she asked.

"If you'll notice, this one has been dead for quite a while."

She nodded. "I got that much. What do you mean? Are you saying it's not the woman you've been connecting with?"

He tapped the side of his head. "I can still hear her breathing."

"Another one?" She looked back at the one in front of them. "Why would he take another one so fast?"

"Maybe because this one died too quickly," Simon suggested. "Maybe there was no fun in it, not enough torture time for him."

She nodded. "We've certainly seen that happen before," she muttered, with a grim tone.

"Jesus," he moaned. "How can any of this be something anyone has seen before? It's just too horrific to even believe that somebody could do this one time."

"Don't look," she told him. "We'll have to do a full workup. So you need to go back to doing whatever it is that you have to do." He stared at her, and she shook her head. "I know you want to stay, but it's not necessary."

"I do want to stay," he agreed. "I don't want her alone, and I don't want you alone."

She stared at him in surprise. "It's my job, you know?"

He raised an eyebrow. "A serial killer's been here. Better off that you're not alone."

She went to protest again, but he reached out, snagged her into his arms, and whispered, "Humor me. I'll just stay until the circus starts. And then I promise I'll stay out of the way."

There wasn't a whole lot she could do to argue with him, particularly when he's the one who had driven her here, and a moment later she nodded quietly.

"But you have to abide by your promise to stay out of my way," she stated. "My team is coming, and so is the coroner."

"They'll be so thrilled with you."

"No, they won't, but, at the same time," she noted, "this is another crime scene, and it's all about the same killer. So this is huge. It really is huge."

"Is it?" he asked doubtfully.

"Yes, every time we get a scene like this, it tells us so much. And it's even more important since this time it's a change in his pattern."

"Are you sure?" Simon asked. "Maybe you just missed the pattern, and you should be looking for more victims."

"Maybe," she agreed, "but the more we find, although it's depressing as all hell, gives us more options to locate this guy."

He stared at her. "Do you think they leave evidence every time?"

She smiled, nodded, and stated, "Every damn time. I get

that this guy is getting better and that chances are there might be something here that we haven't seen before, but there's also always a chance that he made a mistake. And one of the mistakes is that, in this case, he didn't dispose of the body yet. So either he wasn't done or wasn't ready, and now he'll never get that opportunity to clean up whatever he may have left behind for forensics to find. This poor victim is mine now," she stated. "And, as much as I would hope to never ever see one like this again, she's mine now, and I'll do my best for her. And, more than that, I'll take every step I can to make sure this guy doesn't take another victim ever again."

And he believed her.

There was just something so quietly passionate as she turned her already professional gaze to study the scenario. She looked at him and said, "Please, just move back a little bit farther."

He nodded and watched as she went to work because it was a treat to see such professionalism and passion focused on the scene. As long as he didn't spend too much time thinking about what it was that she was focused on, it was pure magic to watch it happen.

He wanted to ask what she was getting from this scene already, but he pushed it back, realizing that, for any number of reasons, she wouldn't respond. All of her reasons would be good, but, at the same time, it was irritating to always be waiting for her to have time for him. He shook his head, smiling, because his complaint with previous girlfriends was that they had been too clingy and had always been asking more of him.

CHAPTER 15

HOURS LATER KATE stepped away from the body. Rodney had been at her side and had been for the last half hour.

"You ready to go home?" he asked her.

She broke her trance, locked on to this poor victim for far too long, looked up at Rodney, slightly confused, then nodded. "Yeah, I need to grab some shut-eye," she murmured, turning resolutely away from the crime scene.

"At least we found ground zero," he murmured.

"At least," she agreed. "Too bad we couldn't get ahead of this guy."

"She's been dead for quite a while," Rodney noted. "I don't know how long. The coroner is not giving us anything to go on yet. But it had to be at least a week."

"Why?" she asked, looking up at him. "Why this victim? Why now? That's more than two, unlike his previous pattern."

"*Hmm.* That puts this woman's capture very close to when we found the last one, when we found Cherry."

"Exactly, so the question is, why so close together? What triggered it?"

"It would be somewhere around the time that you started the case investigation." Rodney stared at her.

"What? So he takes another victim to taunt me?" she

275

asked in disgust.

"No, I guess not. At that point he probably didn't even know you were assigned to these cases."

"I agree"—she nodded—"but he disposed of the other victim, Cherry, and not this one. Why?"

"She didn't deserve it," Rodney guessed, topped with a shrug.

She turned and looked at him. "Why?" she asked, pushing further.

"This one didn't act the way he wanted her to. She wasn't worthy."

"*Worthy*? Simon suggested she died too quickly."

Rodney nodded slowly. "And that makes a weird sense, if you think about it. If she died too soon, he didn't get the same pleasure and satisfaction of the torture he had planned for her. He was too fast, too brutal with this one. Just look at her body, at the damage done to her. I think she probably died very, very quickly. Some of these injuries look like he just lashed out."

"And quite possibly could be postmortem then," Kate suggested.

"That'll be Dr. Smidge's job to confirm," he noted.

She nodded. "He won't be happy with this."

Rodney laughed. "He's never happy with us because we always bring him work."

"And it's not the work any of us want to bring him either. But that's what the job is."

He nodded. "It's not our doing. We're just the delivery boys."

"We're not even that," she argued, with a tired smile. "We're just the ones who come in afterward to sort it all out."

"Come on. Let's get you home." Rodney and Kate trooped downstairs and outside.

"The problem is," she added, as she stood here, staring out at the evening darkness, "Simon says it's not his victim."

"Seriously?" Rodney stopped and looked at her in shock.

She nodded. "He can still feel her connection and knows she's still alive."

He turned and twisted to look back up at the building behind him. "God, that's not good news."

"I know," she agreed in a silent whisper. "It's one of the reasons I was pushing so hard to find this exact church window image because I knew that she was alive. But this isn't her. And if this isn't her ..."

"It means there's another one. Another one with the same church window?"

"You know something," she replied, turning to look at him. "We need to check out the location of the other bodies, those in Alberta and Saskatchewan. To see if they were found in similar locations."

"Well, we know the kid's sister wasn't."

"No, but maybe she was body number one," she stated.

He nodded. "And what? After that he decided there would be a religious reason for this?"

"I don't know if it's something that they take inwardly and actually believe or if, in this case, it's just something to throw us off."

"The trouble is, the bad guys are getting smarter all the time."

"Yeah, they are," she muttered.

"And, as we find the tools to nail their asses to the wall, they find more tools to evade us. The criminal element always moves technology advancements forward." He sighed.

"It's been proven through the ages. We always have to come up with something to combat their methodology."

"I get it," she agreed.

"It still sucks though." Rodney led the way to his car. "So, you sent Simon home finally, huh?"

"He just waited until everybody else arrived," she replied. "He didn't want to leave me alone."

"Nice to see he's protective."

"I charged in, without thinking too much. Once I saw the body, I should have done a full sweep, but I didn't want to leave her."

"Yet you should have," he noted.

"Yes, and we did it as soon as I had backup," she added. "I was standing here, protecting the crime scene, waiting for everybody to show, and Simon stood there to ensure that I wasn't alone," she noted, with half a smile.

"You know he cares."

"I know he cares," she agreed. But she tossed it off almost, with a negligent shrug.

"Don't do that," Rodney said.

She looked at him in surprise. "Don't do what?"

"Dismiss him so easily."

"I wasn't," she protested.

"Yes, you were. You're just making it sound like he cares. And *so what?* It's a *big* so what. To think that he cares like this is massive. I get that you'd find him protecting you amusing because you're the one with the martial arts training, but you also know that you can die just as easily as anybody else can by a bullet or a shove off a building."

"Which is also why I didn't want him hanging around," she argued. "I didn't want him to get in the line of fire in case we weren't alone."

He snorted at that. "I'm sure he'd appreciate that thought process."

"Probably not," she agreed, "but what would you do when you get into a situation like this? He's a civilian, and it's not his job to be here. I came with him because we were looking for his vision, for whatever scenario in his head that he thought he needed to look for, as these symbols were representative of where she was."

"And it worked."

"Not really," she admitted. "Not for the woman he's still connected with."

"Well, even if this wasn't the outcome you and Simon were expecting," Rodney noted, "it's still a good one. Obviously not the best," he corrected. "Since we would prefer to find her alive."

"Absolutely, and that didn't happen."

"No, it didn't, but you're here. You found a crime scene, which hasn't happened since the kid's sister. He may not have cleaned up with this one yet. We could have massive forensic evidence here. And that's all something to keep in mind."

She nodded. "I get it. It's just frustrating to lose another victim."

"No, I hear you. At the same time let's hope that we'll find enough in this case to make this woman's death a viable way to find the killer."

Too tired to discuss it anymore, she fell silent. He drove her home, and she finally spoke. "We need to track dates."

Rodney nodded. "But we've been working on that and should have the board full tomorrow.'

"Yet he's always a step ahead of us."

"Not now," he corrected. "We're catching up fast."

She sighed. "I get it. I really do. It just feels like it's not fast enough, especially when I know another woman's life is hanging in the balance. And, after what he's done to this poor woman, I don't even know that our other victim can survive the torture, even if we do find her."

"We have to believe it," Rodney murmured seriously.

When he pulled up to her apartment building, she nodded and opened the car door. "Did you ever consider—" She stopped.

"Consider what?" he asked.

"That maybe there are two killers?"

He looked at her in surprise. "It's hardly a group activity," he noted quietly.

"I know, but …" Then she shook her head. "I need to think on it and figure out why this would come up right now."

"Because we're grasping at straws, looking anywhere for answers. We need DNA results, and we need answers from Dr. Smidge, and, with any luck, we'll get both tomorrow."

She laughed at that. "I don't know that we'll be quite so lucky to get all that so fast."

"Maybe not but we have to hold out hope," Rodney replied. "Go on now and get some sleep."

She smiled, nodded, and headed up to her apartment. She was too tired to do anything but crash. Fully dressed, she fell face down on the mattress and was out instantly. Unfortunately it led her through wild myriad dreams and nightmares. She woke up several times in a cold sweat, fear running through her veins instead of blood, as she sorted through the panic of her nightmares.

Sunday

FINALLY, WHEN KATE woke up again, a check of her clock confirmed it was already time to get up. She groaned and rolled over. "Why is it morning already?" she whispered to the empty room. She let herself lie here for another few seconds and then got up, stripped out of her old clothes—shaking her head when she realized she was still wearing them—and headed for a shower.

After the initial hot shower, she turned the water temperature to cool before she was done, to really wake up because she was so late already. With that done and now shivering slightly, she stepped out, dressed quickly, grabbed her keys and her wallet, and headed straight to work.

By the time she walked into the bullpen, it was buzzing already. She looked around in astonishment and caught Rodney coming toward her. "What did I miss?"

"Dr. Smidge stayed on and pulled an all-nighter. He's quite pissed at us," he noted, with half a smile.

She nodded. "Good, and what did he say?"

"Same killer as far as he's concerned."

She nodded slowly. "Can't say I'm surprised."

"What is different does support our other theory."

She looked at him. "We have theories?"

He laughed. "Well, yeah, we do. You brought it up last night."

"What was that?" she asked, still trying to catch up mentally with whatever was happening.

"The woman died quickly, and most of the injuries were administered after death."

She stopped and stared. "So that's why he grabbed a third victim in such a short time frame."

He nodded. "Simon was right. It looks like your victim

from last night died too quickly to suit this guy. So our serial killer turned around, snatched somebody else—Cherry, we figure—and probably went easier on her torture but then got worse on her over time."

"Right, he didn't lose his temper, didn't kill her as quickly as the others, just to keep her alive longer." Kate sighed. "And he has another one already, our missing person Chelice, to focus all that rage on."

Rodney nodded. "Smidge confirms our DB last night has been dead longer than a week probably, and his estimate is ten to fourteen days."

"Wow," she replied. "So we found them out of order. This latest one did come before Cherry, just that we found Cherry earlier, and now we have a whole new set of circumstances to go by."

"We've also ID'd last night's victim," he added.

"Wow, that was fast."

"Breast implants," he noted. "We just got the ID a few minutes ago. Already updated the whiteboard."

"Okay, so this is what happens when I actually go home and sleep."

"Yeah." He chuckled. "But that's all right. Remember? We're part of a team."

She smiled, realizing that he was right. It wasn't all on her shoulders to solve. This was for everybody to pitch in and to do what they could to help. And, for once, she was finally seeing the benefit of that. And maybe that was her fault. She was a little bit of a lone ranger when it came to working and had a lot to learn when it came to teamwork. But she was willing, and now, after seeing how much they'd accomplished already this morning, she was more than delighted. "Do we have any updates on the other DNA?"

"Not yet," Rodney stated, "but I put the reminder call in, and they told me that it should be later today."

"That will be interesting too. Any DNA on this victim?"

"Forensics hasn't got back to us yet, but she's been clean so far, per Smidge."

"Yeah, and I wonder when that started."

"Meaning?"

"Well, all kinds of DNA were found on the first victim, the kid's sister."

Rodney nodded. "But that was also because it was done in a home."

"And that's another difference here," she added. "This location, the church window, it matters. My questions are, why and what can we do to learn of the location of the others?"

At that, Lilliana came in, a cup of coffee in her hand. "There you are," she greeted Kate. "Late night, huh?"

Kate nodded. "Yeah, definitely."

"So we did get the locations on the other Alberta cases we have. We're still checking on the Saskatchewan ones. But they were inside and facing churches."

Kate stopped and stared at her coworker. "So, outside of the first victim, all the others were found inside some building, facing a church?"

Lilliana nodded. "What's your take on that?"

Kate shook her head. "Either asking forgiveness or making an offering."

At that, everybody in the place stopped and stared.

"Huh, ... *making an offering*," Lilliana repeated slowly. "I hadn't considered that."

"What's your take on it?" Kate asked, curiously studying the cup of coffee in Lilliana's hand and hoping it wasn't the last one. "I was thinking that it was somebody who couldn't go into a church, for whatever beliefs he may have, and he feels like a sinner or whatever."

"Or I was wondering about making a mockery of the church," Owen suggested, pushing his chair back. "As if to prove to the church that they couldn't control what he did."

"So a heavy religious background? That could also work," Kate agreed.

"Well, I like your idea too," Lilliana added.

Then Rodney interrupted, "The offering thing would also go along with Owen's idea. Because, if he couldn't get into church, was kicked out, or even felt like he was, making an offering might allow him back into God's good graces— or at least in his mind."

"But killing somebody"—Kate frowned, turning to look at him—"and using it as an offering to get back into church does not sound normal. Particularly in a devil's mask, although that would be easy enough to take off."

At that, Rodney looked at her directly and stated, "Is anything about the way those women died normal?"

Kate winced. "Good point," she agreed, rotating her head to get the kinks out. "He really is one sick bastard, isn't he?"

"And then there's the point you mentioned last night just before going home."

"What point was that?" she asked. "I feel like I'm still trying to play catch-up here."

"That's because you haven't got any caffeine coursing through your veins yet."

"Yeah, did you guys leave me any?" she asked, with a growl.

"You can go and find out in a minute."

"So, what point are you talking about?" she called out to Rodney, as she was halfway to the hallway, already heading to where the coffee was.

"Your thought about there being more than one killer. Did you wake up with any more thoughts on that?"

"It would explain some things," she replied. "But I don't know so much if it's more than one killer or more than one killer *vicariously.*"

At that, they all stopped and stared too.

"Jesus," Owen declared, "I didn't even consider that."

"And I still don't get it," Lilliana admitted, looking at Kate in surprise. "What does that mean?"

Kate nodded. "I will, just, ... Jesus, I need coffee." She headed for the coffeepot and thankfully found enough left for her to grab a cup. She put on another pot because no way would just one cup do it today, and she walked back into the bullpen.

"Okay, now explain," Lilliana ordered.

"I'm just wondering," Kate began, holding up her hand, "and I know this will sound really wrong and maybe contrary to what I was thinking earlier, but what are the chances the kid is orchestrating this from a distance?"

They all stopped and stared.

"Well," Rodney spoke, and then he fell silent for a second or three, before continuing on. "You're the one who was thinking the kid was clear, weren't you?"

"I'm trying not to think any limiting things and to just give my mind free rein to ideas that would help this make sense, when nothing makes sense, and all else is canceled out."

"Yeah, but we haven't rejected anything yet," Rodney noted. "Think about it. We have so many people who this could still be, maybe a tag team of killers."

"And yet we did confirm," Lilliana added, turning to look at Owen, "that the Alberta and Saskatchewan murders happened while the kid was in prison in those provinces at those times."

Owen nodded. "And what's your take on that?" he asked, turning to look at Kate.

"Remember how he had day passes too while in Alberta? Don't know if something like that also occurred in Saskatchewan. Yet I'm not sure it allows for the torture this killer enjoys, then the disposal of the body, or even the acquisition of the victim to begin with. Hence the multiple killers' angle. Then alternatively the vicarious killings' theory. So honestly I don't really have one take. I mean, it's too much of a stretch to be a coincidence that the kid was in the vicinity of all these murders, so I'm thinking, either it has to be somebody who knows him or somebody who is wanting to"—she winced—"gain his admiration somehow."

Lilliana sucked in her breath at that.

"That's one idea," Kate noted. "Another option would be that he's potentially directing somebody in that location to do the murders for him. The vicarious element." They just stared at her. "And I know that that would be a whole lot harder to prove," Kate admitted. "I really do know that." She sat down at her desk and added, "I'm also the first one to say my brain isn't functioning this morning, so give it a minute."

"I think it's functioning just fine," the sergeant said from behind her. "Interesting theories. Do you have anything to back it up?"

"Not yet," she admitted. "I'm not even sure I'm on the right pathway. I'm just thinking of ways to explain this," she noted, with her hand out. "Please, somebody come up with some other idea that will make sense."

"Well, that vicarious one does make a sick kind of sense," Lilliana noted, "but I sure hope you're wrong."

"I do too," Kate agreed. "I mean, we put them in prison to stop the killings, not to promote them."

At that, Rodney turned toward her and asked, "Why?" When she frowned at him, he clarified his question. "So, to be clear, you think the kid did this, killing his sister, then went on to recreate her murder through vicarious agents?" She winced. "But why?" Rodney asked her.

She shrugged. "Because ..." But then she stopped. "No," she began again. "I don't even want to toss the rest of this out because I don't have any reason for it. So let's just get to the bottom of what we're working on right now and let me run this around in my brain a little bit longer."

"You could share," Rodney stated. "We won't judge you for it."

She smiled, then nodded and said, "I get that, but I can't even present a logical argument for it yet."

"Has that ever stopped you before?" he asked in a teasing tone.

She laughed. "I get that, and hopefully, when I can wrap my head around it, maybe later today, we can go over it."

Rodney nodded. "Don't wait too long, just in case."

"Got it." She nodded and turned toward her computer and opened up her emails, but her mind was consumed with what had now crossed it. If she was wrong, it would set a dangerous precedent and would send them down a pathway that would take a ton of time that they couldn't afford to waste. And, if she was right, it would be a really bad deal for everybody involved, and she didn't want to go there if she didn't have to.

SIMON WOKE THAT Sunday morning and lay in bed for a long moment. His body was covered in sweat, still trembling from the nightmare. He wasn't just awaking from it, as in jumping out of it, but more of a slow groggy awareness that he was still stuck in the same time frame that this poor woman was. As he opened his eyes, he saw a little bit on the right side—from *her* vision. But everything hurt too much to turn and look. In his head, he whispered, "Turn a bit and let me see. Let me help you. I need some way to find you."

No answer came, as she was heading off into that space in her head where nobody could hurt her. He'd heard of animals and victims in pain finding that space, where they turned and basically gave up, going into a place where they couldn't feel anything anymore.

"You're not done," he told her, willing her to live. "We can find you. We just need time, and we need to know a little bit more about where you are."

Her voice, ever-so-faint, whispered, "It's over."

"No," Simon snapped, sitting up in the bed. "It's not over. Let me see something, anything at all, so we can find you. Is this how you want your family to know that you're gone?"

He felt her weeping, but no tears were on her cheeks, as she had nothing left to cry with. He knew she still had eyes because he could see some shadows, but it was just so hard to sort out what else he was seeing. "Please," he whispered, "please, I know that there's a church window. We saw that through the door, but there has to be something else."

"Are you God?" she whispered.

"No," he replied, realizing that she was starting to lose her grip on reality. "I'm not God, and God is not waiting for you to get there and to join Him," he explained, trying to darken his tone. "What we want is for you to live."

"I don't want to," she whispered. "There's too much pain. I just want to go home now."

He realized that the home she was talking about was the one with God. "I'm so sorry, sweetheart," he whispered. "I'd do anything to help you. But I can't create something out of nothing. I need help from you. Tell me something, anything, like where you were when he caught you. Who is this person? Do you know him?"

Her soft voice whispered, "No."

"You don't know him?"

"No," she repeated. "I don't know why you're punishing me. I don't want to be punished anymore. I just want to die."

He knew all too well that death was coming for her, unless he could get there first. "I'm not punishing you."

"God is," she whispered.

"Why would God punish you?" he asked in confusion.

"He's punishing me," she said again.

"You're not making any sense. Why would God be punishing you?"

"I wasn't supposed to do it."

"Wasn't supposed to do what?"

"It was more of a lark than anything."

"A lark? What was a lark?" he asked.

"A date with a stranger."

He winced at that. "Is that how he found you?"

"Yes," she said on a breath. And she slowly sank deeper under the shadows.

"Wait, wait, please," he cried out. "Stay awake."

"No," she replied. "I'm so tired. I just want to go. Let me come home."

And she started to cry again, deep heart-wrenching sobs that broke his heart. "You don't have to keep paying for this. It wasn't your fault," he told her.

"Yes, I do. I do," she admitted. "This shouldn't be me here. It's not like me at all."

"Did you know who …?" And he stopped because she just said it was a stranger. "Where did you meet him?"

But she didn't answer.

"Can you tell me anything? What does he look like? How old is he? Is he older than you? Is he younger than you?"

"Older," she whispered. "I don't know why I should be punished. It was just a date," she cried out.

"Just a date. But with the wrong somebody. You didn't know until when?"

"Until he caught me. I didn't know until he caught me. I didn't believe it at first, until he hurt me," she whispered through her sobs. "Then how do you forget?"

"You don't," he admitted gently. "Once you're caught by a predator, it's damn near impossible." She started to cry again, and he wished he had words of wisdom to give her. But obviously she was suffering and had been suffering for a long time. "I'm so sorry," he whispered.

"I'm just so ready to go."

"When did he come back?"

"He hasn't been back in so long. Dear God, please, I know that I haven't been good. I know that I probably don't deserve to come to You, but please, make this stop. Please take me with You."

Simon realized that through all this she thought she was talking to the Lord. He didn't care who she was talking to as long as he could get some information. Making his voice deeper, softer, he whispered, "Tell me, child, did you know this man?"

"No," she cried out. "I didn't. I shouldn't have gone with him. I know that now. I was upset. I was depressed and," she added, "I'd had too much to drink."

At that, he wondered if that was a connection between the victims, if the killer sought out women at bars, after having too much to drink.

"Do you know where you are?" he asked in that same soft voice.

"No," she whispered in tears. "I'm alone, always alone."

"You're not alone," Simon argued. "I'm here."

"I want You to take me home." And she started to cry again.

Another voice in the back of her head started yelling at her.

"Shut the fuck up. Just shut the fuck up."

And she tried hard, desperately so, to suck back the tears, but the door slammed open, giving Simon the briefest glimpse of that same window again. Then came a blow to the side of her head, so hard that he heard her neck snap with the force.

"I told you to shut the fuck up," he yelled, and, for the first time, Simon heard that same voice himself.

She tried hard to hold back the sobbing sounds, but it was almost impossible when there was so much pain and when she was suffering so badly.

The second blow knocked her back into unconsciousness, but not before Simon heard the man call her a bitch. A useless bitch. There was something odd about his voice, something off, but then Simon heard the words through a woman who could no longer understand consciousness from unconsciousness—or could differentiate the voice of Simon in her head from the God that she was dearly hoping would save her.

It was all Simon could do to sit here and to hope that something else would happen, but all he sensed was just black darkness, as she sank willingly into the mindless emptiness of unconsciousness. He fell back down on his bed, his head resting in his hands, repeating, "Something had to be there, something useful."

And he thought about it, wondering, was it a church? It looked like a big church, a big rounded window. He thought about it for a long time. However, something was odd about it, yet he didn't know what to tell Kate. What could he tell her now, after she'd wasted all that time looking at churches? Then he had to remind himself that it was hardly a waste since they'd found another victim. And in a building in front of a church. So church was important. He just didn't know if it was the only thing that was important.

As he sat here quietly staring out his bedroom window over the city, he knew he had to get up and get dressed. He had a life of his own, some semblance of normalcy that he had to maintain in his own world. Yet how did one do that when everything else was so destroyed?

Finally he got up, had a shower, and made coffee. When he sat down at his laptop, he checked the news to see if anything was said about the latest victim, and thankfully news of her death was still quiet. He knew it wouldn't last, and, once they caught a whiff of it being a serial killer, the city would be up in arms. And who could blame them? Yet it seemed the city went from one crisis to another.

Was humanity so fucked up that all that they could think about was hurting one another? Causing pain to one another to the extent that they left nothing but broken and damaged people in their wake? How completely wrong was it to think the whole world was so messed up and how all that was out there. Simon knew his own experience was dark and twisted, but he had hoped that other people were having a better time of it. He never really expected his life to be the norm. And it wasn't, and he had to keep reminding himself of that. But, with his association now with Kate—and this same craziness coming up time and time again—he saw ugliness all the time. Not right, not wrong, just the reality of what is.

How did she handle it? Or did she? He hadn't seen her overnight for a couple nights again, and he missed that. He wanted more of that. If nothing else it was a way to ground each other and to let them know that something else was in the world instead of this craziness. That something was precious and special between them. He knew that she needed him as much as he needed her, as he continued on this nightmare pathway.

Only by having that support system—somebody who could understand and could realize how important this need was—could he keep going with this. Otherwise he had to walk away for his own sanity, and, according to his grandmother, that would never happen. There was no sanity left for people like him; it would always be one toe dipped into the dark side.

He didn't ever remember his nan having messages of joy and love and peace. It was always the dark stuff—a child who would die, a serious illness that would take over a family. Was it his inexperience and confusion that let him only see the dark, or was it really all she ever saw as well? Could he change the wavelength somehow so he actually got good news for a change? That might help balance out some of this and make it more tolerable. He didn't know, but it would be something that he needed to work on. He got up, and, carrying his coffee to the big picture window in his living room, he leaned against the wall and stared out.

"Where are you, Kate? What are you doing?"

Almost instantly his phone rang. He fished it from his pocket and stared down, the corner of his mouth twitching when he realized it was Kate. "I was just asking where you are and what you were doing," he murmured into the phone.

There was a moment of silence, and then she replied briskly, "Coincidence."

"If you say so. How are you?"

"Well, I'm at work," she replied, "and dragging ass, but now that I'm into my second cup of coffee, I'm okay. Just checking in on you, before I go to my meeting."

"I'm okay," he noted. "At least I think I am."

"Another dark night?"

"Yes, she's almost done," he relayed sadly. "She thought I was God and kept talking to me as if I were, and she was so ready to go home to God."

"Ouch," she whispered. "That's got to be hard."

"I heard the killer's voice though. He yelled at her, told her to shut the fuck up. That she was a stupid bitch."

"Well, we know he has zero liking and tolerance for women," she noted. "Wait. Does that mean he hasn't cut her vocal cords?"

"I was wondering that myself."

"Anything about the property? Maybe it's remote

enough that he didn't need to keep her quiet."

"I saw the window again," he told her. "But I'm wondering if it could have been on other buildings, not necessarily a church. It's possible, but I'm not sure what else to make of it though. I don't know. I'll take a look around today. I deal with a lot of architects. Maybe somebody would have an idea."

"If you get a lead, let me know," she stated.

"Got it."

"About running out of time—the last thing we want is another victim."

"Do you have anything to go on?"

"Maybe," she replied. "At least I think so. Things are moving now, and, with any luck, we can find her fast."

"Says you," he snapped. "All I can tell you is that she won't last another day."

She whispered, "But that's not unexpected. I'll let you know when we get anything solid. And please let me know if you get anything more."

"I will," he promised and then hung up, staring out at the city he both hated and loved. Right now, it was a toss-up as to how he felt. Always the dark side was present, with so much promise and so much potential, yet, at the same time, so much less than what it could be. All he wanted was to see the good in people and to find and heal the wounds of everyone around him—including the wounds of the buildings he rehabbed.

But he had learned a long time ago not to waste his time, energy, or money on foolish projects. Now he stuck to the ones that he could do something about. And, with that note, he tossed back his coffee and started his day.

CHAPTER 16

KATE WALKED INTO the meeting and dropped her file atop the conference room table. Everybody turned to look at her, and the sergeant smiled.

"Nice of you to join us," he teased gently.

She flushed but stood resolutely. "I know that everybody here understands about Simon, and I get that we're divided on if we believe him or not. But he did just connect with her again."

"Her, the victim?" Owen asked in his decidedly neutral tone of voice.

She appreciated the fact that he was at least being neutral about it. She nodded. "Yes, it seems like in this conversation she thought Simon was God and kept pleading for him to take her home. Essentially that she was done and wouldn't last much longer. He definitely got the impression that she was dying and didn't have more than one day."

A shocked silence came from the others, and then they slowly nodded.

"Given the wounds we've seen on these other victims, it's really not a surprise. Did she say anything more?" Colby asked.

"Not a whole lot. Simon did catch a glimpse of the same window again, but he's wondering if it could be in something other than a church. He said he would take a drive around himself today and talk to some architects he knows."

At that, they looked at each other in surprise.

"You know what?" Lilliana said. "An architect would be a good idea. He's in the building industry, so we'll leave that to him."

"Simon's pretty upset," Kate muttered. "In that latest session, he did hear a man yelling at her to shut up. And called her a fucking bitch."

"So, a degenerative attitude toward women, which also goes along with this torture, then murder MO," Lilliana agreed. "A short temper and likely frustration and finally being done with his prey."

"Yeah, Simon got the idea that the killer was done with her, as in he would get rid of her soon."

"So, either we're out of time or it's already too late?" Rodney asked.

"I don't think it's too late," she noted, "at least not when he talked to her."

"Depends on whether he was talking in real time?" Lilliana guessed.

She shrugged. "I don't know."

"That's the thing about psychics, isn't it?" Owen asked. "One time it's good information, and the next time it seems like it's screwed up. Just like this church thing. We spent how much time—no, you spent how much time looking for windows that matched it?"

"Yet how do I say it was wasted time when it's how we found our latest victim," she reminded him.

"I know. That's what I mean, but it was so vague, and now Simon's wondering if it's a church window after all."

"I get it," she agreed. "I just don't know what I'm supposed to do about it. I can only tell you what he told me."

"So, why don't you fill us in on what you thought you were thinking of earlier," Rodney suggested.

She looked at him in surprise. "Oh, that." She looked down at her paperwork. "Back to the vicarious theory, I guess I'm wondering if the kid has a partner." She looked up from her notes. "And if it's somebody close to him."

"What do you mean?" Lilliana asked.

"I think the kid's directing this. Or at least somebody in his circle is directing this." Kate hesitated.

"So, somebody is actually giving orders, and somebody else is following them?" Rodney clarified.

"Does that fit with the angry man who we suspect has Chelice?" Colby asked.

"I don't know," she admitted, "unless he's waiting for instructions or waiting for a sign or waiting for I don't know what." She raised both hands. "But the fact that the kid was physically there in these provinces at the same time as these women were being killed makes me very suspicious that it's either somebody moving along with him—as in authority figures even, perhaps healthcare individuals, or somebody who came to visit him, or somebody he had contact with on the outside, and the kid was actively participating in the tortures and the murders."

"We're going back to motive then," Colby stated.

"And I don't know what that is. I was doing another check into his sister, who we think is victim zero, but she was a fairly innocent teenager."

"Not that innocent," Owen argued. "She was very heavily involved in church, in *fixing* a lot of things. But she was anti-drugs, anti a lot of stuff on the surface. Did you know that the family was pretty broke?"

She looked over at him and shook her head. "No, I

hadn't heard that."

"They were, and there was talk that they got a life insurance settlement on her."

Her jaw dropped. "On the daughter?"

Owen nodded. "I'm getting confirmation of that now. There was a policy, but I don't have confirmation yet that it was paid out."

"Jesus, but, if it was on a child, it wouldn't be very much, would it?"

"It was ten thousand dollars," he replied.

"I would really hope that nobody would kill her for ten thousand dollars," she replied slowly.

"People have killed for far less," the sergeant reminded her.

"I know," she admitted. "The world sucks, and we don't need any more reminders of that fact. But that doesn't seem like a big enough motive for the torture element."

"No, and I don't know about the torture either, unless it was to throw us off. And then what? Somebody decided they liked it?" Colby asked.

At that, they looked around at each other.

"You know that happens," the sergeant stated. "It's not the most common methodology of developing a serial killer, but, if you actually participate in something, and then you enjoyed it to the extent that you couldn't stop thinking about it, you would turn around and do it all over again. I mean, in the sense that you've already killed once, therefore, the value of life is obviously pretty low."

She added, "It's possible, but it still feels like we're missing something."

"It might *feel* like we're missing something," Rodney noted slowly, "but it does feel like we're getting somewhere."

She agreed with that. "We need to do a full rundown on the kid's whole family," she stated. "The father—who is actually the stepfather—and the mother. His birth father died years ago. The stepfather had been the only father those two kids ever remembered having. The kid himself stated he didn't have any friends, at least none that lasted into jail."

"Does he have any other family though? Any uncles or cousins? Anybody with a rap sheet? Anybody that's bad news?" Colby asked. When nobody replied, he snapped, "Then check it out and get back to me." He left the conference room.

With that, they all split up, grabbed a character out of the family tree, and started a hunt. As she sat down to look at the mother, Rodney walked over to her. "There's an uncle with a rap sheet," he noted. "And it's the mother's brother. The trouble is, he's dead."

She looked up at him in surprise. "Are you thinking he had something to do with any of these?"

"No," he replied thoughtfully, "but I do agree with you. I think it's somebody close to the Lord family."

Kate nodded. "Either somebody close to the kid and his family or somebody who's followed him, like a fan of his work."

"We never did ask him if he got any letters."

"He told me that he did. How he got marriage proposals even."

"Do you think this is the work of a woman?"

"No," she denied flatly. "But nobody said all the marriage proposals were from females either."

"True enough."

She reached for her phone and contacted Rick Lord. He answered, saying, "It's my only day off in like ten days,

Detective."

"We have some more questions. Can I come over and talk to you?"

"Jesus," he moaned. "Do you have to?"

"Yeah, I have to," she snapped. "This is important."

"Fine. Why don't we meet somewhere else? My dad is having a bad day."

She thought about it, except … "I also need to talk to your mom," she stated slowly.

"Oh no, she's got enough on her hands."

"It won't take long."

"Hell no," he yelled. "You leave my mom out of it. I'll cooperate with whatever you need, but keep her out of it."

"Why don't I just come there, and we'll talk outside."

He hesitated. "Fine," but a surliness in his voice came clearly through the phone.

"Hey, we're just trying to solve this."

"Yeah, I wish you'd put this much effort into it last time," he snapped. "When are you coming?"

"We'll be there in about twenty minutes," she said.

"Fine." And he hung up.

"He's not happy about it, and he wanted to meet somewhere else," she explained to Rodney. "I guess his dad's having a bad time."

"And with good reason," Rodney noted.

She hopped up. "I'll go talk to Rick."

"And what is it you'll ask him?" The sergeant raised an eyebrow, as he joined them in the bullpen.

"For any letters that he has from jail. For anybody who may have followed him from one place to the next, and, outside of his parents, any other family members who knew what Rick did or what he confessed to, who he had talked to about it, and who may have seen him in any of the other provinces."

"Right." Colby nodded. "Take Rodney with you."

She looked at him in surprise. "I don't need anybody with me."

"Take Rodney with you," he repeated. "That's an order."

She frowned and looked over at Rodney. "Sorry."

He shrugged. "It's all good."

They headed outside. "Figured I'd drive," she stated.

"You're not too tired?" he teased.

"No, I got enough caffeine flowing through me now," she mentioned. "I should be good for another couple days."

He snorted. "I sure as hell hope not. I don't want to be running for that long."

It took them longer to get to the house than expected.

By the time she pulled up to the front curb, Rick was pacing the sidewalk outside and threw up his hands when he saw her. She hopped out, checked to make sure there was no traffic around and that parking where she did was okay, then she walked around to lean against the car. "Hey."

"Why the hell are you still bugging me?" Rick asked her.

"Because we have another body."

He stopped and stared at her. "Jesus."

She nodded. "So"—she pulled out her notepad—"what I need from you is any letters, any emails, anything along that line that you got from fans or enemies the whole time you were in jail. Hate mail, love mail, whatever, from anybody who might have followed you around to all those provinces."

He shook his head.

"Are you saying there wasn't any?"

He nodded. "Yes, sure there were a few love letters and plenty of hate mail."

"You never told us about the hate mail before."

"I didn't even keep it. It came through the prison email system. And I just hit Delete. Nobody wants that shit."

"Anybody contact you more than once?"

"Yeah, a couple people," he replied. "There was one very persistent female. She was pretty angry and upset."

"Why?"

He shrugged. "What do I know? She seemed to think I was the worst of the worst."

"Anybody else?"

"No, I corresponded with a couple young ladies because they were cute, and it was nice to have something to keep me in good spirits, but it's not like it carried on for very long. It was just fun at the time. More toward the end of my time, when emails were easier."

"Right," she noted. "So, if I understand this, people can contact you via a website?"

He nodded. "And honestly, as much as I'm sure you guys hate it, it does give us a little bit of sanity while we're inside."

"So you don't have any idea of who else might have done these murders?"

"No," he replied. "And I don't understand why you're still looking at me."

"It's not so much that we're looking at you," she explained, "but your sister appears to be ground zero."

"That would be very depressing," he noted. "But, at the same time, you know that's not my fault."

"No, outside of the persisting fact that you confessed, so the entire investigation was derailed."

He raised his hands in frustration. "How long do I have to keep paying for that?"

"I'm not sure." She faced him, studying him carefully. He was a little bit nervous, but then he was being called out on something that he was protesting. Whether you were innocent or guilty, everybody got nervous when they were talked to by the cops like this. "What about your family?" she asked.

"What about them?" he asked. "My mother came to visit me. Both my parents came. At one point in time an uncle came too."

"What uncle?"

He frowned. "You probably already tracked him down since he's got a criminal record of his own."

"For armed robbery?"

"Yes, armed robbery but not murder. And definitely not torture. That should be good then, right?"

"It means they're about power and abuse, maybe even religion."

At the word *religion*, he paled ever-so-slightly and took a half step back. "That just sounds like some fanatic," he said, muttering to himself. He looked back nervously at the house. "Please don't even bring this up to my mother. She's having a tough enough time."

"I get it," she replied. "I definitely do."

"Yeah, what do *you* get?" he asked, with a sneer. "You have no idea and nothing to do with everything in my world."

"No, of course not, but that doesn't mean I don't get all the problems."

He groaned. "Fine, maybe you get some of it. Just please don't get a hold of my mother anymore."

"She believed in you the whole time, didn't she?"

"She did," he agreed. "But she only had two kids, and one was gone."

"And you were doing a lot of drugs back then, right?"

"I already told you that."

"Did any of your friends get into torture like this?"

"No," he stated, "at least not that I know of. How the hell would I know?"

"I don't know," she replied, trying for a neutral tone.

Rodney was just off to her side, studying Rick. "So, how often did your uncle come visit you?"

"You mean, when he wasn't in jail himself? You can check his jail time against the murders. I'm sure it'll probably exonerate him."

"That check is in process now," Rodney confirmed.

"It should be a quick phone call," Rick stated.

She smiled. "So, who else?"

"What do you mean, who else?" he asked.

"Your parents."

"Only them, yes, only my parents came to visit me," he repeated. "And I don't know if people were following me, like some fan club. And, if I didn't know about it, what can I say?"

"Nothing," she agreed.

"Did you ever get any DNA from any of the other sites?" Rick asked.

"One," she replied, "and the current one we're checking right now but haven't heard back from Forensics."

"This guy has been really clean," Rick noted.

"Yes, at least since the beginning."

He nodded. "He was clean then too. It was just me and my family, but then we all lived there." He turned to stare at the house. "I can't imagine what Mom went through."

"Neither can I," Kate noted. "So you have nothing to give us? No names, no dates, no nothing?"

He spun back a little too quickly for her liking. "I already told you that."

"Okay, fine," she stated. "Now I'll talk to your mom. Either I can go knock on the front door or you can send her out to talk to me." He frowned at her, but she held up a hand. "Don't even start. We need to talk to her."

"Fine. Okay, I'll send her out. Please don't upset her." He turned and stormed up the stairs.

She turned to look at Rodney. "What do you think?"

"Something isn't adding up."

"Yeah, we need that DNA," she stated. "You want to make a phone call?"

He nodded. "You already knew the uncle, that his visits and the murders didn't line up with his jail terms, didn't you?"

She nodded. "Yeah, I figured as much."

"Are you still looking at the kid?" Rodney asked.

"It's around the kid. It's about the kid. I just don't know how much of it *is* the kid."

He nodded. "It's pretty sad to think that this could be going on."

As she looked up, Rick's mother stepped out onto the porch and waved them to join her. "I'm not coming down there," she stated. "I can't do stairs at the best of times."

"How do you get up there?" Kate asked.

"Well, the house is built into a hill, in case you didn't notice," she explained. "So the car is on the ground level at the back of the house, with easy access inside for me. So I avoid these front steps that are just hard on my knees."

Kate realized that the older woman walked with a decided limp. "I'm sorry. Are you all right?"

"Nothing that time won't heal," she replied, with a wave of her hand. "Now my son said you have more questions. Have you cleared him yet?"

"I'm sorry," she stated. "We're still working on that."

The woman snorted. "You know he'll be dead of old age before you ever get that fixed, right?"

"We're working on it," Kate repeated gently. "When you visited your son in prison ..." Kate began, and then she asked the mother the same questions that she had asked Rick. Neither were too happy about answering them. Had to be done regardless.

She and Rodney returned to her car. "Let's go check out their previous home, the site of the first murder, and let me just take in the whole scene." And that's what they did.

Unfortunately it led them nowhere.

CHAPTER 17

I N THE DARK of evening, Kate directed Simon to drive to a corner where Kate thought they would be best hidden, where she and Simon had a full view of the back of the kid's house.

"You know they could go out the front door," Simon noted.

She nodded. "I know, but I'm expecting that, wherever they're going, they need to drive, so they'll need the vehicle."

"You're thinking it's all of them?" he asked, horror filling in his voice.

She shook her head. "No, and I don't really know yet," she admitted. "There's only really one viable suspect."

He frowned. "I get that, but you think the killer would have learned that by now."

She smiled at him. "Maybe." She settled back into her seat, sniffed the air, and asked, "What did you buy?"

He snorted. "You said, *coffee and take-out burgers,* so I bought lots of both."

She stared at him. "Lots?" she asked in a surprised tone.

"Well, how long will we be here for?"

"You're into cold burgers?"

"Absolutely," he replied. "After growing up not knowing when food would be available," he explained, "I don't turn down burgers, hot or cold."

She shook her head. "Are you telling me that you'll turn on the engine, open the hood, and warm them in there or something, if needed?"

He grinned. "You know that trick too, do you?"

"Are you kidding? A whole cult of people cook on the manifold," she noted, chuckling.

He reached around into the back seat and pulled up the fast-food burgers. Immediately the smell of salty, greasy fries and burgers filled the air, and her stomach rumbled in joy. "I wish you would feel the same way about smoked salmon and caviar."

"Never had either," she replied, as she reached for a burger.

He reached out and snagged her wrist, staring at her. "Seriously?"

She looked up at him. "Cop job, cop salary. No time, no money. Remember?"

"We'll have to fix that."

She rolled her eyes. "Not everybody has your money, you know? I don't even know how you make your money because no way buying all these shitty old buildings and fixing them up is making you the big bucks."

He chuckled. "You'd be surprised. What's unusable to some is a gold mine for others."

"And what does that do for your conscience then?"

"My conscience is clear because some of them go to low-income housing, some of them go to senior centers, some of them go to families who need a helping hand."

She stopped and looked at him. "Like women's shelters?"

"I support a large number of those as well," he noted quietly. "But they aren't ones that most people know about."

She nodded. "I get it," she replied. "The ones set up by women in trouble, knowing what it's like to be out there on the streets, when they've got an abusive husband or boyfriend after them. Way too many of those kind of men are out there." She unwrapped her burger, looked at it, and gave him a fat grin. "You got pickles and fried onions on the burgers?"

He shuddered. "At least you got the right burger."

"Why? What's on yours?" she asked curiously.

He unwrapped it to see bacon and cheese.

She shrugged. "Well, that's pretty boring."

"No," he argued, "it's not boring. It's conventional."

"Says the man who likes smoked salmon and caviar."

He shook his head. "Absolutely no way you will convince me that what you're eating right now is on the same level as smoked salmon and caviar."

She batted her eyes at him. "You have to be adventurous, you know? If you expect me to try your two items, then you should try this." She handed over her burger.

He shook his head, pushed back the burger, and said, "No way in hell."

She glared and then chuckled. "That's good because I'm really not into sharing." Then she took a huge bite.

He watched in amazement as the burger went down faster than he could have imagined. "Have you eaten at all today?"

She shook her head. "I don't remember," she replied, "so I'll say no. My stomach has been screaming at me all day." She rummaged in the bag, looking for more food and immediately pulled out fries and stuck four in her mouth right off the bat. She looked over at him. "You would share the fries, right?"

"You can have it all," he noted, "if you're that hungry."

"I'd never eat it all," she replied.

"Well then, slow down and pace yourself," he suggested.

She shook her head. "Nope, I'll need fuel soon."

"And why is that?"

"Either you'll do a lot of driving or I'll do a lot of running."

He instantly took in her feet. *Sneakers.* "I didn't come dressed for running," he noted. "I mean, obviously I can do a mile or two," he said, as he looked down at his leather loafers.

She snorted. "You don't worry about that. I'll go after him. You'll have to stay and keep watch on the house, if it comes to that."

At that, he stopped and looked at her. "What are you expecting?"

"Not expecting anything," she said cheerfully. "Yet I'm open to seeing just what occurs."

"And if nothing happens?"

"Then it'll be a damn long tiring night," she stated, "and I'll be frustrated and pissed off come morning."

"But somehow I don't think you'll be that way, will you?"

"I sure as hell hope not," she agreed, "because that poor woman in your visions doesn't have much longer." Immediately his appetite fled. He slowly lowered his hand with the burger; she watched him and whispered, "I'm sorry. You need to eat."

"No," he argued. "Here. You have it."

"You eat it, just in case we need your energy."

"Well, unlike you," he replied, "I had breakfast and lunch, and I think a bagel was in there somewhere as well."

"A bagel?" She stared at him in outrage. "Where the hell are you finding fresh bagels?"

"Did I say it was fresh?"

"It's you," she noted, rolling her eyes. "You don't buy anything but the good stuff."

"I try not to," he agreed. "That doesn't mean it always works that way."

"It works mostly though," she stated. "It's disgusting actually."

"Why is that?"

"Because I really love bagels."

"Oh, I didn't know that," he said. "I could have picked up some."

"You could have," she agreed cheerfully. "But, in the meantime, I'll take care of this." She snatched a second burger.

He did finish off his burger, but now it tasted like sawdust to him, though she was able to eat hers with great relish. "I do appreciate an appetite. I just wish it came from commonsense eating habits and not because your stomach is finally getting fed."

She grinned at him. "It'll be hard to break those habits."

"I'll work on it though," he muttered.

She shrugged. "More power to you, just don't expect any cooperation out of me."

He sighed. "You don't have to be difficult about it."

"I'm not, but I really don't see the point of worrying about it. When the next meal comes, I eat. When it doesn't come, well then, I guess I don't eat."

"You know that you can't keep on like that."

"So people keep telling me," she admitted, feeling the frustration build.

He immediately held up his hand. "Hey, I'm not here to nag you."

"Could have fooled me."

He sighed. "Why don't you just pour some coffee? That'll make you feel better."

She immediately brightened. "You know what? You're right. Can't argue if you've got a coffee in your hand."

He chuckled. "Is that all it takes to stop an argument?"

She nodded. "Pretty much, but, in your case, you need a bottle of wine, a beer, or a shot of whiskey. Me? I'm good with coffee."

"Do you ever think about switching to tea?"

She stopped in the act of reaching for the big jug of coffee in the back seat and stared at him.

"Hey, hey, hey, calm down," he said, interpreting her look as one of complete madness. "It was just a question."

"For the future," she noted, "I have found very little tea that's actually drinkable."

He sighed. "You know that people all over the world would argue with you."

"Then they can drink it," she stated instantly.

He started to laugh. "You're never short of an answer either, are you?"

"Doesn't do me any good to be short on answers," she replied. "People around me are always talking in circles. Or asking endless questions. It's irritating."

"I can't imagine that anybody is doing that," he argued in surprise. "You always seem to be one up on every conversation."

"No, not at all," she admitted. "Sometimes I feel like I'm being completely left out of conversations."

"Is that because you don't get it or because you're so

busy working that you're missing all the joking around you?"

She thought about it seriously for a moment, while she poured coffee. "You know what? It could be the latter. I hadn't really considered that."

"You do know that to make friends, you have to actually be friendly, right?"

"Yeah, that's another fact that's been revealed to me lately," she grumbled. "Who knew being part of a team was such a pain in the butt?"

"Weren't you always part of a team as a cop?"

"Sure, I was," she stated, "but they were used to me. I feel like I have to train these ones all over again."

He stared at her for a moment, and then his shoulders started shaking. She looked over at him, with a quiet satisfaction inside. He didn't know she was joking, but, at the same time, it made her feel good that she could lighten his day. He'd been way too serious and way too sad, when he had picked her up. It worried her to see what all these visions were doing to him, especially when she could do so little to help him.

When he finally calmed down, she held out a coffee and asked, "You want one?"

"Absolutely. It doesn't look like I'll be getting any sleep tonight anyway."

"Nope, you're probably not." She chuckled.

"Are you always this much fun on a stakeout?"

"Oh, hell no," she said. "But I'm here for a reason, and I feel really confident that the outcome will make me happy."

He looked at her. "Do you want to explain?"

"No. I didn't really say too much about it to the guys at work either. I know they were curious, but, having nothing to justify what intuitively I feel is the right answer, won't make me any brownie points."

"You could always suggest it as a theory."

"I do that all the time, but sometimes they don't like hearing them."

"Or is it just that you have a tendency to always be right?"

"It's not my fault," she argued. "Besides, I'm the rookie here, so I have to work twice as hard."

"Why is that?" he asked in surprise.

"Well, I feel like I have to justify my position each time I think these things out loud."

"Oh, I think you've done that already," he noted in amazement. "How could you possibly think that you're not worthy of that job? And it goes along with that whole 'trying so hard to get there' thing. Maybe just calm down and be more of a team member."

"And now you're starting to sound like my boss too."

He winced. "Not trying to."

"No, but I know when multiple people say the same thing over and over again, maybe there's something behind it," she admitted. "And I get it, and I am really working hard on it. I've been working really closely with Rodney on this whole case—and not just us either. The others have really stepped in and have helped out too."

"Is it something that you all work on?"

"Yes, but sometimes we each catch different cases, and we work those too. When we're waiting on whatever and don't have anything to work on at the moment, then we help out the others. We're all supposed to be part of the same team."

"Yeah, when you say, *supposed to*—"

"It's just a carryover from when I first started there.

Honestly the entire atmosphere is very different now, and I really appreciate the change."

"Good." Then he motioned around them. "So how come they're not on the stakeout with you?"

"I would have brought Rodney, but his kid had a birthday today."

"Ah, that's a good reason. Best not to take him away from his family."

"There's very little in our world that allows us to have special moments, except for things like this," she noted. "So we have to honor them when we can get them."

"And I appreciate the fact that you called me instead of one of the other team members."

"Well, honestly"—she winced—"you won't like this."

"What? I was the last choice?"

"Actually I was gonna come out here alone, except my sergeant told me not to."

"Right, so not only was I the last choice," he noted, "I'm the only choice."

At that, she burst out laughing. "No, that's not true. I could have hauled in somebody else from the team, but I thought about who I'd like to spend all these hours with, and you're the one person who came to mind." She leaned over and kissed him gently on the cheek.

He stared at her in surprise.

She shrugged. "What? I'm not allowed to do things like that?"

"Always, of course you're allowed to," he replied, his voice low. "It's just that you never do."

She stared at him nonplussed. "Sure I do."

He shook his head. "No, you don't."

She frowned, feeling like another argument was about to

break, when she glanced at the house and whispered, "Action." She didn't even know if he understood what she meant, but she pointed, and he immediately turned and stared.

"Is that the garage door opening?"

"Yes," she replied. "Now the question will be, who is the driver and where is he going?"

"Well, I sure as hell hope he'll go to the right place, so we can find that poor woman."

"That's the plan," she stated, "so keep the lights off and don't start the engine just yet."

"Fine," he said, "but you should know I've done a little of this in my time."

"Yeah, but probably on the other side of the law."

"What do you know about that?" he asked in surprise.

She shrugged. "I figure anybody who had the history you did probably went wild for a bit."

"I did, but I also came back to the straight and narrow."

"You sure did, which is the only reason you're here right now." She nodded. "Get ready."

He watched as an SUV approached, its darkened windows rolled up. "We won't see the driver, will we?"

"I'm looking," she replied, "but it's damn hard to see anything."

"Isn't that the mother's vehicle?"

"Yes," she agreed, "but did you notice that she has a limp and a hearing aid?"

"No, I didn't," he replied, "but how the hell did you see a hearing aid?"

"She kept fiddling with it, like she couldn't quite get the right tone."

"Damn."

She could tell Simon was pissed off that he had missed it.

"So, just because there's a hearing aid, what does that mean?"

"Maybe nothing," she replied, "but let's go."

Immediately he turned on the engine and eased into the roadway, a good distance behind the vehicle. "No way a woman would do that to another woman," he noted.

"You mean, you're hoping no way a woman would do that."

"It was her daughter. No way. I refuse to believe any parent would do something so horrific to their daughter."

"Yeah, what happened to you?"

"Shit," he muttered under his breath.

She nodded. "Parents of all kinds do not always show themselves as the best people on earth. Some are good, and some are bad. So we learn to deal with both."

"Says you." He followed the vehicle carefully. "Now we don't have anybody watching the house."

"I know," she noted. "I'm putting all my eggs in one basket here. I sure as hell wish I had somebody else to watch back there."

He frowned. "I do know somebody in that area."

She looked at him in surprise. "Yeah?"

"And, if you don't ask too many questions, I could ask him to sit and to keep an eye on the house for me."

She pondered it for a long moment and then said, "Do it."

He pulled out his phone, while driving carefully, and made a call. She listened in on Simon's half of the conversation that made no sense, and, when he hung up, he turned and looked at her. "Done."

"Okay, now do you want to explain that to me?"

"No, remember the no-asking-questions part?"

Frustrated, she glared at him. "I could make you."

"You could, and you would end a great relationship with this guy."

"Shit. Please tell me at least it's not a criminal."

"It's not a criminal," he said instantly.

Unfortunately his reply was a little too instant for her liking. She sighed. "Make sure he doesn't do anything criminal while he's there."

"He won't. He's just keeping an eye on the house to see if anybody comes or goes."

"That's what I need," she stated.

"Exactly, so stop complaining and let me do what I need to do."

She groaned. "Are you always this bossy? Turn, turn, turn."

"Talk about bossy," he muttered, as he followed the vehicle. They were heading closer toward the station. "Interesting direction."

"Well, they'll have to be someplace where there isn't a whole lot of traffic. I suppose if you torture women for fun you don't keep her someplace where anybody'll stumble across her."

"Exactly."

As they kept driving, she said, "It's really important to make sure he doesn't see us."

"And how will he figure that out?" he asked.

"Well, this is a fairly distinctive vehicle."

"I am being careful, plus it's also dark out."

"And yet," she noted, "it's not all that dark."

He thought about it, then nodded and asked, "What do

you want me to do?"

"Depends. Wherever he turns off, we'll have to go past him, so he doesn't suspect, then go around the block."

"Right, I can do that."

She looked over at him, as he expertly handled the vehicle in and out of traffic, staying close but not close enough to be noticed. "You've done this a time or two, haven't you?"

"Sure have. My misspent youth, remember?"

"Yeah, I was trying not to ask too many questions."

"Good. What is it they say? Ask me no questions, and I'll tell you no lies."

She winced. "Please tell me that what you did wasn't too bad."

"Nope, not bad."

But just enough extra brightness filled his tone that she realized she didn't want to know about that time in his life.

They followed the vehicle another few minutes onto Grandview Highway, then Broadway and still on down.

"Interesting," she murmured. "We're heading into a more commercial area."

"Hell, all kinds of buildings are down here," he noted.

"Do you know this area well?"

"Fairly well. I'm just trying to picture in my mind where they would be going."

"Anything with that window you saw?"

"I suspect it'll be a subtle window."

"And yet you saw it."

"I did, and I haven't been able to see it since, other than in the vision."

"Right."

Just then the vehicle ahead of them turned into another lane and made a left off the main road.

He held up a hand as she started to give him orders. "I got this."

She watched impatiently as he did, indeed, have it, and he turned onto the side road, and she whispered, "Goddammit, where are they? Where are they?"

"Up ahead."

"Are you sure?"

"Yes, I can see the lights."

She settled back ever-so-slightly. "I sure hope so. We can't take a chance of losing him now."

"I got it," he repeated. "A little bit of trust will go a long way tonight."

"I'm not used to taking rookies out on stakeouts."

At that, he snorted. "I probably have more experience with nightlife and hunting than all your rookies combined. Including yourself."

"Maybe so. We'll have to talk about that sometime."

"Not unless you can, uh, put aside the cop persona," he said cheerfully.

She sighed. "It's bad, isn't it?"

"Sometimes."

Just then, the vehicle turned right, and then as they came around the corner, they sought a left.

"We're made," she whispered.

"Nope, not at all. That's a parkade."

"What do you mean, *parkade*?"

"It's an old parking garage that is being expanded to support a big set of labs and a residential care facility and some nursing facility—if I remember the briefing I read on it."

"But it's an old building, like empty?"

"Yes, empty. I'm not at all sure about that window

though." He hated the fact that he might have been so wrong about the window because the last thing he wanted to do was find out that there was yet another victim. "Any idea why there are so many victims right now?"

"Partially," she replied, "but I suspect we won't really know until we actually catch him. The last victim was killed quickly, in case I didn't tell you that. I figured, from looking at her, most of the injuries were postmortem."

"That's good for her," he replied.

"I haven't heard yet what exactly killed her, but it could be anything from a heart attack to the drugs he gave them to keep them subdued."

"Right, just because he understands dosing for one doesn't mean it's the same for all, and overdoses are way too easy to administer if you're not familiar with the drugs," he explained.

"Horrible thought," she replied.

"Yes, indeed, and yet, at the same time, this is very helpful if we're in the right area." Just then he pulled into where the car had turned.

"Don't you think they'll see us?" she muttered.

"No, not now anyway. He's up on the second floor. He shut off the lights as he turned into the parkade."

"Well, at least he can't see us now."

"No, he can't see us, but, as soon as he stops, he'll hear us."

She waited and watched as the vehicle circled up higher and higher. "Crap, how high up is he going?" she asked.

"If it was me, I would go all the way up. It is the easiest way to get rid of a body."

She nodded. "In this case it might be just to throw her off the roof."

"I wouldn't be at all surprised."

"I wonder if he just picks old deserted buildings every time," she wondered.

"That brings you back to case number one."

"I know," she admitted. "Case number one, the one that's also important."

Simon pulled into a parking spot. "We're one floor down from the top. I don't think we should go up any higher."

"I got this," she whispered, as she slid out.

"I'm coming with you." She immediately turned to protest, but he held up a hand. "Stop. I'm coming."

She frowned. "You have to stay behind me."

"I got that," he whispered, "I promise I'll do everything you say, but you are not going up there alone."

She just glared at him.

He shook his head. "It's either that or I'll make noise right now," he threatened.

"And he'll kill her," she murmured. "There's no place up there for him to go."

"But this building connects to the one beside it," he explained. "That's the purpose of the parkade. It was for this big complex that was here. It's an old apartment building, and it had the parkade because a lot of other businesses were around here too. So a door here connects to the building that's nearby, and it's deserted as well."

"How do you know that?"

"Because I looked at it at one point, but they were asking way the hell too much money."

"Of course they were," she muttered. "Everybody's hoping to make a buck."

"In this case they wanted to make millions, like a couple

dozen."

She stared at him in shock, and then she gave a quick shake of her head. "Come on. We have to go."

Closing the door ever-so-quietly and leaving it unlocked so the locks being engaged didn't actually *beep*, she raced around to the front end, where the ramp was slightly lit up one way. Climbing up higher and higher, she watched carefully—as soon as they could see over the top of the concrete partitions, to see if there was any sign of anybody. She heard footsteps up ahead. She followed carefully, keeping a respectful distance behind while trying to keep quiet. No sound came from Simon either. She turned to look, and he was walking as smoothly and as quietly as anybody could, yet he didn't have runners on. That suggested a level of expertise that they definitely needed to talk about.

When she thought about that for a moment, she realized it was probably better if they didn't. There were only so many lines she could cross when it came to her work. Something was between them, and she wasn't quite ready to break up yet. Maybe never. But that wasn't something she was even prepared to look at right now.

When she heard a door open and saw a light shining up ahead, she broke into a run. Still no way to tell who the suspect was. A baseball cap was on his head—or hers for that matter. As Kate raced quietly forward, she came to the door and stopped. She looked over at Simon and whispered, "Do you know what's on the other side of this door?"

He nodded. "A long hallway and then it opens into offices."

"Are the walls still here?"

"Some," he whispered, "but not very many."

She nodded and opened the door, but light from the parkade shone into the hallway, and she winced at that. With her handgun out, she couldn't find anybody ahead of her, as she stepped inside. With Simon right behind her, staying close, they quietly raced down the hallway and came up to the first of the offices. She immediately flattened against the wall, and he followed suit. She stared at him.

Quietly she whispered, "Can you think of any place here where they would likely keep her?"

He nodded grimly. "Yeah, I have a damn good idea now." And, with that, he said, "I'll lead."

Not giving her a chance to argue, he bolted ahead, staying close to the wall, until he came to a corner. She was right behind him, as he held back a hand in warning. She waited to see what he would say, when she heard a voice, an angry voice.

"Fucking bitch," he snapped. "Why couldn't you have died yet? Jesus Christ, the last one died in two seconds. I didn't even get a chance to have any fun with her, and you? Jesus, you just won't quit. Do you actually think somebody will come and save you or something?"

Kate barely recognized the voice, but, in her heart of hearts, she knew who it was.

She stepped in front of Simon, raced around the corner, and then, with her flashlight and service weapon drawn together and pointed directly at his face, she yelled, "Police! Hands up!"

He stopped and looked straight at her, then started swearing. She stared into the eyes of a killer, a man who hadn't stopped since the very first time, when his stepdaughter had died in his arms.

She looked at Rick's stepfather and asked, "How do you

keep your wife from knowing all this is going on?"

"She thinks because I take my drugs that she can take hers. She thinks it's safe for her to sleep when I am." He gave Kate a rough smile. "Little does she know what comes out to play when darkness falls."

"She has no idea, does she?" Kate asked.

"No," he said. "How the hell did you figure it out?"

"It got to the point where there were really no other options, and there could only be one choice," she replied quietly.

He shook his head. "No way. I worked really hard to pin these on my stepson."

"Yeah, you did, and it worked the first time, didn't it?"

"Of course, and then I picked two in Alberta at different times," he told her, laughing.

"And two in Saskatchewan."

Immediately the smile fell from his face. "You found those, did you?"

She nodded. "How many overall?"

"I don't know that I counted," he replied, with a sneer. "What does it matter to you?"

"It matters to the families who would like closure." She approached slowly. "Put your hands over your head."

"No, I don't feel like it. What will you do about it?"

She immediately cocked the gun. "I'll shoot you."

"It doesn't matter to me," he told her. "I knew the game would be up soon. You were sniffing around too damn much, and I couldn't figure out how to throw you off."

"Once we found the last crime scene," she noted, "there really weren't too many other options."

He stopped and stared. "You found her? You found Lacy?"

She nodded. "Unfortunately we didn't find her fast enough." She shifted, so she could take a quick look at who he'd been yelling at earlier. And there was her missing persons' victim. As she turned her head back again to see him, he had moved.

"Oh no, you don't," she stated. "I might as well put a bullet through your head right now."

From her side, the woman, her voice faint, said, "Please do, dear God, just do it."

"You just focus on staying alive. I mean it," she snapped. "I mean it. We've worked really hard to find you."

The woman started to cry, and Kate heard Simon's voice gently speaking to Chelice.

Kate aimed her gun and repeated, "Hands up and don't give me any of your shit. Then get down on the floor where I can see you."

"Nope, you'll have to shoot me in cold blood. Of course you can't do that."

"Why do you think that?" she asked, but inside she was just pissed enough, wondering how she would get this guy to cooperate, without ... and then she smiled. "You know what? I don't really need your cooperation."

And, with that, she lowered her weapon and blew out his right knee. Screaming, he dropped to the ground, unable to sustain himself on his feet.

"That's police brutality," he roared.

"No," she replied, "it's a taste of your own medicine." She quickly holstered her weapon and pulled out her handcuffs. Keeping a close eye on him, knowing he was a tricky bastard even now, she quickly moved around behind him, then pulled his arms back and handcuffed him. Feeling better about that, she quickly disarmed him, removing a knife, screwdrivers, scissors, pliers, and some other tool that she didn't recognize, until she realized it was something for cutting off fingers.

She swore as she stacked his stash off to the side and then pulled out her phone and called for backup. "Now your wife will have the worst day of her life."

"Not yet," he said. "Not yet."

"She will when she finds out that you did all these murders," she argued.

"She doesn't want to know. I used to beat her up all the time," he explained. "I'm the one who put her in the hospital when we were in Alberta. I needed her out of the way, so I could go murder a couple more women."

"Why murder them?" Simon asked.

The guy looked over at him. "You don't really understand how much fun it is to torture and murder until you actually get a chance to do it," he explained. "We're built, taught by society, not to do these things, that they're wrong and that they're painful and that they hurt. But they don't hurt us, they only hurt the victims. And, by the time you get dulled to their cries, you actually start to miss it," he shared in a conversational tone. "You just don't understand until you've been there."

"And is that what you did to all your victims? You just missed those feelings, so you had to keep doing more and more murders? I get the last one died on you too fast, so you had to pick our poor girl here to continue your sick hobby," she noted. "But what about your stepdaughter?"

"That stupid bitch," he muttered. "That was a sad deal. I didn't mean for her to die that way. But she caught me with somebody else, so there wasn't anything I could do. I had to take her out. I had been experimenting, you see, on the best ways to keep them alive and to extend the pain. I mean, this latest bitch here is a good example." He pointed at her. "I've kept her alive for a long time. I mean, you should be thanking me."

"Really?" she asked. "That's actually not what I was thinking." She stepped over to look at the woman on the table, both ankles and both wrists broken, with slices across her chest and her belly. Kate reached out and touched the woman's neck, checking for her pulse.

"I'm here," she whispered, "please don't take your eyes off him."

"I blew his knee apart," she told her quietly, "and I'll take out the other one if he moves a muscle. Don't you worry. This asshole isn't going anywhere but jail."

The woman then started to cry in earnest.

Kate looked over at Simon and said, "Keep an eye on her. Help is on the way."

He nodded, and she could see he was already administering first aid. She turned back to the killer. "And your son, what about him?"

"He's built of stronger stuff," he replied. "He helped me with his sister."

She stopped and stared, the sickness inside her coalescing, as she realized that her fears were being proven. "I was afraid of that. He was on drugs, wasn't he?"

He nodded. "He came home, high as a kite."

"But you guys were supposed to be on a holiday."

"Yeah, my wife and I got in a fight. I beat the crap out of her, and I told her that I needed a few days to cool off. She never said a word to anybody and came home meek and mild as always." He sneered. "In the meantime, I picked up a victim, and I kept her at the house, thinking it was safe, but it was just temporary. I just had her there for a day or so. I didn't think about my stepdaughter, but there she was, and she saw me with the other girl. And, after that, all hell broke loose."

"What happened to the other girl?"

"Well, I had to kill her and fast, so that really pissed me off. Then I decided that the stepdaughter had to go because she'd seen too much and would tell," he explained. "So, as much as I was sad about that, it was a pretty obvious answer."

She stared at him in shock. "That was a daughter you had raised."

"Yep, it was," he snapped, "and the bitch should have kept her mouth shut."

"You didn't give her a chance to keep her mouth shut," Kate argued. "You tortured her."

"She kept saying that she would tell, and that somebody would find out, that somebody would help her, and that she would make sure I went to prison. She was always one of those do-gooder people. You know? The holier-than-thou type, always right, while everybody else was wrong. She kept calling me a sinner. I told her that she was a sinner and that she would go to hell."

"And Rick?"

"Rick came home stoned and drunk one day. She was already tied up in the basement, crying and screaming for help. He went down there, and I followed him, and he had a knife in his hand, and he was trying to cut her loose."

"And I said, 'Jesus Christ, boy! What did you do?' He just stopped and stared at me and started yelling, 'I didn't do anything.' He cried out, 'I didn't. I didn't.' Meanwhile I just poured it on, saying, 'You stinking drunk. You're stoned out of your head. Look what you did to your sister.'" The stepfather chuckled, as if delighted with himself.

"Go on," Kate said.

"I told him, 'You don't even know what it's like to kill somebody properly.' He stared at me, as if he was struggling so hard to understand what was going on. I could see the drugs were still in his system. I said, 'When you kill her, you need to kill her clean and make sure that she dies.' At that, his sister started yelling at him to not listen to me and that I was evil and to stop me. But it was funny, like watching a video. He looked at that knife in his hand, and he held it against her neck, as she started screaming and screaming. He freaked out a little, saying, 'Shut the fuck up, just shut the fuck up. I can't think!' And before he knew it, he'd sliced her throat."

"And yet there was a gouge," she noted.

"Yeah, there was. I added that later. Just to make it look a little better." And then he smiled.

"So, Rick did kill his sister."

"He probably doesn't have a clue how it all happened, and I know he's terrified, and he has no idea what part I played in it at all. You can bet he'll never talk."

"But he confessed, just like a good boy."

He laughed. "That was the best part. That and watching my wife have no clue what was going on."

"And you really hate your wife that much?"

"She's completely useless," he noted.

"And yet she's been a patsy for you all this time. She's been your alibi all these years."

"Of course. She has to have some purpose. Even now, she has taken her drugs because she gave me mine."

"And yet you didn't take them, did you?"

"No, hell no. I only make it look that way. I give myself a chance to rest up in between my sessions, and then I'm up all night. It makes me dopey all day. And I can save my drugs for my experiments." He gave her a big fat ugly smile and added, "Works out really well."

"Jesus Christ." Kate stepped back. "I'm tempted to just blow you away now."

He shrugged. "Go ahead. You know something? It'd be good for you. Then there would be no difference at all between us. You high and mighty folks, you think you're so perfect. You're really not. You're just as twisted and sick on the inside as I am."

"No," she argued, "I'm not, but I'm glad to hear you know what a sick bastard you are."

"Nope, I'm not," he stated simply, "but I've listened to enough of my dear stepson's therapy sessions to realize that's what they'll think."

"What started you on this path?"

"Actually it was the woman I took home. I met her on the street. I didn't bring her home in order to kill somebody," he stated. "She was the first, but only because she pissed me off. I mean, she just pissed me off."

"In what way? Were you fighting with her?"

"No, she was a hooker," he explained, "and she'd gotten noisy and then mad because I'd kept her there. But I hadn't intended to kill her, at least not yet," he added. "Then I just killed her real quick because she was just in the way at that point because I had to deal with my holier-than-thou daughter."

Kate shook her head. "Wow, so you killed a hooker because she was in the way, and you killed your daughter because she was in the way too."

"Do you need a better reason to kill?" he asked, twisting his head. "Look at you. I'm in your way, and you just want me out of your way."

"Only to rid the world of evil," she replied quietly. "But I sure as hell have absolutely no wish to kill anybody else."

"Yeah, you do," he said. "You just won't be honest about it. Everybody wants to kill. Everybody wants to know what it's like to kill," he noted, with a half-smile. "But everybody is too scared to do it. Once you've done it, it's a piece of cake. All I wanted to do was make them pay."

"Why? Why do you hate women so much?" And then she looked at him. "Your mother, I suppose."

"Yeah, my mother was a bitch."

"And was your mother the first one you killed?"

"No, I already told you the hooker was my first one. My mother died before I could get there. I think I've been trying to kill her ever since."

That was as good of an explanation as anything she'd ever heard. And explained his chosen "type."

When they heard the sirens outside on the street, she looked over at Simon and nodded. "Go get them and bring them up here, will you? Make sure that ambulance gets here fast."

He hesitated.

She smiled and said, "Don't worry. The next shot will take out his testicles."

Simon winced at that, but he believed her. He raced down the ramp and motioned at the cops and told them to bring the ambulance crew straight up because they had a critical victim. As he raced back, his gaze immediately went to Kate. But she was still standing there, holding her gun on the man on the ground. "At least he's still alive," he noted.

"Yeah, he is," she replied. "It's just so strange to have the case actually over." She looked over at Chelice. "Are you doing okay?"

"I am now," the woman whispered. "I just hurt so damn much."

"The ambulance is here," Kate told her. "Hang on a little longer, and we'll get you out of this hellhole."

Just a few minutes later, the woman was surrounded by the EMTs, and it didn't take long before she was quickly removed from the ropes and whatever support system he had strung her up in. Soon she was cut down and taken away, Kate realized that Simon had been busy taking photos.

She walked over and stated, "I'll need those."

He nodded. "Yeah, I figured somebody needed to take photos of how he had her strung up."

She nodded. "I know, and I couldn't do anything until somebody else had him. Thank you." She looked back to see the killer also being loaded onto a gurney. "He goes into a separate ambulance," she ordered.

The EMTs looked at her in surprise, but she shook her head. "This woman has been tortured by him long enough. He can wait until another ambulance gets here. She gets priority, and the last thing she needs is to be around this asshole another second. He doesn't deserve any medical treatment. Matter of fact, I wouldn't mind if you dropped him a couple times on the way out of here."

The still-bleeding man started to laugh. "See? There's that killer part of you talking right now," he said. "Now if only you'd had the guts to do the job."

"Nah," she replied. "I figure you'll suffer far more in prison for the rest of your life."

"I won't suffer."

335

"Yeah, you will. You'll end up in solitary most of the time," she stated, "because nobody can stand you. And the prisoners will beat the crap out of you when you're in the general population, just as a matter of course."

"I'll kill myself instead," he said, with a casual shrug.

"I couldn't care less, but you won't do it on my watch."

And, with that, she stepped back, and the EMTs loaded him onto a gurney and strapped him down, as another cop handcuffed him in place. She turned to look at Simon. "I'll be here for a while."

"Yeah, you think?" he asked. "Probably all night again, huh?"

"Yeah," she said, with half a smile. "Like all night again. So, if you don't mind making a trip to the car before you go—"

"You want your stuff?"

"Yeah, I'll need my bag. I want my coffee, and some of those cold burgers would be fine too."

He shook his head. "How can you eat after this?"

"Because I'll have a long night ahead," she repeated, with a smile. "Besides, we won this one."

He looked at her and nodded. "You know something? You're right. This is a big win."

"It is, indeed," she agreed. "So maybe you can get some sleep tonight. She's safe. You did everything you could, and we found her."

He smiled. "I wanted to show you something."

She frowned and looked at him in surprise.

He nodded. "Take a look at this."

A door was in front of them. It was barely standing, and it went out to a balcony, and a shutter was over it. But he pulled both open, and there, across the street, was a huge building. And, sure enough, it had the same damn window on it.

She shook her head. "You know that I don't really doubt you," she explained, "but sometimes I do. And then this happens, and I find out that I'm full of shit and that you're right."

He laughed. "Well, in this case, I'm just relieved to see it because the only other answer for me would have been yet another victim out there somewhere, and I couldn't stand that."

"No more victims," she confirmed. "The paperwork will be brutal, however, and it'll take us a long time to get to the bottom of all that he did. Plus I've got a prostitute's body missing somewhere, the true victim zero," she noted, "though, in this case, it's probably sitting in the morgue, unidentified."

"It could have been buried even, as a Jane Doe, since it was so many years ago."

She nodded. "Probably so. Hopefully they took DNA."

"Surely they did," he noted. "You'll run it and test it later."

"Yet we didn't find that at the kid's house."

"Nope. Maybe because he didn't have her there very long."

"Maybe. Or maybe he cleaned up afterward. I don't know. We'll figure it out," she stated. "You need to go home to get some rest."

"I'll go get your stuff first. Be right back."

She nodded and turned to see that Rodney had just arrived on the scene. He walked over, gave her a big fat grin, and said, "So you found Chelice, huh?"

"Yeah, we did." She nodded and pointed out the balcony to the window in the building across the way.

He stared. "Jesus, so Simon was right."

"Absolutely. He's gone down to get my stuff from his car, so he can leave and go home."

"We should probably get a statement from him."

"We'll get that tomorrow," she said absentmindedly. "He's pretty overwhelmed at the moment."

"With good cause, it's a hell of a job you two did. I didn't even think about doing a stakeout because I didn't really expect it would be any of the family."

"Well, if we can believe the stepfather, it sounds like the kid actually did kill his sister. He was drunk and high on drugs, and, at the goading of his stepfather, killed her under the influence, never really knowing what exactly happened. Rick confessed because he killed her," she noted. "Yet it was the stepfather who tortured her."

"Why?" he asked.

"She caught him fighting with a prostitute that he'd kept too long. So he got mad and killed the prostitute, and then he dealt with the stepdaughter before she could turn him in."

"And the torture?"

"She wouldn't shut up about how evil he was and how he would go to hell, and apparently she didn't die easily, and she didn't die fast, and the whole time she gave him shit."

"I like her spirit."

"Yeah, but it also made her life and her death a whole lot harder."

"Yet, in the end, we can still only be who we are," he noted quietly.

She turned and looked at him. "You know what? That's a really lovely thing to say. Because she did her best the whole time. She thought her brother would save her, but instead he's the one who dealt the final blow."

"Asshole."

"I'm not even sure he knows he did it," she murmured, "and he's already been tried and convicted."

"At least now he can get the truth. I wonder how that'll make him feel."

"I rather imagine it'll make him feel pretty shitty, but, at the same time, knowing the truth now should also bring him some relief because I doubt he's had very many nights of sleep since it happened."

"No, that unknown stuff just eats away at you, doesn't it?" he asked.

"Yeah, it does. Now he'll know for sure, and he'll have to live with it. But, like I said, he's already been tried, convicted, and served a sentence. Now he and his mother can begin to heal."

"Jesus, the mother. What a blow for her."

"It's looking like, in many ways, the stepfather was abusive the whole time. The only peace the mother ever got was when he started being medicated for his psychosis or whatever the hell that was, though I think it was largely made up on his part. Anyway, she thought she was getting those drugs into him. However, he has had his nights to play for all these years, while she's taking her drugs to help her sleep. During the daytime then, he's pretty groggy from not sleeping, so he's happy to keep functioning at a minimal level."

"And, of course, now she's all affectionate and loving because he can't beat the crap out of her."

"For the most part," she said. "He went to Alberta and put her in the hospital there, so that he could have some freedom to do what he needed to do with his next two victims, which, of course, would just turn the light on his stepson. He always wanted to keep Rick as an easy suspect, instead of anybody else. Yet, at the same time, he couldn't resist a new hunting ground."

"Asshole," Rodney said.

"Yeah, but now he's a caught asshole, so it's a whole different story."

Forensics arrived just then, and she smiled. "You know something? Smidge will actually be happy with me for a change."

"You think? We've still got bodies in the morgue."

"Yeah, but we didn't bring him a new one," she noted. "This time we kept one alive."

"Thank God for that," he muttered.

"I know." She sighed. "We sure have a bunch of work to do here."

"I can handle this," Rodney stated. "You've done the bulk of it. You need to get your ass home and rest."

"No," she argued quietly. "I'm here to finish it. I'll rest tomorrow. Now that I know everybody is safe and sound, I'll rest then," she said, with a big smile. And, with that, they turned and got to work.

This concludes Book 4 of Kate Morgan:
Simon Says… Scream.
Read about Kate Morgan: Simon Says… Run, Book 5

Simon Says... Run: Kate Morgan (Book #5)

Introducing a new thriller series that keeps you guessing and on your toes through every twist and unexpected turn....

USA Today Best-Selling Author Dale Mayer does it again in this mind-blowing thriller series.

The unlikely team of Detective Kate Morgan and Simon St. Laurant, an unwilling psychic, marries all the unpredictable and passionate elements of Mayer's work that readers have come to love and crave.

Some cases are clear-cut and make sense, and then there's this one. Two women, avid joggers, out for a hard Stanley Park Fun Run. Both dead. Both at the same time. Both on the popular park trail. It's rough when trail running and up hills, but the killer had a unique method for taking out his victims—one that doesn't leave any forensic evidence. Detective Kate Morgan focuses on the victims, ... until two more are killed.

Awakening in the night with horrible nightmares, Simon curses his life and hates having ever traveled down this strange pathway, particularly when the visions come out of nowhere. In this case a much more personal element terrifies him.

As Kate gets closer to finding out the truth, she's also on the same path to becoming the next victim.

Several Days Later, Saturday

S HE WOKE UP early in the morning, still at Simon's. She rolled over and tried to sneak out from the covers. Almost instantly his arm came around her and pulled her onto her belly. Large warm hands slid down over her back to her softly rounded cheeks, only to slide on either side of her hips and onto her thighs, pulling them wide.

A moan escaped, riding on a sigh of joy, as his devious fingers brushed up against her tender flesh, after a long night of sexual satisfaction.

A hot whisper rolled down her cheek. "Okay?" And he shifted his fingers again. She cried out, her hips rising higher, as his devilish fingers continued to tease her.

"Yes, damn it," she cried out in a strangled voice, as she shifted closer to him.

He chuckled, rising up behind her, before entering her in one hard thrust. Her soft cries filled the room, as he picked up the rhythm, until they both crashed over the cliff.

When she could talk, she whispered, "I have to get up."

"It's Saturday," he said.

She froze. "It is?"

He nodded. "It is. You're off work."

"Jesus, I don't even know what day it is anymore."

"Well, if you would take some of the time off that you

have coming and rest a little bit," he noted, "I wouldn't have to worry about you quite so much."

"You worry too much," she said instantly. The arm around her tightened, and she cuddled in closer. "In that case"—she yawned—"I'll just stay here a bit. Maybe we can have breakfast for a change."

"Normally you're up and out of here before breakfast is even possible."

"And normally you're up and out of here buying and selling the world."

"Foreign markets and stock exchanges open up early," he explained.

"So, why the hell are you still here now?"

"It's Saturday. They can go screw themselves."

She laughed. Just then her phone rang.

He froze, tucked her up closer, and said, "Don't answer it."

She rolled over and looked at him. "You know I can't do that."

"I know," he said, with a sigh. He kissed her gently. "Go ahead. Answer it then."

She grabbed her phone and checked her Caller ID. "What's up, Rodney?"

"We got a new case," he stated, his voice grim.

"Yeah, what kind of a case?"

"You mean, outside of dead bodies?"

"Bodies?"

"Yeah, two, on the Stanley Park jogging trails."

"Runners?"

"Yeah, both women, both early twenties."

"Shit. Shot or what?"

"No, we're not exactly sure what happened. But it

343

sounds like something might have been sprayed in their faces. Gassed maybe, but Smidge'll have to tell us what it was," he noted. "Anyway I got the first call. I'm here, and I'm tagging you."

"*Great.* Simon just told me that I needed to take a few days off."

"And he's right. You do. But you didn't set that up."

"Nope, I'm coming," she said. "You know me. Anytime somebody needs me—"

"More than that," he added, "I think this will definitely be your case. At the very least I want you on it with me." And, with that, he hung up.

She smiled down at the phone. "I think that was actually a compliment."

"Remember that teamwork thing?" Simon asked her.

"I'm working on it," she said. "I'm working on it. Oh, and don't plan on jogging the Stanley Park trails today, okay?"

"Not planning on doing any jogging," he replied. "Especially now."

She smiled and got up. "I don't even have time for a shower."

"Yes, you do," he said. "Just make it fast."

She hesitated, but then nodded. She was in and out in five minutes to find him with her clothes all laid out.

"And dirty clothes again," she noted, swearing softly.

"In this case it doesn't matter," he explained, "because we spent most of yesterday sitting around the house doing nothing. So, you'll be good to go in them, if you want. However, these are the ones you wore the day before."

She looked at them in surprise. "Did you wash them?"

"Yeah, I did it last night."

"Shit, you're handy to have around."

She walked over to give him a quick kiss, but he snatched her up into a hug and kissed her thoroughly, then said, "And you remember that."

With that, she was gone.

Find Book 5 here!

To find out more visit Dale Mayer's website.

smarturl.it/DMSSSRun

Author's Note

Thank you for reading Simon Says... Scream: Kate Morgan, Book 4! If you enjoyed the book, please take a moment and leave a short review.

Dear reader,

I love to hear from readers, and you can contact me at my website: www.dalemayer.com or at my Facebook author page. To be informed of new releases and special offers, sign up for my newsletter or follow me on BookBub. And if you are interested in joining Dale Mayer's Reader Group, here is the Facebook sign up page. https://smarturl.it/DaleMayerFBGroup

Cheers,
Dale Mayer

Get THREE Free Books Now!

Have you tried the Psychic Vision series?

Read Tuesday's Child, Hide'n Go Seek, Maddy's Floor right now for FREE.

Go here to get them!

https://dalemayer.com/tuesdayschildfree

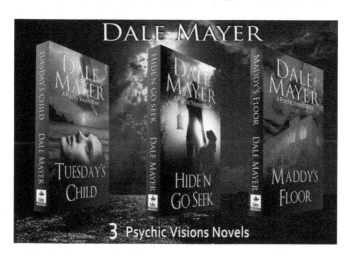

About the Author

Dale Mayer is a *USA Today* best-selling author, best known for her SEALs military romances, her Psychic Visions series, and her Lovely Lethal Garden cozy series. Her contemporary romances are raw and full of passion and emotion (Broken But ... Mending, Hathaway House series). Her thrillers will keep you guessing (Kate Morgan, By Death series), and her romantic comedies will keep you giggling (*It's a Dog's Life*, a stand-alone novella; and the Broken Protocols series, starring Charming Marvin, the cat).

Dale honors the stories that come to her—and some of them are crazy, break all the rules and cross multiple genres!

To go with her fiction, she also writes nonfiction in many different fields, with books available on résumé writing, companion gardening, and the US mortgage system. All her books are available in print and ebook format.

Connect with Dale Mayer Online

Dale's Website – www.dalemayer.com

Twitter – @DaleMayer

Facebook – facebook.com/DaleMayer.author

BookBub – bookbub.com/authors/dale-mayer

Also by Dale Mayer

Published Adult Books:

Shadow Recon
Magnus, Book 1

Bullard's Battle
Ryland's Reach, Book 1
Cain's Cross, Book 2
Eton's Escape, Book 3
Garret's Gambit, Book 4
Kano's Keep, Book 5
Fallon's Flaw, Book 6
Quinn's Quest, Book 7
Bullard's Beauty, Book 8
Bullard's Best, Book 9

Terkel's Team
Damon's Deal, Book 1
Wade's War, Book 2
Gage's Goal, Book 3
Calum's Contact, Book 4

Kate Morgan
Simon Says... Hide, Book 1

Simon Says... Jump, Book 2

Simon Says... Ride, Book 3

Simon Says... Scream, Book 4

Simon Says... Run, Book 5

Hathaway House

Aaron, Book 1

Brock, Book 2

Cole, Book 3

Denton, Book 4

Elliot, Book 5

Finn, Book 6

Gregory, Book 7

Heath, Book 8

Iain, Book 9

Jaden, Book 10

Keith, Book 11

Lance, Book 12

Melissa, Book 13

Nash, Book 14

Owen, Book 15

Percy, Book 16

Hathaway House, Books 1–3

Hathaway House, Books 4–6

Hathaway House, Books 7–9

The K9 Files

Ethan, Book 1

Pierce, Book 2

Lovely Lethal Gardens

Psychic Vision Series

Itsy-Bitsy Spider
Unmasked
Deep Beneath
From the Ashes
Stroke of Death
Ice Maiden
Snap, Crackle...
What If...
Talking Bones
Psychic Visions Books 1–3
Psychic Visions Books 4–6
Psychic Visions Books 7–9

By Death Series
Touched by Death
Haunted by Death
Chilled by Death
By Death Books 1–3

Broken Protocols – Romantic Comedy Series
Cat's Meow
Cat's Pajamas
Cat's Cradle
Cat's Claus
Broken Protocols 1-4

Broken and... Mending
Skin
Scars

Scales (of Justice)
Broken but... Mending 1-3

Glory
Genesis
Tori
Celeste
Glory Trilogy

Biker Blues
Morgan: Biker Blues, Volume 1
Cash: Biker Blues, Volume 2

SEALs of Honor
Mason: SEALs of Honor, Book 1
Hawk: SEALs of Honor, Book 2
Dane: SEALs of Honor, Book 3
Swede: SEALs of Honor, Book 4
Shadow: SEALs of Honor, Book 5
Cooper: SEALs of Honor, Book 6
Markus: SEALs of Honor, Book 7
Evan: SEALs of Honor, Book 8
Mason's Wish: SEALs of Honor, Book 9
Chase: SEALs of Honor, Book 10
Brett: SEALs of Honor, Book 11
Devlin: SEALs of Honor, Book 12
Easton: SEALs of Honor, Book 13
Ryder: SEALs of Honor, Book 14
Macklin: SEALs of Honor, Book 15

Heroes for Hire

SEALs of Steel

The Mavericks

Hatch, Book 16

Corbin, Book 17

The Mavericks, Books 1–2

The Mavericks, Books 3–4

The Mavericks, Books 5–6

The Mavericks, Books 7–8

The Mavericks, Books 9–10

The Mavericks, Books 11–12

Collections

Dare to Be You...

Dare to Love...

Dare to be Strong...

RomanceX3

Standalone Novellas

It's a Dog's Life

Riana's Revenge

Second Chances

Published Young Adult Books:

Family Blood Ties Series

Vampire in Denial

Vampire in Distress

Vampire in Design

Vampire in Deceit

Vampire in Defiance

Vampire in Conflict

Vampire in Chaos

Vampire in Crisis

Vampire in Control

Vampire in Charge

Family Blood Ties Set 1–3

Family Blood Ties Set 1–5

Family Blood Ties Set 4–6

Family Blood Ties Set 7–9

Sian's Solution, A Family Blood Ties Series Prequel
Novelette

Design series

Dangerous Designs

Deadly Designs

Darkest Designs

Design Series Trilogy

Standalone

In Cassie's Corner

Gem Stone (a Gemma Stone Mystery)

Time Thieves

Published Non-Fiction Books:

Career Essentials

Career Essentials: The Résumé

Career Essentials: The Cover Letter

Career Essentials: The Interview

Career Essentials: 3 in 1